GRANDFATHER MOUNTAIN

WYNTON SELLERS

Published in Wake Forest, NC

www.wyntonsellers.com

Cover Designs: Design For Writers

Edits and Interior Layout: BeforeYouPublish - Book Press

Published and printed in the United States of America.

ISBN: 979-8-9863163-1-4

Hardcover first edition: Grandfather Mountain

Sellers, Wynton

GRANDFATHER MOUNTAIN

WYNTON SELLERS

Alexander sat staring at his attorney across a long mahogany table. He noticed all of Julian Hoffman's physical features. He had the face of a man who indulged himself in foods delighting his taste buds without any consideration for its nutritional value. Alexander noticed his finely trimmed mustache, his tailored suit, and engraved cufflinks. There was a diamond ring that seemed to cut off the circulation of Julian's meaty finger. He studied all of Julian's features with steady contempt.

Alexander noticed Julian busying himself on his laptop and looking through a stack of files next to him. He never looked up to see Alexander's penetrating glare. Had he paid any attention to his client, he would have noticed a young man staring straight into his soul.

Alexander had once regarded Julian's well-groomed exterior with admiration and respect. He admired the reverence Julian quietly demanded, and the way sheriff deputies and detention officers accommodated him. He admired Julian's command of the English language—the way complex legal terms vibrated from his vocal cords the way music vibrates from the strings of a cello. However, Alexander was furious when Julian first suggested a plea agreement.

"I am not a criminal," he insisted and then asked Hoffman, "For whom are you working, me, or the Commonwealth of North Carolina?"

"Listen, Mr. Hoffman, I will not allow my son to accept any plea agreement," Emily, Alexander's mother spoke up. "He understands why what he did was wrong, but there is no way any jury would convict him once they have heard all the facts." Emily slapped her hand on the table.

Julian gazed around the visitation room of the Wake County Jail and smoothed back his hair with his large hand. He listened to their protest before speaking, "Ms. Merchant, I understand your frustration with all of this, but North Carolina has a zero-tolerance policy on statutory offenses. The court doesn't care why Alexander committed the offense, only that he did, and they will convict him for it."

"Have you spoken to the D.A.?" Emily asked.

"The district attorney is a snake. He would stop at nothing to get a conviction, regardless of whether Alexander is guilty or not. Nothing is out of bounds for this guy, and if we take this to trial and lose, Alexander could get twelve to fifteen years. Maybe more." He turned to Alexander, "What would you do in prison for fifteen years? Your life would be over." He leaned forward and asked, "How could you recover from that?"

"But I did nothing wrong," Alexander protested.

"Prisons are full of people who have done nothing wrong, and you are no different," Julian said. Sensing he had Alexander where he wanted him, he reached across the table and placed his heavy hand on Alexander's shoulder. "If you accept this plea bargain, you will be out of prison in two years. I'll see to it myself," Julian professed.

"No," Emily slapped the table again. "We're getting another lawyer."

"But we don't have money for another lawyer," Alexander said, slumping his shoulders.

"I don't care. I'll figure it out. We're done, Mr. Hoffman," she said.

"If you wish to hire another attorney, that is your choice. They may take your money and go to trial, but they won't win. I'm doing what is best for him," Julian said.

"Thank you, Mr. Hoffman, but we'll take our chances." Emily picked up her purse.

"Okay, but don't make any hasty decisions tonight. Think about what I said, and call me tomorrow." Julian gathered his things and left.

"Look at me, Alexander. You are not going to prison. Do you hear me?"

Alexander nodded his head. "I'm going home to make phone calls," Emily said, zipped her gray fleece jacket and left.

Alexander sat motionless in the empty visitation room. He fixed his eyes on what appeared to be the Star of David carved into the table. He focused on it until it became a blur. He didn't remember the detention officer escorting him back to his cell, but soon afterwards he was motionless on the flat, worn mattress in his cell the rest of the night. He never moved when the cell grew dark. Sometime between midnight and daybreak, he could remember hearing the detention officer yelling chow time, but he could not remember if he had gone to the chow-hall for breakfast, or if he had simply stayed in the same spot, clutching his knees close to his chest.

On the following evening, Alexander was allowed onto the terrace for recreation. It was a ten-by-fifteen room with a concrete floor and a floor-to-ceiling metal screen used to barricade inmates from the outside world. A detention officer sat watching him.

Alexander stood in front of the metal screen, looking out at the city where his life had been once full of infinite opportunity. He thought about his mother and how she must be feeling about his recent troubles. He thought about her wonderful cooking and wondered what she had prepared for dinner tonight. He wondered if she had even bothered to cook at all, since she was now only cooking for herself. He closed his eyes and pictured her meticulous table settings with her polished silverware, once belonging to her grandmother many years ago. He didn't know why he was thinking about silverware, but he thought about it, nonetheless. He imagined seeing his reflection in his mother's polished spoons, forks, and knives, perhaps because during the past sixty days he spent locked in the Wake County Detention Center, he had grown to hate the plastic sporks accompanying every meal.

Alexander peered down at the street below and fixed his eyes on two men standing directly across the street. He immediately recognized Julian laughing and talking to a man in a dark suit, with a large leather bag hanging from his shoulder. They were clearly old friends. He watched Julian place his hand on the man's shoulder, the same way he'd done him hours earlier, as they both laughed hysterically for about fifteen minutes or so. *He sure has a way with words,* Alexander thought. The two old friends shook hands and departed.

Alexander turned to the officer. "I need to use the phone," he said.

"Don't you want to finish your rec?" the officer asked.

"No, I'm done."

"All right. Let's go." The officer escorted Alexander to the phone.

Alexander placed a collect call and waited for Emily to answer.

"Hi, Mom."

"Hi, honey. Is everything okay?" she asked.

"Yes, I'm fine. I've decided to take the plea bargain," he said.

"What do you mean you've decided? We're getting another attorney. I'm meeting with someone in the morning."

"No, Mom. We can't afford it. You spent all your savings on Julian," Alexander said.

"You let me worry about that." Emily let out a deep sigh.

"No, Mom. I'm taking the plea."

"Wait."

"I have to go. Bye," he said and ended the call.

Alexander went back to his cell, lay down on his bed motionless, and reflected on how quickly his life had changed for the worst.

The following day, Alexander sat on his bed studying the graffiti lining the walls like hieroglyphics.

P Funk was here.

Rolling Sixties baby!

Alexander focused on a lifelike drawing on the wall, created with chalk and a pencil, and it was surprisingly meticulous. The picture was of an urban setting, with a man holding a small boy in his arm. His eyes were dark and penetrating. His face was that of a young man, but his eyes told a story of experience—an experience many people would never understand. They told a story of decisions no young man should ever have to face. Decisions of life, and decisions of death. The eyes were angry, but were also pensive, seeming to follow Alexander from one side of the cell to the other.

Two teardrops were tattooed under the man's eye and Alexander had seen this before. He had seen it on people who were usually on the wrong side of the law. He worked his eyes down the man's torso and observed the left raised pants leg. He noticed the child who was held in the man's sculptured left arm, wrapped around the man's shoulders, holding a pool table ball in his hand. It was an eight ball, and the child held it out as if it was some manifesto of his future life. This disturbed Alexander and he turned away.

A DETENTION OFFICER came to the door. "Hey Merchant, your lawyer is here to see you."

Alexander was taken down to the visiting room where Julian sat waiting. Alexander sat across from him. "Did you speak to my mother?"

"Yes, I did," Julian said.

"So, what now?"

"You'll be going to court in the morning. The district attorney is prepared to offer you a twenty-four-to-thirty-six-month sentence for accepting a plea bargain to indecent liberties with a child."

Alexander fixed his eyes on the floor but did not answer.

"Do you understand?" Julian asked.

Alexander nodded.

"I need you to speak, Alexander. Do you understand?"

"Yes, I understand," Alexander replied.

"You understand that you will have to plead guilty to indecent liberties with a child?"

"Yes, I understand." Alexander shifted in his seat.

The two men were silent for a while.

"It's for the best. I'll see you in the morning." He picked up his briefcase and left the room.

Alexander went back to his cell and fell into a depressed-man's sleep. He awoke at two o'clock A.M. and continued to lie in bed, as still as death. Later, he stood and paced back and forth on the concrete floor, before growing calm and settling in front of the small cell window.

He stared out at the now familiar view of the city, which was calm and quiet. As dawn approached, he watched the half-moon and piercing stars grow softer and softer, until they disappeared into the morning sky. The clouds rushed in and rolled away, and then the morning dew rested gently upon the trees. He watched the morning sky turn orange, and gray, and then blue again.

In the years to come, Alexander would not remember much about this night, but he would remember watching this day's sunrise forever.

TWO

Alexander arrived at the Wake County Court House at 8:15 A.M. He sat in a holding cell for forty-five minutes before Julian retrieved him.

"Good morning, Alexander."

"Good morning."

"How do you feel?"

"Fine, I guess. Did you pick up my suit?" Alexander asked.

"No, you won't need it."

"You want me to go in front of the judge like this?" Alexander gestured to the orange jumpsuit he was wearing.

Julian waved his hand. "It's a plea bargain, Alexander. Your clothes don't matter at this point."

A flash of rage entered Alexander, but he suppressed it and followed Julian out of the cell. A detention officer immediately grasped his arm and escorted him into an elevator. When the elevator ascended to the fifth floor, Alexander was escorted into a conference room and guided to a chair.

Julian sat at the far end of the long mahogany table and

removed several files and a laptop from his leather bag and began typing.

"What now?" Alexander asked.

"We wait," Julian said coldly without looking up from his screen.

Alexander noticed how Julian's usual warm and understanding charm now seemed cold and distant. Alexander concluded Julian was a busy man and under stress from his heavy workload.

Alexander could hear cars and busses passing underneath. He could hear several birds chirping, a dog barking, and the distant whistle of a passing train outside the window. While he listened, he again imagined taking his chances in court and presenting his case to a jury of his peers. *They could not send me to prison after hearing how it happened*, he thought. He imagined Julian's brilliant defense. He knew once the jury heard his case, and examined the facts, their hearts would indeed go out to him. He imagined a long deliberation, and the foreperson handing his verdict to the judge, and the judge handing it back. "We the jury, find the defendant not guilty on all counts." He would shake Julian's hand, hug his mother, and strut out as a free man. He smiled at the idea, but his smile disappeared when District Attorney Ned Williams entered the room.

"Good morning," Ned Williams said.

"Good morning, Mr. Williams," Julian said. "Mr. Merchant, this is Ned Williams, he is the Wake County District Attorney," Julian said.

"How are you, Mr. Merchant?" Ned asked.

"I'm okay," Alexander responded.

Alexander checked out Ned Williams from head to toe. He wore a gray pinstripe suit. His hair was combed to the side, with the sides smoothed to the back. Alexander could not see his shoes, but he imagined they were black, wing tipped, and highly polished. Ned held some documents in his hand, which Alexander figured to be his plea agreement. He watched as the D.A. handed the documents to Julian and Julian looked them over. Alexander sat watching the two men and noticed Julian's stern countenance, and the half smile on Ned Williams' face. Alexander had seen that half smile before. He thought it was a smile of wickedness and cruelty. This is the man whom Julian called a snake. The man who would do anything for a conviction. This is also the man who Alexander observed from the terrace of the Wake County Jail, talking and laughing with Julian.

When he observed the two men laughing and talking, he had known immediately they were old friends. Good friends, and now they acted as if they barely knew each other. He understood these old friends were playing a game. He knew he was playing, too, and was destined to lose.

Alexander was full of rage and hatred for the two scoundrels before him.

"Sit here with me," Julian beckoned, once he saw Alexander shaking with rage and glaring at him intently. "Come on, son," Julian said, sliding back a chair.

Alexander imagined himself leaping across the table and seizing them both, but he knew there was no use. He stood to his feet and calmly made his way over to Julian and sat down at his side.

When Ned Williams sat across from Alexander, Julian cleared his throat and spoke slowly, "You are charged with two counts of statutory rape. Mr. Williams is prepared to offer you a plea bargain for indecent liberties with a child. You will receive a twenty-four-to-thirty-six-month sentence and sixty months of probation. Do you understand?"

"Yes, I understand," Alexander mumbled.

Ned Williams sat quietly—his half smile, now gone.

"Do you have any questions?" Julian asked.

"No," Alexander said flatly.

Julian rested his pen on the document and pointed to a line with his finger. "Sign here."

Alexander reached for the pen as Julian rested a hand on his shoulder. Alexander shook it off and looked at him intently. His eyes moved to Ned Williams, and then back to the document and signed it, Alexander Merchant, October 3, 2006, and then he moved back to his seat at the far end of the table.

Julian picked up the document and handed it to Ned Williams. After they shook hands, the D.A. stepped out, closing the door behind him. Julian watched the wooden door close shut, and he hesitated to look at Alexander. When he did look, he saw Alexander staring at him contemptuously. Julian shuttered, shifted his eyes to his computer, and began typing.

After an hour or so, Ned Williams came back into the conference room and handed Julian two legal documents and said, "The judge will be in shortly."

"We'll be right over." Julian then closed his laptop, placed it in his bag, and stood to his feet. He parted his lips to call Alexander, but before he could speak, Alexander was up and headed towards the door. Julian led the way into the courtroom and entered his client's plea agreement. He handed Alexander a copy of his agreement and kept one for himself. He turned to Alexander sympathetically. "Take care of yourself, son," he said.

The detention officer moved Alexander out of the courtroom, into the elevator, and down to the basement. The stainless-steel doors slid apart, and Alexander was guided into the corridor where another officer stood waiting.

This time he was taken into the transportation office and

locked in a small holding cell. The leg irons felt cold as they closed around his ankles. A chain was wrapped around his waist, and a padlock fastened the chain to a black metal box enclosed over his handcuffs. He rode in silence to the Wake County Jail and was placed in another holding cell, where he remained until the afternoon.

The once white transfer bus was now stained with rust. Division of Prisons and Inmate Transfer Bus was written on the side in large black letters. Alexander tried not to notice. He sat on the third row and imagined he was on a class trip to a historic landmark, but the sound of leg irons dragging along the bus floor pulled him back to reality. This was further realized by the presence of the correctional officer holding a shotgun.

Alexander watched as the bus turned onto the highway, and as it later passed through Chapel Hill, he thought of the Carolina Tarheels. He knew the Duke Blue Devils would soon come to avenge the loss they suffered when the Tarheels visited Durham a few weeks ago. *Why have I never gone to see Duke and Carolina play?* he wondered. A long deep sigh escaped his chest, for this made him sad. He felt he would never get to do anything he wanted, and that, somehow, his life was over. His eyes filled with tears. He gritted his teeth and swallowed hard.

Outside, the sun was setting, the leaves were falling and rustling underneath the bus, as it traveled up into the Blue Ridge Mountains. He watched the trees grow higher and higher, and he knew some of them had been there for centuries. Their autumn leaves seemed to glow as they often do when the sun is setting. The western sky was orange, with silver beams exploding to the east. He took a mental picture of this and filed it away, just as Natalie does whenever she sees something beautiful. Natalie... He filed her away, too, because he didn't want to think about her in the moment. He would think of her plenty later, but not now.

It was growing dark outside, and he could see a long line of red taillights heading up into the mountains. He closed his eyes and tried to rest.

CHAPTER

THREE

The inmate bus slowed to a stop. When Alexander opened his eyes, he saw a large fence covered with barbed wire, stretching forth into the distance. Behind the fence, he saw two flags blowing in the wind, and behind the flags, a tall brown building reached upward into the night's sky. The clouds hung low and seemed to rest upon the roof of the prison like a soft pillow.

In the distance, fog rolled down the side of a mountain like a waterfall. The bus engine idled noisily, and Alexander heard a loud buzzing sound, soon after, a large gate rolled open. The bus inched past the open gate and stopped at another.

After the first gate closed shut, Officer Sanders stepped out of a small building and greeted the two officers sitting in the front of the bus. "Hi, Sanders," the officer holding the shotgun said.

"Cold night, huh?" said the officer, sitting behind the steering wheel.

"Oh, this is nothing. I've seen a lot worse," Officer Sanders said. Smiling, Officer Sanders stepped toward the rear of the

15

bus. He shined his flashlight underneath the bus and examined each wheel. He then made his way back to the front of the bus and pulled open the hood. He shined his flashlight into the engine and inspected it for contraband.

After completing his inspection, Officer Sanders released his transistor radio from his duty belt and brought it close to his lips. "Rear gate to control," he announced.

"Go for control," someone said on the vibrating radio.

"Open the interior gate." Officer Sanders clipped his radio to his belt.

"Ten-four," someone on the radio responded, and the inner gate rolled open.

Alexander saw the driver of a white Ford F-150 was now standing outside of the vehicle and holding his shotgun in a ready position. The butt of the shotgun rested near the officer's hip at the eight o'clock position. The barrel was held at the two o'clock position, silently reminding each new inmate to follow instructions. Alexander shuddered when he saw this.

The bus slowly rolled into the institution and the interior gate closed behind them. An aluminum door rolled up into the stone exterior, and two additional officers came out to the bus.

"Stand up and step off the bus," the driver demanded.

There were 13 inmates on the bus, and each one wore handcuffs and leg irons. As the inmates stood, their leg irons all smashed onto and scraped the floor in unison. The inmates clamored to the front of the bus, stepping off one at a time.

As Alexander stepped off, he was stopped by a correctional officer.

"What's your name?" the officer asked.

"Alexander Merchant."

The officer skimmed through the files he held in his hand and found Alexander's name and identification number typed across the top. He examined the picture attached to the file and studied Alexander's face. The officer examined Alexander's profile, Black male, six feet tall, 170 pounds. "Date of birth?" the officer asked.

Alexander answered.

When the officer became satisfied he was indeed Alexander Merchant, he nodded his head to the other officer.

"Step over here," the second officer commanded. "Open your mouth." He looked in Alexander's mouth and told him to lift his tongue. He looked under his tongue and told him to turn and spread his arms.

Alexander turned around as the officer examined his shirt collar and placed his hands on top of Alexander's shoulders, running them down his arms, stopping at his wrist. He then felt around his wrists, and his hands traveled up to Alexander's armpits, and down to his waist. He checked each leg methodically, sliding his hands up and down each one, lifting his pants legs and feeling around his ankles. Satisfied, he placed his hand on Alexander's arm, and gently pushed him through the doorway and into the institution where another officer stood waiting. He turned to the next inmate and began the same routine.

When the last inmate entered the institution, Alexander watched the aluminum door descend from the ceiling and rest upon the concrete floor. He knew then he was officially a prisoner. The officers removed the handcuffs and leg irons and placed each inmate in a holding cell. The holding cell had cinder block walls, concrete floors, and a concrete bench running along the wall.

The inmates sat quietly for 45 minutes when finally, one inmate stood to his feet and screamed a stream of obscenities at the officers, the institution, and at the concrete floors beneath his feet. He screamed until he grew tired and then stood staring through the Plexiglas with pulsating eyes.

The sergeant stomped over to the holding cell. He removed the baton from his duty belt, opened the cell door, and rested the tip of it upon the inmate's nose. "Open your mouth again, ya hear?" the sergeant said.

The inmate stared at the sergeant contemptuously but said nothing.

The sergeant closed the cell door and returned to his desk.

Later, an officer opened the door to the holding cell. "Alexander Merchant," he said.

Alexander stood to his feet and approached the door.

"Step out," the officer said.

Alexander stepped out of the cell, and immediately, the door closed behind him.

The officer opened the door to a smaller cell. "In here," he said.

Alexander read his name tag and learned the officer's name was Reed. He walked inside with Officer Reed following.

Reed looked at Alexander's waist, shoulders, and the top of his head. "What size do you wear, a large?" Officer Reed asked.

"Large is fine," Alexander answered.

Officer Reed stepped into another room and returned holding a brown jumpsuit, a T-shirt, a pair of underpants, and a pair of white socks. "What size shoe do you wear?" Officer Reed asked.

"Eleven," Alexander replied.

Officer Reed disappeared into another room and returned holding a pair of cloth Converse tennis shoes. "Stand here," Officer Reed pointed to the center of the cell floor, and Alexander obeyed. Officer Reed squeezed his hands into a pair of rubber gloves and stood facing Alexander with his stature towering over Alexander's. His piercing brown eyes stared down on him coldly. "Take off your shirt."

Alexander obeyed.

Officer Reed took and examined the shirt, front and back. He wrapped his hand around the shirt's open neck, and with one hand, and pulled the shirt through with the other, feeling for any hidden objects. Finding nothing, he tossed the shirt into a plastic box. "Take off your shoes," he said.

Alexander did as he was told and handed them over.

Reed examined them and tossed them into the plastic box. "Your pants," he said.

Alexander removed his pants, and then handed them over.

Officer Reed examined the pants and placed them into the box. "Your socks," he said.

Alexander handed over the socks and Officer Reed examined each one thoroughly.

Reed told Alexander to remove his necklace and he placed the necklace with Alexander's other belongings. "Take off your underwear," he said.

Alexander stood motionless.

"Take off your underwear," Officer Reed reiterated impatiently.

Alexander's heart pounded in his chest and his stomach turned, feeling as if his intestines had been tied into knots.

"Come on," Officer Reed scrunched his brow.

Alexander slowly removed his underpants and watched Officer Reed place them into the box.

Officer Reed unleashed a steady stream of commands, "Open your mouth—lift your tongue—raise your arms." Officer Reed inspected his armpits.

Alexander felt humiliated, as if his manhood had been stripped away with each article of clothing he removed.

Officer Reed saw the torment in Alexander's eyes and empathized with him. But that was procedure. Inmates were known to hide contraband in the most unimaginable places, and although his heart went out to Alexander, he had to continue. "Lift your sack," he said, and pointed to Alexander's groin.

Alexander lifted his testicles.

Officer Reed looked carefully and then commanded, "Turn around."

Alexander turned and faced the wall.

"Show me the bottom of your right foot and spread your toes." Then he said, "Now your left... Bend over and spread your butt cheeks and cough."

Alexander obeyed the officer's commands.

"Get dressed," he said.

Alexander dressed quickly.

"Get the box and come on," Reed said.

Alexander was relieved to have this humiliating experience behind him.

Officer Reed was also relieved, because he believed strip searches to be absolutely the worst part of his job. *One down and twelve to go,* he thought.

Holding his plastic box of belongings, Officer Reed escorted Alexander to a long desk where another officer stood waiting.

The officer listed all of Alexander's personal property on two inventory forms. One form listed Alexander's property that would remain within the institution, to be returned to him upon his release. The other form inventoried the property that could not remain within the prison—it read, a handheld radio, headphones, a yellow necklace, a yellow watch, and other miscellaneous items. "Sign here," the officer said.

Alexander looked it over. "My necklace is fourteen-karat gold, not yellow," Alexander said.

"Your necklace is yellow," the officer said flatly. "Would you rather mail your property home, or have it destroyed?"

"Mail it," Alexander said.

"Is your address seven-fifteen Woodburn Road, Raleigh, North Carolina, two-seven-six-o-one?" the officer asked.

"Yes, that's it," Alexander said.

"Sign it."

After Alexander was placed into another holding cell alone, he watched the other inmates enter the room to be searched, and then exit wearing brown jumpsuits identical to his. He watched them decide to either mail their property home, or have it destroyed, and watched the inmates enter the cell where he now sat in silence.

The sergeant checked his watch. It was 7:23 P.M. when he spoke into his radio, "R and D to food service."

"Go for food service," someone on the other end of his radio responded.

"Call extension three-three-six," the sergeant said.

The phone rang and he answered. "I need thirteen pack-outs," he said, and placed the phone back into the cradle.

At 7:55 P.M., a door opened, and an officer entered the receiving area with an inmate carrying a crate filled with 13 brown bags.

"Hello, gentlemen."

"What's going on?" Officer Reed replied.

"Not a whole lot," he said. "Are they all new admissions?" he asked.

"Yes, they are," the sergeant replied.

"All right, well, take it easy," the officer said.

"See ya," Reed said.

Officer Reed handed each inmate a brown paper bag. "You guys missed chow, but this should hold you until breakfast," he announced, exiting the cell and slamming shut the door. Each bag contained a dry bologna sandwich, an overly ripe apple, and a warm carton of milk.

"So, this is a pack-out," Alexander said, laughing lightly. His laughter was contagious, spreading from one inmate to another, until the laughter echoed from the cell, and filled the corridors.

Alexander ate his dinner quickly. When he was finished, he swallowed the milk in four large gulps.

"Slow down, man," an inmate said.

"Who knows how much time we have," Alexander said.

"They feed us this garbage, and they expect us to rush, too? I bet I'll take my time," the inmate said.

Alexander nodded approvingly.

"So, where are you from, man?" the inmate asked.

"Raleigh," Alexander said.

"I'm Calvin. My friends call me C," he said.

They slapped five and locked their fingers together.

"My name is Alexander," he said.

"All right," Calvin said.

"Where are you from?" Alexander asked.

"Laurinburg," Calvin answered.

Alexander looked at him blankly. "Where is Laurinburg?"

"Near South Carolina—in Scotland County," Calvin said.

"Did you attend Scotland County High?"

"Yeah, I did," Calvin said.

"My soccer team played against them a few weeks ago," Alexander said.

"Do you play?" Calvin asked.

"I did, however, I didn't play against you guys, because..." he paused, "...Because of my legal problems," Alexander said.

"So, you were in jail?" Calvin asked.

"Yeah, I was." Alexander lowered his eyes.

"Don't sweat it, man. I played ball at Scotland for two years. At the end of eleventh grade, they kicked me out. There was only two weeks left, and they kicked me out. Can you believe that?" Calvin asked.

"That's messed up."

"It's cool," Calvin said stoically. "I was tired of school anyway, you know what I'm saying?"

The cell door opened, and a barrel-chested man stood holding a clipboard. He called an inmate out of the cell, and the door closed behind him.

The barrel-chested man returned several times before calling on Alexander. When Alexander heard his name, he exited the cell quickly. "Walk straight down the hallway and through that door," the officer directed. He pointed to a door at the end of a long corridor.

Alexander quickly read the man's name tag—Hammond—and proceeded toward the door in silence.

When he entered the room, he saw a short pear-shaped woman standing near a machine.

"Stay there." Officer Hammond passed by Alexander and stepped over to a desk at the far corner of the room. "State your name," Officer Hammond said.

"Alexander Merchant," he replied.

"Date of birth?" Officer Hammond asked.

"September third, nineteen-eighty-eight."

"Social security number?" Officer Hammond asked.

"Three-four-five... Thirty-four... One-nine-three-eight," he answered.

"Come over here," the pear-shaped woman said.

Alexander focused on her weathered name tag—Rogers.

When Officer Hammond handed Officer Rogers a finger-print card, she inserted the card into a machine. "Give me your right hand." Officer Rogers pressed his thumb down onto a glass panel sitting on top of the machine. Pressing a red button, the machine lit up and scanned his thumbprint. She proceeded to scan each finger, and when she completed both hands, she pressed a green button, and a fingerprint card was ejected from the machine.

Alexander signed the card and followed Officer Hammond back to the holding cell.

Later, Officer Sanders opened the cell door. "Step out and line up against the wall," he ordered.

The 13 new inmates lined up along a white cinderblock wall.

"Walk to the end of the hallway, turn right, and stop at the open door," Officer Sanders said.

They walked to the open door quietly. The top portion of the Dutch door was open, and the bottom half remained closed.

"Step up," Officer Reed said.

An inmate standing at the head of the line, moved closer to the door and took the bedroll Officer Reed handed him. It consisted of two sheets and a pillowcase, rolled up tightly in a blue blanket.

"Stand in front of that door." The officer pointed to a closed metal door adjacent to the Dutch door.

Alexander noticed an exit sign above the door and felt relieved. He knew they would soon join the inmates populating the institution. He was anxious to escape the enclosed space and see where he would be living for the next chapter of his life. He thought about the inmates who lived beyond that door, and his relief turned into anxiety, and his anxiety led to pure terror. His mouth went dry, and his knees shook with fear. When the last bedroll was distributed, Officer Sanders pushed a metal button to the right of the door and turned to face a camera mounted on the ceiling above. When the door unlocked, the sound echoed throughout the corridor.

Officer Sanders pulled the door open. "Go to the end of the hallway, turn left, and stop at the first elevator."

The inmates obeyed.

Approaching the elevator, Alexander felt a stirring in his abdomen, and his shoulders felt as though he was carrying an extra 100 pounds.

"Reed to master control. Send elevator one down to receiving, please." Officer Reed held his mouth close to the radio.

"Ten-four," someone on his radio answered.

The elevator door slid open.

Officer Reed read eight names from his clipboard. "If I called your name, come with me. The rest of you stay with Officer Sanders," Officer Reed said.

When Alexander entered the elevator, they ascended to the third floor. He tried to prepare himself for imminent pandemonium. He envisioned stepping out of the elevator and looking up at cells stacked on top of each other and overflowing with seasoned inmates. He imagined a flock of arms hanging through a sea of gray bars, with hundreds of mirrors pushed through the bars, all focused on him. He imagined hearing inmates chanting madly, "fresh meat, fresh meat," as burning toilet paper fell like rain.

FOUR

The elevator stopped on the third floor, and Alexander's stomach tightened. The doors slid apart, and a cacophony of voices permeated the air.

Officer Reed stepped out of the elevator. "Come on out and line up against that wall," he said, pointing at a cinderblock wall.

"Hey, Daniels," Officer Reed greeted.

Officer Daniels stood talking to an inmate then came over to meet Officer Reed. "What's up, Reed?" Officer Daniels responded.

"How are you?"

"I'll be much better at six o'clock," Daniels said.

"You and me both."

"Is this all of them?" Daniels tilted his head in the direction of the new arrivals.

"There are four more, but they're going to the fourth floor," Reed said.

Alexander studied the rectangular dormitory. Unlike he imagined, the dormitory was only one level. Two rows of bunk beds spread out on one side of the dormitory and two rows spread out on the other side. There were bathrooms on both sides of the dormitory. Next to the elevator was a metal door, and above that door sat a small room. Plexiglass surrounded all four sides, and behind the plexiglass sat a gray-haired officer observing the new inmates. Making eye contact with Officer Reed, he brought his hand above his eye and saluted him.

Officer Reed returned the officer's salute and handed Officer Daniels a list of the new inmates and their bed assignments.

"I'll see you tomorrow," Reed said.

"Take it easy," Daniels said.

Alexander watched Officer Reed strut to the elevator and signal to the officer sitting behind the plexiglass before the gray-haired officer pushed a button, opening the elevator doors.

Officer Daniels gave the new inmates their bed assignments.

Alexander was assigned to bed 37 Up and immediately found his bunk. He tossed his bedroll on it and placed his shower shoes in the locker at the head of his bed. Dressing his bed, he saw his mattress was only two inches thick, with cotton protuberating from several holes and the mattress was on a flat metal frame. Suddenly, he was no longer yearning for sleep, but knew he had a big day ahead of him and rest would benefit him greatly.

"What's up, man?" Tony Jenkins called out.

Alexander turned and saw a young man facing him.

"I'm Tony, but they call me Tip," the young man said.

They slapped five and locked their fingers together. "I sleep on the bottom bunk," Tony said.

"It's nice to meet you," Alexander said.

"Is this your first time?" Tony asked.

"Yes, it is."

"I thought so. Just mind your own business and you'll be fine," Tony advised.

"Thanks."

"Have you been in prison before?" Alexander asked Tony.

"Not here, but I did time at C.A. Dillon and Whitaker School," he said.

"Oh, I see." Alexander looked confused.

"They're kiddy camps for juveniles," Tony said.

"How long were you there?"

"I went to Whitaker School for six months when I was thirteen and was sent to C.A. Dillon when I was fifteen—now I'm here," Tony said.

"How old are you now?" Alexander asked.

"Seventeen," Tony said.

"Have you been in prison since you were fifteen?" Alexander asked.

"Well, C.A. Dillon is not really a prison. It's more like a reform school for young teens. Anyway, I left C.A. Dillon when I was sixteen. I stayed in a group home for a while, and then I was allowed to go back home. A few months later, I was caught driving a stolen car, and the rest is history," Tony said.

"Oh, shit. What are you doing here, man." Calvin came up from behind, smiling.

Alexander turned and saw Calvin Dillard rushing over.

"What's up, C?" Tony interjected before they slapped five and embraced.

"I can't believe my man is here," Calvin said, enthusiastically.

"This is my boy, Alex," Calvin introduced.

"We've already met," Alexander said.

"I haven't seen you since Dillon," Calvin said to Tip.

"I know, what's been up?" Tony asked.

"I can't call it," Calvin said.

"How do you know each other?" Alexander asked them both.

"We were at C.A Dillon together," Tony said.

"And Whitaker School, too," Calvin said.

Officer Daniels made his rounds, handing out brown paper bags.

Alexander opened his and examined the contents. He found a toothbrush, toothpaste, a bar of soap, deodorant, and dental floss. With a towel draped over his shoulder, he made his way to the bathroom. The water ran hot and steadily upon his broad shoulders. At home, he would often stand in the shower and let the water massage his shoulders until it ran cold. He closed his eyes and imagined he was at home, standing in his mother's bathroom, safe and relaxed. The sound of a flushing toilet penetrated his thoughts, reminding him this was neither the time nor the place for lingering or nostalgia. He quickly covered his body in a thick lather. The government soap was rough on his brown skin. He rinsed himself off and dressed quickly.

Sitting on his bed, he noticed four phones at the far end of the dormitory. He climbed down and strutted over to the phones. Upon examination, he saw no place to insert a coin. He had no money and was uncertain if he was even allowed to carry any. He pressed zero and waited for an operator. An automated voice instructed him to enter a five-digit code. Frustrated, he placed the phone in its cradle and moseyed back to his bed.

Tony was lying on his side thumbing through a magazine. "You need a code to use the phone," Tony said.

"Where do I get a code?" Alexander asked.

"Your case manager will give it to you in a few days."

"I want to call home and tell my mother where I am."

"Trust me, Alex, I know how you feel, but you'll have to wait," Tony said.

Alexander climbed onto his bed and lay in silence.

"I would let you use mine, but my account is too low," Tony said.

Alexander said nothing and thought about how his life had so drastically gone awry. His emotions swelled deep within his bosom. He took several deep breaths and filed his emotions away for another time. He thought about his mother whose despondency wore deeply on his mind. Knowing he was the cause of her sadness, brought him great despair.

"ATTENTION ON THE COMPOUND, ATTENTION ALL AREAS. IT IS NOW COUNT TIME, COUNT TIME, COUNT TIME," a voice bellowed out of speakers.

The inmates moved to their beds and sat upright.

An officer entered the dormitory and assisted Daniels with counting the inmates. They counted and compared their summations. Concurring on a final number, they proceeded to the control center, and Officer Daniels picked up a telephone and gave the count to the gray-haired man sitting in the control center.

"We have a double count of fifty-three," Officer Daniels said and placed the phone back in its cradle.

The gray-haired officer called the count into Master Control.

"Master Control," a voice answered.

"This is the third-floor control center. We have a double count of fifty-three," he said.

"That's a good count."

"Ten-four," the gray-haired officer said. He pressed a button on his control panel and spoke into a small micro-phone. His voice bellowed out of a small speaker where Officer

Daniels and the other officer stood chatting. "Good count," he said.

The officer was near the door waiting to be let out. The control room officer pressed a button on the control panel and the door unlocked.

"See you later," she said, and the door slammed shut behind her.

"ATTENTION ON THE COMPOUND, ATTENTION ALL AREAS, WE HAVE A GOOD COUNT, GOOD COUNT, GOOD COUNT," a voice bellowed out of speakers.

The inmates cleared their beds quickly.

Tony stood and reached for a towel.

"The lights go out at eleven o'clock, so take care of everything now," Tony said.

The clock read 10:25 P.M. Alexander lay back and clasped his fingers behind his head. His elbows spread out in both directions. He closed his eyes and tried to relax. Once again, he saw Natalie, staring, beckoning. He forced her out of his mind, and she forced herself back in. Frustrated, he moped over to the television, which was in a metal cage mounted high on the wall in the center of the dormitory. He found a vacant seat to watch the Dallas Cowboys play the Washington Redskins.

The inmates watched quietly and cheered sporadically, but Alexander was not a fan of either team. He had nothing else to do, so he watched the game as well. Midway through the third quarter, the Washington Redskins lead by 13. On a punt return, the Dallas Cowboys made it to the Redskins' 39-yard line. Alexander sat up in his seat. On a hand-off, the Cowboys' running back picked up six more yards. On the second down, the quarterback threw the ball to the sideline, the football bounced out of the wide receiver's hands and fell onto the grass. The official threw a yellow flag into the air.

"Pass interference, first down," the official said.

Several inmates cheered and a few yelled obscenities toward the official.

"Lights out, gentlemen. Take it in. Lights out," Officer Daniels announced, standing in the center of the dormitory.

The inmates slowly moved away from the television. Others rushed into the bathroom to relieve themselves and tend to their hygiene. Within a few minutes, all were lying in bed, and the dormitory grew dark. Several lights burned dimly, slightly illuminating the room. Officer Daniels inspected the dormitory, making sure everyone was in bed. Satisfied, he went back to his chair and sat down, listening to a low chatter throughout the dormitory.

"You're crazy," someone yelled, and several inmates laughed loudly.

"Quiet down," Officer Daniels instructed, and the dormitory grew silent again.

Alexander preferred the low chatter, the silence made him uncomfortable. As he lay in bed, listening to the ceiling fans blow hot air around, his palms grew sweaty, and his heart pounded in his chest. Once again, his imagination got the best of him. He fancied several ghastly scenarios that would surely land him in the hospital, or worse. He heard noises around his bed, but when he sat up, no one was there. Feeling silly, he lay back down, closed his eyes, and took several deep breaths.

Alexander's mother had practiced Yoga for many years and he would often come home to find her meditating. Sometimes on their living room floor, sometimes on her bed, and sometimes he found her in her bedroom's oversized closet. She had tried to teach him the art of meditation many times, but Alexander never took it seriously. Now, as he lay behind prison walls, he focused on what he had learned and observed. He lay still, with both hands resting at his sides. He took in deep breaths and blew them out fully. "Breathe through your nose,

Alexander, so that the air is filtered by your cilia," his mother had told him. He cleared his mind, and allowed nothing in. When a thought entered his mind, he allowed it to pass through. He relaxed his temples, his face, his mouth, and his tongue. He relaxed his neck, his shoulders, his arms, his hands, and his fingers. Then he relaxed his chest, his stomach, his waist, his legs, and finally his toes.

When he was fully relaxed, he imagined himself lying next to a small pond deep in the forest. Finally, he prayed and asked God to protect him and see him through this madness. Finally, lying next to a peaceful pond, he dozed and fell asleep.

FIVE

"Wake up, gentlemen," Officer Daniels yelled.

Alexander opened his eyes, but he did not move.

"Wake up, make your beds and get dressed." Officer Daniels strolled past each bed and checked to make sure they were all awake. Several inmates were still fast asleep, so he shook their mattresses until they were awake. One inmate remained fast asleep when Officer Daniels shook his mattress. He banged his baton against the sleeping inmate's metal bed frame. The awful sound made the inmate sit straight up, as though he had been jolted by an electric current.

Alexander climbed down from his top bunk and could see Tony lying on his back, awake. He gathered his toiletries and went into the bathroom. His toothpaste exploded into millions of tiny bubbles, filling his mouth with a taste of fresh mint. Dripping from his mouth, the toothpaste washed down pipes a half century old. Alexander rinsed his mouth, splashed water onto his face, and puttered back to his bed.

"Once your bed is made and you are dressed, you can lie back down," Tony said.

Alexander watched Tony quickly dress himself and make his bed and followed suit. "What time is breakfast?" Alexander asked.

"After count," Tony said.

"When is count time?"

"Six o'clock."

Alexander settled in front of the television and watched the morning news.

"Cold and cloudy for Asheville. Mixed rain and ice overnight," the meteorologist reported. *Asheville? Is that where I am?* Alexander wondered.

He went to a small window and could see the side of a snow-covered mountain. He meandered back to his seat and sat in front of the television. He came to the realization he had absolutely no idea where he was currently located. He did not even know the name of the institution holding him prisoner. He felt lost and despondent. He considered asking someone, but by doing so, he conjectured he might as well write naive on his forehead. He would talk to his case manager soon and decided it was better to wait until then. The popping sound of the unlocking door echoed throughout the quiet dormitory. Alexander turned to see who was reporting for duty.

Two officers stepped through the metal door. Eager to go home, Officer Daniels stood and met them. His countenance showed just how delighted he was to see them.

"Shit, not that motherfucker," an inmate said.

Officer Daniels gave Officer Mahoney his radio, handcuffs, and baton. The other officer entered the control room.

Alexander turned away and continued watching television. Soon after, a loud voice bellowed through the speakers,

"ATTENTION ON THE COMPOUND, ATTENTION ALL AREAS. IT IS NOW COUNT TIME, COUNT TIME, COUNT TIME."

Everyone quickly moved to their beds and sat up, facing the center of the dormitory. Another officer entered and Officer Mahoney methodically counted each inmate, calling it into the control room.

The control room officer recorded the count, called Master Control, and announced, "Good count."

Hearing this, the other officer exited the dormitory, and Officer Mahoney sat in the chair next to the control room.

Alexander, once again, sat in front of the television, trying to determine where he was.

Soon the intercom came back to life. "ATTENTION ON THE COMPOUND, IT IS NOW CHOW TIME, CHOW TIME, CHOW TIME," a voice bellowed.

Officer Mahoney's radio came to life, and Alexander listened closely.

"Compound to the third floor."

"Go for the third floor," Mahoney replied.

"Send your unit to chow."

"Ten-four." Mahoney replaced his radio on his belt. "Chow time, gentlemen," Officer Mahoney announced.

The inmates scrambled for the door, and Alexander followed the crowd. They gathered in front of two elevators. The elevator to the right opened and the inmates packed themselves in like spaghetti in a box. Alexander attempted to squeeze himself in when he felt a firm hand grasp his arm. His muscles tightened, and his mouth went completely dry.

"Hold on, Alex," Calvin said.

He turned and saw Calvin and Tony.

"We'll get the next one," Tony said.

The elevator on the left opened, and the trio rode down

together. Under normal conditions, these two delinquents were not the sort of guys Alexander would associate with, but these were not normal conditions. Alexander knew he had to make alliances fast, and Tony seemed like the sort of fellow he should have on his side. Calvin, however, was part of the package.

The elevator descended to the second floor and when the doors opened, Alexander saw a stream of brown jumpsuits moving into the cafeteria. The cafeteria was the size of a high school gymnasium. Two lines ran along the walls of the cafeteria, extending outside into the corridor. There were four doors. The inmates entered the two outer doors and exited the two doors in the center. The lines moved steadily, and the trio made their way into the cafeteria, along the wall, and eventually to the front. They each received two slices of bacon, two pieces of toast, one serving spoon of grits, and one serving spoon of runny eggs. There was coffee, orange juice, and milk cartons available to wash it down. There was also cold cereal available. In the past, Alexander only ate cold cereal for break-fast when his mother was too tired to cook.

There were eight rows of stainless-steel tables—four rows on each side of the cafeteria. The cacophony of voices made it difficult for Alexander to concentrate. Alexander blessed his meal, but Tony and Calvin wasted no time digging in. When he finished blessing his meal, and picked up his plastic utensils, his friends were halfway done. He began with his bacon and toast. He preferred his eggs well done, and these were too loose for his liking, and they seemed artificial. Suddenly, the cold cereal didn't seem so bad. He contemplated going back for a bowl of cornflakes.

The sergeant standing in the center of the cafeteria, faced Alexander's side. "Let's go! Now," the sergeant yelled, gesturing toward the exit with his thumb.

Calvin stuffed the remaining portion of eggs into his mouth. Tony quickly washed down his breakfast with a cup of lukewarm coffee. Holding a piece of toast in his mouth, Tony stood and picked up his tray.

The sergeant came toward Alexander, discovering he had only halfway completed his meal. "Get up and get out of here."

Alexander stood and followed his friends to the trash can. Waiting his turn, he heard the rhythmic sound of plastic trays pounding against a trashcan and slamming down onto a stainless-steel table. The line moved steadily and marching toward the exit, he saw the barrel-chested officer standing in the middle of the cafeteria reading from a clipboard. He recognized the man as Officer Hammond, one of the officers who had taken his fingerprints. Before reaching the door, he heard his name.

"Alexander Merchant," said Officer Hammond.

Alexander went to see what the officer wanted. "Yes, sir, I'm Alexander Merchant,"

"You are going to Diagnostics. Wait for me out in the hallway."

Alexander exited the cafeteria and looked for his friends. Tony was nowhere to be found, but Calvin was waiting in a line with the group from last night's bus ride. Officer Rogers, the pear-shaped officer who had taken his fingerprints stood nearby.

"Stand in line," Officer Rogers said.

Alexander moved just behind Calvin.

"Are we going to see our case manager?"

"Hell if I know," Calvin said.

Eventually, Officer Hammond exited the cafeteria and counted the inmates who were in line. "They're all here," he said.

"Follow me," Officer Rogers instructed. She led the line,

and Officer Hammond followed from behind. They went up one flight of stairs to the third floor, turned right, and proceeded down a corridor, stopping at a metal door. Officer Rogers waved hello to the officer sitting in a control room. The control room officer pressed a button and the metal door unlocked just before Officer Rogers pulled the door open, leading the inmates into the Diagnostics Center. The door locked behind them, and another door unlocked. Officer Rogers pulled the second door open.

"Step inside," she said.

The inmates crowded into a holding cell. The cement benches aligning the walls were fully occupied, so Alexander stood near the plexiglass window and waited.

A woman came to the door and called the new admissions out into the hallway. "Line up against the wall," she said. "My name is Ms. Coleman, and I'll be giving you several tests today. When you go inside, sit at a desk with a pencil. You will be given an IQ test, also a math, reading, and spelling test. These tests are mandatory, and you cannot finish your processing until they are complete. Which means you cannot see your case manager, get a job, transfer, or do anything until these tests are complete. There is no talking and do not touch anything until I tell you to do so. If you do not follow my instructions, I'll kick you out, lock you up in segregation, and test you at another time." She gave the group a once-over. "Does everyone understand?" Ms. Coleman asked.

"Yes, ma'am," they said together.

"Step inside and have a seat." Ms. Coleman pointed to an open door.

The new inmates did as they were told. She placed a booklet in front of them. "This is the Beta Two IQ test." Ms. Coleman carefully read the directions aloud and asked if anyone had any questions. No one spoke, so she continued, "Pick up your pencils and write your name, date of birth, and today's date on the cover," she said.

When they were done writing, she instructed, "Open the booklet to page one." She explained the practice questions and gave them two minutes to complete them.

"In example one, the correct answer is B, and in example two, the correct answer is C. Does everyone understand why these are the correct answers? Does anyone have any questions?" After there was no response, she said, "Okay. Turn your booklets over to page two and start now." She held a stopwatch in her hand.

The Beta II IQ test consisted of five parts, including picture completion, number works, symbols, and a running maze. Each section was designed to test a category of intelligence, and the combined score of all five sections were used to calculate the intelligence quotient, or IQ, of the subjects.

Alexander recalled riding in the car with his mother and listening to a story on National Public Radio about the Beta IQ test. He recalled the journalist stating the U.S. Army was first to use the Beta IQ test to determine which soldiers were suitable for officer training. They saw the Beta IQ test as a valuable tool for simultaneously testing large numbers of illiterate recruits. The success of the Beta IQ test led to its use by other institutions, who for various reasons wanted to measure intelligence. He wondered if the North Carolina Department of Corrections was using the Beta II IQ test to determine what sort of programs inmates are eligible for. He decided he had better do his best.

At the end of section five, Ms. Coleman collected the tests and administered the Wide Range Achievement Test. The Wide Range Achievement Test was designed to measure what was needed to learn basic reading, math, and spelling skills. Ms. Coleman guided the young offenders through each section of the test.

Alexander finished quickly and awaited her next instructions.

"Time. Pencils down," Ms. Coleman announced.

Alexander scanned the room and saw his new cohorts still writing furiously. "Time. Put your pencils down," Ms. Coleman reiterated. She went around and collected the tests. "Line up near the door," she ordered, and then escorted the inmates back to the holding cell. "Wait here," she said and returned to her office.

Alexander and the other inmates were waiting in the holding cell when a man holding a clipboard opened the door.

"Calvin Dillard," he called out.

"Right here," Calvin shouted from the back of the cell.

"Come with me," the man said.

Calvin stood and strolled out of the cell and followed the man down a hallway. Soon a woman came to the door and called another inmate forward. Following her were more staff calling inmates out of the holding cell, bringing them back, and calling more. Finally, a woman returned to the holding cell and called Alexander.

"I'm Alexander Merchant."

"Down the hallway," she said, and pointed.

Alexander obeyed, and she followed closely behind.

"Turn right and go to the second office on your left."

Alexander entered the office and sat down as he was told. "Are you my case manager?"

"No, I'm not. My name is Ms. Payette." She took a seat behind her desk. "I am going to ask you several questions to begin your processing. When you are done processing, you will be assigned to a case manager."

"How long will that take?"

"A few days," Ms. Payette answered.

"When will I be able to call my mother?"

"Let me ask my questions first, and then I'll answer any questions you have. Okay?"

"Agreed," Alexander said.

Ms. Payette thumbed through Alexander's file. "You have an IQ of one-twenty-eight. That's pretty good, and your achievement scores are perfect," she said.

Alexander nodded.

She turned to her computer and placed her fingers on home row. The cursor was already on a line labeled first name, and she typed Alexander.

"What's your middle name?"

"Manchester," Alexander said.

Ms. Payette typed Manchester and Merchant in the appropriate spaces.

"How old are you?"

"Eighteen," he answered.

"Date of birth?" she asked.

"September third, nineteen-eighty-eight."

Ms. Payette typed as quickly as he spoke, firing off questions rapidly and typing as he answered. "What's your home address?"

"Seven-fifteen Woodburn Road, Raleigh, North Carolina, two-seven-six-o-one," Alexander answered.

"What's your mother's name?"

"Emily Merchant," Alexander answered.

"Her *maiden* name?"

"Manchester."

"Would you say she is in good health, fair health, or poor health?"

"Fair."

"Does she have any illnesses?"

"She was diagnosed with breast cancer a few years ago, but it is now in remission—which is why I was wondering if I could be sent someplace closer to home."

"Let me finish with my questions first." Ms. Payette adjusted in her seat and continued, "What's your father's name?"

"Alexander P. Merchant."

"Would you say he is in good health, fair—"

"He's dead," Alexander said, cutting her off. "He died when I was a child."

"Oh, I'm sorry. What was the cause of death?"

"A car accident," Alexander mumbled.

"Do you have any brothers or sisters?"

"No ma'am, I am an only child."

"What was the last grade you completed?"

"The eleventh grade," he said.

"What is the last school you attended?"

"Needham Broughton High, in Raleigh,"

"Do you have a GED?"

"No,"

"Okay, good. We're almost done," she said.

Ms. Payette turned to a small shelf in the corner of her office and retrieved a box and sat it down on her desk. The box was full of eight by seven fingerprint cards. She found Alexander's and put the box back on the shelf. She filled in his information in the appropriate spaces and wrote his seven-digit OPUS Identification number, his social security number, his date of birth, and his mother's maiden name.

"Sign here," she said, pointing to a cup full of pens reserved for inmate use.

Alexander took a pen and signed as he was told.

"Okay," Ms. Payette turned back to her computer. "Now, I need you to tell me about your crime." She opened Alexander's file and studied it momentarily. "You are here for taking indecent liberties with a child." The disgust was evident on her face.

"I met her in school," Alexander said.

"I am not interested in where you met her. I only care about the details of your crime. Now what is your victim's name?" Ms. Payette asked.

"I do not have a victim," Alexander protested.

Ms. Payette turned to face him. "You're in prison for statutory rape, aren't you? So, who did you rape?"

"I didn't rape anyone."

"So, why are you here?

"I am here because I took a plea bargain—because my attorney is a charlatan, warning me of what would happen if I went to trial—predicting a swift conviction and a long sentence. But it seems I am still convicted."

"Listen," she said in exasperation. "You are here because you had inappropriate relations with a minor. You're convicted because you pled guilty, and I am not concerned with the details of your trial. What I want to know is, what is the name of the person you had inappropriate relations with?"

"Don't you want to hear my side of the story?"

"No, I don't. I only need to know the victim's name."

Alexander sat back in his chair and fought back his emotions. He took three deep breaths and tried to swallow. Collecting himself, he lowered his head and said her name. "Natalie."

"Natalie what?" Ms. Payette asked.

"Agadani."

"Thank you," Ms. Payette said and typed Natalie Agadani

into the database. "How old were you at the time of your offense?"

"It happened on my eighteenth birthday."

"How old was she?"

"She was fifteen at the time, but she turned sixteen two weeks later," he answered.

"The legal age of consent is sixteen in North Carolina. Didn't you know that?"

"No I didn't. No one had ever explained the law to me. Besides, our birthdays are only two weeks apart, so I didn't think it mattered," he said.

"Was she a freshman?"

"No. We were in the same grade. I started school late, because my father died soon before I was scheduled to start the first grade. I took it really hard, so my mother kept me out of school for a year. Natalie, however, grew up in Sweden and later lived in Nairobi, Kenya before coming to the United States. She was academically advanced and skipped a grade. We met in the eleventh grade and started dating," Alexander said.

"I see," Ms. Payette said, her face softening a little. "How long did you date?"

"About nine months."

"Any sexual contact before your eighteenth birthday?" she asked.

"No, ma'am. Only kissing."

"Did you have sex anymore after that?"

"Once more a few days later," Alexander answered.

As Alexander sat before Ms. Payette and heard the words leaving his mouth, he knew their relationship was much more than that. He saw in his mind precisely how they first made love, but he kept the details to himself.

"I was arrested a few days later and I've been in jail ever since. My attorney says that if we had only waited two weeks for her to turn sixteen before being together, it would not have been crime at all. I wish I had known that before," he said, gloomily. "My lawyer convinced me to take a plea, because he said that North Carolina has a zero-tolerance policy on statutory offenses, and claimed that if I took it to trial, I was sure to receive a much longer sentence."

"How did the police find out?" Ms. Payette asked.

"It was a Nancy Drew Spy Kit," he said, shaking his head in disbelief.

"Nancy Drew?"

"Yes. Natalie received a spy kit for her birthday from her aunt in Sweden. She didn't want it, so she gave it to a girl across the street from her. The spy kit included a magnifying glass, binoculars, a flashlight, and a notebook. The girl used the binoculars to peer into Natalie's room and saw us in bed together. She told her father what she saw, and her father called the police."

"Are you serious?" she asked.

"I am," he answered.

"Were you not able to make bail?"

"My mother tried raising the money, but she couldn't," Alexander answered.

"Could she not get a home equity loan?"

"No, that wasn't possible. My mother refinanced our house to pay for her cancer treatments, and there was no more equity available. A family friend had agreed to pay my bail, and would've paid it this weekend had I not accepted this plea bargain," Alexander lamented.

"How is your mother doing?" Ms. Pyette asked.

"Aside from what's happened to me, she's fine." Alexander stared at the ceiling panels and focused on a water stain. His eyes turned red and puffy. "I don't know... Do you think I should have taken my case to trial?"

"Only you can answer that," Ms. Payette said. "Your lawyer was right about one thing. North Carolina has a zero-tolerance policy for statutory offenses. The legal age for consensual sex is sixteen in North Carolina, and the older person cannot be any more than two years older than the minor at the time of sexual contact. So, although Natalie's birthday and your birthday are only two weeks apart, at the time of sexual contact, you were three years older than Natalie, which technically made sexual contact a crime. Had you waited two weeks to have sex, you wouldn't be here now. It would not have been a crime at all. It was only illegal for a total of fourteen days.

"Therefore, if you had chosen to go to trial, there's a chance a sympathetic judge or jury would have given you an acquittal, but there is also a chance you could've been found guilty, which would have yielded a much tougher sentence," she said. "On the bright side, you are still young, and in two years, you will be back home with your family," Ms. Payette said.

"I guess you're right," Alexander said.

"Of course, I am right. You seem to be a smart young man, so I'm sure you'll be fine. Now, get yourself together, dry your tears, and step out of here with your head up," she said.

"Yes, ma'am."

"Do you have any other questions?" she asked.

"Is there any way I could move someplace closer to home?"

"Not until you turn nineteen. This is the only place for offenders in your age group," she said.

"I see." He sighed and looked away.

She entered his crime version into the database. "Are you ready?" she asked.

"Yes, I'm ready."

She stood and stepped to her door. "Come with me," she said.

Alexander followed her back to the holding cell.

"Ms. Payette, when will I receive my pin number? I need to call my mother," Alexander said.

"You'll get it as soon as it's ready. In the meantime, I'll send your mother an information package," Ms. Payette said. She closed the cell door and sauntered back to her office.

CHAPTER

SIX

Alexander entered his dormitory and climbed into bed. He was exhausted and he thought of nothing. The sounds of the dormitory faded into the edge of his consciousness, like a neighbor's loud television, muffled by a shared wall. He desired sleep, but the anxiety of prison wouldn't allow it. Whenever he closed his eyes, he heard heavy breathing and footsteps approaching stealthily. He knew it was only his imagination, but he would open his eyes anyway, to see if anyone was there.

Realizing sleep was hopeless, Alexander got out of bed and settled in front of the television. He had never cared much for television, in fact, there hadn't been a working television in his house since he was six years old. When his father's old floor model burned out, Emily Merchant, his mother, had never replaced it. And she refused to buy him any video games, no matter how much he pleaded. When they wanted entertainment, they read together and played board games such as Scrabble, Checkers, Backgammon and Cranium.

Alexander's father taught him to play chess at an early age.

He would place a dollar in a jar before each game, promising that whenever Alexander beat him, he could have the jar and all the money in it, but he would not allow Alexander to win easily. So, if he wanted the money, he would have to beat him fair and square. He encouraged Alexander to consider the advantages and disadvantages of every move, and to consider how each move would impact his endgame.

After his father's death, Alexander's mother continued the practice. As Alexander's understanding improved, she used Chess to incorporate life lessons, just as his father had planned. Alexander's father believed that a person who understood chess, also understood life, because at the end of the day, the quality of a person's life is a direct result of the choices he or she has made. This simple idea was at the core of every lesson his father had taught him. "Brush your teeth Alexander, or when you're my age you won't have any," he would say, or "eat your vegetables, or you will never grow up to be strong like me."

Emily expanded these lessons for her son. She would tell him to study hard, or you won't get into the college of your choice, and if you don't get into the college of your choice, you may not get the job of your choice, and if you don't get the job of your choice, you may not lead the life you want to live. As Alexander sat in front of the television, all these lessons came crashing back, along with more of his parents' ideas. His father, Alexander P. Merchant, strongly believed in determinism, which is the idea all current and future events are causally necessitated by past and present events combined with the laws of nature. Determinism suggests that the core of a person's being, and his or her ability to make decisions, are controlled by his or her experiences and stimuli in the environment.

Alexander found dozens of his father's books on the

subject, all examining various degrees of determinism. He also found several essays his father had written, arguing the compatibility of determinism and free will. In one article, he argued that in most cases, a person's religious beliefs were determined by where and when he or she was born, recognizing the fact he himself was Christian, because he was born in the United States to Christian parents. Hence, had he been born in Iran or Pakistan, he would probably be a Muslim, and if he were born in India, he would be a Hindu. However, with free will, he could turn away from those religions and become a Christian, if he chose to do so.

In another article, Alexander P. Merchant examined how success was determined by factors such as class, sex, race, and social status. He argued that a person's experiences, social groups, and random interactions with people had more to do with a person's success than some innate traits he or she may have. He suggested that every decision a parent makes for a child, even very early on, will affect the rest of his or her life, and that every action begets a reaction, a chain of events centuries old.

This is the reason Alexander's mother never replaced the television, and why she owned enough books to fill a library. It is why she exposed Alexander to everything imaginable from literature and the arts to world music and foreign films, and why she encouraged him to shed peer and cultural restraints, and to be his own man.

Alexander sat thinking of this and wondered what this chapter of his life would determine for him. *What experiences would this concrete jungle provide, and how would my life be shaped by it?* He focused his eyes on the brown jumpsuit and cloth shoes he was wearing. At that moment, he decided it wouldn't affect him at all. He wouldn't allow it to. He was determined to leave prison just as he had come in, and he would get his life back no matter what it took.

Perhaps he was naive to think he wouldn't be affected by it, but sometimes a little naiveté was necessary. It could be the difference between heroism and victimhood—the determining factor between failure and success. Alexander's father had considered the role of naiveté as well. He had identified examples of when naiveté had proven more valuable than expertise, and other times when it caused destruction, but Alexander had never read that article—and it was good that he hadn't, because who knows how that idea would have affected his plans going forward.

Calvin's voice penetrated Alexander's consciousness, "What's up, Alex?"

"How are you, C?" Alexander asked.

"Where have you been, man? I waited for you to come back," Calvin said.

"I've been in Diagnostics all morning, talking to my case analyst. She gave me the third degree," Alexander said.

"Mine barely asked me anything," Calvin said

"Now I only need to see my case manager," Alexander said.

"Well, you're all set then," Calvin said.

"I'm trapped, is more like it. I cannot move anywhere closer to home," Alexander said.

"Why not?"

"Because this is the only prison in the state for inmates eighteen and under. I can't go anywhere else until I turn nineteen," Alexander said, gloomily.

Calvin didn't respond to him, only staring blankly at the television, pretending not to care, but Alexander knew otherwise. He knew not even the hardest criminals wanted to be far away from home, and Calvin was no hardened criminal. Sure, he had made mistakes, but who hadn't? *And if his attorney was anything like Julian Hoffman, it is easy to see how he ended up in here*, Alexander thought.

"Where's Tip?" Alexander asked.

"He's in school," Calvin said.

"There's a school here?"

"Of course, we all gotta go," Calvin said.

"Is it a GED program or an actual diploma?" Alexander asked.

"GED," Calvin said.

Alexander was disappointed. "I guess that's better than nothing," he said.

"Shit, it's the same thing," Calvin said.

"I guess so." Earning a GED was not something Alexander had ever considered, but it was his only option now. He would have to figure out how to make it work. *I have never heard of an ambassador with a GED. Oh, who am I kidding, The State Department would never hire a felon, neither would the United Nations,* he thought.

Calvin took the remote control and flipped through channels. "Have you seen the gym?" Calvin asked.

"We have a gym, too?" Alexander asked with raised brows.

"Yeah, I checked it out after I left Diagnostics," Calvin said.

"What is it like?"

"It's not bad. There is a B-ball court, pool table, and some weights. There is an outside rec yard too, but it's cold as a bitch out there today." Calvin settled on a movie and crossed his arms.

"Let's go to the gym," Alexander said, rising to his feet.

"We can't. They kicked us out until after lunch," Calvin said.

Alexander sat back down and watched television for a while with Calvin. A detective drama with second-rate actors.

The movie was awful, but they had nothing better to do, so they watched it anyway.

Soon the elevator doors opened, and returning students filed out into the dormitory.

Tony put away his things, and sat next to Calvin and Alexander.

"What's up, Tip?" Calvin said.

"What's up, C? What's up, Alexander?" Tony said.

"Hi, Tip. How was school?" Alexander asked.

"It's something to do. Anything to pass the time," Tony said and strolled over to the bulletin board, read the menu, and came back and sat beside Alexander. "Hot dogs," he said.

Alexander looked at him blankly.

"Hot dogs," he repeated. "It's what we're having for lunch today. The menu is on the bulletin board."

THE HOT DOGS were dry and the French fries were overcooked. Alexander would have to get used to the banality of food prepared by inattentive cooks. He ate swiftly nonetheless, barely finishing before the austere sergeant rushed them out.

They entered the gymnasium, and for a moment, the sound of basketballs pounding on the hardwood floors and the sound of squeaking shoes bouncing off the walls, reminded Alexander of his school gymnasium, but the fleeting expletives flowing from the aggressive ball players were a stronger reminder of where he was.

"Let's get up a game," Calvin said.

"I can't, I have to be back in class," Tony said.

Alexander sunk a shot and trotted off to retrieve the ball. He tossed it over to Tony, who dribbled the ball between his legs and around his back before driving towards the basket and leaping, as he rolled the ball from his fingertips into the basket. They stood in a half circle, passing time by shooting jump shots and free throws—three pointers and layups.

"I gotta go," Tony said.

"I'll see you after class," Alexander said.

"I'm about to put it on this fool, son," Calvin said, as he rolled the ball down one arm and across his back. "We'll play to twenty-one, check," Calvin yelled out and passed the ball to Alexander, and Alexander passed it back.

Alexander lost the first match by seven points. He fared slightly better in the second match, losing only by two.

They were soon joined by other young inmates and spent the afternoon playing pick-up matches with young men who took the game far too seriously.

They were soon sent back to the dormitories, and at 4:00 P.M., they were counted, and they watched television, ate dinner, counted again, and the next three days were the same.

Alexander lay in bed, thinking of his conversation with Ms. Payette. He thought of her words. *If you had chosen to go to trial, there's a chance a sympathetic jury would have given you an acquittal, but there is also a chance you could've been found guilty, which would have yielded a much tougher sentence.* He decided to write a letter to the judge, so he would know who he sent to prison.

Alexander leaned over the edge of his bed and peered down at Tony. "Hey, Tip."

Tony removed his headphones and looked up at him. "What's up?" he asked.

"Do you have paper? I need to write a letter," he said.

Tony reached into his locker, and then handed Alexander a notebook. "Here you go."

"Thanks." Alexander turned onto his stomach and began to write.

Dear Judge Roger Gregory,

My name is Alexander Merchant, and I was
sentenced in your court on October 3, 2006,
to 24-36 months for taking indecent liberties
with a child. My attorney, Julian Hoffman,
convinced me to accept a plea agreement, and
now that I have begun my prison sentence, I
no longer feel that I made the right decision. I know that all plea agreements are
final, and there is nothing to be done at
this point, but I wanted to explain to you
the circumstances of my crime, so that you
would know who you sent to prison.

Alexander wondered how he should begin to tell Judge
Gregory about his relationship with Natalie. He had tried not
to think about her since coming to prison, and now memories
of her filled his mind.

Alexander saw her for the first time while giving an oral
presentation. She had transferred to Needham Broughton High
School in January of his junior year. Two weeks earlier on the
last day of school, before Christmas break, Alexander's English
teacher, Ms. Cummings, had informed the class that they
would have to complete a book report and an oral presentation
when they returned to school. She gave them a list of classic
novels to choose from, and Alexander chose to do his report on
Robinson Crusoe by Daniel Defoe. After school, Alexander
strolled past Wake Tabernacle and saw Reverend Talbert's car
in the parking lot. He found him in his office sitting at his desk.

"Hello, Reverend Talbert," Alexander said.

"Hello, Alexander. What can I do for you?" Reverend
Talbert asked.

"I only stopped by to tell you that I am reading Robinson Crusoe for my English class," Alexander said.

"Wonderful. Are you enjoying it?"

"Well, I haven't started it yet. I only found out about it today, and when I leave here, I'm going to the library to pick up a copy."

"Have you reserved a copy at the library?" Reverend Talbert asked.

"No sir, I didn't think I needed to."

"You cannot expect to find a copy of Robinson Crusoe just sitting on the library shelf."

"I can't?"

"Daniel Defoe wrote it almost three hundred years ago, and it is still among the most read books in any library. There is usually a long waiting list," he said.

Alexander felt disappointed. "I'll just have to buy a copy of my own," Alexander said.

"Nonsense." Reverend Talbert opened a draw. "You will take mine." He pulled out an old copy of *Robinson Crusoe* from his desk and placed it in front of Alexander.

Alexander could tell it was once a beautiful volume. His eyes fell on the engravings once full of vibrant colors. Only traces of gold remained over the engraved letters, reading the title and the author's name.

Reverend Talbert sat smiling.

"Thank you, sir," he said.

"Don't mention it. This book has brought me much comfort over the years. I have read it many times and have a collector's edition at home which I have never cracked open. It only sits on my bookshelf." Reverend Talbert stood to his feet and said, "You must come by and discuss the book with me."

"I will, sir," Alexander said.

"Will I see you on Sunday morning?" Reverend Talbert asked.

"Yes sir, I'll be here."

"Good," Reverend Talbert said.

Alexander went directly home and began reading. Moments later he heard his mother calling him to help her bring in groceries. "I'm coming," he said. Alexander continued reading, and soon after, she was calling his name again. He quickly ran out to her car.

"Hi, baby," Emily Merchant said.

"Hi, Mom." He hauled in bag after bag, until they covered the kitchen table, the countertops, and the floor. He was heading back to his bedroom when she called after him.

"Alexander, help me put the food away," she requested.

He reluctantly turned back to the kitchen. Once all the groceries were put away, he went back to his room and resumed reading. Not even thirty minutes later, she called him to dinner only for him to ignore her as long as he could.

"Come and eat your dinner," she yelled.

"I'm not hungry. I'll eat later," he called out.

"Whatever you're doing in there can wait. Come and eat your dinner," she said.

When Alexander came into the kitchen, he was greeted with a steaming plate of spaghetti. *She's right, Robinson Crusoe can wait,* he thought because his mother's spaghetti was his favorite.

"What were you doing in there?" she asked.

"Reading Robinson Crusoe. Reverend Talbert loaned it to me. I have to do a book report on it," he said.

"You know that's his favorite book," she said.

"Yes, I know. That's partially why I chose it."

"How was school today?"

"It was all right, I guess."

"Just all right?" Did anything exciting happen?"

"No, just an ordinary Friday," he said.

Emily twirled spaghetti onto a spoon. Don't make any plans for next Saturday," she said.

"Why not?"

"We're going to a show."

"What sort of show?" Alexander asked.

"We have tickets to Aida," she said. "It's an opera."

"An opera?"

"Yes, an opera."

"Come on, Mom. I don't want to see an opera," he said, scowling.

"Why not?"

"Because I won't know what they're saying."

"Don't worry. I'll explain everything to you," she said.

"Still," he said.

"Are you going to make me go alone?" she said, puffing out her bottom lip.

"Can you take someone else?" he asked.

"No, I'm taking you, and you need to have an open mind about it. You may like it," she said.

"Probably not," he said.

"You didn't think you'd like La Boheme, but you did."

"That was different. We were in New York and Pavarotti was in it," he said.

"Well, Pavarotti is definitely not in this one, but I'm sure you will like it just the same," she said.

"And if I don't?"

"Then at least you would have had the experience. And if it ever comes up in conversation, you will have something to add," she said.

"Whatever," he said, shaking his head.

"So, are you coming, or must I go alone?" she asked.

"Okay, I'll go," he mumbled.

"Good," she said, smiling broadly.

Alexander finished his spaghetti and went back to his room. He lay across his bed and resumed reading. He read late into the night, before falling asleep. He spent every free moment reading *Robinson Crusoe*, and it proved to be every bit as fascinating as he imagined. He enjoyed stories of sailors and pirates, and Robinson Crusoe kept him entertained night after night for nearly two weeks. *How would I fare if I were ever shipwrecked on a desert island? Could I survive?* he wondered. *Probably not, because I don't know the first thing about farming and hunting. I would probably die a miserable death*, he thought.

On Sunday, service began with a call to prayer, and soon the congregation joined together and sang several hymns. Emily played the piano, the choir sang four selections, and the church followed by giving a financial offering. Finally, Reverend Talbert approached the podium and delivered his sermon.

When service ended, Alexander waited for the opportunity to speak to Reverend Talbert. He watched him shaking hands with everyone as they exited the building, and finally, he went into his office. Alexander gave him time to be alone before he knocked on the door.

"Hello, Reverend Talbert," he said.

"Hi, Alexander. Come on in," he said, joyfully.

"How are you, sir?"

"I'm wonderful. What do I have to complain about?"

"I really enjoyed your sermon today, Sir. It was very inspirational."

"Thank you, Alexander. I cannot take any credit for it. The Lord placed the message on my heart, and he blessed me with the skills to express myself. Now how are you enjoying Robinson Crusoe?" he asked.

"I finished it a few days ago," Alexander announced, and sat the book on Reverend Talbert's desk.

"Wonderful, and what did you think of it?"

"I enjoyed it a great deal. I enjoyed the sailing, the pirates, and I loved the suspense of not knowing how he would survive on that awful island. I wonder if I ever found myself in such dire circumstances, would I have what it takes to survive. I mean would I be strong enough and courageous enough to do what he did?" Alexander said, wondering.

"Of course, you would. God will never give you a burden too difficult to bear. It is up to all of us to find the inner strength to take on our challenges and overcome our obstacles," he said.

"When was the first time you read the book?" Alexander asked.

"Many years ago, far too many to say, I'm afraid," he said, laughing.

Alexander laughed along with him.

"I read it for the first time while I was living in a monastery."

"Were you a monk?"

"Yes, a long time ago," he answered.

"I never knew that. Why did you become a monk?"

Reverend Talbert thought back to the time he spent at the old monastery, before answering, "Many years ago, when I was a boy, there was an old monastery in the foothills of Grandfather Mountain where I grew up. I recall seeing the monks working and walking about the grounds of the monastery. Whenever I attempted to speak to them, they would only smile and continue walking about in silence. The kids in the community would imagine all sorts of strange stories about the monks. Some kids believed the monks were imprisoned crimi-nals who were forced to work and live in silence as punishment for their crimes. Other kids believed they were warlocks, who flew throughout the town at night looking for children. I had many sleepless nights because of these stories. Well, one day, I ventured up there to have a look around. I met the headmaster and he gave me a tour. Monsignor Gilbert explained that the monastery had been built by Christian monks in the early seventeen-hundreds. He gave me a tour and explained the history of the brotherhood," Reverend Talbert said.

"What was the place like?" Alexander asked.

"It was mostly farmland, as they were an agrarian order. They survived solely on what the land provided. They grew many fruits and vegetables and raised some cattle, goats, and chickens. The farm was bucolic in a way that is only found at high altitudes. It had beautiful rolling hills and a tree-covered mountainside, and the autumn season was simply mag-nificent.

It was surrounded by a long stone fence. About one hundred yards inside of the fence were the sleeping quarters. It was a rudimentary structure of stone and wood that included a small chapel, a library, a kitchen, and a dining area. And further up on top of a hill was a small stone church.

I began to visit the monastery several times a week, and when school was in session, I would visit every weekend. Monsignor Gilbert and I discussed many matters of faith. He was such a brilliant man, and unbeknownst to me, my theo-logical training had begun, and my career path was already being forged. After completing high school, I spent my summer preparing for college. I had been accepted to North Carolina Central University in Durham. My father was able to get me a summer job working with him at a local lumber company. I worked six days a week and saved all my money for college. My summer was speeding by, and I began questioning if going to college was God's plan for my life. I considered life at the monastery.

Two days before my departure for college, I told my parents I intended to commit my life to monasticism. They were disappointed, and my father was downright angry. He asked why I wanted to throw my life away. I tried to explain to him I wasn't throwing my life away, I was giving it to God, but they couldn't understand my decision. The next morning, I went to see Monsignor Gilbert, and I told him I wanted to join the monastery. Monsignor Gilbert wasn't sure I was making the right decision either, but I eventually convinced him to let me join.

Everyone in my neighborhood thought I was crazy, but I was sure I was acting under the will of God. After a week of preparations, my parents drove me up to the monastery. Monsignor Gilbert stood waiting for my arrival at the chapel door. He assured my parents I would be taken care of, and he made it clear I was free to leave at any time. My mother was visibly upset, and I tried to comfort her as much as I could. I hugged my mother, and she held on to me as if she would never let go.

I felt my father's strong hand on my shoulder. He pulled me into his embrace. They climbed into my father's truck and left. I stood watching the trail of dust the pickup truck left behind. Monsignor Gilbert showed me to my quarters. It was a five by ten room with a bed, a dresser, a desk, and a small closet. The walls and the floor were made of mason stone, and a small window stood above the desk. I showered and dressed myself in a brown cotton robe and a pair of sandals. When I returned to my room, one of the brothers came to me and said that Monsignor Gilbert was waiting for me in his office. When I arrived, I found him sitting at his desk. I sat across from him and he explained the strict rules of the order," Reverend Talbert said.

"What sort of rules?" Alexander asked, hanging on to his every word.

"The silence. We were only allowed to converse on Saturday mornings before noon. Outside of that, we could only speak about official business, and only during religious instruction," he said.

"What did official business include?" Alexander asked.

"The management of the land, including farming, maintenance and supplies. We could speak when necessary, but not for the sake of conversation. I went to my room and sat on the bed. It was a small room, barely large enough for a bed and a small dresser. I sat still and took in my surroundings. I lay down on my bed and tried to relax, but it was useless. Adrenaline was racing through my body, and I couldn't keep still. I went outside and found Brother Edwards working in a small garden just outside of the chapel. He was planting some trees, but he seemed exhausted, so I asked if I could help.

"Two young lemon trees rested against the building. He handed me a shovel and sat on a pile of dirt and wiped his brow with a rag. I began digging and continued until he told me to stop. He directed me to dig a hole equal in size. I did so quickly, and soon we lowered the lemon trees into the ground. Brother Edwards took advantage of my youthful energy, assigning me tasks such as de-weeding the garden and hauling heavy equipment. I worked hard for Brother Edwards well into sunset, and we accomplished more that day than he would have in a week's time working alone. He seemed to be so happy, and I left him sitting quietly in the garden, admiring our work for as long as the itinerant sunlight allowed.

I went inside and took a cold shower before supper. Rice, mixed vegetables, and lentil soup was served for dinner. I learned that meat was seldomly served, and in just a few weeks, I found myself wanting nothing more than one of my dad's grilled hamburgers.

In addition to the vegetarian diet, the silence was maddening. On most days, the only voice I heard was my own. When I did speak, it only concerned matters of religious instruction. Three months into my stay, the reality of my hasty decision became apparent. I wanted to run for the hills and scream until my vocal cords went numb. I felt like a failure. It was the first adult decision of my lifetime and I had fought to protect it and convince everyone who had foreseen the consequences of my indiscretion.

Although I wouldn't dare express my shame to anyone, I would wear it on my face like a scarlet letter, and my shame was suffocating. One evening, Monsignor Gilbert summoned me to his office and asked how I was doing. Several brothers had expressed concern about me, as I was growing more melancholy each day. My stomach turned and my mouth became as dry as a desert.

I told him that I was having a wonderful time, but he wasn't convinced. He watched me incredulously for a moment. I diverted my eyes and studied his bookcase. He asked if I would like some reading material, and he retrieved a book from his bookshelf and handed it to me. The book was *Robinson Crusoe.*

I went back to my room and prepared for bed. My workload was light that day, yet I was exhausted, and moments after lying down, I drifted off into a deep sleep. Hours later, a storm passed over Western North Carolina. The heavy rain, thunder, and lightning woke me from my sleep, keeping me awake for the remainder of the night. I lit a candle and began reading. I found *Robinson Crusoe* to be fascinating and continued reading the tale well into the morning. Due to the storm, we were forced to cancel all outdoor duties, so I stayed in my room most of the day reading.

After completing the book, I found a new energy. I knew that if Robinson Crusoe could endure that hellish island, I could certainly endure a year living as a hermit. Robinson Crusoe's reference to Hebrews 13:5, in which God says: 'I will never leave thee nor forsake thee,' proved to be a catharsis, and it gave me just the strength I needed to see my commitment through.

At the end of the year, I told Monsignor Gilbert it was time for me to leave. He thanked me for the time I had spent with the brotherhood and told me to go back home and live my life. He then told me I would always be welcome there if I should choose to return. The next morning, I said my goodbyes to everyone, and after breakfast, I set off towards home," Reverend Talbert concluded.

"Were your parents happy to see you?" Alexander asked.

"They were ecstatic, especially my mother. I immediately applied to seminary school and stayed with them for six months before leaving for school. I never saw the old monastery again."

"Is it still there?" Alexander asked.

"As far as I know. I haven't received any news from the old monastery for some time," Reverend Talbert said.

Alexander wrote his report and prepared for his return to school. The winter break seemed to fly by as it always does, and before he knew it, school was back in session. On the day of his return, he was confident and well prepared. He showered and dressed and came into the kitchen, where he found Emily preparing eggs, grits, and toast.

"Good morning, honey," she said.

"Good morning."

"Have a seat. Breakfast is ready." She brought over his

plate, and they ate while listening to the news on National Public Radio.

"Rainy and cold in the triangle. It's currently thirty-eight degrees, and warming up to a high of forty-three today," the newsman said.

Alexander stood and darted to a window. Peering out, he could see the dripping leaves and shiny streets.

"It's nasty out there. Would you like me to drive you to school?" Emily asked.

"That would be great, Mom," he said, and returned to the kitchen table and finished his breakfast.

They quickly cleaned up the kitchen and rushed out the door. Shortly after leaving, the rain fell heavier and soon it seemed as if the sky had burst wide open, and the rain poured down upon them with an awful fury.

"Take us safely, Lord," Emily prayed.

When they arrived at school, Alexander sat in the car hoping the rain would let up, just long enough for him to make it through the school doors, but the rain continued to fall hard and steadily. "Drive safely, Mom," he said and pushed open the door and ran as fast as he could. He entered the school building and walked to his locker.

"What's up, Alexander?"

Alexander turned and saw his best friend, Howard Connerly approaching.

"Hey, Howard. When did you get in?" he asked.

"Last night."

"I called you around nine o'clock and left a message. Did you get it?" Alexander asked.

"No, when I came home, I went right to bed."

"What time did you get in?"

"Around eight o'clock," Howard said.

"I guess I'll let you off the hook then," he smiled.

"Now that I am absolved, I can go on with my life," Howard said, sarcastically.

"You are absolved, my child," Alexander said.

They laughed before departing. "I'll see you at lunch," Alexander said.

"I'll be there," Howard said.

Alexander's day began with homeroom at 8:00 A.M., where everyone pretended to be upset about returning to school, but they were happy to be back. His first three classes were Social Studies, Biology and English. He felt Social Studies and Biology were banal as usual, and he entered English class with only two thoughts: his book report and lunch.

He settled into his seat and greeted his friends. Pre-class discussions were the same all day. It consisted of Christmas gifts and holiday travels.

The bell rang, and Ms. Cummings closed the classroom door. "Settle down, everyone," she said. She passed out a syllabus, detailing their assignments for the remainder of the year. She sat behind her desk and took attendance. Calling each student and placing a small check by each name as the students answered.

"Class, we have a new student, Natalie Agadani."

Alexander turned to see the new student.

"Welcome, Miss Agadani. Class, make Natalie feel welcome," Ms. Cummings said.

Natalie smiled and said, "Thank you." Natalie sat at her desk, her legs were crossed, and she was writing in her notebook.

"I hope you all came prepared for your presentations," Ms. Cummings continued.

The students grunted and squirmed in their seats.

"Pass them to the front, please."

A trail of white paper floated to the front of the class, and then towards the middle, where Alexander sat. He gathered them into a neat stack and gave them to Miss Cummings.

"Who would like to go first?" Miss Cummings asked, and when her smile turned into a look of disappointment, Alexander raised his hand.

He made his way to the podium and stood facing the class. He gazed at the new student and his heart nearly jumped out of his chest. Public speaking had always come easy to Alexander, so he couldn't understand why he was feeling so nervous. He started off smoothly, explaining the story of a young man who took up sailing in pursuit of adventure and riches. He explained all of Crusoe's misfortunes, including the two years in which Crusoe was captured by a pirate and forced into slavery. He explained how after two years of slavery, Crusoe had managed to escape and made it to Brazil, where he built a plantation and became rich and prosperous. He discussed Crusoe's expedition to Guinea, where he had planned to bring back Africans to enslave them, but found himself the sole survivor of a shipwreck on an uninhabitable island, where he was miserable and destitute for twenty-eight years. He explained how through his misfortunes, God provided him everything he needed to survive.

Alexander looked out at the class. "Many readers enjoy this novel for its action and adventure, but Defoe's primary purpose for writing this novel was not so much to entertain his readers, as it was to offer religious instruction. Defoe wanted to convey to his readers, if we live according to God's will, He will provide us with everything we need, and it is up to us to recognize all God has done and continues to do for us," Alexander concluded.

At that time, Natalie Agadani raised her hand. "You say that Robinson Crusoe's misfortunes, was punishment for his disobedience and lack of gratitude, but it seems to me that

Crusoe's biggest sins involved his treatment of other people. Wouldn't you agree?" Natalie asked.

"Well, no. That's not the message I believe Daniel Defoe was trying to get across. You see Defoe was a minister, and he used the story to spread the gospel," Alexander said.

"What I mean to say is, in the story," Natalie said, leaning forward in her seat. "Robinson Crusoe is captured and forced into slavery. When he was delivered from slavery, and he arrived in Morocco on the brink of starvation, he was given food and water from Africans correct? Yet, he goes back to Africa in hope of enslaving the same people who had saved him from starvation. It seems to me, that was the bigger affront against God, more so than disobeying his parents," she challenged.

"I suppose so, but in the book, Defoe uses Crusoe's own interpretations to pass religious principles onto his readers, and slavery is just not a topic he explored," Alexander said.

"I am well aware of who Defoe was, and his purpose for writing this book, but I think if a picture is worth a thousand words, then surely a book is open to various interpretations, and I think Defoe missed the mark by advocating for enslaving people," Natalie said.

"I don't think he was advocating for slavery," Alexander said.

"Sure, he did," she said, cutting him off. "He refers to Africans as wild men and savages who were capable of eating him, and in doing so, Defoe was justifying Crusoe's desire to enslave them, and we are supposed to accept this as religious instruction?" Natalie said.

Alexander looked to Ms. Cummings for help. He wanted her to tell Natalie to lay off, or at least to hold her questions until he was done with his presentation, but Ms. Cummings just sat there smiling, as if she was overjoyed to see such a spirited debate taking place in her class. Alexander felt himself getting angry, but he wasn't sure if he was angry with Natalie for her interruptions, or mad at himself for leaving it to Natalie to point out what he should have seen all along.

"Daniel Defoe, like many ministers of his time, was influenced by his culture, that was flawed in many ways," Alexander retorted. He felt like an idiot. *Is that all you could think to say?* he thought. Alexander thought it best to resume his presentation before Natalie could respond. He went on to explain the final years of Crusoe's life on the island, his battle with the cannibal savages, and how after twenty-eight years on the island, God had provided Crusoe with companionship and a way off the island. "I do not want to spoil the book's ending for those of you who are interested in reading it. However, I will say the book ends with a climax of adventure that will not disappoint. In the end, Crusoe manages to find his way home," Alexander said.

Natalie, peering at him through her rectangular shaped glasses, raised her hand and spoke, "Why do you think Crusoe only chose to intervene when he saw a white man was among the victims the savages were planning to kill?" she asked.

"Well, when Crusoe first discovered the savages, as he called them, he had planned to kill them if they had ever returned, but he decided he did not have the right to play judge and executioner. He knew it was only God's right, and God's alone. Therefore, he resolved to not intervene."

"So, it was not his right to intervene when these cannibals were killing natives, but when they planned to kill a white man, they deserved to die?" she asked, indignantly.

"Well, Crusoe saw the white prisoner as someone from his own community," Alexander said.

"He was not from Crusoe's community, he was a Spaniard, and Robinson Crusoe was English," she said.

"Yes, but he was European," Alexander responded.

"And according to the Minister Defoe, the European's life was more valuable than the native's," she said, sarcastically.

"As I said before, Defoe was a product of his society, and although this book was intended for religious instruction, he was flawed in many ways."

Once again, he was left with no logical rebuttal. Natalie had dissected his arguments like a prosecuting attorney, and Alexander could only concede. He sat in his seat and began packing his books.

"Thank you for that, Alexander. It was very well done," Ms. Cummings said, clapping her hands. Taking her cue, the class clapped enthusiastically. Roger, Marianne, and Michele, you are presenting tomorrow," Ms. Cummings said.

Demonstrating his disappointment, Roger forcefully closed his textbook and sighed.

"If more of you had volunteered, I would not have to decide for you," Ms. Cummings said.

The bell rang and the students filed out of the classroom as Natalie made her way to the front of the room.

"Welcome again, Natalie. We are so glad to have you," Ms. Cummings said.

"Thank you," Natalie said.

"Now don't worry about the book report, you can just make it up later," Ms. Cummings said.

"Thank you, but I've already begun working on my report," Natalie said.

"Really?"

"Yes, ma'am. I recently read *Anna Karenina*, and when I saw it was on the list, I began writing my report," Natalie announced.

Alexander left the classroom and went to his locker. He was starving and he was glad it was time for lunch and

Howard was leaning against his locker, already waiting for him.

"What's wrong with you? You look like you've seen a ghost," Howard said.

Not only did Alexander look like he had seen a ghost, he felt as though he had been possessed by one. "I'm fine," he said. He put his books inside of his locker and went to lunch. They were served square pizza and carrot sticks.

Alexander and Howard were the first to arrive at their regular table.

"How was New York?" Alexander asked.

"It was fantastic. I think I want to live there," Howard said.

"Really?" Alexander asked.

"That's right, I visited NYU. It was so cool man, believe me, you would love it up there. That is where we should go to college," Howard said.

"What are you talking about? I thought we were going abroad to study," Alexander said.

"My parents can't afford that," Howard said.

"You could get a scholarship," Alexander said.

"No, you could get a scholarship. I don't have your grades. I have a much better chance here at home," Howard said.

"Let me guess, you saw NYU with Allyson," Alexander said.

"Well yes, but that's not why I like NYU," Howard said, smiling.

"You suck, you know that?" Alexander said.

"Is anyone sitting here?" Natalie asked.

"No," Howard said, jumping out of his seat and pulling back a chair for her.

Natalie sat her tray on the table and sat across from Alexander.

"Hi, I'm Howard. Are you new here?"

"Yes, I am." Natalie opened a carton of milk.

"Howard, this is," he paused and looked at her, "Your name is Natalie, right?" Alexander asked.

"Yes, it's Natalie. It's nice to meet you, Howard. It is nice to meet you both." She looked at Alexander and said, "I want to apologize for today. I didn't mean to give you the third degree," Natalie said.

"I felt like I was defending my thesis," Alexander responded. They both laughed.

Howard looked confused.

"I'm sorry," she apologized again, pursing her lips together and smiling sympathetically. "It's just that stupid book. People make such a big deal about it, but I don't see what's so great about it," she said.

"What book?" Howard asked.

"Robinson Crusoe," Alexander answered.

"Oh, you didn't like it?" Howard asked Natalie.

"I hated it. It is so disparaging," she paused, "Oh, there I go again, I'm sorry," she said.

"No, you're right. I was so focused on the religious principles of the story, that I didn't see what an imperialist he was," Alexander said.

Alexander turned to Howard, "I did my book report on Robinson Crusoe, and during my presentation today, Natalie really let me have it."

Howard sat back and smiled. "I'll be back." He got up and sat with some other friends.

"Where are you from?" Alexander asked.

"Where am I not from?" she said.

"I cannot place your accent is all."

"That is because I am from everywhere, and nowhere. I was born in Stockholm. It's in Sweden," she added.

"I know where Stockholm is," he said, smiling broadly.

"I know you do, I was just making sure," she laughed.

"When I was five years old, my parents moved to London. We lived there for seven years before moving to Kenya, and we have been here now for three weeks," she said.

"Wow, that's amazing. What were you doing in Kenya?" he asked.

"My father is Kenyan. He and my mother are doctors. My father wanted to return to his village to offer medical assistance so they joined Doctors Without Borders and went to Kenya. They spent two years traveling around to the most rural areas, giving much-needed medical care to people."

"That's so awesome. What part of Kenya is he from?"

"It's a small town," she said.

"What's the name of the town?" he pressed.

"Do you know any towns in Kenya?" she asked.

"I know where Nairobi is," he said.

"Oh, great." She smiled. "It is about thirty minutes from Nairobi," she said.

"So, it's somewhere in the center of Kenya, or South-Central?" he asked.

"Wow Alexander, I am impressed. Most students at this school have never heard of Nairobi," she said.

"Is that all it takes to impress you?" He smiled.

"This time, yes." She returned the smile.

Alexander gazed at her smiling face and felt himself being carried away. He thought she was the most beautiful girl he had ever seen. He saw no blemishes on her cool bronze skin. She wore no makeup, no lipstick, and her hair was in a frizzy ponytail. She dressed well, but never in the latest fashion or fads, as though she did not want to be noticed, but Alexander had noticed it all.

"I had better be getting to class. It was nice talking to you, Alexander."

"Thank you. It was nice meeting you," he said.

She smiled and carried her tray to the trash.

Alexander felt Howard's hand grasping his shoulder.

"You can put your tongue back in your mouth now," Howard said.

Alexander laughed.

"You were smiling so hard, I thought you had won the lottery," Howard said.

"Not quite," Alexander said, "Not quite."

Alexander was unable to concentrate for the remainder of the day. Natalie was all he thought about. She had fascinated him. She had already seen most of the world, just as he had always dreamed of doing. And unlike most of the girls at Broughton High, she seemed to have depth.

When he arrived at trigonometry, which was his last class of the day, he was delighted to see Natalie sitting in the third row. He was delighted, but also miserable, because he knew she would occupy his mind even more. Instead of listening to his teacher, who prided himself as a fastidious educator, he spent most of the class deciding what he would say to Natalie at the end of class, and had Mr. Norwood called on him, he would have been at a loss for words.

When class finally ended, he slowly packed his belongings, hoping to position himself in Natalie's path, but Mr. Norwood stopped her and spent several minutes talking to her about class assignments and his expectations. Alexander realized how foolish he must have looked rumbling through his bookbag as though he was looking for something of great importance. So, eventually he left and found Howard waiting out front. They walked home as they did every day, and Howard told Alexander of his experience in New York.

Alexander teased him about wanting to attend NYU to be closer to Allyson, the so-called love of his life, and whom he only sees twice a year. Once, when his family goes to New York to visit his grandparents, and once when her family comes to Raleigh to visit hers.

In the past, whenever Allyson's family made summer visits, Allyson would persuade her family to allow her to stay with her grandparents for an extra week or so after her parents left, but when her father realized the reason for her wanting to stay, he would no longer allow it.

After Allyson's and Howard's scheming was discovered by her father, Howard would try to convince his parents to allow him to stay on after their visits to New York. Although Howard's father was unaware of his motivations, his answer was always no. Howard's father, Orlando Connerly had moved out of New York to escape the madness of the city, and he would be damned if he would leave his son there to get into God knows what. So, Howard and Allyson were resolved to only seeing each other twice a year, and for no more than a few weeks at a time.

When they were away from each other, Howard would never want for company. At 6 feet and 4 inches tall, broad shoulders, brown skin and a Hollywood smile, dating came easy for him. And before he had grown into such an impressive young man, Howard had developed an eloquence with words and was always at the center of attention.

In his early years, Alexander could have been called a social maladroit. His father, Alexander Poindexter Merchant and Orlando Connerly had been best friends. The two mechanical engineers had met each other during the early development of Research Triangle Park. They served as best man in each other's weddings, and when they could afford it, they bought houses in the same neighborhood.

Five years after young Alexander was born, Alexander Sr. was driving home from a lodge meeting with the Prince Hall Masons when he was struck by a drunk driver. He died two hours later at Wake Medical Center. From that moment on, Orlando Connerly included Alexander in everything he and Howard did—fishing trips, sporting events, and even family vacations.

Over the years, Howard and Alexander were inseparable. More than friends, they were brothers in every sense of the word. They knew all there was to know about each other, and to the observer, it seemed as though they could read each other's thoughts.

The socially inept Alexander never felt comfortable around unfamiliar faces. For him, using small talk to break the ice, felt like breaking an iceberg. So, for that sort of thing, he depended on Howard, who always knew what to say and how to say it.

When Howard made friends, Alexander made friends, and each one would use each other's strengths to his advantage. With all his charisma, people liked Howard immediately, and if they liked Howard, in time, they loved Alexander. They came to Howard for fun, and to Alexander for advice. Howard knew what to say, and Alexander knew what to do, and together they felt unstoppable.

Walking home, absorbed in their teenage reflections, Alexander would not notice the pearl white Lexus waiting at the stoplight. He wouldn't see Natalie's countenance turn into sheer delight as she learned that Alexander, her first American friend, had lived so close, so he would spend the remainder of the evening agonizing over what she thought of him.

On the following day, when Alexander and Howard arrived at school, they were standing near their lockers when Alexander saw Natalie navigating through the crowded hallway alone, and when her eyes connected with his, her face lit up and she smiled.

"Hi, Alexander. Hi, Howard," she said, removing her headphones.

"Hi, Natalie," Alexander spoke up.

"Do you live on St. Mary's Street?" she asked.

"No, I live on Woodburn. It's a few blocks over."

"Okay, I saw you two headed home yesterday," she said.

"Where do *you* live?" Alexander asked.

"On Pineview Street," she answered.

"That's only a few blocks away," Alexander said.

"Yes, it is." She smiled.

"You should walk home with us," Howard offered.

"Yes, we walk home together almost every day." Alexander said, "You should join us."

She smiled. "That sounds nice. I'll see you in class."

"I'll be looking for you," Alexander said.

Howard wrapped his arm around Alexander's neck. "You're one step closer, my friend," he said.

"To what?" Alexander asked.

Howard laughed and strutted down the hallway.

Alexander looked forward to seeing Natalie in class. First and second periods seemed to drag on forever, and when third period finally came, he couldn't wait for it to end. Natalie joined Alexander and Howard for lunch, and later, the three of them gathered to go home together.

"I'm glad you could join us," Howard said.

Natalie smiled.

"I hope it's not too cold for you," Alexander said.

"No, not at all. I'm from a cold climate, remember," Natalie said.

"I thought you were African," Howard said, as they started down St. Mary's Street.

"My father is Kenyan, and my mother is Swedish," Natalie said, gazing into the flower shop across the street.

"How did your parents meet?" Alexander asked.

"They met in college. My father was born in a village

outside of Nairobi. He was an exceptional student and he wanted to study medicine. He earned a scholarship to the University of Stockholm to study Biology and Chemistry, which for him was like winning the lottery. When he arrived in Sweden, my mother, who was also a Biology major, was assigned to him as his peer mentor, and she helped him get acclimated to the University and the City of Stockholm. They became friends and eventually started dating, and the rest his history," she said.

"Is your dad a doctor?" Alexander asked.

"They both are. After undergrad, my parents went on to study medicine at Karolinska Institute, and they later trained together at Karolinska University Hospital. They do everything together," she smiled proudly.

Alexander was amazed by Natalie's storytelling and wanted to know every detail of her life. "Howard, I'm going to walk Natalie home. I'll catch up with you later."

"Take your time, man." He gave him a half smile. "Bye, Natalie."

"Bye, Howard." Natalie threw up a hand.

Crossing over Wade Avenue, the couple slowed to a more leisurely pace.

"How do you like America?" Alexander asked.

"It's nice," she said, sighing. "I have always wanted to come to America, but I imagined living in New York or California, not here."

"Why did your parents choose Raleigh?"

"My parents are researching H.I.V., that is partly what they were doing in Kenya. Duke University contacted them and said they were interested in my parents' study. The university made my parents an offer to bring the study here, and they accepted," Natalie said.

"Tell me more about Kenya," he said.

"I love Kenya. It is a beautiful country. Naturally beautiful, you know? And the people are so nice, the nicest people on earth."

"I imagine meeting your family made it even more special," he said.

"Yes, yes, that was the best of all. My mother was raised just outside of Stockholm where I was born, therefore, I knew my Swedish family very well. My father talked about Kenya often, and I had read many books about it, but not knowing my Kenyan relatives left a void neither my father's stories or any book could fill," she said, pensively.

"I know all about that," Alexander said. "I would love to know where my ancestors came from, but I wouldn't know where to look."

The orange hue of the setting sun rested softly on Natalie's face, and Alexander was mesmerized by her beauty. "This is my phone number," Alexander said, handing her a small sheet of paper. "In case you need to call me," he said.

Natalie reached in her bag and produced a small phone. She typed in Alexander's number. He heard the phone ringing in his pocket. Her phone number appeared on the screen.

"That is my number. Call me anytime you like," she said.

Alexander and Natalie talked often after that, sometimes late into the night. Their conversations covered a broad range of topics. Social issues, politics, world news, sports, movies, television, and music. No subject was too banal, and in time they became inseparable.

As Alexander lay in bed thinking about all that happened between him and Natalie, and how he should present his story to Judge Gregory, he formulated his thoughts and continued writing his letter.

CHAPTER
SEVEN

Emily Merchant sat in her driveway staring at her empty house. The place she had always loved was now cold, lonely, and forbidding. She fixed her eyes on the steps leading up to the porch, and dreading the effort it would take to reach her front door. She eventually climbed out of her car and checking the mailbox, she found the envelope she had been waiting for. It contained information about Morganton Youth Institution, the prison where Alexander was being held.

On the day of Alexander's conviction, she sat in the courtroom, furious with Alexander's attorney, Julian Hoffman, who had only made a cursory effort to prepare for her son's trial, and had convinced Alexander to accept the plea agreement.

On the evening prior to Alexander's plea bargain, she came home from a long day of teaching, and found a voice message from Julian. She had left message after message for him, and he had finally returned her call.

"Hello, Ms. Merchant. This is Julian Hoffman, your son's attorney. Although I empathize with your concerns, the particulars of your son's case make it difficult for us to defend his charges success-

fully. For this reason, I strongly believe it is our best option to accept a plea bargain, which will be finalized tomorrow at nine o'clock A.M. Please, call me if you have any questions. Bye now."

Emily arose early the following morning and went to the Wake County Court Building, and found the courtroom where Alexander was scheduled to appear. She watched as Alexander was brought into the courtroom wearing an orange jumpsuit and shackles, not the suit she assumed he would be in. She saw him scanning the room for her, but not seeing her until he was standing before the judge. "I love you," she mouthed to him. He entered his plea and was swept away. Emily found a Sheriff's Deputy and asked if she could see him but was told it was against policy to see him before transport. It was also against policy to disclose where he was being transported.

"How do I find out where my son is going?" she asked, tightly clenching her purse straps.

"He'll call you when he gets to his destination," the deputy said, coldly.

Emily was as angry with Julian Hoffman as she was with herself. She had wanted to be angry at Reverend Talbert as well, but she found when she relished in that anger, she also became angry at her faith, and in these difficult times, her faith was all she had.

Four years earlier, Reverend Talbert, founded the Upward Bound Christian Academy. He told his congregation he was establishing a school out of obedience to God's will, and he asked his members to do all they could to ensure God's will was done.

As time grew near for the Upward Bound Christian Academy to begin teaching its first students, Reverend Talbert desperately needed an English Teacher, so he asked Emily Merchant to consider the position. Emily Merchant had been an English teacher at Wake County Public Schools for thirteen years and was apprehensive to leave the public school system for a start-up private school. Not only was she apprehensive about the $12,000 pay cut and lacking retirement program, but there was no health insurance for six months. He explained that money for health insurance was simply not in the budget, but after six months of collecting tuition, he promised to offer it to all the teachers.

Emily was more concerned with Alexander's health than her own. Her daily routine was basic, she went to work, came home, and graded papers. Her physical activities mostly consisted of using the treadmill and practicing yoga, with no health concerns she knew of. But Alexander, she considered a fearless young man who lived for soccer, was a different matter. She knew Alexander, like most athletes, could sustain an injury at any time, so she decided to continue teaching in public schools, until Reverend Talbert could offer health insurance.

After one Sunday morning service, Emily met with Reverend Talbert and explained her decision to him. She could see he was visibly disappointed.

"Don't you know God will not allow anything to happen to you or Alexander if you're working for him?" Reverend Talbert said.

"Yes, but I have to take care of my son. I'm sure you can understand that," Emily said.

Reverend Talbert acquiesced, "Of course, Sister Emily. The job is here for you whenever you're ready."

The following Sunday, Reverend Talbert began a series of sermons titled, Step Out on Faith and See Thy Will be Done. He stood with his hands grasping the sides of the podium. His eyes moved slowly over the faces of his audience.

"If you believe in God, say amen. If you believe in God," he repeated, "Say amen. If you have faith, the way Abraham had it, say amen," Reverend Talbert yelled out.

"Amen," said the congregation.

"Say amen, if you have faith the way Moses had it when he stood boldly before the pharaoh and said, let my people go," he said.

"Amen," said the congregation.

"Really?" He smiled. "I must be doing a fantastic job. But, before I pat myself on the back too much, let's talk about Moses' faith. In Matthew seventeen and twenty, Jesus said: *because of your unbelief, for verily I say unto you, if ye have faith of a mustard seed, ye shall say unto this mountain, move mountain, and it shall move, and nothing shall be impossible unto you.* Did Moses have the faith of a mustard seed? Did Moses not move mountains? Did he not part the Red Sea? But why was Moses so powerful? Moses was human, just like you and me, so how did he perform such miracles? It was because of his faith," he grunted, shaking his fist.

"Moses was human, and like all humans, he had doubts, but seeing is believing. Moses saw God with his own eyes. He saw Him as a burning bush, but he saw Him nonetheless, and God stood before Moses as clearly as I stand before you. He heard His voice as clearly as you can hear mine. Is that why his faith was so strong?

"Did Peter not have faith when he raised Tabitha from the dead? Sure, Peter had walked with Jesus. He had witnessed the miracles of Christ personally, so how could his faith not be greater than others, but is that what it will take for us to reach that level of faith? Is that what we are waiting for to do God's work?" He smiled.

"We shall never know why God chooses to reveal Himself to some and not to others, but we cannot wait for empirical revelations to do God's work, for there is too much to be done, and the hour is too short.

"Faith is the substance of things hoped for, and conviction in the evidence of things not seen. When you stand up for God, God will stand up for you. He would not allow any harm to come your way, and no weapon formed against you shall prosper. Let us pray.

"Lord, we come before you today, asking for strength, the strength to step out on faith and do Your will. Lord, Your word tells us that without faith, it is impossible to please You. For he that cometh to God must believe He is all powerful, and He is a rewarder to those that diligently seek Him. Lord, we ask that You lay hands on every one of your children, that we may desire to do Your will. Amen," Reverend Talbert concluded and stepped down.

Emily felt as though she was sitting in the pews alone. She could feel Reverend Talbert's message tugging at her heart. She believed he was a true man of God and she believed in his vision and very much wanted to help him. She went home and prayed for guidance.

"What is Your will, Lord?" she prayed. "Tell me what You want me to do," she pleaded, but she received no definitive answer. She only felt a greater desire to acquiesce.

She searched for an individual healthcare provider for Alexander. When she found suitable coverage, she typed a letter of resignation, and sent it to the Wake County Board of Education.

Emily Merchant was a gifted educator, and although she could have taught at any private school, she believed in public education and it was where she desired to stay. She believed that education was essential to the future of mankind. She also believed education was the right of all people, and how do you charge a person for something rightfully his or hers? But she also wanted to please God, and she believed it was God's will that she help Reverend Talbert to build his Christian Academy.

Emily's students mostly consisted of church members whom she had known all their lives. Many of whom she had taught in Sunday school, and some she had even babysat. She used these relationships to her advantage and challenged the young minds in ways often too difficult in public schools. For the first time, she experienced the increased commitment of parents who paid for their children's education, and she was pleased.

Reverend Talbert delivered health insurance as he had promised, and soon after, Emily scheduled a physical. As she prepared for her visit, she noticed how bright the sun shone in the winter sky and since the doctor's office was nearby, she thought a brisk walk would do her some good. She kicked off her heels and slid her feet into a pair of crisp white tennis shoes. Dressing warmly, she stepped out of her house and filled her lungs with a breath of cold air.

As she strolled up the sidewalk, the sun illuminated her face and warmed her skin, and then disappeared behind dark and ominous clouds. The clouds moved swiftly, as a strong wind shook the bare trees. She saw thick drops of rain falling in the distance, rain that would eventually consume her. She turned and hastened back towards her house. A plastic bag swirled violently before her, as the rain moved in closer. Emily quickened her pace, making it to her car only moments before the rain consumed everything around her.

The storm blew violently. Lightning crawled across the sky, and thunder shook the ground beneath her. Her windshield became opaque with the bullets of exploding rain, which fell on her vehicle like the hooves of sprinting mustangs.

Gail force winds rocked her Toyota Prius and in an instant, it was gone. The bare trees glistened in the sunlight, and the streets glistened like rivers of black gold. The experience made Emily nervous, and she feared the fleeting storm was a harbinger of something worse to come, but what, she didn't know. *So much for exercise*, Emily thought. She started her engine, whispered a silent prayer, and drove to the doctor's office.

Emily sat in a small exam room, wearing a thin blue gown made of paper, and her clothes were folded neatly on a wooden chair.

A nurse entered the room and closed the door behind her. "Hello, Ms. Merchant."

"Hi." Emily smiled.

"The nurse washed her hands and looked over some forms. "Let's get your height and weight please," the nurse said.

Emily stood on the scale.

"One-thirty-five," the nurse reported, and recorded her weight on a form. "Over here, please."

Emily moved over to the height chart on the wall and stood with her back against it.

"Five-fo five," the nurse said, and wrote it on the form.

Emily sat on the exam table.

The nurse wrapped a sphygmomanometer around Emily's arm and pumped a few times. "Looks good," the nurse said. She wrote down Emily's blood pressure on the form. "Dr. Castaneda will be in shortly," she said, and left the room.

Emily sat waiting.

"Hello, Mrs. Merchant," Dr. Castaneda said, entering the room.

"Hi, Doctor Castaneda. How are you?" Emily said.

"Very well," Doctor Castaneda said, smiling. "How is that handsome boy of yours?"

"Alexander is very well," Emily said.

"He is in the ninth grade now, yes?" Dr. Castaneda asked.

"Yes, he is—and getting straight As," Emily said.

"You must be proud of him, yes?"

"Oh, yes," Emily said smiling.

"Wonderful," Dr. Castaneda said, as she studied Emily's file. "Have you seen a doctor since I've seen you last?"

"No," Emily said.

"Are you on any new medications?"

"No."

"Has there been any change in your health since your last visit?" Dr. Castaneda asked.

"No, not really. Although, I have experienced some discomfort in my right breast," Emily said.

"What sort of discomfort?"

"It's almost not worth mentioning. However, at times, I feel something has changed." Emily placed her hand where the discomfort was.

"Are you experiencing any pain?"

"Fleetingly," Emily said.

"How would you rate your pain on a scale of one to ten?" Dr. Castaneda asked.

"Two maybe three," Emily said.

"How often?"

"It has occurred on three occasions in the past two months," Emily said.

"Any excretions?"

"No, not at all," Emily said.

"Have you examined yourself?" Dr. Castaneda moved closer and motioned for her to lie back.

"Yes, but I felt nothing unusual."

"Let's have a look." Dr. Castaneda examined Emily's breast, looking for any irregularities. "I don't feel anything unusual. When was your last mammogram?"

"It's been three years," Emily said.

"Are you planning to have a mammogram?" Dr. Castaneda asked.

"I plan to make an appointment soon," Emily said.

"Triangle Radiology recently opened a satellite office next door. They can probably see you today if you like," Dr. Castaneda said.

"How long has it been there?" Emily asked.

"Only since last week. I can call for you if you like. Women your age should have a mammogram every one to two years. It's very important," Dr. Castaneda said.

"I suppose I could have it done today if they'll see me," Emily said.

"The business is still slow. I'll have the nurse call for you when I am done with your exam," Dr. Castaneda said. "Everything looks good to me, Ms. Merchant, but the nurse will take your blood samples, and we'll be finished," Dr. Castaneda said. "I will contact you in a week with the results of your blood work, and I'll call Triangle Radiology and see if they can fit you in. Wait here," Dr. Castaneda said, and left the room.

The nurse returned and filled a syringe with Emily's blood and filled four glass tubes.

Emily dressed herself and sat studying a pamphlet about osteoporosis.

"Good news, they can see you in thirty minutes," Dr. Castaneda said, when she returned.

"Thank you," Emily said.

"You are very welcome. You should never put off for tomorrow what you can do today. Especially in matters regarding your health," she said, in a motherly way.

Dr. Castaneda's tone was what Emily liked about Maria Castaneda. She had never known any doctor to treat patients the way Maria Castaneda did, genuinely caring about her patients.

Emily sat in the waiting room of Triangle Radiology alone. She was the only patient in the building from what she could tell. She filled out several forms and was quickly taken into an exam room. She was impressed by the new facility. The smell of new lumber and fresh paint complemented the pristine décor.

"Hello, Ms. Merchant. I'm Dr. Haun." Dr. Haun shook Emily's hand.

"It's nice to meet you," Emily replied.

Dr. Haun smiled. "I see it's been three years since your last mammogram," Dr. Haun said.

"Yes, it has."

"Do you do self-examinations regularly?" Dr. Haun asked.

"No, not regularly," Emily said.

"How often?"

"Periodically. Maybe every three or four months," Emily said.

Dr. Haun stretched a pair of rubber gloves over her small hands and stood facing Emily. "Would you undo your gown, please?" Dr. Haun asked.

Emily untied her gown, exposing her thirty-six C-cup caramel-colored breasts.

Dr. Haun observed Emily's breasts and saw nothing of concern. There were no dimples or secretions, and they had perfect symmetry, by what she could tell. She warmed her hands and placed her fingertips on Emily's soft flesh, feeling for lumps. "Raise your right arm," she said, as she continued her examination. "Raise your left arm, please." Dr. Haun asked, "Do you know how to conduct a self-examination properly?"

"Yes, I do," Emily said.

"It's important that you examine yourself on a regular basis. If you do it at least every thirty days, you can detect changes more easily," Doctor Haun said.

Sensing Dr. Haun's concern, Emily felt uneasy.

"Come with me across the hall," Dr. Haun said.

Entering the adjacent room, Emily saw the mammogram machine and felt a chill. She had seen mammogram machines many times, but on this occasion, she didn't want to go near the thing.

The mammographer attempted small talk, as the machine closed on one of Emily's breasts, pressing it flat. "Hold your breath for a moment," the mammographer said.

Emily did as she was told.

"Now the other side," the mammographer instructed. When it was done, the mammographer escorted Emily back into the adjacent room.

"When should I expect the results?" Emily asked.

"Not long. We don't have many patients now. Wait here," she said.

Emily sat for what seemed like an eternity before Dr. Haun returned.

Dr. Haun sat before a computer, studying the images of Emily's breast.

Emily watched Dr. Haun furrow her brow and bite her lower lip, so she braced herself for what she presumed to be an unwelcome diagnosis.

"You have what looks like a tumor on your right breast," Dr. Haun said.

Emily stared at Dr. Haun blankly.

"I need to do an ultrasound to be sure," Dr. Haun said.

"How soon can you do it?" Emily asked.

"Right now," Dr. Haun answered.

Emily followed Dr. Haun into another exam room and climbed onto the exam table, lying on her back.

Dr. Haun pressed the probe against Emily's breast and focused on the monitor. "I think it's hiding under some tissue here, so let's see," Dr. Haun said, sliding the probe downward. "There it is," she said.

Emily opened her eyes and focused on the monitor.

"Do you see here?" Dr. Haun said, pointing to a spot on the monitor. It's hard to say at this point, but it seems to be about one-point-four centimeters, which is the size of a pea," Dr. Haun said.

"Is it malignant?"

"I need to conduct a biopsy to answer that," Dr. Haun said.

Emily felt her throat tightening. "I know you have many questions, but there is a lot we don't know right now," Dr. Haun said.

"Not knowing is the worst part," Emily said.

"Let's see if we can find it. Raise your arm," Dr. Haun said, placing her fingers at the spot where she thought the intruder was hiding. "Found it. Feel here," she said, guiding Emily's fingers. "Do you feel it?"

"No, I don't feel anything," she paused, "Yes," Emily said.

Dr. Haun washed her hands and reviewed her calendar. "I can do the biopsy tomorrow morning," she said.

"I can do that," Emily said.

"Okay. I'll have the nurse set it up." Dr. Haun placed her hand on Emily's knee. "Don't worry too much. We found it early," Dr. Haun said.

Later, the biopsy confirmed Emily's worst fears. The tumor was malignant, and aggressive action was needed. The oncologist, Dr. Johnson, was optimistic. He assured Emily that a lumpectomy, along with radiation treatments, would cure the illness.

"I'm scheduling your surgery for the eleventh, at Rex Hospital," Dr. Johnson said.

"That's in five days," Emily said.

"Yes. We must move quickly," he said.

"How long will I have to stay in the hospital?"

"A lumpectomy is an outpatient procedure, so an overnight stay won't be necessary. Just take it easy for a few weeks, and you should be back to normal activity quickly," Dr. Johnson said.

"When will I begin radiation?"

"In about three to four weeks. It depends on the condition of your lymph nodes. It's good we found the tumor early. Early detection lessens the probability of your lymph nodes being affected."

"What if they *are* affected?" Emily asked.

"In that case, I'd recommend chemotherapy, but let's not get ahead of ourselves," Dr. Johnson answered.

"Should I prepare for any hair loss?"

"No. Radiation only causes hair loss to the treated area. I wouldn't worry too much about it," he said, smiling.

Emily's eyes became saturated. "I'm sorry," she said, wiping her eyes. "I am asking you questions I already know the answers to. I've been researching this mess ever since I was diagnosed. It's just better hearing it from you," Emily said.

"It's quite all right, Ms. Merchant. I understand. Do you have any further questions?" Dr. Johnson asked.

"No, I suppose not," Emily said.

"Okay. Kathy will give you prep instructions, and I'll see you in five days," Dr. Johnson said.

After he left the room, and the nurse escorted Emily to the front desk, she handed Emily a package of information. "All of your instructions are here," she said. "Please, do not eat or drink anything after 6 P.M. You must arrive at Rex Hospital by 6:30 A.M. on the eleventh, okay?" the nurse instructed.

"Yes," Emily said.

"You will need someone to drive you to the hospital and wait during the procedure. This is very important. We cannot do the procedure if you do not have anyone with you," the nurse said.

"I'll have a friend drive me," Emily said.

"Do you have anyone at home who can help you?"

"My son will help me," Emily said.

"How old is he?"

"He's fifteen," Emily said.

"That's good. Now don't you worry, dear. Everything will be just fine. Dr. Johnson does this procedure all the time, so you're in good hands, okay?" The nurse smiled and patted Emily's hand.

"Thank you," Emily said, smiling.

On the following afternoon, Emily was home resting in a Padmasana pose. For Emily, the combination of yoga and prayer was the perfect remedy to a stressful day. She sat on her living room floor practicing Pranayama, the art of yogic breathing. She was aware of life pulsating through her body—her feet, her hands. She was escaping the madness of the world—a world where a cluster of cells could ravage a person's life. In this place of consciousness, she talked to God with uncompromising faith so He would see her through this difficult moment. The ringing phone brought her back, and she moved across the room and lifted the phone to her ear.

"Hello, may I speak to Mrs. Merchant, please?" a voice said.

"This is she."

"My name is Ms. Clyburn. I am calling from Rex Hospital."

"Yes," Emily said.

"There seems to be a problem with your medical insurance."

"What sort of problem?"

"Well, your insurance has only been effective for three weeks. Is that right?"

"Yes, it is."

"I'm sorry dear, but your insurance is claiming your tumor is a pre-existing condition and is refusing to pay for your treatment."

"They have to pay for it," Emily exclaimed.

"I'm sorry Ms. Merchant, but do you have any other means of paying?"

"No, I don't," Emily said, dropping into a chair. "What am I going to do?"

"Don't worry, Ms. Merchant. We will try our best to help you."

Emily sat in disbelief.

"We have a counselor who specializes in helping patients in your situation. I'll have her call you, okay?" Ms. Clyburn said.

"Yes, thank you," Emily said.

"Okay, bye Ms. Merchant, and don't worry. We deal with this sort of thing all the time."

"Thank you, bye," Emily said, ending the call. She spent the remainder of the afternoon, and several weeks to come, fiercely disputing the insurance company's claim.

Reverend Talbert was outraged. "Those scoundrels will not elude their responsibility. God will not allow it," he declared.

However, despite all their efforts, the insurance company would not acquiesce.

Emily sat across from Wanda Smith, one of Rex Hospital's financial counselors. "What are my options?" Emily asked.

"It is not our policy to deny services to someone in your condition, so your surgery will take place as scheduled," Ms. Smith said.

"How much is this going to cost?"

Wanda Smith placed a file in front of Emily. Inside was a list of service charges totaling $136,000.

Emily sat in disbelief as Wanda Smith explained the figures before her.

"And this," Wanda Smith said, turning over a page, "is your payment schedule. You will pay an eight percent interest rate over sixty months, a monthly payment of two-thousand-seven-hundred-fifty dollars."

"I don't know how I can pay for this," Emily said.

"We will worry about payments later. Right now, we need to get you well," Wanda Smith said.

Emily wiped away a tear. "Thank you so much. I don't know what I would have done without you."

"You're welcome, Emily. We deal with this sort of thing all the time. These insurance companies are all crooks if you ask me, but God sees us through, doesn't He?" Wanda Smith said.

"Yes, he does," Emily said, her tears flowing steadily.

Wanda Smith stepped around her desk and pulled Emily into her embrace. "Soon this will all be behind you."

Emily's doctors recommended a lumpectomy, followed by radiation therapy. She made all the necessary preparations, choosing a substitute for her students, and transportation for Alexander to and from school.

She explained the details of her surgery to Alexander, speaking to him matter-of-factly, in a nonchalant sort of way. "It is only a routine procedure, and I'll be back home when you get in from school," she said, trying to calm his nerves, but it was no use. She listened as Alexander fired off a series of acute questions, interested in every detail. Emily understood how Alexander's mind worked, finding comfort in the details, no unknown variables—surprises made him nervous, so Emily answered each question honestly and patiently.

She explained the difference between a mastectomy and a lumpectomy, and chemotherapy versus radiation. He inquired about the advantages and disadvantages of each treatment.

"Are you sure you won't lose any hair?" Alexander asked.

"I may lose some, but not a significant amount," Emily said.

"What will you do if you began to lose a significant amount?" Alexander asked.

"I don't know, cut it all off, I suppose," Emily concluded.

Alexander looked confused. "Why would you do that?"

"Control," Emily said thoughtfully, "Control." She kissed Alexander's forehead and tucked him into bed.

At age 15, Alexander had grown beyond his mother tucking him in at night. Like most teenage boys, he was embracing adolescence with fervor, but on this occasion, as he snuggled in the cocoon of bed sheets and blankets his mother had created, he found himself wanting to be a child once more. He imagined climbing out of bed in the still of night, and tip-toeing barefoot across the cold wooden floors, carrying his pillow and dragging his favorite blankie. He saw himself climbing into his mother's bed and burying his head beneath her chin. "Sleep, Alexander," she would say, "Sleep."

Emily emerged from a hot shower and wiped herself dry. She wiped the mirror clear, and her towel fell to the floor. She stood naked, gazing at her reflection in the mirror. She observed her breasts, which still sat up straight and full. She thought of her dead husband, who at times seemed to think of nothing other than her breasts. She thought of his touch, and how he made her feel. He was the only man she had ever loved. The only man she had ever given herself to, emotionally and physically. Observing her bare breasts, of which in a few hours, would be changed forever, her mind filled with thoughts of her self-image, womanhood, and sexuality.

Emily had been out on a few dates since her husband's passing, but nothing too serious. She wouldn't allow serious. *Will I ever find love again?* she wondered. *Will anyone want me?*

For many years, her beauty was an afterthought. She was oblivious to the effect she had on men and had taken her beauty for granted. It had never defined her—she was much more.

THE SURGERY WAS A SUCCESS, Emily was told. She was at home resting when Alexander burst through her bedroom door. She opened her eyes and met his gaze.

"Are you okay?" Alexander asked.

Emily smiled broadly. "I'm fine," she said, grasping his hand.

"Do you need anything? Do you want something to drink? I can make you some soup," Alexander offered.

"No dear, I only need rest. You should get started on your homework."

"I don't have any."

"You always have homework," she admonished.

Alexander retrieved his books and sat down next to Emily's bed.

In the days that followed, Alexander almost never left his mother's side. He tended to her every need and was relieved by her speedy recovery. However, her radiation treatments, which began weeks later, were particularly difficult on them both.

Emily took her radiation treatments in stride, a necessary duty like getting up for work, or once again carrying a mortgage on a home which she has rightfully owned for over seven years. Emily's inexorable medical bills left her with two options, bankruptcy or securing a home equity loan, which she would use to pay her medical expenses. After the countless lessons of fiscal responsibility she had bestowed on Alexander, bankruptcy was not an option. She secured a home equity loan and transferred her $136,000 of medical debt into a 15-year mortgage.

Emily was lying across her bed reading *O Magazine* when she heard her doorbell ring. Moments later, Alexander came to her bedroom door and said, "Mom, Reverend Talbert is here."

"Tell him I'll be right down," she said. Emily found Reverend Talbert sitting on her living room sofa.

"Hello, Emily. It's good to see you," the Reverend said.

"Hi, Reverend Talbert." She embraced him. "Thanks for stopping by," Emily said. Would you like some tea?" Emily asked.

"Yes, that would be nice," he said.

She poured Reverend Talbert a cup of green tea and sat down across from him.

"How are you feeling?" Reverend Talbert asked.

"I feel okay. The radiation therapy has been tough, but I'll get through it," she said flatly.

Reverend Talbert sipped his tea. "I haven't seen you in church in a while. Is everything okay?" Reverend Talbert asked.

"I've been there five days a week. Is that not enough?" Emily said.

"Well, of course you have been there with your students, but I haven't seen you in service," he said.

"I haven't found the strength to go," she said.

Reverend Talbert smiled warmly. "What better place to find strength than in the house of the Lord, among friends and family who love you," he offered.

Emily felt an influx of mixed emotions: comfort, nerves, love, and anger. She patted her tight cornrows, which irritated her scalp. "I need a little time is all. I need space."

"Space from whom?" Reverend Talbert asked, amiably.

In a moment of uncontrollable exasperation, Emily screamed out, "You, Pastor Talbert. I need space from you."

Reverend Talbert sat back and crossed his legs. He then uncrossed his legs and sat up again. "What do you mean?"

"I'll tell you what I mean. You convinced me that leaving my government job and taking a pay cut and no health insurance to work for you was God's will. You said that by doing so, by stepping out on faith, God would protect me. Well, was it God's will for me to get cancer—to almost lose everything? The church raised five hundred dollars to help me, when my medical bills amounted to one hundred and thirty-six thousand dollars, over two hundred and fifty thousand dollars with interest. Had I listened to my mind, not my heart or my faith, but my own reasoning, perhaps I wouldn't be in this mess. Perhaps I wouldn't be in debt up to my eyeballs," Emily screamed, and then stood and began straightening a room that was already immaculate.

Reverend Talbert was aghast, sitting in silence for what seemed an eternity.

Whether he was praying or choosing his words carefully, Emily didn't know.

"Emily," he finally said warmly, "if I misled you in any way, I am truly sorry. I only said what God had placed on my heart or maybe what I thought or wanted Him to. I had no way of knowing this would happen. That the insurance company would cancel your policy when you needed it most. Please, understand that I never intended to deceive you in any way," he said.

Emily stood listening with folded arms.

Reverend Talbert continued, "Emily, if your faith is being tested due to something I've done, I," he paused, "I cannot even bear the thought of it."

Emily felt the tension in her muscles relax. "I only need time, Reverend, I need space." She made her way to her front door and opened it. Upon doing so, she noticed Alexander, who had been sitting on the front porch listening to every word. She saw the horror in Alexander's eyes—the obvious confusion. She didn't want to feel responsible for compromising her son's faith, as much as Reverend Talbert didn't want to compromise hers. Taking this into account, she turned to Reverend Talbert and said, "I'll see you on Sunday."

EIGHT

Emily arrived at Morganton Youth Institution on a Saturday at 8:30 A.M., visiting hours began at nine. She filled out a form and was escorted into the visitation room. When Alexander entered, wearing a brown jumpsuit and cloth shoes, she wrapped him in her arms and held him tightly.

Alexander could feel her heart pounding in her chest. "Hi, Mom," he said.

"Hi, honey. Are you okay?"

"Yes, Mommy, I am fine," Alexander said.

They sat at a small square table next to each other. "I tried to call you, Mommy, but they wouldn't let me. I need a pin number to make phone calls, and I haven't received it yet."

"When will you get it?"

"Monday, I hope. I had no way of telling you where I was." Tears burned Alexander's eyes.

"That's okay, sweetie. They sent me a letter. Julian Hoffman was no help—I am so angry with that man I could scream," she said.

Alexander leaned in close. "Julian is a charlatan, Mommy. He led me to believe he was working towards my best interest, but he never cared what happened to me. Do you remember what he said about the district attorney—how he despised him? Well, it turns out they're close friends," Alexander said.

"I am so sorry, honey. I trusted Julian in the beginning, too. I didn't realize who he really was until it was too late. I feel like all of this is my fault," Emily said.

"It wasn't your fault," Alexander said. Seeing her pain was excruciating. "It's not too bad here, Mommy. I have a job and everything."

"A job doing what?"

"Unit orderly."

"How much does it pay?"

"One dollar a day."

She shook her head and lowered it.

"It keeps me busy, and I've been tutoring on the side," he reassured her.

"Tutoring who?"

"My classmates. We are all mandated to take GED classes, which I don't really need, but they won't allow me to test out, so I'm in class for most of the day. A lot of students desperately need extra help. In fact, many students can barely read at all."

"That's so sad."

"Yes, it is."

"I am glad you're able to help."

"It feels good, and it keeps me busy."

"Pastor Talbert says hello—and Howard says he is coming to visit next Saturday. He wants you to call him."

"I mailed him a letter yesterday."

"He stops by to check on me every day," Emily said. "He offers to take out the trash and rake the leaves."

"I asked him to look after you," Alexander said.

"I thought as much." She smiled. "But I can look after myself."

"It makes me feel better—I worry about you."

"I know, but don't worry so much. You need to take care of yourself in this place."

"He enjoys it, Mom. Besides, I couldn't stop him if I tried," Alexander said.

"I know." She smiled. "Did you get the money I sent you?"

"Yes, thank you."

"I'll send you more next week," Emily said.

Alexander looked away and squinted his eyes.

"What's wrong?" Emily asked.

"How's Natalie?"

"I hear she's doing better. This situation has been tough on her."

"I know," Alexander said.

"She's been depressed, as you know, but doing much better," Emily reported.

"I'm not allowed to contact her in any way. They read all my letters and monitor my phone calls. Please, tell her I would contact her if I could."

"She already knows that."

"Would you tell her that I love her?"

"She already knows that, too," Emily said.

"Tell her anyway."

"I don't think that would be appropriate," Emily said.

Alexander looked away.

"Are you okay?" Emily asked.

"Yes, I'm fine. How are things at home?" Alexander asked.

"Much too quiet. I'm used to you and Howard clamoring through the house"

"Is that why you look so well rested?" Alexander said, laughing.

Emily laughed, too. "Rest is the least of my worries," she said.

"Enjoy it now, because in twenty-three months, things will be back to normal," Alexander said.

"Take one day at a time honey, and you'll be home before you know it." Emily rested her hand on his.

Alexander lay in bed thinking about his mother for most of the night. He was pleased to know Howard and his parents were looking after her. Alexander had also asked Howard to look after Natalie. Alexander wondered how Natalie was coping with the situation. He wondered how she was feeling, and what people were saying about her. He had spent the week anxiously awaiting Howard's visit and the day finally arrived. He wondered what message Howard would bring him from Natalie.

Upon entering the visitation room, Alexander and Howard embraced before sitting at a small table.

"How are you?" Howard asked.

"I'm fine."

"What's it like in here?" Howard's eyes roamed around the room.

"It's awful, Howard. I never thought I would end up in a place like this. It's a living nightmare."

"I can imagine," Howard said.

"No, you cannot imagine how bad it is. This place is filthy, the food is awful, and there is never a moment of privacy."

"What's your room like?"

"I don't have a room. We all sleep in one big room together. We even have to shower together."

"What do you mean you have to shower together?" Howard asked shockingly.

"The shower room has twelve shower heads in it."

"Do you have to shower with eleven other guys?"

"Sometimes, yes."

"That's awful." Howard was clearly horrified. "We have to get you out of here."

"I'm afraid that's impossible. I'll be here for at least twenty-three months."

"Nothing is impossible. We could appeal your case."

"No, we can't. Plea bargains are next to impossible to appeal. Besides, even if I were to appeal, I'm likely to be out of prison before my case even went to trial. All I can do is make the best of my time while I'm here."

Howard grew quiet, sitting with his shoulders slumped.

"Enough about my situation. How's Natalie?" Alexander asked.

Howard sighed. "I have some bad news."

"What sort of bad news? Did something happen? Is she okay?"

Howard looked pensive. "I don't know how to say this, but..." he paused.

"Spit it out, Howard." Alexander leaned forward.

"Natalie's parents sent her to Stockholm to live with her uncle," Howard said.

Alexander sat up straight. "Why would they do that?"

"They wanted her to have a fresh start," Howard said.

"Is that what she wanted?"

"Of course not, but she was having a difficult time. What happened with you two was all everyone talked about, and some even made-up stories about her."

"What sort of stories?"

"Silly gossip of no importance—but it added to the pressure she was under."

"Could she not handle it?"

"Of course, she could handle it, but her parents saw no reason why she should have to. Natalie fought against them as much as she could, but she eventually acquiesced. This situation had taken a lot out of her, and I don't think she had the strength to fight them too," Howard said.

"How long has she been gone?"

"Four days."

"So, she left on Wednesday?"

"Yes, on Wednesday. Perhaps it's for the best. She lives in Stockholm, where she was planning to return eventually anyway," Howard said.

"But she was supposed to return with me," Alexander said gloomily. He leaned back in his chair and rested his eyes on the white cinderblock wall. "Did she leave a message for me?"

"She said that she loves you, and no matter what happens, she'll never forget you," Howard said.

Alexander's eyes swelled with tears.

Howard made several attempts at small talk, but Alexander was lost in his own misery.

The two friends sat quietly before the visit came to an end. The visitors said their goodbyes and lined up near the door, and an officer escorted them out of the room.

Alexander went back to his dormitory and lay across his bed. His melancholy mood deteriorated into a long period of depression. For several weeks, he rarely ate anything or spoke to anyone.

EMILY'S CONCERN for Alexander increased with each visit. She noticed his wrinkled clothing and his unmanaged hair. She took note of his melancholy conversations that no longer considered his future, but increasingly focused on the here and now.

"I'm so worried about him," Emily told Howard and Orlando when they were over for a visit.

"Have you spoken to the psychology department?" Orlando asked her.

"No, I had a conversation with his case manager. She promised to refer him to psychological services. However, she tried to convince me his behavior was quite normal," Emily said.

"It isn't normal for Alexander," Howard said, pacing the living room floor.

Sitting on her sofa, Emily crossed her legs and embraced a pillow. "His case manager explained that people in Alexander's situation, whose lives have been so abruptly changed, will often have more difficulty adjusting to life in prison," Emily said.

"I imagine she's right," Orlando said, sitting across from Emily. "Kids who live a more deviant lifestyle are more prepared for prison. For some, it's considered a rite of passage, but for kids like Alexander, this shocking turn of events could only be distressing," Orlando said.

"I wish there was something I could do—I feel so helpless." Emily hugged the pillow tightly.

"Perhaps I could cheer him up this weekend with some news from Natalie. She emailed me a message for Alexander," Howard said, before detecting a flash of anger on Emily's face.

"What sort of message?" Emily asked.

"She wants him to know about her new life, new school, and new friends," Howard said.

"I don't see how that would help him. I wish he had never met that girl," Emily said.

"You're certainly not blaming Natalie for this, are you?" Howard said.

"Be careful, Howard," Orlando admonished.

"Please, forgive me, Ms. Merchant. I only mean to say that this situation has been hard on Natalie, too. In fact, she feels like she is in a prison of her own," Howard said.

"I fail to see how her privileged life is at all commensurate to a prison," Emily scolded. "I know this situation has been hard on her, but she's in Sweden. Therefore, the sooner he forgets about her, the better. Alexander has to move on with his life."

"You're right, Emily, but I think Alexander is as much depressed about losing Natalie, as he is about being in prison. So, I think an occasional correspondence between the two may do him some good," Orlando offered.

Emily folded her arms. Her legs were crossed, and her flip-flops swayed delicately over the floor. "I ran into Natalie's mother yesterday," she said.

"How did that go?" Orlando asked.

"It was fine. We had no hard words. She claims that they were willing to testify on Alexander's behalf, but they never got the chance. None of us did," Emily said.

"Her father, too?" Orlando asked.

Emily sucked her teeth and said, "According to her, yes, but who knows." She crossed her arms and gazed out of the window.

"Well, we had better get going." Orlando stood and made his way to the door.

"Okay. Say hi to Vivian for me," Emily said.

"I will," he smiled and followed Howard out and onto the porch.

~

Howard's news of Natalie lifted Alexander's spirits considerably and he was happy to share. "She said her new school was over two hundred years old. It was once a nineteenth century castle before it was converted. She says the school is filled with mysterious passages, and the exterior is decorated with ghastly gargoyles," Howard said.

"That sounds like a place Natalie would love. She likes architecture you know," Alexander said.

"Is that right?"

"Oh, yes. She often gazed at photos of old European buildings and marveled at the beauty—particularly buildings in Edinburgh and Moscow," Alexander said. "Has she made any friends?"

"She has three cousins who attend her school and mostly hangs with them. But she says she's made a few new friends, too." Howard said.

"I'm glad she has family to help her adjust," Alexander said thoughtfully. "Listen Howard, whenever you talk to her, don't tell her how miserable I am, nor what a terrible place this is. Only tell her that I am doing well, okay?" Alexander said.

"She has to know this place is no hotel," Howard said.

"I suspect she knows that already, but you should only report good news. I don't want her to worry so much about me. She will eventually need to get on with her life," Alexander said.

"So must you," Howard said.

"We all will, Howard, in due time," Alexander said.

Howard sighed.

"Ask her about the weather. After living in Kenya, I know she must be freezing there, and ask her to send pictures of Stockholm and this school of hers," Alexander requested.

Alexander and Natalie corresponded in this way for many months, careful to code their messages in a way to disguise their continued relationship. Their correspondence, including greeting cards and personal letters, were all filtered through Howard.

When Howard received the pictures Alexander had requested, he packaged them and sent them to Alexander labeled random shots. The package included photos of landmarks, parks, snow-covered fields, and frozen lakes. In one of the photos, Alexander was able to make out Natalie's reflection in a window. In another photo, Natalie was seen inconspicuously placed among pedestrians on a busy street. There was a picture of a charming brick house, where on the back of the photo, "home" was scribbled by Natalie's delicate hand. Included in these treasures, was a photo of a bedroom. Inside of this photo was a twin sized bed, a small desk, a dresser, and most prominently, a mirror mounted on her bedroom wall. Hanging on the left side of the mirror, Alexander recognized the prize Natalie had won on the day she set a new state record in the 200-meter. Hanging on the right side of the mirror was a white cotton bathrobe, which Alexander also recognized. He had last seen this bathrobe on his 18th birthday. It was the bathrobe Natalie had worn on the evening of her big race. It was the bathrobe she had worn when they first made love.

More memories of Natalie filled his mind, and he was reminded of the beginning of their relationship. He reached for the letter he had started writing to Judge Gregory and read it over, thinking about what else he wanted to say.

TEN

On an unseasonably warm day, Alexander and Natalie played tennis together. Alexander thought he should take it easy on her, but that proved to be a critical lapse in judgment, as Natalie was an excellent tennis player. She was fast and decisive, and when Alexander realized what a formidable opponent he was facing, she had already taken the first set by a score of six to four.

Alexander fared better during the second set, as he resolved to show her no mercy, but to his dismay, Natalie had returned his best serves with ease, and using her lanky frame to her advantage, she ran down his would-be winners and returned them as well. Alexander managed to win their second game in a tiebreak of seven to six, but it took all his energy to do it.

Alexander realized his win seemed to awaken Natalie's competitive spirit, as she no longer smiled or laughed at her mistakes, and she grunted as she powered passing shots by him, spinning the ball just out of his reach. At times, he found himself distracted by the sun glistening against her perspiring bronze skin, and her toned legs and sculptured arms, and although he gave it his all, she ended the match with a score of six to three.

"A warning would've been nice," he said.

She laughed. "You played well."

"Oh, rub it in, why don't you?" he said, and collapsed on a nearby bench.

"I mean it, you play well. It just so happens that I have had a private coach for most of my life." Natalie took a seat beside him.

"That doesn't make me feel any better," he said.

She pushed his arm playfully.

"Do you play competitively?" he asked.

"I tried, but I wasn't good enough," she answered.

"You look good enough to me," he said, flirtatiously, drawing from her a smile.

"I'm better than average, but not good enough to stand out," Natalie said.

"You could still improve," he said.

"I could, but I know I'll never be good enough to really compete, so I quit competitive play and focused on track and field instead," she said.

"What events do you run?"

"I run the two hundred and four hundred meter, and the three-hundred-meter hurdles."

"You should join Broughton's track team," Alexander said.

"I start practice on Monday. Do you play any sports?"

"Soccer," Alexander said.

"What's your position?"

"Striker and goalie."

"I love soccer. In Kenya, the kids play football every day. They would play all day long sometimes," Natalie said.

"Did you ever play with them?"

"Oh yes, I would play whenever I could, and in Nairobi, the kids play right in the street, and many would play barefoot," Natalie said.

"Doesn't it hurt their toes?"

"I suppose they get used to it," Natalie said.

Walking home with Natalie, Alexander considered the possibility of them becoming exclusive. He tried to broach the subject several times but struggled to find the right words.

"Natalie, I like you, a lot, actually," he said.

"I like you, too," she said.

"Ever since meeting you, you're all I think about. And I always look forward to seeing and talking to you. I was thinking, if you feel the same way, then maybe we shouldn't see anyone else," he said nervously.

"So, you want to be my boyfriend," she responded, candidly.

"Well, yes," he said.

In her countenance, Alexander saw a look of contentment. Saying nothing, she crossed her arms, and moved her shoulder against his. When her arms fell to her side, Alexander reached for her hand and wrapped his pinky finger around hers. Soon, she grasped his hand firmly, silently affirming her affection. They walked on in silence, both calm and ebullient. Reaching her doorstep, Alexander felt the palms of her hands pressing against his back. With a curled index finger, he raised her chin and kissed her as softly as he knew how. She pressed her lips firmly against his, drawing the energy right out of him. They stood for a while, looking at each other, but still silent, as if afraid that uttering one word would awaken them from a dream.

From that moment on, Natalie and Alexander were inseparable. They would converse about many subjects, and sometimes they would just sit together, listening to the same songs over and over again.

Alexander sat on his back porch talking to Howard about his budding relationship with Natalie.

"I knew you were right for each other from the beginning," Howard said.

"And how did you know that?" Alexander asked.

"Because, you are so cosmopolitan and idealistic, that frankly, I don't think anyone else could hold your attention," Howard said.

"I'm not an idealist," Alexander said.

"Sure, you are. There is nothing wrong with idealism if you are equally pragmatic. Besides, I knew her accent would get you if nothing else. I could see it in your eyes every time she spoke," Howard said, laughing

"You have to admit, the accent is pretty cute," he said.

"Face it, my man, she has you wide open," Howard said, holding his stomach as he laughed loudly.

"And you have room to talk, Mr. NYU? *It is such a cool school,*" Alexander said, mocking him.

"Touché," Howard responded.

"Dinner is ready," Emily called out from the kitchen. "Howard, are you hungry?"

"Yes, ma'am," Howard said.

"How does lamb chops, sweet potatoes, and asparagus sound?" she said.

"Awesome," Howard said, as he took long strides towards the kitchen.

"Wash your hands," she commanded.

Howard, who is known for his garrulous nature, was only silent on two occasions, when he is sleeping or eating a good meal, and he hadn't said a word since he sat at the table.

"What are your plans for the summer, Howard?" Emily asked.

"Work," Howard said.

"Have you found a job?"

"No, ma'am, I am still looking," Howard said.

"Have you thought of an internship?" she asked.

"No, ma'am, I haven't."

"My friend is looking for an intern to help out around the office this summer. She asked if Alexander was available, but since he has already committed himself to Raleigh Parks and Recreation, I thought maybe you would be interested," she said.

"How much does it pay?" Howard asked.

"It is only six dollars an hour, but it will enhance your college application," she said.

"You will be working at the Orion Institute. It's in Cary, which should not be a problem once you get your car back," Alexander said.

"What happened to your car?" Emily asked Howard.

"His grades dropped below a three-point-five, and Mr. Connerly took it," Alexander interjected.

"Oh, my. What happened?"

"I got a three-point-three last quarter, and he had a fit. You would have thought I flunked the eleventh grade," Howard said. "He can be such an..." he paused. "He can be so..."

"Fastidious," Emily said, finishing his thought for him.

"Yes, fastidious," Howard said.

"When Orlando gave you his car, didn't you agree to maintain a three-point-five grade point average?" Emily asked.

"Yes," Howard said.

"Well, if you agreed to those conditions, you shouldn't be angry with him if you didn't keep your end of the bargain. So, I advise you to work harder and bring your grades back up," she said.

"Yes, ma'am," Howard said.

"How are your grades this quarter?"

"Straight As so far."

"He will end the year on a high note," Alexander said.

"That's good news," she said, smiling, "And shall I tell Ms. Lawson to expect a call from you concerning the internship?"

"Yes, ma'am, you may. Thank you," Howard said.

"You are gonna like her," Alexander said.

"Gonna is not a word," Emily said.

"It's just slang, Mom," Alexander said.

"I don't care. Use proper English," she admonished.

"Proper English is subjective. There is really no such thing as proper English, only the established version of it, and no version of English is any more proper than the other. In fact, dialect gives us great insight into a person's heritage," Alexander said.

"If you want to get ahead in this world, you must learn to speak properly, otherwise, you are only holding yourself back," she said.

"Give up, man," Howard said.

Alexander laughed.

"Would you mind taking care of the dishes for me?" Emily asked Alexander. "I'm too tired and need to lie down."

"Thank you for dinner, Mrs. Merchant."

"You're welcome, Howard."

Howard helped Alexander clear the table and load the dishwasher. "How was Aida?" Howard asked.

"It was nice. I enjoyed it more than I thought I would."

"Really?" Howard said. "You usually complain about your mother dragging you to Broadway shows."

"I know, but it was different this time. The story of the

African princess resonated with me and the singers were first rate. You should see it," Alexander said.

"I don't do the opera. I'll wait for the Broadway version to come," Howard said.

"Why wait? You could walk to Broadway from NYU," Alexander said.

"Funny," Howard said.

SUMMER MOVED QUICKLY, and Emily's roses were in full bloom. It was mid-July and Alexander spent his days working as a counselor in a youth camp and playing soccer in an indoor summer league. Natalie spent her time training and competing in various track meets. She had spent the summer flirting with two state records, and in her quest for breaking those records, she pushed herself to get faster and develop the form of a champion. In his spare time, Alexander watched her practice and attended her local competitions.

"You were looking good out there today," Alexander said, as they strolled home.

Natalie smiled. "I could do better," she said.

"I am sure you could."

"I just have a few kinks to work out."

"You shouldn't put so much pressure on yourself. Learn to relax," Alexander said.

"I do relax," she said.

"I know, but when you're running, you look as though you are thinking through every step. I think if you would clear your mind and run freely, you would do a lot better," he said.

"Listen at you, Coach Alexander," she said playfully.

Alexander laughed.

"How is Howard?" she asked.

"He's excited out of his mind," Alexander said.

"Excited about what?"

"Allyson is coming on Thursday, and the poor guy doesn't know what to do with himself."

"Aw, that is so sweet. It's hard to imagine Howard that way about anyone," she said.

"Anyone, but Allyson," he said.

"I hope I get to meet her?"

"You will. We're going out to movies on Saturday. Are you free?"

"Sure," Natalie said.

Standing on her porch, Alexander leaned in to kiss Natalie goodbye, and at that moment, as if driven by some fatherly intuition, the door opened, and Abasi Agadani stood in the doorway. Alexander quickly stepped away from Natalie, not knowing if he should speak or run away.

"Hi, Alexander. How are you?" he asked, smiling.

"I'm doing well, sir. How are you?" Alexander asked.

"I am well, thank you for asking."

Mr. Agadani spoke to Natalie in a foreign tongue and Natalie responded in the same language. They went back and forth for a moment, speaking rapidly. Their words, which were incomprehensible to Alexander, sounded smooth and melodic. He concluded it must have been some tongue of Kenya, of which Natalie would have learned directly from her father.

"It was nice to see you, Alexander," he said, smiling broadly, teeth gleaming. With that, he placed his hand on Natalie's back, guiding her into the house, closing the door behind them.

Moments later, the door opened again, and Helena Agadani stood there. "Come in, Alexander. I want to give you something." She said, "You must forgive my husband. I don't know where his manners have gone."

Alexander didn't know how to respond to that, so he smiled and followed her into the kitchen.

"Here, try one of these," Mrs. Agadani said.

"It's a Swedish cinnamon twist," Natalie said, coming into the kitchen and standing next to Alexander.

Alexander took a bite, and immediately took another one. "These are delicious," he said.

Mrs. Agadani smiled. "I am glad you like them."

"Yes ma'am, it's really good," he said, just as Natalie handed him another cinnamon twist, and a glass of milk. Alexander smiled.

"It is an old family recipe. I made far too many, and I don't want them to go to waste," Mrs. Agadani said.

"She is feeling a little too nostalgic," Natalie said.

Mrs. Agadani gave a soft chuckle and said, "I got a little carried away, so please take some home to your mother." She handed him a bag filled with a dozen Swedish cinnamon twists. "Please, say hello to her for me," Mrs. Agadani said.

"I will. Thank you, ma'am," he said, just before Natalie saw him to the door.

"Do you really like them?" Natalie whispered.

"Yes, I do."

"Okay, you do not have to eat them," she said.

"Of course, I will eat them, they're delicious."

Natalie smiled and let out a sigh of relief.

"What language were you speaking to your father?" he asked.

"Swahili. It is my father's native tongue. I learned to speak it as a child," she said.

As Alexander left her yard, he saw Natalie still standing in the doorway watching him. He blew her a kiss and watched Natalie blow him one back.

"I'll call you in an hour," she yelled out.

ALLYSON ARRIVED ON THURSDAY, and she and Howard were nowhere to be found. Alexander knew they were taking advantage of the short time they would have together, wanting nothing more than to be alone together. Away from the world, away from the living. He imagined they would have stopped time if they could, but despite their best efforts, Saturday arrived, nonetheless.

Natalie found Alexander sitting on a stone wall on the corner of Peace Street and St. Mary's. He sat listening to music and bobbing his head. She sat beside him and pulled an earbud from his ear and popped it into hers. She listened for a moment before asking, "Who is this?"

"Little Brother. They're a local group out of Durham," he answered.

Natalie glanced at the Needham Broughton Clock Tower high up above and saw it was 3:00. "What time does the movie start?" she asked.

"Six-thirty," he said.

"Where are Howard and Allyson?" she asked.

"We're meeting them later. There's something I want to show you first." He grabbed her hand and started off up Peace Street.

"Where are we going?"

"You'll see. It's a surprise," he said.

"Girls like surprises," she said, raising an eyebrow and giving a wink.

They continued steadily along, passing through Cameron Village, a shopping center consisting of boutiques and eateries, until they arrived at their destination.

"Close your eyes," Alexander said, and led her by the hand

for several yards and stopped. "Okay, you can open your eyes now," he said.

Natalie gasped. "This is beautiful. Where are we?"

There were over 1400 individual rose bushes. It was six acres of the most beautiful, landscaped garden in all of Raleigh. In the shape of a bowl, the garden sat 600 feet below street level, offering the impression of stepping down into paradise.

"This is the Raleigh Rose Garden. I know how you love roses, and since it is such a pretty day, I thought you would enjoy a picnic," he said, patting his knapsack.

"This is so nice," she said. Her countenance displayed a look of pure pleasure, as they stood looking out at a sea of roses.

"This is the largest rose garden in all of North Carolina. It has over sixty varieties of roses. These trees are redwoods, that one is a boulevard cypress." He pointed and said, "And that one is a China fir."

Natalie admired every bush. Smelling while smiling pleasantly.

"By mid-September, some of these roses will stand close to six feet tall," Alexander shared.

They strolled under the stone archway, which stood at the top of the flowerbeds like a noble crown, proud and meaningful. They sat on a bench and Natalie gazed at the numerous roses, climbing and covering the archway.

"I often come here when I want to be alone. It is my favorite place in the world," he said.

"I think it is mine, too," Natalie said. She closed her eyes and filled her nostrils with the heavy scent of rose petals. "What is that building?" she asked.

"That's the Raleigh Little Theatre. It's a community theater that offers many small productions, workshops, and acting classes. There is an amphitheater on the other side of the garden where they often have outdoor productions," he said.

"Can I see it?"

"Sure." Alexander led her to the amphitheater, where they stood on the stage taking in the idyllic setting. She admired the rows of sandstone benches climbing upward to the rear sandstone wall.

"Thanks for sharing this with me," she said. She took his hand, and Alexander kissed her softly. They sat near the garden shelter and ate turkey sandwiches he had prepared.

"What are your plans for college?" Alexander asked.

"I don't know, really. I planned to attend the University of Stockholm, but now that my parents are employed by Duke University, I am eligible for a grant covering most of my tuition," she said.

"I bet your parents are happy about that," he said.

"You bet they are. It would save them almost thirty thousand dollars per semester," she said.

"What will you study?"

"Medicine, like my parents," she said.

"I want to study abroad," Alexander said.

"Where?"

"England, France, Germany, or any place I can earn an international scholarship. I want to study anthropology and international relations," he said.

"Do you want to teach?"

"No, I want a career in Diplomatic Services, as an ambassador," he said.

"For the State Department?"

"Either the State Department, or the United Nations. However, I think I would be a better fit for the United Nations," he said.

"How so?" she asked.

"Well, I think working for the United States is the patriotic thing to do, but I worry that if I choose to work for the State Department, U.S. interest would take precedence over any humanitarian policies I pursue," he said.

"Isn't that the nature of any government's diplomatic policies?" Natalie said.

"Yes, it is. And there is nothing wrong with that, but I also consider myself to be a citizen of the world. As an ambassador for the United Nations, I would have more freedom to work for the interest of all of humanity."

"Where would you live? New York?" she asked.

"That's the beauty of it. I want to see the world you know, and as an ambassador, I could live anywhere in the world, a different place every year if I wanted."

"That sounds exciting," Natalie said, but then looked pensive.

"What's wrong?" he asked.

Natalie bit her lower lip. "I was just thinking that if you go overseas to study, we will never see each other," she said.

"I know, I thought about that," he said, and gathered up the wrappings from their sandwiches.

"What would we do?" she asked.

"I don't know," he said, and the two sat quietly for a while.

"Why don't we apply to the same schools, both here and abroad, and whichever school we are both accepted to is where we will go?" she suggested.

"But what about your scholarship?" he asked.

"It's a grant. Besides, I can get a scholarship anywhere, and if all else fails, my great uncle is the chancellor of Stockholm University. We could go there," she said.

"It's not that easy," he said.

"Sure, it is," she said confidently. "My uncle would do anything for me. What is your GPA?" she asked.

"I have a five-point-o weighted," he said.

"That's good," Natalie said, excitedly.

"What about your parents? I don't think they would like us moving to Stockholm together," he said.

"Let me worry about my parents, you just nurture that five-point-o," Natalie said.

Alexander could see the wheels turning in her head. She wrapped both hands around his arm and lay her head on his shoulder.

Alexander's phone rang and he answered Howard's call.

"Are you ready?" Howard asked.

"Yes, we are," Alexander said.

"I'll be in front of the Little Theater in fifteen minutes," Howard said.

"We'll be there," Alexander said, and ended the call.

Alexander took a swig of water and lay back on the blanket.

Natalie lay beside him, looking up at the roses towering above.

"I love nature. There is nothing else like it. Look how beautiful," she said.

"It's lovely," he said.

"No, look at it," she said. "Look how the sunlight is shining through the trees, and how the scattered sunlight rests on the flowers, reflecting off the water falling from the fountain. Do you see?" she asked.

Alexander sat up and took in the scene. The sound of the water falling from the fountain was amplified along with the birds singing in the distance. He watched a bird bathing in the fountain, feathers wet and glistening. The scent of roses filled the air, and at that moment, he knew he was in love.

They made their way out to the theater and waited for Howard and Allyson. "They should be here soon," Alexander said, but noticed Natalie seemed unconcerned.

"I wonder what is playing," she said.

They looked at the Little Theater's schedule and discussed which shows seemed interesting and which did not.

"When's your next track meet?" Alexander asked.

"September third," she said.

"Are you kidding? That's my birthday," Alexander said.

"No way, my birthday is September eighteenth," she said.

"Our birthdays are only two weeks apart?"

"That is awesome," she said.

"We should have a party."

"That sounds fun, but all of my friends are in Nairobi and Europe. Who would come?"

"You have made plenty of friends here," Alexander said.

"No one I would want at my sweet sixteen birthday party," she said.

"Are you really turning sixteen?" he asked.

"Yes," she said.

"But you are going to the twelfth grade this year," he said.

"I skipped a grade, when I came here," she said.

"How did you pull that off?"

"I don't really know. I took a placement test, and they skipped me," she said, nonchalantly.

"That's cool."

"How old are you?" she asked.

"I am turning eighteen. As you know, my father died when I was five years old, and I took it really hard, becoming seriously withdrawn. So, my mother thought it best to hold me out of school for a year, therefore, I am graduating a year late," he said.

A horn blew, and Alexander saw Howard's car sitting a few feet away.

"I don't know what you lovebirds are discussing, but we have been sitting here for five minutes," Howard said.

"Hi, Allyson," Alexander said.

Allyson leaped from the car, her arms out wide.

Allyson embraced Alexander. "It's so good to see you."

"It is good to see you, too," Alexander replied.

"And this must be Natalie." Allyson said.

"It is good to finally meet you," Natalie said, as they embraced.

"It is so good to meet you, Natalie. I've heard so much about you, it feels like I have known you for years," Allyson said.

They climbed into Howard's car and made their way to the movie theater.

"I'm glad you're finally here, Allyson. Howard has been a lost soul without you," Alexander said.

Allyson touched Howard's arm as he laughed.

"He has been quite exuberant all week," Natalie offered.

They all laughed some more.

"Aw, that's sweet," Allyson said, pinching Howard's cheek and he blushed.

They approached the box office and looked over the start times of all the movies.

"May I help you?" the box office attendant asked.

"Four for Batman at seven o'clock," Howard said, as he slid his credit card under the plexiglass window, and the box office attendant slid his credit card and four tickets back. Howard gave everyone a ticket and they went inside.

"I'll get the refreshments," Alexander said.

"Cool," Howard replied.

Alexander bought two large buckets of popcorn and four medium cups of Coke and they made their way into the theater and settled into their seats.

"He really likes you, you know?" Allyson whispered to Natalie.

"I like him, too," Natalie whispered back.

"How was the picnic?" Allyson asked.

"It was so nice." She smiled some more. "That place is so beautiful."

"How did you guys meet?" Allyson asked.

"In school. What about you and Howard?"

"We met through Jack and Jill," Allyson said.

"What is that?"

"It's a social club for kids. My date to a cotillion got sick and couldn't make it, so Howard escorted me, and we've been together ever since," Allyson explained.

The lights in the theater dimmed, and the movie started soon after. Natalie and Allyson chit-chatted throughout the film, and when the movie ended, the two couples strolled over to the Burger Barn for dinner. Stepping inside, they saw Brett Collins and Samantha Fields in line to be seated.

"What's up?" Brett said to the group.

"Hey, Brett," Alexander replied.

"I saw you guys in the theater," Brett said.

"What did you think?" Howard asked.

"Best Batman ever, bro," Brett said, holding out his fist to Howard.

"For sure," Howard said, and bumped his fist against Brett's.

"This is my girlfriend, Allyson," Howard said. "This is Brett and Samantha."

"Brett is my boyfriend," Samantha said.

Natalie rolled her eyes and turned away.

"How many in your party?" the hostess asked.

"Do ya'll wanna get a table together?" Brett asked.

"Sure," Howard said.

"Party of six," Brett said.

The hostess gathered six menus, and said, "Right this way."

Brett and Samantha followed the hostess to the table, while Natalie lingered.

"I think I am going to be sick," Natalie whispered to Alexander.

"What's wrong?" Alexander asked.

"Brett, he makes me sick," Natalie said.

"Brett is all right. He's a mindless jackass, but he's all right," Howard whispered.

"He is a Neanderthal, always hitting on me and making comments," Natalie said.

"Why haven't you told me?" Alexander asked.

"He isn't worth the trouble," Natalie said.

"We'll be sure to ditch them after dinner," Allyson said.

"That sounds like the right idea," Howard said.

The three couples sat and looked over the menu, which consisted of a variety of ground beef, turkey, and vegetarian burgers. They placed their orders and waited for their meals.

"Tell me about New York. What is it like?" Natalie asked Allyson.

"I can't imagine living anywhere else," Allyson said.

"I want to see Broadway," Natalie said.

"Do you like the theater?" Allyson asked.

"I love the theater," Natalie said.

"I loved New York. I was there last summer," Samantha interjected, "There's so much to do."

"There's no place like it," Allyson said.

"I don't care for it, personally," Alexander said.

"How could you not like New York?" Brett asked.

"We have everything here that New York has, just on a smaller scale," Alexander said.

"Are you crazy? This whole city shuts down at two A.M.," Brett said.

"How often do you want to stay out past two?" Alexander countered.

"I'd like to have the option," Brett said.

"Not me, I am happy where I am. Although I did enjoy Broadway," Alexander said.

"What shows have you seen?" Natalie asked.

"La bohéme , The Lion King, and Aida," Alexander answered.

"Did you enjoy it?" Natalie asked.

"It was cool," Alexander said nonchalantly. He winked at Natalie and flashed his pearly whites. Natalie smiled back.

"I'm moving to New York next year," Howard said.

"We're attending NYU," Allyson said, happily.

"However," Howard continued, "this area is full of New Yorkers, and although they all complain about how much they hate it here, they never seem to leave."

Alexander chimed in again. "I hate the traffic up there. They start blowing the horn and cussing at people as soon as the red light turns green. In fact, when I was there last, I was sitting at a red light, while this elderly lady was crossing the street. She was directly in front of our car, when the light turned green, the guy behind us started blowing his horn and yelling at me to go. I asked if he wanted me to run the old lady over?"

"I think I will have to see it for myself," Natalie said.

"You've been everywhere else," Howard said.

"Oh, where have you been?" Samantha asked Natalie.

"I lived in Nairobi, Kenya, Stockholm, Sweden, and London," Natalie said.

"She has also been to almost every major city in Europe," Allyson interjected.

"How have you been able to travel so much?" Samantha asked.

"My parents are itinerants," Natalie said, downplaying her travels as much as she could.

The server arrived with their burgers and set their plates on the table.

Natalie gazed at the half-pound burger in front of her and rubbed her chin.

"Can you handle all of that?" Alexander asked.

"I'll give it my best shot," Natalie said, and pulled her thick, curly hair away from her face and bit into the burger with fervor.

"What do you think?" Alexander asked.

"We need a place like this in Stockholm." Natalie ate as much as she could, before giving up and sliding her plate over to Alexander. She then excused herself and went to the restroom.

Moments later, Brett slithered towards the restroom as well, so when Natalie exited, she found Brett waiting in the corridor. She tried to move past him, but he blocked her path.

"What do you see in Alexander anyway?" he said.

"What is it to you?" Natalie said.

"He's cool and all, but I think you need more," Brett said.

"I suppose you are the right boy for the job," Natalie said.

"Who else?" Brett said.

"Let's see what Samantha thinks of that," Natalie said, pushing herself past him.

When Natalie returned, she was scowling and she was breathing hard, and Alexander was certain that Brett had something to do with it.

"What's wrong?" Alexander asked.

"It's nothing. Can we go now?" she requested.

"Sure, just let me finish up," he said.

Brett returned to the table as nonchalantly as he had left it. He sat and wrapped his arm around Samantha's shoulder.

Alexander watched him with stern eyes.

"What are you guys doing later on?" Brett asked.

"We're just gonna ride around a bit," Howard said.

"Ya'll should come back to my house. My parents are out this weekend, so you could have your privacy," Brett said.

"No. I need to get Natalie home," Alexander said.

"Suit yourself. I guess we know who is not getting laid tonight," Brett said.

"You're such an asshole," Natalie said.

"Don't be mad at me," Brett said.

"Why don't you shut your mouth?" Alexander said, angrily.

"Why don't you make me?" Brett said.

Alexander jumped to his feet and rushed towards him.

"Whoa," Howard said, jumping between them. "Everybody just calm down. Brett, you and I have always gotten along, so let's keep it that way, okay?"

"Then tell your boy to watch his mouth," Brett said.

"No, I'm telling you," Howard said forcefully. "You need to chill." Howard eyed him intently.

Brett gazed at Howard and sat without saying a word.

"I think we should be going," Allyson said to Howard. "It was nice to meet you, Samantha."

With that, they left the diner and climbed into Howard's car and rode away.

"He's so obnoxious," Natalie said.

"What happened when you went to the restroom?" Alexander asked.

"He tried to come on to me again," Natalie said.

"If he ever again says anything to you that's out of line, and I mean anything, you tell me immediately," Alexander said.

Howard drove Natalie home, and Alexander saw her to the door.

"Thanks for standing up for me," she said, under the illumination of the porch light.

"You're welcome."

"You were not actually planning to fight him, were you?" she asked.

"I would fight him and the whole football team for you," he said.

They embraced and Alexander kissed her softly on her forehead before she gazed up at him affectionately. He kissed her good night, before he hopped off the porch and trotted over to Howard's waiting car.

CHAPTER

ELEVEN

"Yo, this shit tastes like dog food," Calvin said, sitting in the cafeteria with Tony and Alexander.

"I wouldn't feed this slop to anyone." Alexander pushed the tray away from himself.

"*I wouldn't feed this slop to anyone,*" Calvin repeated, mockingly.

"What's your problem?" Alexander asked.

"You're my problem. You and your uppity bullshit," Calvin said.

"If you don't like the way I speak, you can go to hell," Alexander said.

"You speak like a bitch, Alex," Calvin said.

"Chill, C," Tony interjected. "Look, Alex, this is prison, not college. So, you gotta let that bourgeois shit go," Tony said.

"So, I should walk around blissfully ignorant like him?" Alexander asked Tony.

"I got your *ignorant,* motherfucker," Calvin said.

"Shut the fuck up, C," Tony said. "Look, Alex, that preppy

141

shit makes you vulnerable, which makes me vulnerable. You feel me?" Tony said.

"How does it make us vulnerable?"

"It makes you a target," Calvin said.

"These cats think you're weak, which means sooner or later, someone is gonna try you, because you stand out," Tony said.

"This is who I am. If I pretend to be someone I'm not, wouldn't I stand out even more?"

"I'm not telling you to get all gangster and shit, just tone it down a little," Tony said.

"You got it, *Alexander*," Calvin said deliberately.

"That's the other thing, you need to change your name," Tony suggested.

"What's wrong with my name?"

"Nothing, except that you're the only Alexander in this joint. So, when some shit goes down, and one of these snitches blames you, you will be too easy to find. But if someone says C did it, well, C, could be anybody," Tony said.

"And Tip could be anybody," Calvin said.

"So, like I said, homeboy, you need a new name," Tony said.

"Call him A-Rod," Calvin said.

"My father's name was Alexander."

"Your bitch-ass father ain't here," Calvin said.

Alexander sprang to his feet and reached across the table for Calvin's neck.

Calvin laughed. "Chill out, man, damn."

"Sit down, Alex," Tony said, and placed his hand on Alexander's shoulder. Tony noticed Alexander's rage—his passion. He wondered how he could manipulate that passion to work in his favor.

"Do you like A-Rod?"

"No, not really," Alexander said.

"Well, get used to it, because *A-Rod* it is," Tony said.

At that moment, Alexander felt a crushing grip enclose around his right arm.

"Get up," Sergeant Campbell ordered. With brute force, Sergeant Campbell drove Alexander through the cafeteria door. "Get your ass out of here, boy."

CHAPTER

TWELVE

Alexander focused on helping his fellow students prepare for their GED exams. He tutored students in mathematics and language arts, and due to his encouragement, some students embraced education with a new fervor. Alexander paid close attention to the students and was delighted by their measured improvements.

Alexander's teacher encouraged him to pursue a career in education. "Teaching comes natural to you. Your charisma is an asset," she had said.

He had never considered becoming a teacher, and the idea excited him.

In his spare time, Alexander immersed himself in literature. He sought after books that explored world culture. He read, *Things Fall Apart, White Teeth, The Good Earth, Native Son* and *Invisible Man,* which was his favorite. He read the tragic tales of Charles Dickens, John Steinbeck, and Toni Morrison.

He nurtured his sadness with tales of human suffering and failure, which aided to his literary escape from prison walls. He relished in his sadness, and often sat contemplating the failures of his young life.

～

HOWARD ENTERED the visitation room and sat down, now comfortable with the routine. "Is there a chess set available?" Howard asked an officer standing by.

"I don't know. You can check in there." The officer pointed to the game room.

Howard retrieved a chess set, returned to his seat, and began setting up the board. As Alexander entered the visitation room, Howard stood and embraced him. "Do you want white or black?" Howard asked.

"Black," Alexander answered.

Howard sat and started the match with the English opening. "How is the competition in this place?" Howard asked.

"Not very good. They're all mostly beginners," Alexander said.

"What's good, A-Rod?" Tony said, as he passed Alexander's table.

"What's going on, man," Alexander responded.

"Did he just call you, A-Rod?" Howard asked.

"Apparently, calling a man by his proper name is too much to ask these fucking idiots," Alexander said.

Howard raised a brow.

"What?" Alexander asked.

"Nothing. I just noticed you've been cussing a lot lately," Howard said.

"So would you if you were locked up in this fucking place," Alexander said defiantly.

Howard felt chagrined, but smiled and said, "I guess you're right."

Alexander captured Howard's rook. "You should pay more attention to the game, instead of my language," Alexander said.

"I have some good news." Howard said proudly, "I was accepted to NYU."

"That's fantastic. Congratulations," Alexander said, losing interest in the chess game.

"Thanks. It's exciting. I'm glad everything seems to be working out," Howard said.

"Are you planning to live on campus?"

"I'll be living in the dormitory, but NYU is not a traditional campus. Much of it is spread throughout the city," Howard explained.

"I see, so where will you live?"

"The freshman dorms are mostly near Washington Square, which is in Greenwich Village."

"You're going to live in The Village..." Alexander said, exuberantly. "Isn't that where all of the freaks are?"

"No, that's a misconception. I hope," Howard said.

They both laughed.

"Well, I'm very excited for you, Howard. This *is* great news," Alexander said.

"Thanks, man," Howard said, studying the board.

Regaining his interest in the game, Alexander captured one of Howard's pawns before Howard took his knight.

"Was Allyson accepted, too?" Alexander asked.

"Yes, she was, but she also got into Columbia," Howard said, proudly. "She has a tough decision to make."

"That's not a tough decision, it's a no-brainer. She has to go to Columbia," Alexander said.

"No, she doesn't. NYU is a good school," Howard said.

"NYU is a great school, but if *I* had a choice, I would choose Columbia."

"Well, the choice is hers, not yours," Howard snapped.

Alexander glared at Howard. Vile and harsh words raced through his head. He swallowed hard and looked away. "What do I know," Alexander acquiesced. "You two will attend the colleges of your dreams, and I have capitulated to a GED program for convicts."

Howard's face softened. "It shouldn't be this way," Howard said.

"These are the cards I was dealt, or perhaps the cards I dealt myself. I don't know," Alexander said, gloomily.

Howard leaned forward. "This is only a bump in the road. This place doesn't define you, and it never will."

They sat quietly for a moment before Alexander broke the silence, "Who are you taking to the prom?"

"I don't know. I haven't decided if I want to go just yet," Howard said.

"You have to go," Alexander said.

"Why?" Howard said.

"Because, from where I'm sitting, it's not so insignificant. I would give anything to go, and you shouldn't take it for granted. Besides, don't you know I'm living vicariously through you? How else will I find out what went on there?" Alexander said, smiling.

"We will see," Howard said.

"Checkmate," Alexander said.

Howard studied the board and surrendered his king.

CHAPTER

THIRTEEN

Emily Merchant sat reading the New York Times on her Carolina-blue sofa. Her legs were crossed, and her dangling flip-flops swayed in a delicate dance. She heard the mail lady's truck accelerating and stopping, and accelerating again, as she made her way down the road. Expecting a letter from Alexander, Emily rose and made her way outside. She sifted through an endless stack of bills and junk mail before recognizing Alexander's steady handwriting. She strolled up her driveway and climbed the stairs onto her porch, where she stopped and grabbed her chest. She felt as though she had just completed a marathon. She sat on the steps and attempted to calm herself, but as her breathing steadied, she couldn't shake the feeling something was terribly wrong. Emily entered her house and immediately called her doctor's office.

"Wake Urgent Care," a voice answered.

"Hello, this is Emily Merchant. Is Dr. Castaneda in?" Emily asked.

"She's with a patient right now. May I help you?" the receptionist asked.

"Yes, I need to make an appointment."

"I can help you with that. When would you like your appointment?"

"Today, if at all possible," Emily said.

"Okay, let's see," the receptionist said, as she checked for availabilities.

Emily could hear her fingers striking the keyboard.

"Will two-forty-five work for you?" the receptionist asked.

"Two-forty-five is fine," Emily said.

"Okay, we'll see you then," the receptionist said.

Emily slipped into a tan sundress, with blue embroidered flowers wrapping around her waist and down one side. She pulled her hair back into a ponytail and went into the kitchen. Pouring herself a cup of piping hot green tea, she settled down at the kitchen table and opened Alexander's letter.

```
Hello Mom,


    I hope this letter finds you in good spir-
its. It is hard to believe that spring has
already arrived. Time here moves slowly, yet
the winter season seems to have whisked right
by. The mountainside is now green, and the
valley across the road is now covered with an
assortment of wildflowers. I cannot tell what
type of flowers they are, and I could not
convince the officers to let me out to inves-
tigate. They are worried that I won't return
(smile). Isn't it ironic that the state of
North Carolina reserved the prettiest part of
Morganton for a prison? There should only be
```

a small bungalow here, with smoke rising from the chimney and a herd of sheep grazing the fields. It is surprisingly beautiful here, but I pray that you and I will never have to see this place again.

Family day is scheduled for Saturday, May 12th. I am on the planning committee and being forced to deliver a speech. I hope you can make it, but please, don't feel obligated to come. It's not a big deal. I will see you soon, and I love you.

Alexander

Emily placed the letter on her lap, sat back, and sipped her tea. It was still hot, but bearable. She contemplated Alexander's words for a moment, before reaching for the *New York Times* again. She turned to a scathing report by the urban affairs columnist, who detailed how the United States was failing America's students—particularly low-income students. The columnist admonished Congress for what she described as legislative missteps and unwarranted hubris.

"She is awful," Emily said, laughing.

The columnist pointed out how teachers lacked the necessary resources to educate students in overcrowded schools. She argued that out-of-date policies such as the anachronistic school year, built around farming communities' harvest schedule, must be changed.

Emily had touted similar ideas for many years. She had fiercely debated these necessary reforms with many of her coworkers, who for one reason or another, had dug their heels in the sand, and categorically opposed all attempted educational reforms.

Emily understood that the fight for reforming education was taking place in the public school system. The system she loved and longed for. She enjoyed teaching at the Christian Academy, where the students were motivated to learn and always respectful, but she wasn't content. She saw how easily she could become complacent there, and as Emily became increasingly doubtful of Reverend Talbert's claim that God had wanted her teaching at the Christian Academy, she began to wonder if her true calling was in the public schools.

Emily glanced at her watch which read 2:17 P.M. She slipped on her shoes and made her way to the doctor's office. She sat in the waiting room flipping through an edition of *O Magazine* when a nurse called her name. She was escorted into an exam room where the nurse measured her weight and blood pressure.

"Dr. Castaneda will be right in. Please, remove your clothes and put this on," the nurse said, handing Emily a blue gown.

Emily slipped on the gown and sat down on the table.

Dr. Castaneda entered the room with open arms. "Emily, how are you, dear?" she said, taking Emily's hand in both of hers.

"That is what I'm here to find out," Emily said.

"Tell me what is bothering you."

Emily explained what had happened when she retrieved her mail—the shortness of breath—the discomfort.

Dr. Castaneda placed her cold stethoscope against Emily's chest. "Breathe deeply," she said as she listened, moving the stethoscope to Emily's ribs and back. She placed the stethoscope around her neck and used her fingers to examine Emily's ribs. "How does this feel?"

"Fine."

"And this?"

"Fine, too."

"And this?"

Emily grimaced and pulled away.

"Did that hurt you?"

"It feels a little tender," Emily said.

"Okay, let's get an X-ray," Dr. Castaneda said, and led Emily into another room, and filled in the radiologist on Emily's condition.

"Stand here," the radiologist said.

Emily stood with her chest to the machine.

"Hands on your hips, elbows pointed out," the radiologist instructed, before stepping into another room.

Emily disliked X-ray machines. Far too often, they were the bearer of bad news. As she stood facing the machine, she could feel her stomach churning on the inside.

When the X-rays were completed, she went back to the exam room and waited for Dr. Castaneda to return. She sat on the exam table swinging her feet and staring at the floor.

Dr. Castaneda entered the room and fastened the X-rays to the illuminator. "How is Alexander?" she asked.

"He's okay, considering our situation," Emily said, with sadness in her eyes.

Dr. Castaneda's eyes softened. "It breaks my heart to think about it. He is such a fine boy." She stood, studying Emily's X-rays, and furrowed her brow. "Come here," she said.

Emily slowly made her way, feeling as though she was wearing lead boots.

Dr. Castaneda took Emily's hands and gazed at her with soft eyes.

"Just tell me," Emily said, bracing herself for the worst.

Dr. Castaneda sighed. "Do you see this?" she said, pointing to the X-ray. It looks like the cancer has come back," she said.

Emily felt sick. The room was spinning, and she thought she would pass out.

Dr. Castaneda held Emily's hand firmly. "Look here, it's in your lungs, and here in your ribs. It explains the shortness of breath and the pain you felt when I pressed against your ribs," she explained.

"What am I going to do?" Emily said.

"You are going to fight it," she said, looking deep into Emily's brown eyes. "You are going to fight this, yes?" Dr. Castaneda asked.

Emily nodded her head.

Dr. Castaneda pulled Emily into her embrace.

A wave of emotions poured forth, and Emily's tears flowed like the Euphrates River. All the stress and anxiety she had bottled up inside, the pressure she felt to stay strong for Alexander, and for herself, was now released onto Maria Castaneda's shoulder.

"You need to see Dr. Haun immediately," Dr. Castaneda instructed, and led Emily over to a desk, picked up a phone, and dialed a number. "This is Dr. Castaneda at Wake Family Practice. I need to speak to Dr. Haun." Holding Emily's hand, she said, "Dr. Haun, this is Dr. Castaneda. I am here with Emily Merchant. She needs to see you today." She filled Dr. Haun in on the details of Emily's condition. "I will send her right over, bye," she said.

For several hours, Emily was poked and prodded and she had more X-rays and an MRI. She thought about Alexander and his father, who she missed so much. She prayed to God for a miracle, asking God to heal her body completely.

Dr. Haun sat across from Emily with weary eyes. "The cancer is in stage four and very aggressive. It has metastasized to your lungs, your rib cage, and your liver," she said.

"What are my chances?" Emily interjected.

"Not good," Dr. Haun said, matter-of-factly.

"Give me a number, a percentage—a guess," Emily requested.

"I cannot say at this point," Dr. Haun said. She sighed and added, "In my experience, I would say you have a twenty-five to thirty percent chance of surviving this."

"I see," Emily said, with moist eyes. The news hit her like a ton of bricks and she wondered how this could be possible at her age. *I am only forty-one years old,* she thought. She wondered if this was only a bad dream she would suddenly awake from, but she knew it wasn't. It all felt too real—the pain—the sadness.

"Your treatment starts first thing in the morning. I need you to report to Duke Oncology Center at six o'clock A.M. After tomorrow, you will start your second round of chemotherapy in six weeks. We must be aggressive," Dr. Haun said.

"How many rounds of chemo will I have?"

"You will have three rounds of chemotherapy, followed by radiation treatment."

"And if it doesn't work?" Emily asked.

Dr. Haun considered her words. "If the treatment is unsuccessful, you will die, Emily."

Dr. Haun's words stung Emily's heart. Eminent mortality is never easy to accept. The words "twenty-five to thirty percent" resounded in her head.

"You can either complete your paperwork now or you can do it at home. I know it's been a long day," Dr. Haun said.

"I will complete them at home," Emily said.

Emily left Dr. Haun and drove around town with no certain destination when she found herself at Wake Tabernacle.

Reverend Talbert was not at the church, and neither was anyone else. She decided to call Reverend Talbert when she got home. Sitting at a stoplight, she noticed a barber's pole spinning in the distance. Emily parked her car and went inside.

"May I help you?" the barber asked, smiling broadly, looking her over with hungry eyes. He noticed her small frame and the way her sundress tightened around her curvy hips, indicating a full derriere. He liked what he saw, but Emily barely noticed him at all.

She settled into his chair.

"What can I do for you?" he asked.

"Cut it off," Emily announced.

"How much do you want me to cut?"

"All of it, and do it quickly before I change my mind," Emily said.

"You have beautiful hair, why do you want to cut it off?"

"Just do it," Emily snapped. Feeling chagrined, she contrived a smile.

"It's your hair," he said coarsely. He reached for a cape and prepared to drape it around her neck, when his eyes fell on the pink medical band fastened on her wrist, and suddenly, he understood. *Why else would a woman looking like her, part with her crowning glory?* he thought.

"Emily saw the barber's reflection in the mirror and noticed him looking at her wrist. She saw his eyes soften and the angry wrinkles in his forehead fade away. The barber delicately placed the hair cape around her slender frame and gently snapped it around her neck, treating her with tenderness. For the barber, Emily realized, was the first person to know her condition. He was a total stranger, and she didn't even know his name.

She kept her eyes fixed on him. She watched him as he gently and almost playfully ran his fingers through her thick shoulder-length hair. She heard the buzz of the clippers, and watched her hair fall away.

At home, Emily stood in the shower. Hot water massaged her head, her shoulders, her back. She thought of the barber.

"My name is Jeffrey," he had said. *He seemed nice, and was handsome,* she thought.

She stepped out of the shower and stood in her bathroom mirror drying herself. "Not bad," she said, looking at her bald head. *I can wear one of Alexander's ball caps,* she thought. She ran her fingers across the scar remaining from her first battle with cancer and observed her right mangled breast. Her left breast was so far unaffected by the intruder, and the soft brown flesh stood as a monument to the power her womanhood once possessed. She thought of the reconstructive surgery she had been saving for. It no longer seemed important.

Lying in bed, she thought of her deceased husband. *Will I see him again?* she wondered. *Not yet,* she thought, *not yet.* She thought of Alexander. *I have to be strong for my son. I have to fight this and get through it for him,* she thought. She turned to God and prayed herself to sleep.

CHAPTER

FOURTEEN

Alexander stood before a window, staring out at the mountains surrounding the institution. He was transfixed by the beautiful spring day. The trees clinging to the mountains stood tall, as proud monuments of a past life. The leaves stood still, no breeze blew at all, but the clouds moving above told a different story. Below was a soccer ball spinning into the air and bouncing from swift feet. *I haven't played soccer in forever,* Alexander thought, and then changed into a pair of shorts and a T-shirt and tied his shoes.

Calvin sat watching television.

"I'm going outside to play soccer," Alexander said.

"Soccer?" Calvin said, with disgust. "With them damn Mexicans?"

"What do you have against Mexicans?"

"Nothing personally, but they stick with their own kind, and we stick with ours. If you go out there by yourself and they flip on your ass, you're on your own," Calvin said.

"I'll take my chances," Alexander said.

"Suit yourself," Calvin said, turning back to the television.

Alexander made his way outside where a group of young men stood in a circle booting a soccer ball to one another. "Que pasa? Estás jugando un juego?"

Alexander's greeting was met with silence and stern faces.

Manuel stood, dribbling the ball from foot to foot. Tattoos covered his neck, and two teardrops were tattooed under his left eye.

Alexander glanced over his shoulder and noticed two young men had positioned themselves behind him.

He heard Manuel's foot striking the ball and then saw the soccer ball rocketing towards his head. In a flash, Alexander leaped into the air and blocked the ball with his inner thigh, directing it down between his legs. With his foot, Alexander rolled the ball up his calf and flipped it into the air, flicking the ball behind his back and over his head. He quickly moved under the ball and booted it back to Manuel.

Manuel settled the ball under his foot. "You played soccer before, A-Rod?" Manuel asked.

"Sí, yo jugaba al fútbol para mi escuela," Alexander responded, knowing that the best way to gain a man's trust is to speak to him in his own language.

Manuel nodded and booted the ball over to Oscar, who settled the ball and sent it over to Sergio. Sergio popped the ball onto his head and balanced it like a seal, moving his head back and forth—side-to-side. He let the ball fall towards the ground and bounced it off his knee over to Juan, who redirected it back to Manuel.

"We need another man, A-Rod. You play on my team," Manuel said.

Alexander trotted over to Manuel.

"Let's go," Manuel said.

No one moved. The footballers kept their eyes fixed on Alexander.

"Vàmonos," Manuel Barked, and the players fanned out into two teams of five.

The game was more physical than Alexander anticipated. The opposing team missed no opportunity to slam themselves into Alexander, knocking him to the ground. His grass-stained knees and back were a sobering reminder of Calvin's warning.

Alexander and Manuel were on the move. As Manuel approached the goal, he saw Alexander running parallel to him. Manuel passed the ball to Alexander.

As Alexander moved towards the goal, he saw Rigoberto barreling down on him. Alexander passed the ball back to Manuel and lowered his shoulder. Alexander and Rigoberto slammed into each other. The impact sent Rigoberto crashing to the ground and Alexander stood over him triumphantly as his teammates began yelling, "Goal!" Manuel had scored.

Alexander extended his hand to Rigoberto, who was slow getting up.

Two of the opposing team members circulated Alexander like wolves.

Manuel quickly stepped between them and wrapped his arm around Alexander's shoulder. "Don't worry, amigo. Keep playing. Let's go," Manuel said.

As the opposing teams faced off, Alexander heard his name bellowing across the compound. "Alexander Merchant, report to your case manager's office."

Alexander continued playing. The game was tied four to four, and he was determined to see it through. *I will go in on the next move,* he thought.

Both teams had opportunities to end the game, but neither could convert the winning goal.

"Hey, Merchant," an officer yelled.

"Yes, sir," Alexander said.

"Your case manager is looking for you. Go inside," the officer said.

"Okay."

Alexander was running backwards, noting Sergio had an open shot. As he booted the football, Alexander stopped and allowed Sergio's shot to slam against his bare shins. Alexander won the ball and sprinted up the sideline. He moved in and around his defenders in full strides, no longer holding back. Three defenders stood between him and the goal. As one drew near, Alexander whipped his feet around the ball and cut to the inside. He kicked the ball, whipping his leg in a circular motion. He watched the soccer ball spin outward, and then bend back towards the top corner of the goal. The fooled goalie was unable to recover. The score was five to four—the game was over.

"Good shot," Rigoberto said. The players collapsed on the field. Each one tried desperately to catch his breath—they were exhausted.

"I have to go," Alexander said.

"We're playing tomorrow at the same time," Manuel said.

"I'll be here," Alexander said.

Alexander made his way upstairs where Calvin and Tony were watching television.

"How was your soccer game?" Calvin asked, sarcastically.

"It was good," Alexander said, as he rushed off to change his clothes.

"What's wrong with that brother?" Calvin asked Tony.

"The hell if I know," Tony replied.

"I'll be back in a few," Alexander said.

"Your case manager has been calling for you," Tony said.

"That's where I am going." Alexander rushed over to his case manager's office and knocked on the door.

"Come on in, Merchant. Have a seat." Mr. Henderson said angrily, "I've been looking for you all morning,"

"I am sorry sir, but I was outside, and I didn't know you were looking for me," Alexander said.

Mr. Henderson leaned back in his chair. "I'm afraid I have some bad news," Mr. Henderson said.

"What sort of bad news?"

Mr. Henderson leaned forward. "It's your mother, Mr. Merchant. She was diagnosed with cancer."

"My mother had cancer years ago. She's fine now," Alexander said, not understanding what Mr. Henderson was trying to tell him.

Mr. Henderson sighed. "Your mother was diagnosed recently and is in the hospital," he said.

"In the hospital? Is it serious?"

"I don't know how serious it is. I only know what she told me," Mr. Henderson said.

"Have you spoken to her?"

"Yes, she called this morning and said she was starting her treatment today. She wanted you to know she won't be able to attend Family Day," Mr. Henderson said.

Alexander sat in disbelief. He felt as though the walls were closing in on him. Beads of sweat formed on his forehead.

"Are you okay, Mr. Merchant?"

"I cannot believe this is happening. I need to make a phone call." Alexander stood and staggered towards the door.

"Wait a minute. You can use my phone. Have a seat," Mr. Henderson said.

Alexander sat again.

"What's the number?"

Alexander gave him Howard's number and Mr. Henderson dialed. "Who is it you want to speak to?"

"Howard Connerly."

"Hello, may I speak to Howard Connerly? He's not?"

"Ask for Orlando Connerly," Alexander said.

"Is there an Orlando Connerly available? Hi, this is Mr. Henderson calling from Morganton Youth Institution. Alexander Merchant would like to speak to you. Is that all right? Okay, here he is," he said, handing Alexander the phone.

"Hello," Alexander said into the phone.

"Hi, Alexander. How are you?" Orlando said.

"I just found out about my mother. Can you tell me what's going on?"

"Emily wasn't feeling well yesterday, so she went to the doctor. Her doctor ran some tests and discovered the cancer had returned and it's spreading rapidly," Orlando said.

"Well, how bad is it?"

Orlando sighed. "Stage four, Alexander," Orlando said.

"Will she be all right?"

"I don't know," Orlando said.

"Is anyone at the hospital with her or is she by herself?"

"When I left the hospital, there were seven or eight church members there. They're coming in shifts," Orlando said.

"Was Reverend Talbert there?"

"No, he's coming this evening, and Vivian and I will go back in the morning."

"Where is Howard?"

"He's at the library working on a project. He'll be back this evening."

Alexander held the phone in silence.

"Are you all right?" Orlando asked.

"No, I'm not. I feel so helpless because there is nothing I can do from here."

"We will do all that we can, Alexander. You know that," Orlando said.

"I know you will, but it's my responsibility to take care of her, and I can't do that from here," Alexander said.

"I know you feel compelled to do something, but no one is blaming you for not being here," Orlando said.

"I'm not concerned about what people think of me. I only care that my mother has no one to take care of her."

"She has plenty of people who care about her, and she will not have to go through this alone," Orlando said.

Alexander fell silent.

Orlando continued, "Just give me time to talk to her. Call me tomorrow evening, and in the meantime, just worry about taking care of yourself."

"I will call tomorrow at seven o'clock. Bye." Alexander turned his attention to Mr. Henderson. "Listen sir, I need to be moved someplace closer to home. Due to my mother's condition, there's no way she could continue visiting me here, but I know she'll try no matter how bad she's feeling. And that won't be good for her."

"I'm sorry Mr. Merchant, but this is the only place for you until you turn nineteen. And your visitation is not something I can take into consideration," Mr. Henderson said.

"It's not about my visitation, sir. My mother doesn't have anyone to help her. I am the only family she has, and if I were closer to home, I could use my resources to manage her affairs more effectively."

"There's nothing you could do differently from any other prison, Mr. Merchant. The same rules would apply."

"Please, Mr. Henderson. She's all I have," Alexander said.

Mr. Henderson sighed. "When do you turn nineteen?"

"September third."

"The only place I could send you is Rolesville Correctional Center, but they may not accept you until after you turn nineteen," Mr. Henderson said.

"If my age is the only problem, I assure you I can handle myself."

"That is not the point. Rolesville is a rough place, and no one wants to be responsible if something were to happen to you there."

"I can handle myself," Alexander said.

"Can you really?" Mr. Henderson challenged.

"Yes."

"Are you sure?"

"Yes, I'm sure."

Mr. Henderson looked pensive. "I'll make a special request for a hardship transfer and let you know if it's been approved in a few days," Mr. Henderson said.

"Thank you, sir."

ALEXANDER MADE his way back to his dormitory and climbed onto his bed.

"What the hell happened, man?" Tony said, "You look stressed."

"It's my mother, she's sick," Alexander said.

"What's wrong with her?"

"She has cancer."

"Is it bad?"

"Stage four."

"Damn, son. That's fucked up." Tony climbed onto his bed and sat next to Alexander. "Are you and your moms close?"

"Of course, she's my mother," Alexander said.

"Shit, I barely knew my mom."

"What do you mean?" Alexander asked.

"My mom was always either high, on that shit, or chasing some dude. I pretty much raised myself."

"How did you do that?"

"I did what I had to do. I got my hustle on, and if I caught some cat slipping, I flashed a burner on him and took his shit, you know."

"Wow. I can't imagine living like that," Alexander said.

"You'd be surprised what you'll do when you're hungry. Hey, a brother's gotta eat," Tony said.

"Where was your father?"

"The hell if I know. I ain't never seen that motherfucker. I could end up sharing a cell with him and I wouldn't even know it."

They sat quietly for a moment—each contemplating his young life.

"I'm trying to get transferred to Rolesville," Alexander announced, breaking the silence. "I put in for a hardship transfer."

"For real?" Tony sat back.

"Yeah—I heard Rolesville is off the hook though," Alexander said.

"Man, don't even sweat that shit. Prison is prison—you know. Whether they are young or old, it's just the same motherfuckers locked up for the same shit. You feel me?" Tony said.

"Yeah, I feel you." Alexander let out a long breath.

"Besides, me and C will be there by the end of the year, and it will be business as usual," Tony said.

The next week seemed like an eternity. Alexander spoke to his mother as often as he could, squeezing in phone calls between each break in his schedule. Preparing for Family Day had served him well. It had allowed him to focus on something other than his mother's condition. Although he was happy to have the event behind him, the additional free time only provided worrisome days and sleepless nights.

Tony and Calvin were as sympathetic as prison culture allowed.

"We're going downstairs to play ball. You coming?" Calvin asked Alexander.

"I don't feel like playing basketball," Alexander said.

"Come on, man. Are you gonna lay on your bed all day?" Calvin said.

"Just for now," Alexander said.

"A'ight, man. We'll be back before lunch," Tony said.

"I'm going to see Mr. Henderson at eleven o'clock. I will meet you in the cafeteria," Alexander said.

"That'll work," Tony said.

Alexander lay on his bed until 11:00. He stood and rushed over to his unit officer. "Excuse me, sir, I need to see Mr. Henderson," Alexander said.

"Did he call for you?"

"Well, no, but I..."

"Then you're not going anywhere," the officer said.

"I've been trying to see him all week, but he's been too busy. I just need to know if I'm leaving or not," Alexander said.

"If he didn't call for you, I cannot send you," Officer Brantley said.

"Come on, sir. You know I don't ever give you any problems. He came in at eleven o'clock today, and I want to see him before he gets tied up again," Alexander said.

The officer sighed. "How's your mother doing?"

"She has not improved much," Alexander said.

"Oh, all right. Go ahead," the officer said. He turned to the control room officer and said, "Let him down."

Alexander stepped into the elevator and descended two floors and waited outside Mr. Henderson's door.

Eighteen minutes had passed when Ms. Robinson noticed him loitering. "What are you doing?" she asked.

Her challenge startled him. "I'm waiting for Mr. Henderson, ma'am," Alexander said.

"Mr. Henderson isn't here. So, you need to leave, and don't come back unless someone calls for you," Ms. Robinson said.

"But I really need to see him, Ms. Robinson."

"Get out of here before I throw you in the hole," she said, pointing to the door.

Alexander did as he was told and staggered towards the cafeteria in a daze. He was preoccupied with his problems and his grim future, never noticing the four young men blocking his path.

"Watch where you're going, man," J-Rock said.

"Excuse me," Alexander said.

"Well, if it isn't Benedict Fucking Arnold," Face said.

"Where the fuck you going?" J-Rock said.

"Are you going to let me by or what?" Alexander said.

"Let you by," Courage mocked.

Boo moved behind Alexander.

"I ain't gonna let you do a damn thing," J-Rock said.

"What the fuck is your problem?" Alexander said.

"You're my problem. You're always walking around here like you're better than everybody, motherfucker. You ain't shit," J-Rock said.

"I never said I was better than anyone," Alexander said.

"Fucking Oreo," Courage mumbled.

The situation was quickly going from bad to worse, and Alexander knew he had to take control. He looked past his adversaries for anyone who could help him but saw no one. "Whatever, man," he said, pushing himself past J-Rock, but taking his eyes off of his adversaries proved to be a painful mistake.

J-Rock planted his knuckles squarely on Alexander's jaw. The pain numbed his skull before he felt a barrage of punches from every direction. *Fight back*, he told himself, but the narrow corridor limited his options. Boo grabbed him from behind and tried to throw him on the floor. *Stay on your feet,* Alexander thought. *Do not go down.* Alexander threw his head back into Boo's nose and pushed him back into the wall. Boo's grip loosened and Alexander broke free. He returned several punches before taking a shot on his nose. He felt warm blood pouring into his mouth and soaking his shirt before stumbling backwards.

At that moment, Calvin came crashing into the group. Calvin drove Courage into the wall and slammed his knee into his groin. Tony took on both Boo and Face. Tony slammed his fists into their faces, their heads, their necks. He adroitly avoided their punches, and with each blow he delivered, his opponents lost their will to continue fighting.

Alexander and J-Rock faced each other and traded punches. Courage lay on the floor looking at his opponent, who was drunk with rage.

"I'll kill you, motherfucker," Calvin screamed, as he stomped Courage mercilessly.

"Get down, get down," the responding officers yelled.

Tony and his opponents were tackled and placed in handcuffs. Tony watched Alexander deliver a crushing blow—fracturing J-Rock's jaw.

J-Rock held his face and screamed in agony as he fell to the floor. "Fuck 'em up, A-Rod, yeah," Calvin screamed as an officer drilled his shoulder into the small of Calvin's back.

"Get over here," Mr. Henderson said. He pushed Alexander through the corridor. "What the hell are you doing?" Mr. Henderson said.

"They jumped me for no reason. I was only defending myself," Alexander said.

"Shut your mouth," Mr. Henderson said. He was furious.

"Here I am busting my ass to get you moved, and you and your friends want to fight?" Mr. Henderson said.

"They attacked me for no reason. Calvin and Tony came to my rescue," Alexander said.

Mr. Henderson wrapped his large brown hand around Alexander's neck and shoved him into the wall. "Didn't I tell you to shut your damn mouth. Do you think Rolesville is going to take you now with an assault on your record?" He grabbed Alexander's elbow and dragged him through the corridor and into the elevator, taking Alexander to Receiving.

"Damn. What the fuck happened to you?" Officer Mahoney said.

Alexander stood quietly, breathing heavily.

"Go in there and get cleaned up." Officer Mahoney pointed. "You were scheduled to transfer out today," Mr. Henderson said.

"I didn't know," Alexander said.

"Of course, you didn't know," Officer Mahoney said.

"Give him some clean clothes and leave him here until I'm done reviewing the cameras. I'll let you know if he can still leave," Mr. Henderson said.

"What about my stuff?" Alexander said.

"Your unit officer will get it," Mr. Henderson said, and he left.

Alexander sat in a holding cell for several hours, and then was put on a transfer bus and taken to Rolesville Correctional Institution.

CHAPTER

FIFTEEN

All eyes were on Emily as she entered the church sanctuary. Sunday morning worship was in progress and the congregation sang devotionals a cappella. Emily wore a white knee-length dress, which accentuated her curves. She wore white stilettos and a white wide-brimmed hat. She sat at the organ and began playing and singing as though she didn't have a care in the world. The church erupted into praise and worship. Some prayed quietly and others cried out and embraced each other. They continued in this manner for more than an hour, altering the order of service.

Reverend Talbert stood at the podium egging them on. "Somebody ought to praise Him," Reverend Talbert said, tapping his hands and stomping his feet. "Call on the Lord. Invite Him in," he said.

Emily was playing the organ and praising God.

"Invite Him into your life. Invite Him into your home, your family, your work. Walk with Him. Talk with Him. Praise Him, praise Him, He is worthy of your praise," Reverend Talbert said.

The congregation clapped their hands in a continued rhythm.

"Sister Sandra, come forward. Sister Elizabeth, come forward. Brother Charley, come forward. Sister Marie, come forward," Reverend Talbert called out. He addressed each one individually, offering words of comfort and encouragement. He led them in a prayer that seemed to be designed specifically for each individual.

Sister Mary broke out in a dance. Tears streamed down her face—her hands raised over her shoulders—her head pointed upward—her feet pounded the floor in a rhythmic dance.

Reverend Talbert's brown skin glistened under the lights. He wiped the sweat from his brow and wiped his graying mustache, which matched the short graying afro on his head. "I feel the Holy Ghost in here. Do you feel Him?" Reverend Talbert said.

Sister Veronica started dancing in the middle aisle.

"You better praise Him," Brother Joseph said.

Emily played the organ even more loudly, while Howard and Orlando followed suit with Howard playing the drums and Orlando playing the bass guitar.

"Let the Holy Ghost in. Go on and praise Him," Reverend Talbert said.

Reverend Talbert moved over to the organ and stood watching Emily with her head tilted upward and her eyes closed as she praised God loudly and enthusiastically. He watched her hands continue to play as if they had a mind of their own. "That's it, Sister Emily. Praise Him. Let the Holy Ghost play the music. You just keep praising Him."

The praise team formed a circle around Emily. The congregation all raised one hand to the sky and pointed one hand towards Emily as she continued to play and praise God loudly.

Reverend Talbert placed his hand on Emily's forehead.

"Father God, in the name of Jesus, we come to You right now, Lord, asking You to shower down Your blessings on one of Your most faithful servants. For we know that the doctor's report she has is only a test. We know it is only a test because You said so, Lord. Lord, we know that You are a healer, we know You are a way-maker. We know that You are a deliverer. Lord, we ask You to heal Emily's body. We ask You to heal her from the crown of her head—to the soles of her feet. We ask You to bind those cancer cells and cast them out. Because we know You are not done with her yet. We know that You have more for her to do. We know that You are a healer, Lord. We know that You are the great physician. We know that through You, all things are possible, Lord Jesus. Bind it. Bind it, Lord," Reverend Talbert said.

"Yes, Lord," Emily joined in.

"Bind it."

"Yeah," the congregants screamed.

"Bind it!"

"Yeah."

"Yes, Lord. Yes, Lord," Emily said.

"Oh, I wish I had some believers in here today," Reverend Talbert said, looking out at the church.

"Yeah!"

"I said, I wish I had some believers in here today. I wish I had some praying folks."

"You better preach, pastor," someone yelled from the back.

"I wish I had a church with some faith. A church that believed in healing like you believe the sun will rise tomorrow morning."

"Yes, Pastor."

"Do you believe it?" he screamed.

"Yes, Lord," the congregants screamed.

"Do you believe it?"

"Yeah."

"Do you believe it?"

"Yeah,"

"Then praise him like you do."

Several congregants danced and shouted amongst the pews. Others filled the center aisle, shouting and praising the Lord loudly. Some stood, jumping into the air, and some fell to the floor praising the Lord.

"I feel the Holy Ghost in here," Reverend Talbert said.

"Yes, Lord."

"Holy Ghost," Reverend Talbert said.

"Yeah."

"Holy Ghost."

"Yeah."

"You are healed, Sister Emily. I've seen it. And I believe it. Do you believe it?" Reverend Talbert asked.

"Yes, Lord," Emily said.

"Do you feel it?"

"Yes, Lord."

"Then praise Him for it."

"Yes, Lord. Hallelujah," Emily said, still playing the organ, Howard and Orlando playing in sync.

They went on this way for some time before Reverend Talbert brought the service to a close. He stood at the podium smiling broadly. "Our God is a good God, is He not?"

"Yes, He is," the church responded.

"Our God is a good God, is He not?"

"Yes, He is."

Sister Marie handed Reverend Talbert a handkerchief, and he wiped the sweat from his face. "I've been doing this a long time, and God has not failed me yet," he said, smiling. "When He says He will do something, He does it. When He shows me the future, it comes to pass. That is why I can stand here before you today and speak with confidence. Amen."

"Amen," the church said.

"Amen," he repeated, smiling.

"Amen."

"Raise your hands where you are and say along with me: Thank God, thank God, thank God. Now hug your neighbor and tell him: I love the Lord and I love you, too."

CHAPTER

SIXTEEN

Alexander sat on his bed, watching the inmates occupying his new dormitory. Some were getting dressed and making their beds. Some were brushing their teeth and grooming themselves, and others were settling in front of the television to watch the morning news. He watched their interactions, seeing whom they associated with and separated themselves from. He watched a young man the inmates called Buff, swagger away from his fully ajar locker, a locker which was always ajar whether Buff was in the dorm or not. Buff strutted over to the television and sat down. His thick dreadlocks rested on his shoulders. An inmate watching television placed the remote control on the arm of Buff's chair.

It was clear to Alexander that Buff was in charge, and nothing happened in Dorm 1 without his knowledge and approval. Alexander considered marching over to Buff and punching him in his face as hard as he could to show the other inmates he would not seek the approval of anyone. But Buff's massive arms and chest made him envision Buff wrapping his hand around Alexander's neck and slamming him onto the concrete floor. Alexander decided it would better suit him if Buff had never noticed him at all.

"ATTENTION ON THE COMPOUND. ATTENTION ALL AREAS. IT IS NOW CHOW TIME, CHOW TIME, CHOW TIME," a voice bellowed from the intercom.

The inmates lined up near the door, but Buff and eight other inmates remained seated, watching television. When Officer Williams entered the dormitory and yelled, "Chow time, line up," Buff and his henchmen remained seated. The inmates filed out of the dormitory and lined up along the wall. Finally, Buff stood and strutted out of the dorm and the remaining others followed.

Officer Williams counted the inmates and wrote the number in her booklet. She leaned against the outer door and gave the thumbs-up sign to the control room officer. The control room officer pressed a button, and a loud clicking noise filled the area before the door she leaned against swung open. She pushed it fully open and held it with her foot. "Let's go," she said.

The inmates marched out of Dorm 1 in a single file.

Officer Smith, the yard patrol officer, stood at the end of the sidewalk, waiting to escort the inmates to the cafeteria. "Hey, Williams," Officer Smith said.

"Hi, Smith," Officer Williams responded.

"What happened to you last night? I thought you were coming out with us," Officer Smith said.

"I was too tired. I went home and went to sleep," Officer Williams said.

Officer Smith smiled broadly.

An inmate called Trouble eyed Officer Williams' breasts, waist, hips, buttocks, and her thighs. He imagined how her body looked underneath her blue uniform. He looked at

Snoopy and shook his head. "Boy, if I ever get my hands on that."

"You ain't never lied," Snoopy whispered.

Officer Williams launched her ballpoint pen towards Trouble's head. The pen bounced off his head and landed on the ground.

"What the fuck you doing?" Trouble yelled.

"Keep walking," Officer Williams ordered.

"What you do that for?" Trouble said.

"Keep walking," Officer Williams repeated.

Trouble looked at Snoopy and said, "Man, that bitch crazy."

Officer Smith rested the tip of his baton against Troubles' face. "You have one second to get your ass back in line."

Trouble complied with Officer Smith's order immediately.

Alexander felt a chill across the compound, seeing hundreds of inmates streaming out of their dormitories in single file lines. Each line was escorted by two officers. One near the front of the line, and one near the rear.

"I hope the food is better here than it was at my last spot," Alexander said to the inmate in front of him.

"Keep quiet," Officer Smith said.

Alexander nodded and marched on.

"CODE YELLOW, DORM TWO. CODE YELLOW, DORM TWO," bellowed out of Officer Smith's radio.

"Get on the grass," Officer Smith yelled.

The inmates stepped off the sidewalk, onto the grass, and stood in line.

Alexander saw Officer Williams sprinting towards Dorm 2. He watched as a stream of officers followed behind her, and Officer Smith took off and ran towards the incident. The other escorting officer stayed with the inmates. Alexander read the officer's name tag. It read Davis.

Eventually, Officer Smith and three other officers exited Dorm 2, carrying a handcuffed inmate. Each officer held on to one of the inmate's limbs. Moments later, several other officers exited the dorm carrying another inmate on a stretcher.

As they passed by, Alexander saw the inmate was covered in blood, with his face mangled like ground beef.

"What happened?" Officer Davis asked the officers carrying the injured inmate.

"Lock in a sock," an officer said.

"Damn," Officer Davis grimaced.

Alexander felt sick.

Officer Davis' radio lit up. "Lieutenant Price to dorm two, what's your status?"

"All clear, sir."

"All right, let's get these inmates moving."

"Let's go," Officer Davis said.

The inmates moved back onto the sidewalk and resumed marching towards the cafeteria.

Inside the cafeteria, Alexander moved through the serving line and sat at a table. His eggs were dry and overcooked, and his grits were soupy, but he ate as much as he could stand.

"What the fuck are you doing here?"

Alexander looked up and saw Moe from Broughton High School sitting across from him.

"Moe, what's up, man?"

"What's up, Alexander?"

They slapped five and locked fingers.

"What the fuck are you doing here, man?" Moe repeated.

"I got caught up in some B.S.," Alexander said.

"Word? I know it's fucked up out there if you're in here," Moe said.

"Yeah," Alexander said.

"Man, I never thought I'd see you in a place like this," Moe said, disappointedly. "I know your mom whipped your ass, didn't she?"

"Nah, man," Alexander said, looking away shamefully.

"How *is* your mom?"

"Not well. She's sick, unfortunately."

"Word?"

"Yeah. She has cancer," Alexander said.

"For real? That's fucked up," Moe said.

"Yes, it is."

"You know what, man? Out of all my teachers, your mom was the only one that gave a fuck about me, man. I swear, when I got locked up, she was the only one I didn't want to face."

"For real?"

"That's my word, son," Moe responded.

Alexander sat twirling his plastic spork in his soupy grits.

"When did you get here?"

"I arrived yesterday from Morganton Youth."

"Oh, word? I was at that ratchet-ass spot. Man, they need to tear that shit down."

"Yes. This place is much better," Alexander said.

"Nah son, this place is newer, but don't get it twisted. You gotta have eyes in the back of your head at this bitch, 'cause somebody will snuff your ass out at this motherfucker, you feel me," Moe said.

"Yes. I saw that this morning," Alexander said.

"Oh, that motherfucker had it coming. He couldn't pay his debts. That's another thing. Don't gamble, and don't borrow shit from nobody. Not no money, not a cigarette, not even a potato chip, you hear me? If you need something, you come to me, a'ight?" Moe said.

"Yes. Thanks, Moe."

"Don't sweat it, man. I got you. What dorm you in?"

"Dorm One," Alexander answered.

"A'ight, bet. That's my man Buff's unit. I'll tell 'em you're my boy, and he'll look out for you. Won't nobody fuck with you if he's got your back. You'll have to show him some appreciation, but other than that, you're good."

Alexander swallowed hard. "What sort of appreciation?" he said, nervously.

"Nah, man. Nothing like that," Moe said, laughing. "You just make sure you keep his commissary stocked and do whatever favors he needs you to do. I'll tell him you're a civilian, and you not into that crazy shit, and he won't have you do nothing too crazy. If so, just come to me, and I'll talk to him."

"Thanks, Moe. I really appreciate it."

"Don't sweat it, man."

"They called me A-Rod at Morganton."

Moe laughed. "A-Rod," he said, shaking his head. "A'ight, man. I'm out."

They slapped five and locked fingers before Moe stood and left.

An officer read Alexander's name from a list.

"Here," Alexander said.

"Diagnostics—line up outside the door," the officer said.

Alexander joined the other inmates standing outside the cafeteria door.

The officer came out and escorted the inmates up a flight of stairs, through a sally port, and into a holding cell. A short, bald man came to the holding cell and pressed a button outside the cell door and waited.

The control room officer pressed a button and the door popped open. "Merchant," he called out.

Alexander stood and stepped out of the cell.

"Go all the way to the end of the hallway, turn right, second door on the left," the man instructed.

Alexander followed his directions and the man trailed closely behind him.

"Have a seat," the man said.

Alexander sat across from him.

"My name is Mr. Peterson," he said, looking at his computer screen. "State your full name."

"Alexander Manchester Merchant."

"I see you have a birthday coming up."

"Yes sir, in two weeks."

"Happy birthday."

"Thank you."

"I have your mother, Emily Merchant, listed as your emergency contact person. Is that correct?"

"Yes, sir."

Mr. Peterson slid a piece of paper across his desk and pointed. "Is this her correct address and phone number?"

"Yes, that's correct," Alexander said.

"Is that your social security number?"

"Yes, sir."

"Wait a minute," Mr. Peterson said, staring at his computer. "How old are you?"

"Eighteen."

"Shoot, you're too young to be here."

"I turn nineteen in two weeks," Alexander said.

"It doesn't matter. Right now, you are too young. Crap," he said. He picked up the telephone and dialed his supervisor. "Ms. McDowell, step over for a minute, please." He hung up the phone and sat tapping his fingers on his desk.

Alexander saw a light-skinned, curvy woman with micro-braided hair appear in the doorway. "What's up?" she asked.

"This inmate is only eighteen," Mr. Peterson said.

"What? We have to lock him up," she said.

"I turn nineteen in two weeks," Alexander offered.

"It doesn't matter. Call the lieutenant," she said.

"Hold on. I'm sorry, ma'am, Ms. McDowell, is it?"

"Yes," she smiled.

"Mr. Henderson, my case manager at Morganton, made an exception for me. My mother is sick, you see. She has stage four cancer, and I needed to be closer to Raleigh."

"I'm sorry about your mother, young man, but we are not allowed to make exceptions. It's for your own safety," she said.

"So, what are you going to do, send me back for two weeks?"

"No, but we will have to put you in segregation until you turn nineteen," she said.

"Please, Ms. McDowell, don't lock me up. I haven't seen my mother in weeks because she couldn't travel that far. If I am locked up, she still won't be able to visit me."

Ms. McDowell sighed. "When you finish with him, bring him to my office," she said to Peterson.

"I'm done. You can have him," Peterson said.

Alexander followed Ms. McDowell into her office and sat across from her.

"You say your mother is sick?"

"Yes, ma'am."

"How bad is it?"

"I'm not sure, really. I know her cancer is stage four, but that's all."

Ms. McDowell considered Alexander's words for a moment and picked up her phone. "What's your mother's phone number?" She dialed the number and held the phone to her ear.

"Hello," Emily said.

"Hello, may I speak to Ms. Merchant?"

"Speaking."

"Hi, this is Mrs. McDowell at Rolesville Correctional Institution. I have your son, Alexander Merchant, sitting in my office."

"I didn't know he had already been moved," Emily said.

"Yes, he arrived yesterday. But first of all, how are you doing? I understand you are ill."

"I am well under the circumstances. Better than expected, actually."

"Well, I want you to know I will be praying for you, and so will my church, okay?"

"Thank you, Ms. McDowell. I appreciate that."

"You're welcome. Now, your son tells me you are planning to visit him here. When are you planning to come?"

"Saturday, if possible," Emily said."

"Well, you may need to hold off for a bit. We may need to place your son in segregation until his birthday."

"Why? Is he in some sort of trouble?"

"No, nothing like that. This institution only houses inmates from the age of nineteen to twenty-two. Therefore, we may need to segregate him for his own safety—until he's of the appropriate age."

"Is it dangerous there?"

"No more than anywhere else, but it is prison, ma'am, and things happen in prison."

"Oh, Lord. Can I visit him in segregation?"

"Not without approval, ma'am. I'll have your son call you once a decision is made."

"Okay. Can I speak to him?" Emily asked.

"Sure. Hold on." She handed the phone to Alexander.

"Hey, Mom."

"Hi, baby. How are you?"

"I'm fine. Don't worry about me. How are you feeling?"

"I'm doing well. I'm going to beat this thing. I promise."

"I know you will."

"What's it like there?" Emily said.

"It's nice here. Everything looks brand new. Not like Morganton," he said, cradling the phone in both hands.

"I'm worried about you, Alexander."

"Don't worry, Mom. Correctional officers are omnipresent here, and most of the inmates just want to do their time and go home. There isn't anything to worry about, I promise."

"When will I know if I can visit?"

"I'll call as soon as I know, okay?"

"Sure. Be careful in there."

"I'll call you soon."

"Okay. I love you, baby."

"I love you, too, Mom. Bye." He handed the phone back to Ms. McDowell, and she placed it back on the receiver. She reached for her radio and called the captain, who was also her husband. "Diagnostics to Captain McDowell."

"Go ahead."

"Call me, please." When her phone rang, she answered, "Hey, Cap. We have an issue."

"What kind of issue?" Captain McDowell asked.

"We got one in yesterday who is underage."

"Well, how the hell did that happen?"

"Someone dropped the ball. We need to lock him up."

"We can't lock him up. Segregation is full, and we're still locking up inmates from the incident this morning."

"So, what do we do with him?"

"I don't know. Let me think about it and call you back."

"Don't worry, I'll handle it," she said.

Ms. McDowell hung up the phone. She sat back in her chair, tapping her pen on her desk. "It looks like we're going to have to keep an eye on you. Have you ever done any janitorial work?"

"No, ma'am."

"Well, we're looking for a new janitor, so I guess you're it. Come back here after lunch, and I will have someone show you what to do. You are to report to work every morning at seven-thirty A.M. You'll work until three-thirty. After business hours, for the next two weeks, you are to stay in your dormitory where an officer can see you."

"Yes, ma'am," Alexander said.

"Don't look so excited," she smiled. "Have you seen your case manager yet?"

"No, ma'am. I was hoping to see him today."

"His office is in your dorm. Go ahead and see him now. I'll call and fill him in."

"Thank you, ma'am. I'll see you after lunch."

Alexander found Case Manager Cunningham in his office and knocked on his door and waited.

"Come on in, and have a seat," Mr. Cunningham said. "Are you Merchant?"

"Yes, sir."

"You just have everything working out for you, don't you?"

"Sir?"

"Well, you came here before you should've. You already have a job. You're not in segregation. Everything is working out for you, isn't it?"

"No, sir, I would not consider any of this working out."

"Hmm," Mr. Cunningham grunted. "I see you dropped out of high school."

"No, sir. I was arrested before I could graduate."

"Well, for the next two weeks, you will report to Diagnostics as Ms. McDowell told you, but after that, you get in school and get your GED. If you do a good job, Ms. McDowell may allow you to work around your school schedule, but that's up to her."

"I will," Alexander said.

"Have you gotten into any trouble since you've been in prison?"

"Ahhh, yes."

"What kind of trouble?"

Alexander swallowed hard. "I was involved in an altercation yesterday morning."

"You were fighting, and yet you still got your transfer. How did you manage that?"

"It wasn't my fault, sir. Four guys attacked me for no reason. I was only defending myself," Alexander said.

"Is that right?"

"It's the honest truth, sir."

Mr. Cunningham stared at Alexander dubiously. "I'm glad you had the sense to tell me the truth. I've already spoken to Mr. Henderson about it, but let me be very clear. You will get no special treatment from me. This is your last pass. If you get into any trouble here, you are going to wish you had never met me, you understand?"

"Yes, sir."

"Now, why do you still have those bus clothes on?"

"I have not been to laundry yet."

"Come on here. Let's get you some clothes. You're standing out like a sore thumb."

Alexander followed him to the laundry room, where he received two sets of clothes—two pairs of pants, two button-up shirts, two T-shirts, two pairs of underwear, two pairs of socks, and a pair of brown cloth shoes. He followed Mr. Cunningham to the door and they waited for the control room officer to let him in.

Dorm 1 was designed in the shape of a horseshoe, fanning out into four individual pods. Each pod was designed as two-tiered open dormitories. The bottom tier had 25 bunk beds and 25 lockers stacked along the back wall. A set of stairs led up to a loft aligning the back wall. The loft had an additional 25 bunk beds and lockers. The control room sat in the center of the dorm. The control room was surrounded with large plexiglass windows, which allowed the control room officer to see into each individual pod. Surrounding the control room was a corridor with four doors allowing access into the pods.

Once the control room officer allowed Alexander inside, he changed his clothes and went to lunch. He ate quickly and reported back to Diagnostics. Ms. McDowell retrieved him from the holding cell and escorted him over to the Diagnostics officer.

"Are you ready to work?"

"Yes, ma'am. Thanks for the opportunity," Alexander said.

"He doesn't look like he's ready to work," Officer Benson said.

"Mr. Benson, this is inmate Merchant. He is our new orderly. Please, show him around, okay?"

With his eyes fixed on Alexander, Officer Benson asked, "Are you sure about him, Ms. McDowell? He looks lazy." He turned to Alexander. "Are you lazy?"

"No, sir. I'm a hard worker."

"We'll see about that. Don't think I won't fire your ass," Officer Benson said.

"Benson, stop cussing," Ms. McDowell admonished with a smile.

"You just remember what I said. Come on here," Officer Benson said.

Alexander followed.

Officer Benson led Alexander to the men's restroom. "First things first. Clean the bathrooms twice a day. Clean the toilets and urinals, the sinks, empty the trash, sweep and mop the floor. Do it first thing in the morning and after lunch. You got it?"

"Yes, sir."

"Good. Make sure no one is in the women's restroom before you go in there. Knock, wait, knock again. Open the door and announce yourself loudly. Make sure it's empty. Once you enter, prop the door open with the wet floor sign or the trash can to let the ladies know you are in there. Got it?"

"Got it."

"Okay, come with me."

They stepped across the hallway to a closet, and Officer Benson opened the door. This is the janitor's closet.

"All of your supplies are in here. Let me know when you're getting low on anything, and we will get you more supplies. You should never run out of anything if you let us know in advance."

Alexander nodded.

"Before you leave every day, make sure the janitor's closet is locked. If anything is stolen, or if any contraband is found in here, it's on you. You got it?"

"Yes, sir."

"Okay. This is the break room. Clean it twice a day just like the bathrooms, more if necessary. Sweep and mop the hallways and empty the trash in each office. Knock before entering and never go into any office without permission. And never go in any office if no one is in there to watch you."

"Yes, sir."

"You will clean the offices upon request and empty the shredder once a day. That is pretty much it. Do you have any questions?"

"No, sir," Alexander said.

"What are you standing there for? Get to work," Officer Benson ordered.

Alexander made his rounds to each office. He introduced himself to all the staff members and emptied their trash cans.

He emptied the shredder, cleaned the bathrooms and the break room, and swept and mopped the hallways. He went back to Officer Benson's office and knocked on the door. "Mr. Benson, I finished everything."

"You did?"

"Yes, sir."

"Did you clean the sink?"

"Yes, I did."

"Did you?"

"Yes, I cleaned all the sinks in the bathrooms and the break room."

"What about this one?" Officer Benson asked, pointing to a sink and coffee station in the hallway.

"You didn't tell me to clean this one," Alexander said.

"Damn, do I have to tell you everything? Can't you think for yourself? Clean it and the coffee pot, too."

Alexander cleaned the sink and rinsed out the coffee pot as told. "Okay, I'm all done now."

"Are you?"

"Umm. I think so."

"Benson, stop messing with that boy," Ms. McDowell said.

"All right, you failed the first test. We'll see how you do tomorrow. Go on back to your dorm and remember to stay where the officer can see you." Officer Benson said.

"Okay. I'll see you tomorrow," Alexander said.

"Good job, Merchant. We'll see you tomorrow," Ms. McDowell said.

"Okay, bye."

"Is the closet locked?" Officer Benson asked.

"No, I was just about to ask you to lock it," Alexander said.

"Sure, you were. Get on outta here," Officer Benson said.

Alexander made his way back to his dormitory and lay across his bed. He watched Officer Williams make her rounds, checking the bathrooms and the showers. She looked inside trash cans and underneath the beds. Finally, she picked two inmates to sweep the dormitory, and stack all the empty chairs against the wall.

Officer Jackson arrived to relieve Officer Williams, handing him her radio, her pepper spray, her handcuffs, and her baton. She picked up her bag and left. Officer Jackson positioned himself where he could see the entire dormitory.

Buff stood peering into his locker, "Shit," he said, slamming it shut. It slowly swung back open. "Yo Skip, you gotta Coke?"

"Nah, man, I'm out," Skip said.

"Shit," Buff said.

"Count time. On your bunks," Officer Jackson commanded.

"They haven't announced anything yet," Chi-Town said.

"Get on your bunks," Officer Jackson ordered.

"Man, that's bullshit," Skip said.

"ATTENTION ON THE COMPOUND, ATTENTION ALL AREAS, IT IS NOW COUNT TIME, COUNT TIME, COUNT TIME," a voice bellowed from the intercom.

Officer Jackson stared at Chi-Town and pointed towards his bunk. Chi-Town leisurely went to his bed and sat down. Officers Jackson and Taylor counted the inmates of A-pod, B-pod, C-pod, and D-pod. Officer Jackson picked up the phone and gave the total number to the Dorm 1 control room officer. The control room officer called in the number to the Master Control Center. Upon receiving confirmation, the control room officer gave Officer Jackson two thumbs up.

Officer Jackson stepped back into A-pod and yelled, "Good count."

The inmates climbed off their bunk beds and went about their normal routines.

Alexander hurried to the television, grabbed the remote control, and turned the television to *Sports Center*. Moments later, Buff sat in front of the television and Alexander placed the remote control and a bottle of Coca-Cola on the arm of Buff's chair.

"Appreciate that, homie," Buff said.

"Not a problem," Alexander said.

"You Moe's boy?"

"Yeah, we went to school together," Alexander said.

"A'ight, cool," Buff said.

They slapped five and locked fingers just before Buff's henchmen gathered around the television.

"Yo, this is A-Rod. He's cool," Buff said.

Alexander slapped five with Chi-Town and Beats. The others acknowledged Alexander by nodding their heads.

"What 'hood you from, man," Chi-Town said.

"I'm from Raleigh," Alexander said.

"I know that, but where about?"

"Are you from Raleigh?" Alexander asked.

"Yeah, I'm from Garner Road. You know it?"

"I think so. I live near Cameron Village," Alexander said.

"In those new apartments?"

"No, we have a house."

"Oh, y'all own that shit?"

"Yeah," Alexander said.

"Oh, your people got money, huh?" Chi-Town said.

Shit I'm talking too much, Alexander thought. "No, not really. My parents got in when it was cheap."

"It was never cheap over there," Chi-Town said.

"Yeah well, that was before my dad passed away. My mom has been able to hold on to it, but it hasn't been easy," Alexander said, hoping to downplay what Chi-Town obviously considered a privileged upbringing. Though living on a teacher's salary in North Carolina was far from privileged, he would have a hard time convincing Chi-Town, who grew up in public housing, of that. He was happy to see Chi-Town turn his attention to *Sports Center's* highlights.

Beats wrote down all the scores from yesterday's games and handed the list to Buff.

Buff looked them over and stuffed the list into his pocket.

Teardrop studied the newspaper for more detailed statistics. He compiled a list of individual points scored, rebounds, assists from the NBA, and touchdowns, yards gained, sacks, pass completions, and interceptions from the NFL, and handed that report to Buff also.

Alexander wondered if Buff was running a gambling ring. *We're not allowed to have any money, so what would be the point,* Alexander thought. He planned to observe more and find out.

"Chow time," Officer Jackson announced.

The inmates lined up in the corridor and marched to the cafeteria.

SEVENTEEN

For Alexander, Saturday could not come fast enough when thinking about seeing his mother. After breakfast, Alexander ironed his uniform, shaved his face, and brushed his teeth. He dressed, brushed his hair, and waited for Emily to arrive. Time moved excruciatingly slow. The long hand on the clock seemed frozen in place.

Eventually, Officer Williams entered the dorm. "Merchant, inmate Merchant," she yelled.

"Here, ma'am."

"Visitation," she said.

Alexander stepped out into the corridor and waited in line. "Yard Patrol to Dorm One." Officer Williams answered her radio. "Go for Dorm One."

"Send them out."

Officer Williams leaned her shoulder against the outer door and waved at the control room officer. The door popped open, and she sent the inmates out to meet Officer Smith. Officer Smith escorted the group to the visitation room.

When Alexander entered, he saw Emily waiting at a small

square table. He was shocked to find her clothes hanging off her shoulders, too big for her small frame, and her skin sagging on her face. He hugged her tightly and felt her brittle frame. Tears filled his eyes and his throat tightened. He wiped his face before loosening his grip.

Sitting across from her, Alexander composed himself and smiled broadly. "It is so good to see you, Mom. You look great."

Emily smiled. "It's good to see you too, baby."

"Did you have a hard time finding this place? I know it's in the middle of nowhere."

"No, not at all. The GPS led me straight here."

"Good," Alexander smiled.

"How are you getting along here?"

"Things are going well. Do you remember Milton Fogle?"

"Sure, I remember him. That boy was always getting into trouble."

"He's here, too."

"That's no surprise."

"He's sort of well-connected here and has been looking out for me."

"Looking out for you how?" Emily inquired.

"Nothing major. He sort of vouched for me, if you will, and is seeing to it that no one bothers me. He asked me to say hello to you."

Emily grimaced. "I'm not sure what to think about that," she said.

"It's fine, Mom. Everything is fine."

"Well, tell him hello, I guess."

"I have a job."

"A job doing what?"

"I'm the janitor in Diagnostics. Ms. McDowell, the woman who called you, hired me. It was mostly to keep an eye on me since I'm underage, but I think she's fond of me."

"What does it pay?"

"Ten cents an hour," Alexander smiled.

"How can they get away with paying you so little?"

Alexander laughed. "Labor laws don't apply here, and trust me, there are worse jobs to have."

"What about school?"

"I start next week."

"It's good you can leave here with your diploma."

"I'll leave with my GED, not a diploma."

"It's the same thing, Alexander. You'll go to community college, transfer to the university of your choice, and get on with your life."

"Sure, I will," Alexander said, gloomily.

"You will. One day you will look back on this as a mere bump in the road," she said. She reached for Alexander's hand and held on to it.

Her hand felt cold and brittle, and Alexander had a terrible feeling he had yet to see the worst of his declining fortunes.

Alexander was in a sour mood for the rest of the weekend, keeping mostly to himself. He lay on his bed reading a book and watching the dynamics of his dormitory. He observed Buff's gambling operation, observing multiple inmates placing bets with Beats, Chi-Town, and Teardrop. Bets were placed in the cafeteria, on the recreation yard, and in the dormitory. He watched Beats, Chi-Town, and Teardrop record each bet on a piece of paper and hand the list over to Buff. *These guys are begging to get caught,* Alexander thought.

Alexander reported to work on Monday morning. He cleaned the bathrooms, and the break room, before making his rounds emptying trash cans. "Good morning, Ms. Solas," Alexander said.

"Good morning," she replied.

Alexander removed the trash bag from her trash can and replaced it with a new one.

"I'm gonna need you to clean my office this afternoon," she requested.

"Yes, ma'am," Alexander said.

He entered Mr. Jackson's office. "How are you doing today, sir?" Alexander said.

Mr. Jackson shifted in his seat and let out a thunderous fart. "That's how I'm doing," he said.

The stench was awful, so Alexander grimaced and left the office.

"What about my trash?" Mr. Jackson asked.

Laughter was heard throughout the building.

"Got one," Benson said.

More laughter filled the air.

Ms. McDowell stepped out into the hallway. "Damnit, Richard. You need to check your drawers," she said.

Richard Jackson laughed loudly.

"Come on in here, Merchant," she said.

Alexander entered her office and removed the trash bag from her trash can and replaced it with a new one. "Do you have a minute, Ms. McDowell?" Alexander asked.

"Sure, what's on your mind?"

"I turn nineteen on Thursday and will have to start school on Monday morning."

"Yes, I'm aware of that," she said.

Alexander felt a presence behind him. He turned and saw Captain McDowell, Ms. McDowell's husband, filling the doorway. "Good morning, sir," Alexander said.

Captain McDowell nodded.

"Go on, Merchant," Ms. McDowell said.

"Well, I was wondering if it will be possible to keep my job?"

"You can't be in two places at the same time," she said.

"Yes, but my duties don't require me to be here all day. I can do it in half the time, really."

"Then why am I paying you for eight hours?" she asked.

"Don't penalize the man for working hard," Captain McDowell said.

"You mind your business," she said, pointing her finger at her husband.

He winked at her and smiled.

"I understand that exceptional students can qualify for independent study, and I see no reason why I shouldn't," Alexander said.

"Is that right?" the Captain said.

"Yes, sir," Alexander said.

Captain McDowell laughed.

"I'll have to think about it," she said.

"Only I can make that decision," Captain McDowell said.

"You don't run anything up here," she said.

"You don't believe that do you, son?" Captain McDowell winked and smiled.

Ms. McDowell stared at Alexander and awaited his answer.

Alexander did not respond.

Captain McDowell sat and crossed his legs.

"Should I check back in a few days?" Alexander asked.

"I'll let you know," she smiled.

Alexander completed his duties and went to lunch.

EIGHTEEN

O ver the next few days, Alexander found himself falling into the regular routines of prison life. He awoke early and remained on his bunk until count time. After count time, he showered and brushed his teeth, dressed himself, made his bed, and stood in line to exchange his laundry. He went to breakfast, reported to work, went to lunch, reported back to work, and went back to his dorm, where he either read books or watched television until the evening meal. He didn't like going out onto the recreation yard, because the officers watched him like a hawk, and the other inmates took notice. Being watched was not something he wanted to be known for, so he spent time in his own pod until he turned 19.

On his birthday, Alexander awoke feeling melancholy. It was the worst birthday of his young life, and it was only getting started. He had been looking forward to breakfast all night, *Wednesday's evening meal wasn't fit to feed a dog,* he thought. He was standing in line outside of the cafeteria when an officer pulled him out of line and told him to place the palms of his hands against the wall. She proceeded to pat search him, starting at his collar, and placing her hands against his shoulders, his chest, his back, and waist. She reached between his legs and grabbed a hold of his genitalia.

Alexander jerked upward.

"Move again and I'll put you on the ground," she said, squeezing his genitalia, checking for weapons, drugs, or any other form of contraband. She pressed her hands against one thigh, his knee, his calf, and pressed her fingers into the edges of his cloth shoe. She then proceeded to check his other leg in the same manner. Satisfied, she sent him on his way, and randomly selected the next inmate to do the same.

Alexander ate quickly and reported to work. He stood in the Diagnostics holding cell for several minutes before Officer Benson came to get him. "Good morning, Mr. Benson," Alexander said.

Officer Benson looked at his watch. "You were supposed to be to work ten minutes ago," he said.

"I've been waiting in there for fifteen minutes," Alexander said.

"Don't think you're going to get out of work because it's your birthday." Benson smirked and laughed, losing his composure.

Alexander laughed and made his way over to the janitor's closet and waited for Officer Benson to unlock the closet.

"Set up the conference room for a staff meeting. Wipe everything down and make sure there are at least sixteen chairs around the table," he requested.

"What time does the meeting begin?"

"Nine o'clock."

"Yes, sir." Alexander started with the bathrooms and the break room, before setting up the conference room. He wiped down all the furniture and swept and mopped the floor. He washed out the coffee pot and set it up in the conference room.

Ms. McDowell entered the conference room, carrying bags of bagels and cupcakes. Other staff brought in bottles of soda, cookies, and bags of potato chips. Ms. McDowell arranged all the food on a table and locked the door.

During the staff meeting, Alexander busied himself by sweeping and mopping the corridors and washing the plexiglass windows. At the conclusion of the meeting, staff took what leftover food they wanted and tossed the rest into the trash. However, a plate with two vanilla cupcakes and two chocolate chip cookies was left on the table.

"Merchant," Ms. McDowell said.

Alexander stepped into the conference room and saw Ms. McDowell and several other staff sitting around the conference room chatting.

"Yes, ma'am," Alexander said.

"Clean this place up, but first take these cupcakes and cookies and dispose of them," she said.

"Yes, ma'am. Let me get the trash can," Alexander said.

"No, Merchant. Take these cupcakes. Go into the janitor's closet, close the door behind you, and dispose of these cupcakes and cookies."

The staff sat around laughing.

Alexander knew it was against the rules for staff to give him any food, and it was against the rules for him to eat anything that did not come from the inmate cafeteria or commissary.

"Yes, ma'am," Alexander said, cautiously picking up the cupcakes and cookies.

"Happy birthday," Ms. McDowell said.

"Thank you, ma'am," he said, and left the conference room,

making a beeline straight to the janitor's closet. He closed the door behind him and stuffed an entire cupcake into his mouth.

Later, Alexander lay in bed thinking about his nineteenth birthday, and how he had come to spending it in prison. He thought about his letter to Judge Roger Gregory and decided he should finish it and send it off. He found himself stuck on the act that had led him to his current predicament. He wasn't sure how to explain it to the judge, how to put it into writing. His mind went back to Natalie, and the details of the act filled his mind.

SUMMER ENDED and Alexander and his friends prepared for what they hoped to be the best year of their lives—senior year. For Natalie, this simply meant a continuation of what she had always done. Of what her family had always done, pursuing excellence as a way of life. Thanks to her family's position, her future was virtually solidified. However, for Alexander and Howard, performing at a high-level was critical to their success.

At the end of Howard's junior year, he had restored his GPA to respectable standings, and Alexander had scored a respectable 1520 on the SATs. That, along with maintaining a 5.0 weighted GPA would earn him a scholarship at many of America's most coveted universities, but Alexander feared it wouldn't be enough to earn the international scholarship he desired. With that in mind, he decided to try for an SAT score of 1600. Natalie agreed that a score of at least 1600 would better his chances, but she assured him her uncle will do all he could to help.

"My mother has promised to call my uncle on your behalf," Natalie said.

"What does your father think?"

"He doesn't know yet. We will tell him when the time is right," Natalie said.

They were entering their second week of school, and the three friends spent their daily lunch hour strategizing how to enhance their college applications. They decided that Howard should run for president of the Student Government Association, Alexander would run for vice president, and Natalie would manage their campaigns.

"We will start campaigning on Monday. For now, I must focus on Saturday," Natalie said.

"Are you putting that much thought into Alexander's birthday?" Howard asked.

"I have a track meet," Natalie said.

Over the last three weeks, Natalie had twice broken the state record for the 300-meter hurdles by 100th of a second, and she tied the state record in the 200-meter sprint. She had realized these achievements in practice, and she hoped that on Saturday, her competitive adrenaline would give her the boost she needed to officially enter her name into the book of state records.

Alexander awoke to Natalie's phone call. "Happy birthday," she said.

"Thank you, baby. What time is it?" he asked.

"Seven-thirty. I have to meet the team at eight."

"What time is your first event?"

"Eleven-twenty," she said.

"Okay, I'll see you there," he said.

"I'll see you there, bye-bye."

Alexander made his way to the meet and sat among a handful of spectators. He spotted Natalie, lying on the field, wearing her purple and gold uniform. Her legs were crossed, and two white earplugs flowed from her ears. Her first event was the 400-meter and as the event drew near, she sat up and went through her pre-competition ritual. She stretched and jumped, ran in place, and shook her muscles loose. Seeing Alexander in the stands, she smiled and waved. When Alexander blew her a kiss, she pretended to catch it. She lined up for the race, and when the race began, a short, busty girl took the lead and controlled the race for the first 300 meters. Natalie ran third behind a slim blonde. With 100 meters remaining, Natalie quickened her pace. She moved alongside the blonde, and the leader was forced back into third. Moments before crossing the finish line, the blonde runner moved slightly forward taking first place. Natalie spoke to her coach briefly and came over to where Alexander sat.

"Hi, honey," she said, breathing heavily.

"What was your time?" Alexander asked.

"Forty-eight point fifty-one," she said.

"You've run faster than that," he said.

"I'll get her next time," she said nonchalantly, I have a record to break in twenty minutes.

"Did you let her win?"

"Not exactly, but she won't win anymore today," Natalie said, displaying her usual confidence.

"Where are your parents?" he asked.

"They're out of town attending a conference. They'll be back late tonight," she said, now breathing normally. She raised a bottle of water to her lips and drank. "I better go and focus," she said.

"You are going to do great," he said.

As she turned away, Alexander succumbed to a powerful impulse and reached for her hand. "Hey," he said, and she met his gaze. "I love you," he said.

She gazed at him, and her countenance showed a look of

astonishment, but then slowly her lips widened into a smile. "I love you, too," she said, "I love you, too."

She trotted back to midfield, lying down on her back, knees raised, feet flat on the grass. Minutes later, she was back on her feet and taking her position in lane three. Seeing her in uniform, Alexander saw that years of tennis and track and field had sculptured her body in a way that Michelangelo himself would have envied.

Natalie stretched and jumped in place, all while maintaining a look of focused determination. She kneeled into position and at the sound of the gun, she exploded out of her starting block. Natalie had gotten off to a great start, and after clearing the second hurdle, she emerged from the group, taking a commanding lead, but when she attempted the third hurdle, her left leg slammed against the hurdle, sending it crashing to the ground. Her form was broken, and she struggled to stay in her lane, and when she took the fourth hurdle, her leg had struck it, and left it rocking back and forth. She was now running in fifth place.

It was painful for Alexander to watch, and he lowered his head in disbelief. He felt it was his fault. *Why did I tell her that I loved her? It was a distraction,* he thought. At that moment, Alexander heard a familiar voice yelling, "Go Natalie, go." He looked in the direction of the voice and saw Samantha standing, fist clenched, yelling words of encouragement.

Looking back to the race, he saw that Natalie had moved back into second place. Somehow, with will and determination, she had brought herself back from near disaster, and had developed the form of an Olympian.

With gritted teeth, ponytail swinging, she cleared the eighth and final hurdle, and landed in a dead heat for first place. Sprinting to the finish line, Natalie leaned forward, retaking her position, and claiming victory. She slowed herself into a hasty walk, never stopping to see her official time, because it wasn't the time she had wanted. Natalie marched directly off the field and disappeared beneath the aluminum bleachers.

"Alexander," Samantha called, and gave him two thumbs up.

Natalie returned to the field for her next race, the 200-meter. Never looking in Alexander's direction, she took her place next to the blonde runner who had beaten her early on. With her hands on her hips, she stared out at the lanes, her eyes blazed with intensity. Natalie took her mark and exploded from the starting blocks like a woman who was on a mission. Taking the lead early, she never let up and crossed the finish line a full body length ahead of everyone else. She joined her coach and waited for her official time.

Natalie's official time was posted. It read 22.06. Seeing this, Natalie darted across the track, pumping her fist into the air, her teammates running behind her.

Natalie's teammates gathered around her, hugging each other, and slapping fives. Natalie ran over to Alexander. "Did you see it?"

"Of course, did you break it?"

"Yes, I broke the record, I hadn't even planned on it. I was going for the other one," she said, bubbling with excitement. "Do you see the woman sitting behind my coach? She's from Stanford," Natalie said.

She trotted back over to her coach, embraced her, and settled in next to her teammates. When the meet ended, Alexander waited for Natalie outside of the women's locker room.

Natalie emerged carrying her awards in a small box.

"I'll take that," Alexander said, and they climbed into Emily's car. "How should we celebrate?" Alexander asked.

"When must you return your mother's car?" Natalie asked.

"I have it all day," he said.

"Surprise me," she said, settling back into her seat. "Just take me home first. I need a shower," she said.

They arrived at her house and went inside, with Alexander following Natalie into the den.

She turned on the television and handed him the remote control. "Would you like some lemonade?"

"Yes, I would," he said.

Natalie exited the room and returned carrying two glasses, which she placed on the coffee table. She reached into her pocket and produced a small box wrapped in a ribbon.

"Happy birthday," she said.

Alexander opened the box and was greatly surprised and delighted by the iPod.

"Do you like it?"

"I love it, thank you, but isn't this expensive?" he asked.

"Not really. Besides, you're always messing with my iPod, so I thought you should have your own," she said.

"But this is the most expensive model," he said.

"It's fine. Don't worry about it." She kissed him and Alexander kissed her back. She pressed her weight against his chest until his back rested on the sofa. Sitting there, they kissed and held each other for a while.

Eventually, Natalie leaned back, biting her bottom lip, and stared at him intently.

"What is wrong?" he asked.

"Nothing, I need to go upstairs and shower. My laptop is in my bedroom if you want to load your iPod. Come on up," she said.

They entered her bedroom, and Alexander saw her laptop on her bed.

Natalie pulled a pair of white shorts and a pink halter top

from her closet and held it under her chin. "How does this look?" she asked.

"It looks great," he said.

She gathered some more of her things and went into the bathroom.

Moments later, Alexander heard the shower running. He lay across her bed and looked through her library of music.

Natalie came out of the shower wearing a white cotton bathrobe, her wet curly hair resting on her shoulders. She lay across the bed with him, as he downloaded songs onto his iPod. She climbed onto his back and rested her chin on his shoulder.

"Download all of it. You can erase what you do not want later," she said.

Alexander felt the weight of her lean body resting on his back, her toes resting on his heels. He felt her soft lips kissing him just below his ear lobe. He tried to keep his eyes fixed on the monitor, until he felt her lips once more at the base of his jaw. He turned his head towards her and pressed his lips firmly against hers. His lips parted slightly, and he felt her warm tongue slip into his mouth. Alexander rolled onto his back and sat up, as Natalie brought her knees forward, straddling his hips. With her hands on each side of his head, she kissed him deeply and passionately. She brought her hands down to his sides and with one motion, she pulled his shirt over his head, tossing it onto the floor.

Alexander reached for the belt that had held her bathrobe together. He stopped for a moment and wondered how far he should go.

Sensing his hesitation, Natalie pulled away and stared at him intently. She climbed under the covers and tossed her bathrobe onto the floor. She pulled the cover underneath her chin and smiled.

"Are you sure?" Alexander asked.

"I am," she responded.

Alexander climbed under the covers and moved himself into position. Their love making ended quickly, but they were both satisfied with the experience. The lovers would lie there for hours, their legs intertwined, arms wrapped tightly around each other, neither wanting to move, both wanting to stay in the moment. So, they did until the last rays of sunlight faded away.

In the days to come, the observant eye would have noticed a slight shift in the couple's relationship. There was evidence of a new closeness, and a deeper bond that hadn't existed before. It was the kind of change that only occurs when two people discover love in a way most people never will. Hemingway said it only happened when the earth moved, and it only moved once in a lifetime, never twice.

On Monday morning, the three friends worked on their campaigns. They hung posters and flyers all over the school, announcing their candidacies. The campaign would last for three weeks, and it included two debates.

There were two other students running against them, and although they were fine candidates, they were less organized by far, and they lacked Howard's popularity.

Judging from the positive response Alexander and Howard were receiving, they were certain they would win the election by no less than 80 percent of the vote. However, the first debate was quickly approaching, so they met at Natalie's house to prepare.

Sitting at her kitchen table, they wrote the first draft of their opening speeches, and sharpened their talking points. They worked steadily for an hour or so before Howard announced he had to leave.

"I have a ton of homework," Howard said, as he gathered his things.

"So do I," Alexander said.

"I think we've gotten off to a good start," Howard said.

"We have eight days to get it right," Natalie said, trying to keep them focused.

"I'll tell you one thing, if I ever run for president of the United States and need a campaign manager, I'll know who to call," Howard said.

They all laughed.

"Interested in politics, are we?" Natalie asked.

"I could make a run at it," Howard said.

"And what of your running mate?" Alexander asked.

"Are you up for it?" Howard asked.

"He would make a fine secretary of state," Natalie said.

"I think you're right," Howard said.

Howard left, and Alexander and Natalie worked on their calculus homework together.

Mrs. Agadani entered the kitchen carrying a box. "Hello, Alexander," she said.

"Hi, Mrs. Agadani."

"Happy belated birthday," she said.

"Thank you, ma'am."

She handed Natalie a box. "This came in the mail for you today. It is from your Aunt Edith in Sweden," she announced.

Natalie opened the box and found a present. She opened her card first and read it aloud. "Happy birthday, Natalie. Your uncle tells me you are interested in attending Stockholm University. We would be delighted to have you back home. We miss you terribly. I hope you enjoy your gift," she read, while holding the card.

"When did you talk to Uncle Filip?" Natalie asked.

"Last week," Mrs. Agadani said, as she poured a cup of tea.

"Did you ask about Alexander?" Natalie asked.

"Yes, I did," she said. Mrs. Agadani joined them at the table. "He said as long as you meet the international requirements for admission, he would help you. However, he cannot give you a scholarship. You will have to apply for an international scholarship and compete against other students," she said.

"I wouldn't have it any other way," Alexander said.

"However, if you are unable to earn a scholarship, you can take advantage of a program allowing you to attend Stockholm University, if you are willing to work fifteen hours a week on campus. By doing so, you can qualify for several grants that will cover most, if not all your tuition costs," Mrs. Agadani said.

"That's fantastic," Natalie said.

"I don't know how to thank you, Mrs. Agadani. Please, tell Mr. Larson I will do whatever it takes," he said.

"I know you will," she said.

Helena held his hand and smiled as her eyes shifted between his and Natalie's. Although she smiled, her eyes showed a look of concern. It was a mother's concern for her daughter who was growing up right before her eyes.

Alexander wanted to assure her that he should not be the cause of her concern. He wanted to tell her he would love and care for Natalie for as long as she would let him, but he thought it inappropriate to say so in the moment.

Natalie opened her gifts and found a Nancy Drew spy kit. "What is this?" she said, with a furrowed brow.

The kit included a magnifying glass, binoculars, a flashlight, walkie-talkies, and a notebook. "What does she think I am, a child?" Natalie said. She stood, and tucking the gift under her arm, she marched out of the kitchen and directly through the front door.

"Where are you going?" Mrs. Agadani asked.

The door slamming behind her was Natalie's only response. Alexander and Helena went to the window and watched as Natalie marched across the street and rang the Collins' doorbell. Katie opened the door, and Natalie handed her the spy kit. Moments later, Natalie was back inside.

"Why did you give it away?" Helena asked.

"You didn't expect me to play with it, did you?" Natalie asked.

"No, but Aunt Edith went out of her way to send it to you," Mrs. Agadani said.

"Katie would enjoy it more than I would. She's the neighborhood detective anyway," Natalie said.

"Is that so?" Helena said.

"I'm afraid so, ma'am," Alexander said.

"She is the nosiest child I have ever met," Natalie said.

Helena finished her tea and returned to her bedroom.

"I can't believe I may actually have a chance to study abroad. I'm so excited," Alexander said.

"Isn't it fantastic? You are going to love Stockholm. It is the most beautiful city. I cannot wait to show you around," Natalie said.

They finished their homework, and Alexander went home to study for his upcoming French exam. He sat on the couch half studying French and half watching reruns of the Boondocks.

"How was your day?" Emily asked.

"It was good. You'll never guess what happened."

"What?"

"Natalie's uncle says he will help me get into to the University of Stockholm."

"The University of Stockholm?" Emily folded her arms.

"Yes. And Mrs. Agadani says if I worked fifteen hours a

week on campus, I could get a grant to cover most of my tuition cost," he said.

"I thought you wanted to go to Morehouse like your father?" Emily said.

"I never said that," he said. Alexander detected the same look of concern which he had seen in Helena. There were no words of consolation for her uneasiness. In fact, he was not sure of what precisely she was uneasy about, so he simply said, "Don't worry, Mom. I'll be fine."

"Sweden is a long way from home," she said, gloomily.

"I know it is, but studying abroad is what I've always wanted to do," he said.

"I just worry about you, dear."

"I can take care of myself. Besides, I'll be there with Natalie."

"That's what worries me," she said.

"What does that mean?"

"Natalie is a wonderful girl, and you know how I adore her, but you're still young, Alexander. Both of you are, and I just want you to be careful," she said.

"I'll be careful. I promise," he said.

As Alexander approached the conclusion of his letter to Judge Gregory, he thought about how he should explain the unfolding of the final act, which sealed his fate and changed the course of his life forever.

He recalled walking Natalie home after school and peering at the low-hanging clouds.

"I think it's going to rain," Natalie said.

"I wish it would. It has been like this all day," Alexander said.

The wind blew and the leaves rustled above. The clouds broke in the western sky, and rays of light shined through and rested on the tops of distant trees.

"It's pretty, don't you think?" Natalie said.

"It's very nice," Alexander said, distantly.

"What's wrong?" Natalie asked.

"It's nothing, just something my mother said."

"What did she say?"

"She's worried about me going to school in Sweden," Alexander said, looking pensive.

Natalie pushed open her front door. "Come on in," she said.

"Where are your parents?" Alexander said.

"They're working."

"Are they working late?"

"Very late," she said, softly.

Alexander wrapped his arm around her waist and pulled her in close. Their knapsacks crashed on the floor as they kissed each other long and hard. They ascended the stairs and moved into Natalie's bedroom, closing the door behind them.

They kissed and slowly undressed each other and kissed some more. Lying on her bed, Alexander kissed her neck and her shoulders. He ran his fingers across her well-defined abdominal muscles and took his time kissing each one.

OVER THE NEXT FEW DAYS, Alexander and Howard prepared for the debates, and when the day of the debates arrived, Alexander was a nervous wreck. The day started just like any other. It was a brisk and gloomy morning, and the cold air stung his nostrils with each breath.

Alexander, Natalie, and Howard entered the auditorium and made their way backstage. The master of ceremonies explained the order of events to all of the candidates. The vice-presidential candidates were to each deliver a five-minute speech. Afterwards, the student body presidential candidates would deliver a ten-minute speech, which would be followed by a question-and-answer session from the audience.

The master of ceremonies informed Alexander that he would be the first to speak, so he sat and studied his flashcards.

Mr. Andrews, the dean of students, entered the auditorium. "Alexander," he called.

"Yes, sir," Alexander said.

"You're needed in the principal's office," Mr. Andrews said.

"May I go after my speech?"

"I'm afraid not. It's urgent," he said, solemnly.

Alexander entered the administrative office where two police officers stood waiting.

"Are you Alexander Merchant?" asked the officer in front.

"Yes, I am."

"We need you to come with us," he said.

"Come with you where?"

"To the police station."

"I can't go to the police station, I have to make a speech," Alexander said.

"Your speech will have to wait," the officer said.

"Am I being arrested? I haven't done anything," he said.

"You're not under arrest, but we need you to answer some questions," the officer said.

"Questions about what?"

"We would rather not discuss it here," the officer said.

His name tag said Adams, and his partner's said Smith, Alexander noticed. "Look, Mr. Adams, there must be a misunderstanding. Just let me finish my speech. It's important for me to give it today," he said.

"You won't be making any speeches today, now shut your mouth and come with us," Officer Smith said.

"I'm not going anywhere with you," he said.

"Turn around and face the wall," Officer Smith said, and reached for his handcuffs.

"Wait a minute," Mr. Andrews said, grasping Alexander's arm. "Listen Alexander, this is not a joke. You need to go with the police, or you will only make matters worse."

"But I haven't done anything," Alexander said.

"I know you haven't, but you cannot disobey the police. We will notify your mother. Follow commands and don't make any sudden movements. Do you understand what I'm saying?" Mr. Andrews asked.

"Yes," Alexander nodded.

Mr. Andrews turned to face Officer Smith. "Are those handcuffs necessary?"

"No," Officer Adams said. "Let's go," he commanded.

Alexander was led outside with the police and shoved into the vehicle. He was taken to the police station and led into a room.

"Have a seat," Officer Adams said. Alexander sat at a small table, and Officer Adams left the room. Alexander sat alone for a while before a man entered the room and sat across from him.

"Mr. Alexander Merchant?" he said.

"Yes," Alexander answered.

"I am Detective McNeal," he said.

"Can you tell me why I'm here?" Alexander asked.

"I will get to that, but first I need to ask you some questions," he said. He opened a file in front of him and examined its contents. "Do you know a young lady named Natalie Agadani?"

"Yes."

"How long have you known her?"

"For almost a year," Alexander answered.

"How long exactly," Detective McNeal asked.

"Ten months."

"How well do you know Miss Agadani?"

"Very well. Why, is she in some sort of trouble?"

"No, she's not," Detective McNeal said.

"Has something happened to her?" he asked.

"I'll ask the questions. Now, how well do you know her?"

"I've already told you, I know her very well," he said.

"Describe your relationship with her."

"She's my girlfriend."

"Your girlfriend," he repeated, and wrote something in the file. "How long have you been dating Miss Agadani?" Detective McNeal asked.

"Nine months," Alexander answered.

"How many times have you kissed Miss Agadani?"

"I don't know."

"You don't know," he said, inquisitively.

"No, I don't, and I don't like your tone," Alexander said.

"More than five?" he asked.

"Five what?"

"Have you kissed her more than five times?"

"I suppose so," Alexander said.

"More than ten?"

"Yes."

"More than twenty?" Detective McNeal asked.

"I said I don't know. How many times have you kissed *your* girlfriend?" Alexander asked.

Detective McNeal stared at him momentarily in silence. His eyes were cold, and he was breathing heavily. "Have you had sexual intercourse with Miss Agadani?"

"That is none of your business," Alexander said.

"Answer the question," the detective screamed and threw his pen into Alexander's chest.

"I don't have to answer anything, and what business is it of yours?" Alexander said.

Detective McNeal jumped to his feet and with two long strides, stepped around the table and grabbed Alexander's shirt collar. "Everything is my business, and you will answer my questions, or I will throw your scrawny ass in jail," he said.

Alexander was terrified and thought it best to tell him everything he wanted to know. "Twice," he said, "we had sex two times."

"When?" McNeal demanded.

"Last week," Alexander said.

"On what day?"

"Last Saturday was the first time, and then again on Thursday," he answered.

"How old are you?" McNeal asked.

"I'm eighteen."

"And how old is Ms. Agadani?"

"She's fifteen," Alexander answered.

"Do you like having sex with fifteen-year-old girls?" McNeal asked.

"What does that mean?" Alexander asked.

"It means you are under arrest, you pervert. Get up," he said, pulling Alexander out of the chair.

"*Under arrest?* Under arrest for what?"

Detective McNeal spun him around and pressed Alexander against the wall.

"What did I do?" he asked.

"You have the right to remain silent," he said, as he pressed handcuffs around Alexander's wrists. "Anything you say can and will be used against you in a court of law. You have the right to an attorney. If you cannot afford an attorney, one will be appointed to you." He secured the metal restraints, and then brought Alexander out of the room and put him in a holding cell.

"What are you arresting me for?" Alexander asked, with panic rising in his chest.

Detective McNeal would not answer. He locked the door and left Alexander alone in the cold musty cell.

NINETEEN

After Monday morning chow, Alexander reported to education. He waited inside a holding cell for fifteen minutes before the education officer came to retrieve him.

Finally, Officer Carmichael filled the doorway of the holding cell. "Inmate Merchant," he said.

"Here," Alexander said.

"Come with me," Officer Carmichael said.

Alexander stood and came out into the corridor.

"Down the hallway, last door on the left," Officer Carmichael said.

Alexander did as he was told.

When he arrived, Officer Carmichael said, "Stop right there." Carmichael knocked on the office door, as he stepped inside.

"Hi, Ms. Perez."

"Carmichael, how are you?"

"I'm good. I have inmate Merchant here."

"Okay, he can come in," Ms. Perez said.

Alexander entered and sat across from her.

"Good morning."

"Good morning," Alexander replied.

"I hope you're ready to get started."

"Yes ma'am, I am. Although... Have you spoken to Ms. McDowell?"

"Spoke to her about what?"

"Well, I think I should qualify for independent study, and if so, I wanted to keep my job in Diagnostics, and work around my class schedule," Alexander said.

"No, that won't be possible. GED classes are mandatory. Therefore, you will need to participate full time like everyone else."

"Yes ma'am, I know it's mandatory, but I don't think I would benefit much from these classes."

"No? Perhaps if you had stayed in school instead of running the streets, you wouldn't be in prison."

Alexander sighed. "That's not what I mean. I wish I could test out altogether, but I know that's not possible, so I was hoping to get independent study so I could keep my job, that's all."

Ms. Perez glared at Alexander. She opened his file and noticed his IQ scores. She pursed her lips. *Impressive,* she thought. His math, reading, and spelling test scores were perfect on all three. Her face softened, but she remained resolute. She turned to her computer, printed out Alexander's class schedule, and handed it to him. "Your first class begins in five minutes. Be sure to arrive on time, or you'll receive an incident report. Do you understand?" she said.

"Yes, ma'am."

"Do you have any questions?"

"No, ma'am."

"Okay, get moving. She picked up her phone and dialed a

number. "Hey, Carmichael. I'm done with him. Will you show him to Purdic's class?" she said.

Alexander stepped out into the corridor and met Officer Carmichael.

"Follow me," Carmichael said.

He led Alexander down the hallway and stopped at a door before he spoke into his radio, "Education door two, Control."

The door popped open, and they passed through.

"Second door on your right," Carmichael said.

Alexander entered the classroom and stood near the door.

"This is inmate Merchant," Carmichael said.

"All right, have a seat," Mr. Purdic said.

Alexander settled into his seat and gazed at the blackboard, where he saw a few basic algebraic equations. His classmates were busy completing a quiz.

Mr. Purdic pulled a math textbook and a workbook off a shelf and sat behind his desk. "Merchant, over here," he said, as he wrote Alexander's name and number down in a logbook.

Alexander stood and went over to Mr. Purdic's desk.

"Here you go," he said, handing the books over to Alexander. "Don't worry about the quiz, we'll get you caught up later. Turn to page fifty-four in your workbook and begin working on today's homework assignment. Just do the best you can," Mr. Purdic said.

"I can take the quiz," Alexander said.

"That won't be necessary."

"I want to," Alexander persisted.

Mr. Purdic handed Alexander a sheet of paper. "Suit yourself. Bring it back when you're done," he said.

Alexander sat and looked over the quiz, consisting of simple algebraic equations:

$$4x + 5x = ?$$

$$3x \ (-9x) \ =?$$
$$10x + 3x \ (-2) \ =?$$
$$45x - 25x \ / \ 2=?$$

Alexander pursed his lips and sighed while quickly solving the equations and returned it to Mr. Purdic.

"Giving up already?" Mr. Purdic said.

"No, sir. I'm finished," Alexander said.

Mr. Purdic glared at Alexander and snatched the sheet of paper from Alexander's hand. He examined the quiz, and to his surprise, he found all ten equations answered correctly. "Hmm. Okay, have a seat," he said.

Alexander sat at his desk and started on his homework. The other students sporadically made their way to the front of the class with their quizzes in hand.

"Five minutes," Mr. Purdic announced.

Alexander surveyed the room and saw students furiously writing and erasing equations, brushing away debris, and writing again. *They seem to be trying their best, but struggling nonetheless*, Alexander thought. A bell rang loudly outside the classroom door. "Times up," Mr. Purdic said.

Alexander saw English 101 was next on his schedule. He entered the class and sat in the front row near a narrow rectangular window. While Ms. Thurmond busied herself writing sentences on the blackboard, Alexander peered out the window, watching puffy white clouds lounging in the Carolina-blue sky.

1. Mary and Sally _____ walking in the park. A. was B. were.
2. John _____ lying down. A. was B. were
3. Anne and I _____ planning to see a movie. A. was B. were

What are we, fifth graders? Alexander thought. He closed his eyes and rubbed his brow.

When he finished his classes, he reported to Diagnostics.

"Do you still work here?" Benson said.

"For now, I do. Is Ms. McDowell in?" Alexander asked.

"She's in her office."

Alexander found Ms. McDowell sitting behind her desk reviewing documents when he knocked on the door. "Hi, Ms. McDowell. Do you have a minute?"

"Come on in, Merchant. How was your first day of school?"

"It was a colossal waste of time."

"School is never a waste of time."

"Have you seen the curriculum over there? They must think we're all a bunch of retards."

"Not everyone had your upbringing, Merchant."

Alexander shrugged. "I suppose so. I spoke to Ms. Perez today, and she said it wouldn't be possible for me to test out of the program, and I cannot take independent study courses."

"Yes, I know."

"Can you talk to her?"

"I already have. She says we can't make any exceptions for you if we're not willing to do it for others," Ms. McDowell said.

"That's right," a voice said, from the hallway.

Alexander turned and saw Mr. Murphy, the Administrator of Rolesville Correctional Institution, standing in the doorway.

"Hi, Mr. Murphy," Alexander said.

Mr. Murphy nodded his head.

Alexander turned back to Ms. McDowell. "So, am I out of a job?"

"I'm afraid so," Ms. McDowell said with soft eyes. "Just empty the trash and tidy up the restrooms, and we won't need you anymore after today."

"Yes, ma'am." Alexander stepped out and began working.

He cleaned the restrooms and made his rounds to each office, emptying trash. He heard loud voices coming from Mr. Davis' office.

"English. Do you speak English?" Mr. Davis said to the inmate sitting across from him.

"Pas d'anglais, pas d'anglais," the inmate said loudly. "S'il vous plait laissez-moi appeler la maison," the inmate continued.

"What the..." Mr. Davis said, in exasperation. He stood and stepped out into the hall. "Ms. McDowell, this is useless. I can't communicate with him."

Ms. McDowell and Mr. Murphy stepped out into the hallway. "What's going on?" she said.

"This inmate doesn't speak any English—I can't understand him."

"Have you called the interpreter service?" Ms. McDowell said.

"He's speaking some African language. The interpreters don't cover Africa," Mr. Davis said.

"Where is he from?" Ms. McDowell asked.

"Guinea," Mr. Davis said.

"He's speaking French," Alexander interjected.

"What?" They all said and turned to face Alexander.

"They speak French in Guinea. He has a heavy accent, but he's speaking French, not an African language," Alexander said and turned to the frustrated inmate. "Calmer. Qu'est-ce que vous voulez?" Alexander asked in French.

"S'il vous plait laissez-moi appeler la maison," the inmate said.

Alexander turned back to Mr. Davis. "He wants to call home."

"Can you interpret the interview?" Ms. McDowell asked.

"Yes, I can."

"Tell him we will allow him to call home, but he has to answer Mr. Davis' questions first."

Alexander turned to face the inmate. "Quel est ton nom?" he said, asking his name.

"Je m'appelle Amadou."

Alexander relayed the message to the inmate while Mr. Davis sat behind his desk. He interpreted Mr. Davis' questions and Amadou's answers.

Mr. Murphy and Ms. McDowell stood in the hallway listening to the interview.

"What's his story?" Mr. Murphy nodded his head towards Alexander.

"He doesn't belong here," she said. She filled him in on Alexander's criminal conduct, his mother's health, and his desire to continue working in Diagnostics to stay out of trouble.

Mr. Murphy listened and nodded his head. "There's not much we can do. He has to do his time," he said.

"I know," Ms. McDowell said.

"It is not for us to decide who should be here and who shouldn't. It is our job to make sure they leave here better than they came. We must lead them all to the water and let them drink what they will."

"Yes, I know, sir, but some have more potential than others," she said.

When the interview ended, Alexander exited Mr. Davis' office into the hallway.

"Where did you learn to speak French?" Mr. Murphy asked.

"I've studied it since the ninth grade. My Spanish is much better. My goal was to work for the State Department or the United Nations one day, but I know that's unlikely now," Alexander said.

"Not necessarily," Mr. Murphy said.

Alexander looked incredulously.

Mr. Murphy continued, "The State Department is a long shot, but the United Nations is a bit more forgiving. It won't be easy, but if you play your cards appropriately, and patiently, you can get there," Mr. Murphy said.

"Thank you, sir. I appreciate that," Alexander said.

Mr. Murphy nodded.

Alexander turned to Ms. McDowell. "Thank you, Ms. McDowell, for everything."

"You're welcome." She smiled.

Alexander turned to leave.

"You know, Mr. Merchant, we have a teacher's assistant program in the education department that I think you would be a good fit for," Mr. Murphy said.

Alexander stopped and spun around to face him.

"The position would require you to assist the teachers with various tasks, including grading assignments and tutoring other students. The pay is commensurate to what Ms. McDowell is paying you. We don't currently have any participants, but I could make a recommendation if you're interested."

"Yes sir, that sounds awesome. Thank you," Alexander said.

Mr. Murphy nodded and walked away.

Back in his dormitory, Alexander was excited to share the news with his mother. He attempted several calls, but they went unanswered. Finally, he lay across his bed to pen her a letter. As he wrote, he heard Buff's voice fill the air.

"What the fuck you mean?"

Alexander saw Buff's open hands slamming into the chest of Chi-Town, sending him crashing into a row of plastic chairs. Alexander hopped off his bunk and ran down the stairs. "What's going on?" he said to Beats.

"Chi-Town got shook down today, and he lost the

gambling slips, and now some motherfucker don't want to pay up," Beats said.

"That motherfucker owes me, and you gon' let that shit slide?" Buff said in a rage.

Chi-Town kept his distance.

"Fuck it. I don't want his money. Y'all beat his ass. You too, A-Rod. It's time you earn your keep."

"What do you want me to do?" Alexander asked.

"Did I stutter, motherfucker? Put his ass in the hospital," Buff ordered.

"I can't do that," Alexander said.

"Motha…" Buff said, making long strides towards Alexander, his dreadlocks swaying behind him.

Alexander held up his hands and backed away. "Hold up, wait. Listen, I could be of better use to you than that."

Buff stood in his face. "How?"

"I have a good memory. From now on, if you tell me who has placed bets, you won't have to write anything down. I'll keep it all up here," Alexander said, tapping his temple with his finger.

"What you got a photographic memory or some shit?" Buff said.

"No, not photographic, it takes more work than that, but I can remember what I need to," Alexander said.

"You better not be fucking with me," Buff said.

"I'm not, I promise. Just give me a chance," Alexander said.

"All right. Y'all make that bitch bleed. A-Rod, you stay here with me," Buff said.

Alexander breathed a sigh of relief.

After the dormitory released for the evening meal, time passed slowly. Alexander and Buff sat watching *Sports Center*. Alexander took note of all scores and stats and filed them away for later.

"So, how's that shit work?" Buff asked.

"How does what work?" Alexander said.

"Your memory."

"Well, again, it's not photographic. I use pneumonic devices to remember things."

"What the fuck is that?"

"It's a technique to help me remember things. I create mental files for everything I need to remember, and whenever I need to recall that information, I just open the file and pull it out."

"Man, what the hell are you talking about?" Buff asked.

"All right, imagine this dorm as one big storage room, and each bed in this storage room represents a filing cabinet. Now, you have been in here long enough to have every inch of this place memorized. Right?"

"Yeah."

Alexander continued, "Well, let's say Dizzy, who sleeps on bunk one, bet twenty postage stamps that the Giants would beat the Cowboys this week by seven points. And let's say Kwame, on bunk nine, bet forty postage stamps on the Panthers beating the Eagles by fifteen points. Are you with me?"

"I'm with you," Buff said.

"Okay, now close your eyes and imagine," Alexander said.

Buff interjected, "Close my eyes?"

Alexander laughed. "Bear with me, man. Close your eyes and picture this entire room. Visualize a group of cowboys running around the dorm, riding horses and lassoing bulls. Now picture yourself walking over to bunk one and pulling back the covers. Visualize seven giants, at least ten feet tall, jumping out of bunk one and stomping those cowboys to death. Also, visualize each giant having the number twenty painted on his chest. Can you see it?"

"Yeah, I see it," Buff said.

"Now as absurd as that vision may be, I can almost guarantee you that when I ask you about Dizzy's bet three days from now, you will recall that vision of seven giants, with the number twenty painted on their chests stomping on those cowboys, and you will remember that he bet twenty postage stamps on the Giants beating the Cowboys by seven points," Alexander said.

"Really?"

"I guarantee it my, man. It takes practice, but the more you practice, the easier it will get."

"And what about Kwame's bet?"

"Just visualize your own scene that represents the panthers feasting on the eagles. The more outlandish the better," Alexander said.

Buff shook his head slowly and imagined his own scene. He saw fifteen black panthers wearing golden collars with the number forty dangling from the collars. The panthers leaped from bunk nine, and devoured Kembo, who owed him money from a foolish bet. He smiled at the vision and settled his eyes on the television.

Alexander heard a voice bursting from the officer's radio, "Code Yellow in the cafeteria. Code Yellow in the cafeteria."

The dorm officer took off running towards the chow hall while Alexander watched, feeling his heart rate increasing quickly. He looked at Buff, and saw him calmly watching television, as if nothing was happening at all.

EMILY MERCHANT SPENT the day with her students at the North Carolina Museum of Natural Sciences. She was feeling better than she had in weeks, but as the day waged on, fatigue set in.

Emily's students stood in a semicircle, gazing up in awe of the Tyrannosaurus Rex. They marveled at the creature's massive jaws and sharp teeth. Feeling dizzy, Emily peered across the room at an empty bench. As she staggered across the floor to sit down, James, one of her students, took the opportunity to creep across the velvet rope.

James had intended to reach out and touch the foot of the prehistoric creature. As he prepared to stretch out his fingers, Emily called his name, "James, get over here."

He heard her and froze, not knowing if he should leisurely step back or run away.

"Get over here now, James," Emily warned.

James Michael moped over to where Emily was standing.

As he approached, Emily pointed to the bench. "Sit down and do not move," she said.

James did as he was told, and sat beside Emily. He looked up at her with pitiful eyes. "I wasn't going to touch it," James said.

Emily waved her hand and James fell silent.

Soon Emily and the chaperones gathered all the children together and escorted them down to the parking lot. The children gathered into several vehicles provided by the chaperoning parents. Emily checked to ensure all the children were wearing their seatbelts. Satisfied, she climbed into her car, fastened her seatbelt, and started the engine.

As she drove the children back to the academy, her mind wandered. She thought about how difficult it was becoming for her to climb out of bed each morning and face her day, and how she often did not have the energy to check the children's homework, and how on a few occasions, she did not assign any homework at all just because she did not want to have to grade it later. She wondered if she was doing her children a disservice and if the time was coming for her to step aside.

The sound of a police siren brought her back. She looked in her rearview mirror and saw blue flashing lights. She checked her speedometer and saw that she was driving four miles over the speed limit. *I know he is not pulling me over for this*, she thought. She saw a gas station and drove her car into the parking lot and stopped. Emily rolled down the window and waited.

The officer pulled in behind her. He climbed out of his vehicle and made his approach. The officer looked into the vehicle and observed the children before speaking.

"Ma'am, do you know why I pulled you over?"

"I was only doing four miles over," Emily said.

"That isn't why I pulled you over," he said.

"Then why?"

"One of your passengers is not wearing his seatbelt."

Emily turned to the three children sitting in her backseat. She saw James Michael not wearing his seatbelt. "Did you remove your seat belt?"

James did not answer.

She turned back to the officer. "Sir, I assure you that I made sure they were all wearing their seatbelts before we left the museum. He must have removed it while I was driving."

"Are these your children?" the officer asked.

"No, sir. I'm their teacher. We were on a field trip."

"What school?"

"Upward Bound Christian Academy."

"Wait here," the officer said. He went back to his vehicle and climbed in.

"James, why did you remove your seatbelt?"

James looked at her with wide eyes. His mouth opened, but nothing came out.

"Answer me," she ordered, but he said nothing. Exasperated, she turned around and gripped the steering wheel, and rested her head against it.

The officer tapped on the window, and she looked up at him. He held a pink sheet of paper in his hand. "I am sorry ma'am, but I have to give you a ticket. You cannot drive children around without their seatbelts on."

At that moment, a motorcycle pulled into the gas station and slowly rolled past Emily's vehicle. Emily saw a small child sitting on the back of the motorcycle with his arms wrapped around the man driving the motorcycle.

The police officer followed Emily's eyes and gazed at the motorcycle. He turned back around to face her. "That is not against the law," he said halfheartedly.

"Are you serious?" she said.

The officer shrugged.

"Just give me the ticket, please," she said. Emily took the pink slip of paper from his hand, rolled up her window, and drove away.

When Emily arrived at home, she checked her mailbox and was delighted to find a letter from Alexander awaiting her. She plopped onto the couch and began to read.

```
Hello Mom,


    I hope this letter finds you in good spir-
its. I have good news and bad news. Which one
would you like first? Smile. The bad news is,
I was unable to keep my job after all. Ms.
McDowell was willing to keep me on, but the
education supervisor would not allow it. Now
for the good news: first, I have started
school, and I will have my GED before I come
home. Second, Mr. Murphy is recommending me
```

for a job as a teacher's assistant. Any recommendation from him will be followed swiftly, so I am sure it will only be a matter of time before I start. I am not sure what my responsibilities will entail, but I will fill you in as soon as I find out.

As Emily read Alexander's letter, she heard a lawn mower start up in her yard. She turned to look out of the window and saw Orlando cutting her grass. She set the letter down on the coffee table and arose to open the door. "Hi, Orlando," she said, and waved.

Orlando threw one hand in the air while pushing the lawn mower with the other.

Emily went into the kitchen, washed her hands, and grabbed four lemons ripening in the window-seal. She rolled the lemons under the palm of her hands until they were soft. She filled a pot with water, poured a cup of sugar into it, and placed it on the stove. As the water heated, she shaved some lemon zest into the pot, before cutting the lemons open and squeezing the juice into a pitcher. She leaned against the counter and watched tiny bubbles form at the bottom of the pot.

She heard the lawn mower on the side of the house and in the back yard. When the pot began to boil, she filled the pitcher with ice, placed a strainer over the pitcher, and poured the liquid syrup into it. She stirred the fresh lemonade rapidly and placed the pitcher into the freezer.

When Orlando finished cutting the grass, he placed the lawn mower back in the shed, and knocked on the back door.

"Hi, Orlando. Come on in," Emily said.

Orlando entered and embraced her. "How are you feeling?" he asked.

Emily shook her head and sighed. "I started out feeling

really good today, but as the day waned on, I went from bad to worse," she said, and handed him a glass of lemonade. "Fresh off the press."

Orlando drank it down and smiled. "You make the best lemonade."

Emily leaned on the kitchen counter and folded her arms.

Orlando refilled his glass and drank some more.

"Thanks for cutting the grass. It's a big help."

"Don't worry about it. It's the least I could do," he said.

"I think I'll need to stop working soon. It takes too much out of me and everyday it's getting harder to get out of bed."

"If that's what it takes to get better, then do it."

"I am not getting any better, Orlando."

"Sure, you are. It's been prophesied, and God doesn't break his promises."

"If God was going to heal me, he would have done it by now. Otherwise, what would be the point of all this?" she said.

"Emily, don't talk like that. You cannot lose your faith. God will heal you; I know it."

"Just promise me that when I'm gone, you will look after Alexander, please," she requested. Tears filled her eyes and streamed down her face.

Orlando wrapped his arms around her small frame. "Of course, I will Emily, you know that."

Emily looked up at him. "Thank you, Orlando. Thanks for everything," she said.

Orlando looked down at her. Even in her illness, she was beautiful. He sighed and turned towards the door.

CHAPTER

TWENTY

Alexander reported to the education department on Monday morning. He waited in the holding cell for Officer Carmichael to retrieve him. "Good morning, Officer Carmichael," Alexander said.

"Morning."

"I'm supposed to start work today."

"I know," Officer Carmichael said.

"What am I supposed to do?"

"I don't really know. Check in with Ms. Perez."

Alexander proceeded to her office and knocked on the door.

"Come in, Merchant," she said.

"Today is my first day of work, but I'm not quite sure what I should be doing," Alexander said.

"Neither am I. The program was not designed for students. I don't know how you can work on your own GED and help other students at the same time, but if that's what Mr. Murphy wants, then so be it."

Alexander kept quiet.

"Just report to your regular classes for now, and do whatever your teachers need," Ms. Perez said.

Alexander reported to his math class and found Mr. Purdic sitting at his desk. "Good morning, Mr. Purdic," Alexander said.

Mr. Purdic handed Alexander a sheet of paper, without looking up at him. "Write these equations on the board," he said. The sheet of paper contained five algebraic equations, which Alexander copied onto the blackboard.

"I'm finished, sir."

"Have a seat."

The morning bell rang, and Alexander sat at his desk. Soon the room was filled with students who would rather be somewhere else—anywhere else.

Mr. Purdic explained the equations on the board. "Does anyone have any questions?" he asked. When no one answered, he handed Alexander a stack of worksheets. "Pass these out, please," he said.

Alexander passed out the assignments and sat at his desk. He quickly completed his own worksheet and turned it in.

Killer B. raised his hand.

"Yes, Mr. Rasnick?" Mr. Purdic said.

"I don't get number two," Killer B. said.

"I got it, sir," Alexander said, and went to Killer B.

"What up, A-Rod?"

"What up, B?"

They slapped five and Alexander sat beside him.

"What the fuck he send you over here for?"

"It's my job, man. I'm the teacher's assistant."

"How the fuck you get that?"

"Man, I don't know. These lazy bastards don't want to do anything," Alexander said.

"Sweet gig though, son," Killer B. said, holding out a closed fist.

"Yeah, I guess."

They bumped their fists together.

Alexander saw that Mr. Purdic was watching him from his desk. "All right, man. What do you need help with?"

"This one here," he said.

Alexander looked over his work. "Okay. Remember when multiplying, two negatives equal a positive. Therefore, negative three-x times negative nine-x will equal a positive twenty-seven-x. Now subtract seventeen-x from that, and you will have your answer," Alexander suggested.

"Right. Appreciate that, homey."

"Not a problem."

They slapped five, and Killer B. pulled him in close. "Let me get five stamps on Miami tonight," he said.

"Got it," Alexander said.

Later that evening, Alexander sat on the recreation yard watching inmates do their best to entertain themselves. Some played basketball, some were exercising and lifting weights, some strolled around the perimeter, and others stood in groups. Alexander attempted to recall the names of everyone. He studied the faces of the inmates whose names escaped him and made learning their names a top priority. Beats and Chi-Town went around collecting bets. They recorded the bets on sheets of paper and delivered them to Alexander. Alexander studied the bets and committed them to memory. He tore up the sheets of paper and discarded them in the trash can.

Buff strutted out onto the recreation yard and sat next to Alexander. They slapped five but didn't speak. They just sat there in silence, both watching the dynamics of the yard. An inmate they didn't recognize was coming toward them.

"What's up?" he said.

Buff and Alexander nodded their heads in unison.

"Are you A-Rod?"

"Who's asking?" Alexander responded.

"I'm Meth," he said. He held out his hand and Alexander slapped five and locked fingers with him.

"What you want, cuz?" Buff asked.

"Put me down for ten on the Knicks tonight," Meth said.

"I got you," Alexander said before Meth turned away.

"You ever seen that dude before?" Buff asked.

"Nope. First time," Alexander said.

"Then how the fuck you gon' remember his bet without writing it down?" Buff asked.

"Oh, I'll never forget his bet, and neither will you."

Buff looked dubious.

Alexander snapped his fingers and rapped, "*Cash rules everything around me, cream gets the money, dollar dollar bills y'all,*" he smiled. "Have you ever heard that before?"

"Of course."

"And who sings it?"

"Wu-Tang," Buff answered.

"Exactly. Now what you don't know about Meth over there is that Method Man is his uncle," Alexander said.

"You're shitting me," Buff said.

"Yes, I am, but from now on, every time you see him, what song will you hear in your head?"

"C.R.E.A.M," Buff answered.

"Sung by who?"

"Wu-Tang."

"And who is Meth's Uncle?"

"Method Man."

Alexander smiled. "Now how can you ever forget that his name is Meth?" Alexander commented.

Buff laughed. "Okay, I see it now. But what of his bet?"

"Well, that's the easy part. Meth bet ten stamps on the New York Knicks, and Wu-Tang is from New York, right?" Alexander said.

Buff nodded.

"Now, do you remember how many members were in the original Wu-Tang?"

"Ten," Buff said.

"Ten stamps on the New York Knicks," Alexander said.

"That's good," Buff said, shaking his head. "That's good."

Alexander sat alone in Mr. Purdic's class grading tests. The other teachers used him sparingly, mostly for manual duties, such as reorganizing spaces, taking inventory of office supplies, and cataloging library books. Mr. Purdic, however, utilized him like a university teacher's assistant. He graded papers, tutored his fellow students, and on one occasion, to Alexander's great surprise, Mr. Purdic allowed him to teach the class lesson on long division.

Alexander stood before the class nervously, without knowing where to start. He went over to Mr. Purdic's desk and quietly voiced his trepidation, "Are you sure about this, sir? What if I teach them incorrectly?"

Mr. Purdic smiled. "Mr. Merchant, you have not gotten a single equation wrong since you've arrived here. I doubt you will start today."

"But I've never taught a class before," he said.

"Math is math, Mr. Merchant. It's either right or it's wrong. There is no in-between. Just work out the equations on the blackboard, verbalize the process, and if you say anything wrong, I'll stop you. Okay?" Mr. Purdic instructed.

Alexander felt more at ease, so he turned his back to the class and talked his way through the first equation. He answered a few questions and continued. He soon settled in, and teaching mathematical equations felt as natural as the morning dew.

"That wasn't so bad, was it?" Mr. Purdic said.

"No, sir. I enjoyed it very much."

"Good. You know Mr. Merchant, my college mentor had been to prison, before working his way into academia. He's the reason I chose to work in a prison, rather than public schools."

"How did he accomplish that?"

"He acquired multiple degrees and wrote a few books. He had to kick his way through the door, but he did get in," Mr. Purdic said.

Alexander nodded his head and thought about it as he graded tests. He wondered about the opportunities he would have when he got out of prison. What doors could he kick through himself? What barriers could he expect to face, and how should he start planning for those barriers today?

Ms. Perez stepped into the room. "Mr. Merchant."

"Yes, ma'am?"

"You have a visitor."

"Today is not a visitation day," Alexander said.

"It's a special visit," she said.

"But I have to finish grading these tests."

"Don't worry about the tests. Go on to your visit. I'll tell Mr. Purdic you needed to step away," she said softly.

Alexander noticed Ms. Perez was not her regular forbidding self. She seemed more pleasant and sympathetic and it gave him an uneasy feeling.

Alexander entered the visiting room and found Orlando sitting alone. "Hi, Mr. Connerly," Alexander said.

"Hey, buddy," Orlando said.

They embraced and sat at a square table.

"How are you doing?" Orlando asked.

"I'm fine, but why are you here?"

Orlando lowered his head and looked away.

Alexander felt short of breath. "Just spit it out," Alexander said.

Orlando gathered himself before he spoke, "It's your mother Alexander—she passed away last night," he said.

And before the words finished escaping Orlando's mouth, tears burst from Alexander's eyes, landing on the table, and splashing onto Orlando's hand.

Orlando reached for his hand, but Alexander pulled away and stood. He immediately felt dizzy and stumbled backwards, crashing into the table behind him.

Orlando rushed to wrap his arms around him and steadied him on his feet.

"You need to separate," the officer said.

"Just give us a minute," Orlando pleaded.

Alexander collapsed in Orlando's arms as he cried uncontrollably. All the pain and suffering he had managed to bury away since being sentenced, forced itself to the top, and waves upon waves of emotions poured out of him, rendering him helpless.

"Thanks for everything, Mr. Connerly. I have to go," Alexander said.

They embraced each other again.

"You call me anytime you want," Orlando said.

"I will, thank you." He turned to Officer Evans. "I'm ready, C.O."

Officer Evans stood from his chair. "Stand by the door," he said.

Alexander moved to the back of the room and waited.

"You can come with me, sir," Officer Evans said to Orlando. They stood by the front door.

Officer Evans spoke into his radio, "Visitation to control, pop door five."

The sound of the hydraulic locks clicking open filled the room. Once Orlando left the secured room, Officer Evans met Alexander in the back. He spoke into his radio, "Door six, control." The door opened, and he and Alexander entered a rectangular-shaped room.

Alexander backed up against the wall, removed his shoes, and handed them to Officer Evans for inspection. He removed his socks, his pants, and his shirt.

Officer Evans examined each article of clothing carefully. "Your drawers," he said.

Alexander removed his underwear and handed them over.

Officer Evans stepped in closer.

"Raise your arms," he said. Evans inspected Alexander's armpits, looking for any contraband he may have tried to conceal. "Spread your fingers, open your mouth, raise your tongue." He inspected his mouth, and without finding anything suspicious, he stepped back. "Lower your head, and run your fingers through your hair vigorously, now pull your earlobes forward," he said.

Alexander did what he was told.

"Turn around, raise your feet, wiggle your toes. Bend over, spread your butt cheeks, cough," he said.

Alexander coughed.

"Get dressed," Officer Evans said.

Alexander dressed as quickly as he could, but as he clothed himself, the tears came back, flowing down his face in streams, and mucus clogged his throat and nostrils.

Officer Evans pursed his lips, and spoke into his radio, visitation to control, door eight." He turned to Alexander. "Do you need a minute?"

"No," Alexander said.

"I know you're hurting young man, but you need to get

yourself together before you go out on that compound. In fact, you need to go and see the chaplain."

"I don't want to see the chaplain—I'm going to my dorm," Alexander said.

"Get your ass upstairs and see the chaplain," Officer Evans ordered. He spoke into his radio, "Evans, to the chapel."

"Go for the chapel."

"I am sending one to you," Officer Evans announced.

"Copy."

Alexander entered the chapel and sat, staring blankly at the pulpit.

Chaplain Donahue sat beside him but the two didn't speak, they just sat at the altar in silence.

"What brings you here, Mr. Merchant?" the chaplain said, finally breaking the silence.

"My mother passed away last night."

"I'm so sorry to hear that."

Alexander's eyes stayed fixed on the altar.

"How do you feel?"

"I suppose I feel the way most people would after losing a mother. I wouldn't expect you to understand."

"Oh, but I do understand. I know firsthand how it feels to lose a mother. I lost mine six years ago," Chaplain Donahue said.

Alexander didn't respond.

"It was the worst pain I have ever felt," Chaplain Donahue added.

"How long did it take you to get over it?"

"One never gets over the loss of a mother, Mr. Merchant, but it gets easier."

Alexander let out a loud sigh.

"Let us pray," Chaplain Donahue said.

"Pray for what?"

"For strength, for courage, for understanding."

"I mean no disrespect, Chaplain, really, but I have been praying my whole life, and where has it gotten me? Where did it get my mother?"

"Oh, Mr. Merchant, your faith is being tested and with good reason. But now is not the time to give in to doubt. Now is the time to be even stronger in your faith, even more resolute. God will never give you more than you can bare."

Alexander turned to face him. "Are you saying all of this is a test?" he said loudly. "I'm in prison for a test? My mother is dead because of a test?"

"No, Mr. Merchant, that's not what I mean," Chaplain Donahue said.

"Well, if this is a test, I have failed, okay," he said, standing to his feet. "I've failed." He turned and staggered to the door.

"I'm praying for you, Mr. Merchant."

"Do what you like," Alexander said, as he left.

ALEXANDER FOUND Case Manager Cunningham sitting in his office, and watched as he motioned him in.

"Have a seat, Mr. Merchant," he said.

Alexander sat across from him.

"I'm sorry for your loss, Mr. Merchant," he said.

Alexander nodded and looked away.

"Is there something I can help you with?" Mr. Cunningham asked.

"I would like to make a request to go to my mother's funeral."

Mr. Cunningham pressed his lips together and sighed. "Mr. Merchant, only the warden can approve a furlough, but I have to tell you that as a medium security inmate, it will be difficult to get it approved," he said.

"Why? It's a legitimate request."

"Yes, but D.O.C. policy only allows for low security inmates to go on furloughs, and medium security inmates are left to the warden's discretion. And this warden has not approved any furlough requests to attend a funeral since I've been here. That being said, I would be happy to make the request on your behalf, but approval is highly unlikely," Mr. Cunningham offered.

"I understand, but please make the request anyway."

"Okay, I'll send it up today."

"Thank you, sir." Alexander stood and went to his dorm to lay down across his bed, where he would remain for 26 hours.

On the following afternoon, he was awakened by Mr. Cunningham. "Merchant."

"Yes, sir?"

"Did you not hear me calling you over the intercom?"

"No sir, I didn't." Alexander rubbed his eyes and sat up.

Mr. Cunningham handed him a sheet of paper. "The warden's response to your request."

Alexander took the sheet of paper and sat up.

"Again, I'm sorry for your loss," Mr. Cunningham said.

Alexander wiped his eyes and unfolded the sheet of paper. The letter read:

Dear Mr. Merchant,

This is in response to your Inmate Request to staff, in which you request a furlough to attend funeral services for your mother, Emily Merchant. An investigation into your request reveals that you are currently serving a 24-to-36-month sentence for Indecent Liberties with a Child. Additionally, you are a Medium-security level inmate with In custody. Per Department of Corrections policy on Furloughs, the warden may grant a furlough only to an inmate with community custody and only an emergency furlough for an inmate with more than two years remaining until the inmate's anticipated release date. While we empathize with your situation, your request for an emergency furlough is denied as you are a medium-security inmate and you do not have community custody.

To assist you during this time of bereavement, you may contact Religious Services regarding the process of receiving and reviewing a video/DVD of your mother's funeral services. Also, your case manager will provide you with additional phone calls for you to maintain family ties during this difficult time. I trust this addresses your concerns.

George Murphy, Warden.

AFTER THE CRUSHING blow of not being able to see Emily being laid to rest, the days and weeks to come all blended together like fields of wheat for Alexander. Each stem indistinguishable from the next. Besides going to education and chow, Alexander mostly lay in bed sleeping, reading, or staring into space.

Buff sat in front of the television, side-eyeing Alexander. He leaned over to Chi-Town. "Go get his ass out of bed."

Chi-Town made his way over to Alexander.

"What up, bro?"

"What's up, man?" Alexander responded.

"Buff wants you downstairs."

"For what?"

"No reason. He just doesn't want you lying around all damn day."

"I'm good, man."

"He doesn't care if you're good. Look man, I know you are hurting right now, but lying around like this makes you look weak, and this ain't the place to be looking weak. So, get your bitch-ass downstairs," Chi-Town said.

Alexander made his way downstairs and parked in front of the television near Buff and Beats. Beats sat listening to music with folded arms and staring at the floor.

"You good bro?" Buff asked.

"Yeah, I'm good," Alexander said.

Beats handed Alexander one of his ear buds. Alexander popped it into his ear and heard Tupac Shakur blazing from the tiny speaker.

"I reminisce on the stress I caused, it was hell
Huggin' on my mama from a jail cell.
And who'd think in elementary, hey
I'd see the penitentiary, one day?
...I wish I could take the pain away
If you could make it through the night, there's a brighter day
Everything will be alright if you hold on
It's a struggle every day, you gotta roll on
And there's no way I can pay you back, but my plan
Is to show you that I understand; you are appreciated"

TWENTY-ONE

Alexander and Buff sat in the recreation yard when Alexander noticed Buff fidgeting and breathing hard. "What's up with you?" Alexander asked.

"My man on the street and half my squad got locked up yesterday. Our numbers are down enough as it is. You know what I'm saying?"

"What happened?" Alexander asked.

"I'm not sure, but it was some sort of sting operation. They sold some weight to multiple undercovers throughout the day from what I heard, and eventually the cops rolled in from every direction. There was nothing they could do," Buff said.

"So, they were just standing on the street selling drugs to strangers?"

"Yeah."

"And I suppose you're worried that some rival crew will push your boys out and take over?"

"That's what I would do."

Alexander turned away and shook his head. "Look man, I'm not trying to tell you how to run your business, but it seems to me like they were asking for it. I mean, I wouldn't run an operation like that. Not that I would ever do that sort of work anyway, but if I did, I would operate much differently."

"How so?" Buff inquired.

"Well, for starters, I wouldn't be standing on any street corner waiting to get popped by the police or some rival gang. You need to transition to a courier service and do business with a higher clientele. You know people use drugs in North Raleigh too, but you don't ever see the police kicking down their doors, do you? So, those are the people you need to do business with. They can call or text you their orders, and you deliver the product right to their doorsteps," Alexander said.

"There's more money to be made on the streets," Buff said.

"What does it matter how much money you make if you're in prison or constantly fighting to maintain your territory? It may be more profitable in the short term, but in the long run, you're better off flying underneath the radar. In addition, you shouldn't have anyone working for you who fits the profile of a drug dealer or gangbanger. You need people that no one would suspect to be involved in such an enterprise. You need someone who looks like a privileged college student. Someone who doesn't look out of place in upper-class neighborhoods," Alexander advised.

"I can't do anything about that. Your crew is what it is, and you have to roll with who you have at any given time, because at the end of the day, those are the guys who have my back. Not some yuppie who's only in the game to rebel against his rich parents," Buff said.

"I get that, but your current operation is obviously not working, so you need to figure out a new strategy," Alexander offered.

Buff nodded his head and stared out onto the field.

An inmate stepped onto the recreation yard, surveying the

area, and stood with his back against the wall. His eyes fell on Alexander, and a fleeting smile appeared on his face and disappeared. He made his way over to where Alexander was sitting.

"What up, A-Rod?" he said.

Buff placed his hand on the inmate's chest and stopped him. "Yo, back up, man," Buff ordered.

The inmate slapped Buff's hand away. "Get off me, man," he said.

Buff clinched his fist and drew back to strike him.

Alexander grabbed ahold of Buff's arm. "No, hold up. This is my boy, Tip from Morganton," Alexander said, slapping five with Tony and embracing him. "What's up, man?" Alexander said.

"I'm good, man. I'm good," Tony said, cheerfully.

"Tip, this is my man, Buff," Alexander said.

"Oh, you're Buff. I heard about you," Tony said.

"What did you hear about me?"

"Just that you were the man here, and I should look you up," Tony said.

Buff eyed Tony incredulously. "Yo, who you roll with, man?" Buff asked.

Tony lifted his shirt sleeve and showed Buff his shoulder tattoo.

"Oh, my man," Buff said smiling.

He and Tony slapped five and embraced.

"Where you sleeping?" Buff asked.

"I'm in Dorm Two," Tony said.

"Okay, I'm gonna need a man over there soon. Holla at Red. He'll get you set up, a'ight?" Buff said.

"A'ight, bet," Tony said.

"How's C?" Alexander asked.

"He's good. We got caught up in some shit after you left.

We had to put it on these motherfuckers, and afterwards, they sent me here. They locked up C in seg until his release."

"It wasn't those same guys we got into it with before I left, was it?" Alexander asked.

"Nah, man. They didn't want any more after you broke that motherfucker's jaw," Tony said.

"Who broke someone's jaw? This motherfucker," Buff said, pointing at Alexander.

"Hell, yeah. That motherfucker is still eating through a straw," Tony said, laughing.

Alexander felt embarrassed.

Buff looked at Alexander and wondered.

"I have to get to work, bro. It's good to see you." Alexander shoved his hands into his pockets and headed toward the door.

"Work? At this time of day?"

He stopped and turned back. "Yes, I tutor at study hall this evening. We have GED testing in three weeks," Alexander said.

"Okay," Tony said.

Alexander and Tony slapped five and embraced before Alexander left for work.

At study hall, Alexander found himself distracted. He thought about all he had seen and experienced since coming to prison. He could feel himself changing, and not for the better. Things that would have shocked and terrified him a short time ago, now felt normal. The stench of prison was no longer noticeable, witnessing violence was a normal occurrence, and he was no more affected by the sight of blood and blunt force trauma than an emergency room nurse. He thought about Tony's arrival. He wasn't sure if Tony's presence was a blessing or an omen, but he was glad to have another ally, nonetheless.

Alexander left work and ambled leisurely across the compound. He was lost in thought and overwhelmed with sadness. Graduation was quickly approaching and the person who had been his biggest supporter and cheerleader, and who had never missed any of his life events, would not be there. He missed Emily tremendously, and not even Lake Superior could fill the void left by her demise.

He entered his dormitory and lay across his bed. He reached for Toni Morrison's *Song of Solomon* and opened the book to where he had stopped reading earlier. He took in a few paragraphs before slamming the book shut and stuffing it back into his locker. He found it too difficult to concentrate, and Morrison's writing required concentration. He lay on his back and stared at the ceiling. Melancholia enveloped him, pressing down on his chest and suffocating him. He saw the ceiling fan rotating slowly. He grimaced as he struggled to move his arms and legs, which were held motionless by a shadowy figure above. Beads of sweat formed on his face, arms, and his chest. He tried to scream for help, but nothing came out. His jaws were held shut by this shadowy figure, who sucked the air from his chest. In his mind, he cried out to God for help. *The blood of Jesus. The blood of Jesus. The blood of Jesus,* he prayed.

"Hey man, wake up," Beats said, shaking his arm.

Alexander sat up and gasped for air.

"What the fuck, man? What, were you having a nightmare?"

"Yes, I guess I was. I think a witch was riding my back," Alexander said, breathing heavily. He settled himself and swallowed hard.

"Come on down, man. Buff needs you," Beats said.

Alexander gathered himself and went down to where Buff was sitting in front of the television.

"Hey, Buff. What's going on?" Alexander said.

"What's up, man?" Buff replied.

"Did you need to see me?"

"You see that motherfucker up there in the bathroom?"

Alexander saw Reese shaving in front of the bathroom mirror.

"Yes," Alexander said.

"That motherfucker needs to pay up. Go up there and get my money," Buff said.

Alexander climbed the stairs and entered the bathroom. "Hey Reese, how are you?" Alexander asked.

"What's up, A-Rod?" Reese said.

"I just came to see if you had the money to cover your bet," Alexander said.

"Nah, I ain't got it," Reese said, turning back to the mirror, and continuing to shave.

Alexander sighed. "Look man, it's been three weeks since you lost, and now you need to pay your debts," Alexander said.

Reese sat his razor down and pressed his nose against Alexander's. "Look motherfucker, I said I ain't got it. Now get the fuck out of my face."

"Chill out, man," Alexander said, placing his hand on Reese's chest to create separation.

Reese slapped Alexander's hand away and shoved him.

Alexander shoved him back.

Chi-Town noticed the confrontation and started towards the stairs, but Buff held him back.

"Hold up. Let's see how he handles it," Buff said.

Reese clenched his fist and punched Alexander above his left eye. He lowered his shoulder and drove it into Alexander's stomach, driving him backwards. Alexander wrapped his arms around Reese's torso and used his momentum to toss him against the wall. Reese hit the wall and crashed to the floor. Reese sprung to his feet and rushed towards Alexander. He threw a left punch and missed, and Alexander backed away. He threw a right punch, and Alexander ducked and smashed his right fist into Reese's jaw. Reese's legs went limp, and he collapsed on the floor. He lay on his back and looked up at three Alexanders where there had been only one.

Alexander stood over him with clenched fists. "Give me the fucking money," he screamed.

Reese reached into his pocket and handed Alexander two books of postage stamps.

Alexander snatched the postage stamps from his hand and stormed out of the bathroom.

Buff sat watching as Alexander dropped the postage stamps into his lap.

Alexander stomped over to his bunk and sat and stared blankly for a moment. Finally, Alexander closed his eyes and prayed between clenched teeth, "Father God, in the name of Jesus, please get me out of this place. Get me out of here before it is too late. Please, Lord."

CHAPTER
TWENTY-TWO

Alexander and his fellow graduates marched into the visitation room and sat along the wall. Alexander studied the visitors for familiar faces, but he found none. He had almost expected to see Emily sitting in the audience. She would have arrived early and sat in the front row near the center, but she wasn't there. The only person who had come to witness Alexander's achievement was Tony, who sat in the back of the room near the door. Alexander sighed.

Principal Harding approached the podium. "Good morning," she said.

"Good morning," the audience responded.

"On behalf of our administrator, Mr. Murphy, assistant administrators, Ms. Favors and Mr. Young, education supervisor, Ms. Perez, and all our staff, I would like to welcome you all to our commencement ceremony here at Rolesville Correctional Institution." She waited for the applause to end before she continued.

"I am Mrs. Harding, the Principal of Education here at

Rolesville Correctional Institution, and it is my great pleasure to welcome you all here today to celebrate the achievement of our graduating class. I have worked as an educator for well over twenty years, and out of all the commencement ceremonies I have participated in throughout my career, today's ceremony is extra special. Now why do I say this?" She smiled. "I say it because this year has presented us with a unique set of challenges, and to be honest, at the beginning of this academic year, we were not sure how many of our graduating class would be with us today," she said, laughing. "But despite that, they worked hard, and they persevered. They attended study hall in record numbers, and supported and encouraged each other every step of the way. And due to their hard work and their determination to succeed, I am immensely proud to report that one hundred percent of our General Education Diploma candidates are graduating today," she said excitedly.

The staff of Rolesville Correctional Center stood and applauded loudly. The audience followed suit and cheered on the graduating class. Ms. Harding stood behind the podium, smiling broadly. The graduating class clapped and nodded their heads with appreciation.

Kevin Williams held out his hand to Alexander and they slapped five.

Alexander placed his hand on Paul Owens' shoulder and shook it affectionately.

Ms. Harding turned to face the audience. "If we are to take anything away from today's achievement, it should be this," she paused and surveyed the crowd for dramatic effect. Satisfied that she had everyone's attention, she continued, "I believe with every fiber of my being that with hard work and determination, there is nothing these young men cannot achieve. No goal is too high, and no dream is too big if they focus their minds and work hard for it," she said.

This statement brought another round of applause and congratulatory handshakes from the graduating class, but Alexander was annoyed. He crossed his arms, leaned back in his chair and stared at Ms. Harding with disdain. *How dare you?* he thought. *How dare you sell us false hopes, when you know everything you just said is a lie. No one is lining up to give us decent jobs or decent places to live, because whenever they look at us, they will always, first and foremost, see a felon. I will never work for the State Department, and I will never be an ambassador for the United States. Of course, I will fight like hell to carve out some decent life for myself and some measure of success, but my original goals are forever lost to me, and I don't appreciate you selling us your fantasies,* he thought.

Alexander tuned out the rest of Ms. Harding's speech. He tuned out the rest of the entire ceremony. He heard no part of the chaplain's prayer. Nor did he hear any part of the Rolesville Correctional Institution choir's performance. He only heard murmurs as he sat staring blankly at the floor.

"Hey, man," Kevin Williams said, nudging Alexander's leg. "Hey."

"What?"

"Your speech."

"My what?"

"She's calling you for your valedictorian speech," Kevin Williams urged.

Alexander saw Ms. Perez motioning him towards the podium. "Oh, thanks," Alexander said, and went to the podium, removed his speech from his pocket, and unfolded it in front of him. He looked at the audience and swallowed hard.

"Good morning," he said.

"Good morning," the audience responded.

"To friends, family, faculty and staff," he paused and took in several deep breaths.

"It's okay, young man," a woman in the audience said.

Alexander gathered himself and started over. "To friends, family, faculty, and staff, we are thankful you are here to witness this monumental occasion," Alexander said. He paused again and looked out into the audience. He looked at the seat where Emily would have certainly occupied if she had been present. He imagined she was sitting there witnessing his accomplishment. The elderly woman who was sitting in Emily's place returned his gaze. She pleasantly nodded her head in encouragement. Alexander crumbled his speech into a tight ball, and with his best impersonation of Michael Jordan's jump shot, he tossed the crumpled speech across the room and into a trash can. He heard a few gasps from the audience. He returned their gaze and swallowed hard. He readjusted the microphone and gathered himself before speaking again.

"I want to start by congratulating my classmates on their accomplishment today—as well as my own. Although, I must admit when I arrived at this institution, I had no intention of obtaining my GED. I simply did not see the value in it. I did not understand how obtaining my General Education Diploma from prison would help me to obtain the goals I had set for myself before coming to this godforsaken place. However, my mother, Emily Merchant, encouraged me to do so. She made me promise to not leave here without it. So, I did it for her. My mother was my first teacher. Teaching was her profession. In fact, it was her first love.

My mother is not here today. She would have been here if she could, but after a long battle with cancer, she has left the suffering of this earth, and has moved on to a greater place. A place where there is no suffering. A place where she could be with the Lord. So, Mom, I hope you are happy. I hope that I have made you proud, and I hope one day, I will see you again.

Thank you," Alexander said, and stepped down and went back to his seat.

As the ceremony ended, Alexander slowly made his way to the exit. Along the way, he received words of encouragement and random pats on his back. The elderly woman who sat in the front row, wrapped her arms around Alexander and held him for a moment.

"You are going to be okay, son. You are going to be fine," she said.

Alexander's throat tightened. He swallowed hard and respectfully thanked her for her encouragement.

Tony stood waiting by the door. "Congratulations, bro," he said.

"Thanks, man," Alexander said.

"Let's roll," Tony said.

They dashed across the compound to their dorms.

"Meet me on the rec yard near the handball court in ten minutes. I have something for you," Tony said.

"All right," Alexander said, and entered his dorm and went to his bunk. He removed his shirt and placed it in his locker. He pulled a white T-shirt over his head and strolled out onto the recreation yard. He made his way over to the handball court and sat on the grass, leaning against the wall. Some inmates were playing kickball on the softball field. Alexander looked up and watched the clouds moving across the blue sky. He focused on a cloud shaped like a medieval knight. It reminded him of *King Arthur and The Knights of the Round Table*—a book he had first read in the third grade. He read it three more times over the years. It was one of his all-time favorite stories.

A kickball slammed against the wall just above Alexander's head, taking him away from a pleasant memory. He ducked down, raising his arms over his head.

"What's up now, motherfucker?" Reese said.

Alexander focused his eyes and saw Reese and two other inmates standing in front of him. The three inmates spread out on three sides.

Alexander stood and backed up against the wall. Reese and his henchmen closed in on him, and Alexander raised his fists and prepared for battle.

Tony and Buff trotted over, and Tony shoved Reese backwards. "What y'all want, motherfuckers? What y'all want?" Tony said.

Reese and his henchmen backed away. Reese pointed to Alexander. "You better watch your back, motherfucker," he said.

"Get your bitch asses outta here," Buff said.

"Thanks, fellas," Alexander said.

"Man, fuck them bitches," Tony said.

"Yo, you good, bro?" Buff asked.

"Yeah, I'm good," Alexander said.

"He's still mad 'cause you beat his ass," Buff said, laughing.

Alexander laughed too.

They slapped five and sat on the grass. Tony reached in his pocket and pulled out a marijuana cigarette. He lit the joint and filled his lungs with smoke. He closed his eyes and leaned back against the wall. He inhaled again and passed the joint to Buff.

Buff filled his lungs with smoke and held it for a few seconds before blowing the smoke out of his nostrils. He inhaled again and formed his mouth into a circle, blowing the smoke out in a series of rings.

Buff attempted to pass the joint to Alexander, but Alexander refused.

"No thank you, bro. I don't smoke," Alexander said.

"What?" Buff said.

"I don't smoke."

"You mean ever?" Tony asked.

"No, I have never tried it. I've never had the interest."

"Take a puff, man. It ain't gon' kill you," Buff said.

"We're in prison, bro. What other fucking means of celebration do we have?" Tony said.

Alexander took the joint in his hand and looked it over.

Buff nudged him with his elbow. "Come on, man. It's gonna go out," he said.

Alexander placed the joint in his mouth and pulled the smoke into his lungs. He grimaced and coughed as if he had pneumonia.

Tony and Buff laughed.

Alexander attempted to pass it over to Tony.

"Nah man, hit it again," Tony advised.

"It is not doing anything for me," Alexander said.

"Hit it again," Tony repeated.

"Alexander brought the joint back to his lips and inhaled again. "Whoa," Alexander said, as he felt his torso and arms going numb, and a cloud of haziness rushed to his head.

"Yeah, that's it," Tony said, nodding.

Tony and Buff laughed hysterically. Tony took the joint from Alexander and inhaled again.

Alexander laughed, too. "Where did you get this from?"

"I have a connect," Tony said.

"Who is it?" Alexander asked.

"Don't worry about all that, bro," Tony said.

"Come on. Tell me, Tip," Alexander said.

"Chill, man. Just enjoy it," Tony said.

Tony and Buff laughed again.

"All right. You never cease to amaze me, brother," Alexander said.

Tony wrapped his arm around Alexander's shoulder. "Congratulations, man. I guess I'll go ahead and get mine, too. You're gonna help me, right?" Tony said.

"Anything you need, my man," Alexander said, and laughed with Tony and Buff.

CHAPTER
TWENTY-THREE

With graduation behind him, Alexander occupied himself by cataloging library books, reorganizing storage closets, and purging materials left over from the graduating class. As his work slowed, he took on custodial duties, such as cleaning windows, taking inventory of damaged furniture and equipment, and spot-painting walls. He intended to stay as busy as he could. School was out, inmates were bored, and the summer's heat made the dormitories feel like an inferno. The sweltering heat had everyone on edge. Inmates were easily agitated and were lashing out at each other with increasing frequency and Alexander wanted no part of it, so he removed himself from the cesspool of anger, helplessness, and despair.

Back in his dormitory, Alexander sat on his bunk and waited to be counted.

When the count cleared, Case Manager Cunningham entered the dormitory. "Town hall meeting, gentlemen. Town hall meeting," he announced.

The inmates gathered around him and waited unenthusiastically for Case Manager Cunningham to speak. When everyone was in place, Cunningham held up a sheet of paper for everyone to see. "This memorandum regarding the new policy on postage stamps, will be posted on the bulletin board shortly. Read it and familiarize yourselves with it."

"What's in it?" Beats asked.

"Basically, postage stamps will no longer be sold at commissary. Starting on the first of the month, you will drop your letters in the mailbox without postage stamps. When your letters are processed at the institutional post office, they will weigh it and the appropriate amount of postage will be applied to your letters, and the cost of postage will be deducted from your account," Cunningham said.

He stepped over to the bulletin board and fastened the memorandum to it with four staples and listened to the inmates groan and complain, as he expected. He ignored their discontent and made his way back to the door, leaving their complaints behind.

The new policy had an immediate impact on Buff's gambling business. Inmates no longer had a currency they could use to wage their bets, and over the next few weeks, Buff's business had slowed to a trickle.

Alexander passed a joint to Tony while watching Buff slam a basketball onto the ground as hard as he could, bouncing it high into the air.

"These motherfuckers are fucking with my money," Buff said.

Tony passed the joint to Buff. "Chill out, man," he said.

"What the fuck you mean, chill out? We 'bout to be broke, man." Buff pulled on the joint and passed it to Alexander.

Alexander filled his lungs with marijuana smoke and blew

it out slowly. "There may be a way around this problem," he offered.

"Yeah, what's that?" Buff said.

"We can no longer barter and trade with stamps, at least not at the volume we were used to. Therefore, we need to figure out a way to allow people to continue placing bets and making good on those bets when they lose. We should tell people to have their family and friends deposit what they owe in our accounts," Alexander suggested.

"How the fuck are we gonna pay them when they win? And how am I gonna pay all of you?" Buff asked.

"We have to figure that part out," Alexander said.

"That many deposits going into your account would raise red flags," Tony said.

"True." Alexander considered their questions. "Is there anyone on the street whom you could trust to hold the money for you? Those who owe us could have their family make payments to someone on the street and that person could disburse money into the accounts of those who win, and then disburse money to our accounts, too," Alexander said.

"Ain't nobody going through all that shit for no damn gambling slips," Buff said. He filled his lungs with smoke and focused his eyes on the smoldering joint. "But you might be on to something, bro... But not for that nickel and dime shit, though. Tip, how good is this connect of yours? Is it reliable?" Buff asked.

"Yeah, it's good," Tony said.

"It's time we expand into a new business—cigarettes and weed," Buff said.

Alexander felt sick. He felt the weight of despair pressing down on his shoulders. He raised his knees to his chest and gazed at the ground, sighing deeply.

A few weeks later, Buff and all his crew sat at a table in the cafeteria.

"All right, listen up. Our new operation starts next week. You'll bring your orders to A-Rod like you did before. A-Rod will bring those orders to me at the end of each day. I'll get word to my man on the street to expect payments. My man will let me know when the payments have been made. I will relay that information to A-Rod, and he will let you know when it's okay to deliver the product."

They all nodded in agreement.

Alexander looked pensive, sucking in a long breath of air.

"What, man?" Buff asked Alexander.

"I don't know about this, man. Gambling is one thing, but I'm not a drug dealer. We could get into serious trouble for this, and I'm not comfortable with that," Alexander said.

"Motherfucker, I didn't ask you what you was comfortable with. This is what we doing now, you heard?" Buff said.

Alexander sat quietly.

"Don't make me ask you again, motherfucker. You heard me or not?"

"Yes, I heard you," Alexander said.

"All right, our first shipment comes in this weekend. Ain't that right, Tip?" Buff asked.

Tony nodded and said, "Yeah, that's right."

"All right. Everybody's good?" Buff asked.

"We good," they all responded.

Buff stood and emptied his tray and the crew followed.

ALEXANDER STOOD IN THE LIBRARY, organizing books and magazines.

"What's good, A-Rod?" Moe said.

"I'm good, brother. How are you?" Alexander said.

"I'm real good, bro. I'm going home next week," Moe said.

"Congratulations, brother."

"The first thing I'm gonna do is go to my girl's house, and I ain't leaving 'til I'm satisfied. You feel me?" Moe said.

"Yeah, I feel you," Alexander said.

They slapped five and laughed.

"What are you doing up here?" Alexander asked.

"Buff sent me. He said I needed to talk to you."

Alexander looked away and sighed.

"What's going on with you?" Moe asked.

"Do you know what he's doing?" Alexander asked.

"Yeah, I heard about it."

"I can't do it. I could never sell drugs," Alexander said.

"You also can't be in here on your own. If you're not aligned with anyone, you won't make it outta here in one piece."

"I know it's dangerous, but I just can't do it, Moe. That's not me."

"Look bro, I'm not tryna tell you what to do, but after next week, I won't be here to look out for you no more. Buff may be all you got—you feel me?"

"Yes, I know…" Alexander said, "I know."

Alexander trudged on with his duties. He gritted his teeth in anger when he came across a magazine lying on top of a water fountain. *Freaking heathens,* he thought. He grabbed the magazine and sat at a table to wipe it dry. The magazine fell open to a story about a theology school dropout turned chef in Crown Heights, Brooklyn, where the menu is comprised of Caribbean recipes he learned while growing up in St. Vincent and the Grenadines. The descriptions and photos of high-lighted menu items made his mouth water. He committed the address to memory, 355 Rogers Avenue, and added it to his list of places to visit. He wondered if Howard had been there. He had not spoken to Howard in several months and wondered how New York City was treating him. He decided to pen him a letter. He wrote:

Hello Howard,

I pray you are doing well, and I hope NYU is all you dreamed it would be. I must come up for a visit when I get out of here. I am well, considering my circumstances, and in five months, this long nightmare will be over. How are you getting along up there? Have you settled on a major? Have you been to Broadway or Yankee Stadium? I know you must be incredibly busy with your studies and all, but whenever you visit any of those places, please take pictures and send them to me. I am still living vicariously through you, buddy. Please, give Allyson my love, and I hope to hear back from you soon.

P.S. I know I said I am doing well, but that is not entirely true. I am currently facing an incredible dilemma, and I don't quite know what to do.

Please understand, Howard, that it is not simply a matter of choosing between right and wrong. I wish it were that simple. The fact of the matter is, you would be shocked by the decisions we must make on a daily basis. I can feel myself changing and not for the better. Sometimes when I look in the mirror,

I don't recognize the person staring back at
me. That is what prison does to you, Howard.
It assaults your humanity. It attacks your
soul.

Sincerely,
Alexander

TWENTY-FOUR

lexander and Chi-Town were standing guard outside of the shower while Buff and Beats bathed themselves when Poo arrived with a towel draped over his shoulder.

Chi-Town held up his hand and stopped him. "Yo, hold up, man. You gotta come back later," he said.

Poo peered into the shower stall. Seeing Buff, he turned away without protest.

"Can I ask you something?" Chi-Town said to Alexander. "What reason did they give you for not letting you go to your mother's funeral?"

"They claimed my custody level was too high, but they wouldn't have allowed it no matter what my custody level was," Alexander said.

"Why is that?"

"Funeral furloughs are up to the warden's discretion, and this warden has not approved any funeral request since he's been here."

"Seriously?"

"Yup. Essentially, they will always find a reason to say no," Alexander said.

Chi-Town looked pensive.

"Why do you ask? Is someone not doing well?" Alexander asked.

"My grandmother is under hospice care. I don't know how long she has left, and I was hoping to go to the funeral, but it seems there would be no point of asking," Chi-Town said.

"Ask anyway. Make them look you in the eye and say no. Make sure they feel what fucking assholes they are," Alexander said.

Buff and Beats exited the shower.

"You can go in. I'll keep watch for you," Chi-Town said.

"Thanks. I'll be quick," Alexander said.

Alexander quickly covered himself in lather. As he washed his feet, he grasped the handrail to steady himself. The handrail shook in his hand and plaster fell to the floor. *They still haven't fixed this,* he thought. Alexander's mind was racing. The shipment of marijuana and cigarettes had come in as planned. Buff had set the price at $5 per cigarette, $100 per nickel bag of marijuana, and $200 per dime bag. Ten days had passed before they sold their first cigarette. Cigarette sales slowly increased over the next few weeks, but they had not sold any marijuana. The cloud of despair was beginning to lift, and Alexander wondered if they would eventually move on from the foolish venture. The consequences for possession of tobacco would pale in comparison to what they would face if found in the possession of marijuana.

He rinsed away the soap and exited the shower. He dressed himself and moseyed over to the door. He waved his hand at Officer Williams, who stood on the other side of the plexiglas.

Officer Williams came to the door and looked at the officer

sitting in the control room. The control room officer unlocked the door, and Officer Williams pulled it open.

"Yes," she said.

"Good morning, Ms. Williams. Will you please put in another work request for the handrail in the shower? They still haven't fixed it," Alexander said.

"There's no need to put in another one. They'll get to it eventually," Officer Williams said.

"It's been three months since I first reported it. Maybe they've forgotten about it," Alexander said.

"They didn't." She closed the door in his face.

Alexander shook his head disappointedly. He sat in front of the television and awaited breakfast. The morning news was predictably depressing. It consisted of weather predictions, traffic accidents and a home invasion in Cary, North Carolina.

Officer Williams opened the door and yelled, "Chow time. Line up."

The inmates lined up and trooped over to the cafeteria.

Alexander looked over his breakfast and sighed. His eggs were again overcooked, and his grits again were like soup. He ate his toast and pushed his tray away.

Chi-Town sat beside him. "I got an order for you. Fame wants two dimes. His boy is gonna drop the deposit tomorrow," Chi-Town said.

Alexander nodded.

Officer Martin pointed to their table. "Let's go," he said.

Alexander emptied his tray and left the cafeteria. He trudged up the stairs towards educational services. Each step felt like he was treading in mud, and a throbbing pain settled above his left eye. He held his left eye closed and gritted his teeth. The migraine swelled and pushed against his skull. He entered Mr. Purdic's class and sat with his hands covering his face.

"Is everything all right, Merchant?" Mr. Purdic asked.

"Yes, I'll be fine," Alexander said.

Mr. Purdic dropped a stack of quizzes on Alexander's desk. "Grade these," he said, and then stepped over to the blackboard and began his lecture on multiplying mixed numbers.

Later, Alexander pushed a squeaky cart through the library, returning books to the shelves. He noticed Beats standing in an aisle thumbing through a magazine. The library was not a place where Alexander expected to ever find Beats. He knew he was there for a reason. "What's up, man?" Alexander asked him.

"I'm good, man." Beats moved his lips close to Alexander's ear. "Quick wants a dime bag today."

"Not until he pays," Alexander whispered.

"He already did," Beats said.

"I'll check with Buff, and if the money is there, you can deliver it tonight," Alexander said. He pushed the cart to another aisle. As he moved through the stacks, the migraine headache returned, and he felt his heart pounding in his chest. *Enough of this shit,* he thought. He found Ms. Perez sitting in her office chatting on the phone. He waited outside of her office until she ended the call.

"Come in, Merchant," she said.

"Ma'am, I'm not feeling well today. Do you mind if I take off a little early?" he requested.

Ms. Perez looked at the clock and rubbed her chin. "I suppose so. Will you be back tomorrow?" she asked.

"Yes, ma'am. I will."

"Okay. I'll see you in the morning," she said.

Alexander went back to his dorm and lay down across his bed. He sat up for a while and lay back down. He sat up again and placed his hands underneath his thighs. The dorm was mostly empty, with mostly everyone outside on the recreation yard. Alexander went to the door and knocked on the plexi-glass window.

The officer opened the door. "You going to rec?" he asked.

"Yes, sir." Alexander found Buff sitting on a bench.

"What up?" Buff said.

Alexander sat beside him. "Did you get a payment today?"

"Yeah, two hundred," Buff said.

"That's from Quick for a dime," Alexander said.

"A'ight, go on and break 'em off," Buff said.

Alexander caught Beats' eyes and nodded his head. He turned back to Buff. "You should also have four hundred dollars deposited tomorrow from Fame. He wants two dimes," Alexander said.

Buff rubbed his hands together and nodded.

"One more thing," Alexander said.

"What's that?" Buff replied.

Alexander measured his words and swallowed hard. "I'm out after today. This isn't for me," Alexander said.

"What the fuck you mean, this isn't for you?" Buff said.

"I told you before that I'm not a drug dealer. Anything else that you need is fine, but not this," Alexander said.

Buff pressed his lips together and nodded. "That's cool," Buff said, and grabbed ahold of Alexander's arm, pulling him in close. "But I tell you what, motherfucker, you're on your own. I don't wanna see or hear from your bitch ass again or I'mma stomp your fucking teeth out, you heard me?" He shoved Alexander backwards.

Alexander stumbled and fell to the ground but quickly stood and brushed himself off.

Everyone stopped what they were doing and stared at the spectacle.

"Now get the fuck outta here," Buff ordered.

Alexander went back into his dorm and sat alone.

On the following day, Alexander skipped breakfast and reported directly to educational services where Mr. Purdic had him lead the class lecture on dividing and multiplying fractions. After concluding his lecture, Alexander graded homework and quizzes. He decided to work through lunch, staying behind to organize a bulletin board and rearrange a bookshelf. He removed all the books, wiped the shelves clean, and replaced the books in their proper order. He removed trash and dried bubblegum from the desks and wiped them clean.

Mr. Purdic sat watching Alexander and wondered why he was working so hard. "Are you wrapping up, Merchant? It's almost time for recall," he said.

Alexander looked at his watch and sighed. "Yes sir, I'm finishing up," Alexander said.

"Is everything okay?"

"Yes. Everything is fine," Alexander said.

Alexander returned to his dorm and sat on his bed until the evening meal was called. He was starving and skipping dinner was not an option. He went to the cafeteria where the slow-moving lines snaked out of the door. He eventually received his tray and sat at the table for inmates who were not affiliated with any group.

Tony looked at Alexander as he passed by holding his tray.

Alexander returned his gaze and nodded his head, but Tony did not acknowledge him, proceeding by and sitting next to Buff.

Over the next few weeks, Alexander stayed to himself. He only had three months until release and wanted to stay under the radar as much as possible. He spent his days working at educational services, offering evening tutoring classes a few days per week—anything to stay away from the dormitory. Weekends were dreadful because there was nothing for inmates to do but stay in the dormitories or go out on the recreation yard. He devoured every available genre of litera-ture, including books on history, biographies, classic novels, and detective dramas for an escape. He even read the occasional romance novel, which he found to be surprisingly popular among the inmates. He only watched television when no one else was using it, and he only watched it from afar, careful to not give the impression that he was attempting to control it.

Cabin fever was setting in and Alexander felt restless. Books were no longer holding his interest, and he thought a little physical activity would do him well. He stood by the dormitory door and waited for the officer to come and open it.

"What do you want?" the officer asked.

"I'm going to rec." Alexander strolled over to the soccer field, hoping to join a game, but to his dismay, the soccer field was empty. He, instead, sat on a bench near the softball field where two teams were involved in a game.

In the bottom of the third inning, Pimpie trotted over to Alexander. "What's up, A-Rod. I got a visit. You wanna take my place?"

"Sure," Alexander said, taking Pimpie's glove and trotting out onto left field.

Red stood on the pitcher's mound waiting for Alexander to take position. When he was in place, Red turned around and stared down the batter for a moment before winding up for his next pitch. With an underhanded toss, the ball arched upward before dropping down towards the batter's knees.

Coozie hit the ball high into left field.

Alexander ran towards the infield, trying to get under the ball, but realizing he had misjudged it. He stopped and peddled backwards, but it was too late. The ball sailed over his head and rolled towards the fence. He ran it down and threw it to third base, holding the runner at second.

The next batter grounded out to first. The next batter again hit the ball deep into left field. Alexander stood still, watching the ball's trajectory. He trotted forward, but the ball dropped in front of him. The runner advanced to third.

Red raised both arms in frustration. "What the fuck, man?" he said.

"My bad," Alexander said, embarrassed.

"They're hitting to you on purpose," Red said.

"All right," Alexander said.

The next batter followed suit, hitting a line drive into left field. The ball landed a few feet in front of Alexander, and the runner took off towards home. Alexander scooped up the ball and threw a bullet to home plate. The ball sailed over the shortstop's and pitcher's outstretched arms, and flew directly into the back catcher's glove, who caught the ball and tagged the runner out.

"Yes," screamed Red, with a clenched fist, as the team ran off the field.

Rizzo hit a fly ball into right field, which was easily fielded by the first baseman. Dizzy hit a ground ball to third and was thrown out at first.

"Two down, one to go," Birmingham said.

"Let's go," Nino said, clapping his hands.

Red stepped into the batter's box and settled into his stance. The pitch hung high, and Red hit it into center field. He ran to first base and stopped.

"Let's go, A-Rod. Bring him home," Dizzy said.

Alexander took the first two pitches. The first was a ball, and the second was called a strike. Alexander didn't like the call, but he didn't protest. He waited on the pitch he wanted, and when it came, he hit it hard into right field. The ball sailed over Birmingham's head and rolled towards the fence.

Candy ran behind it. The ball bounced off the fence post

and rolled awkwardly into the corner. Alexander rounded second and looked back towards right field. He saw Candy bending over to pick up the ball, and Dizzy running towards third base, waving him home.

Alexander rounded third as the first baseman waited on the ball to reach his glove. He caught the ball and with one fluid motion, he turned towards home plate, and threw a bullet to the back catcher. The ball sailed high, and the back catcher leaped off home plate and stretched his glove high into the air. He caught the ball and stretched his arm down towards Alexander who was sliding headfirst underneath.

Alexander's hand tagged home plate a split second before he felt the back catcher's glove striking his back.

"Yeah, that's game," Red said, clapping his hands.

"Fuck that. He was out, wasn't he?" Birmingham said to the catcher.

The back catcher shrugged and stepped away. "Tell 'em, man. You tagged him out," Birmingham shouted.

"Nah, he was safe," the catcher said.

"Come on, man," Birmingham said, throwing up his hands in disbelief.

"Game over, bro," Red said.

Alexander and his team stood in a circle slapping fives. "Line up," Alexander instructed.

The teams formed two lines and shook hands.

"Where's the brew?" Birmingham inquired.

"A-Rod, come with me," Red said, as he trotted over to the bathroom. "Keep watch for me," Red said.

Alexander stood outside the bathroom door. Red went into the bathroom and climbed onto the toilet. He slid a ceiling tile to the side and reached his hand on top of the fluorescent light, where a bag of homemade wine was fermenting. He pulled the orange hooch from the ceiling and replaced the ceiling tile.

"Grab some ice," he said to Alexander.

Alexander trotted over to the ice machine and filled a bag with ice. He returned to the field where both teams sat around holding Styrofoam cups.

Alexander sniffed his brew and grimaced. It smelled awful, but he chugged it down anyway.

Red immediately grabbed Alexander's cup and refilled it.

"Thanks, bro."

"You earned it, A-Rod. You can't play defense worth a damn, but you can hit. I'll give you that," Red said.

"Well, we don't use designated hitters, so your ass better learn how to catch," Dizzy said.

Alexander laughed.

"We'll get y'all back tomorrow," Birmingham quipped.

"What time?" Alexander asked.

"After chow," Red said.

"All right. I'll be here," Alexander said, as he stood.

"Five-O," Birmingham announced.

The group hid their cups from view.

"Hi, Ms. Thompson," Alexander said.

"Hey, Merchant," Officer Thompson said, as she passed by.

"Damn, she fine," Dizzy said, gazing at her small waist and thick thighs.

"Yes, she is," Alexander agreed.

"You know your boy smashin' her right?" Birmingham whispered.

"Who?" Alexander asked.

"That light-skinned motherfucker," Birmingham answered.

"Tip?" Alexander asked.

"Yup."

"How do you know that?"

"She comes around after hours and takes him somewhere

to clean," Birmingham said, with *clean* in air quotes. "But it's always someplace where no one else is around. What do think is going on?" he asked, with a raised brow.

"Interesting," Alexander said, rubbing his chin. *So she's the connect,* he thought. He smiled and shook his head. "I'm heading inside. Good game, fellas," he said. He slapped five with everyone and went to his dorm. He was feeling good. It was the best he had felt in weeks. *That was just what I needed,* he thought.

Alexander removed his sweaty clothes and trotted into the shower and turned on the water. He placed the palms of his hands against the wall and let the hot water run on his head and down his body. He placed a small bar of soap in the palm of his hand and rubbed it against his skin until a thick lather formed on his brown torso.

Reese, Skinny, and Jigga stealthily moved towards the shower. Reese stopped and looked towards Buff to see if he would object. When he caught Buff's eye, he nudged his head towards the shower. Buff shrugged his shoulders and turned towards the television. Reese and his two henchmen continued, entering the shower and seized upon Alexander without warning.

Reese wrapped his arms around Alexander's waist, and Skinny and Jigga grabbed ahold of both of his arms and stretched them outward, and then their punches rained down on Alexander from all sides.

Alexander screamed for help, but no one came. A blow to the back of his head made him dizzy, and Jigga forced his head down towards the floor. Alexander felt Reese's penis pushing inside of him. He struggled to break away, but the more he struggled, the more kicks and punches fell upon him. He felt blows slamming against his head, his neck, his back, and his kidneys. He felt Reese thrusting himself in and out of his body in rapid succession. Tears flowed down his face as he continued to cry out for help. Reese continued thrusting his hips until he relieved himself.

"I told you, bitch," Reese said.

"My turn," Skinny said.

Reese took control of one of Alexander's arms, as Skinny moved behind him and lowered his trousers, when Reese lost his grip on Alexander's arm, Alexander quickly grabbed ahold of Jigga's scrotum and sank his teeth into his hand.

Jigga screamed out in agony and released his hold.

Alexander took Jigga's penis in his other hand, and with all the strength he could muster, he twisted and pulled his penis and scrotum in opposite directions, trying to sever both organs from Jigga's body.

Reese and Skinny rained punches down on Alexander, but he wouldn't let go. He continued to pull and twist until Jigga collapsed on the floor, convulsing. Skinny kicked Alexander and knocked him against the wall.

Alexander grabbed ahold of the handrail and tried to steady himself, but it shook in his hand and plaster fell to the floor. The handrail still had not been repaired. Seeing this, Alexander grabbed the handrail with both hands and ripped it from the wall. He swung the metal bar hard into Skinny's jaw. The blow shattered the left side of his face and sent his teeth flying across the room. Alexander drove the metal bar into Reese's stomach. As Reese keeled over, Alexander swung the bar against his shoulder, knocking Reese to his knees. Alexander raised the metal bar high above his head and brought it down hard on the back of Reese's neck. The blow crushed his vertebrae, and he collapsed on the floor, motionless.

Alexander stood over his three assailants breathing hard.

Blood and a mixture of body fluids trickled down Alexander's leg.

Officer Mason ran into the bathroom and drove his shoulder into the small of Alexander's back. They collapsed on the floor and Officer Mason cuffed Alexander's hands behind his back. Additional staff arrived and secured the scene.

"Get him outta here," Sergeant Cooper said.

Officer Mason pushed Alexander out of the bathroom and down the stairs.

Buff, Chi-Town, and Beats stood, watching wide-eyed—their mouths gaping.

Alexander looked into Buff's eyes and silently mouthed, "I'm gonna kill you."

Alexander was taken to the special housing unit and placed in a holding cell.

Officer Mason handed Alexander a set of clothes. "Put these on," he said.

Alexander dressed himself and sat with his back against the wall.

An hour or so later, Officer Mason returned and opened the trapdoor. "Come on."

Alexander stood and went to the door.

"Turn around and cuff up," Officer Mason instructed.

Alexander turned his back to the door and reached his hands back through the trapdoor.

Officer Mason placed handcuffs on Alexander's wrists and held his arm as he spoke into his radio, "Open door H-one, control."

The door slid open, and Alexander backed out.

"This way." Officer Mason escorted Alexander down the corridor and spoke into his radio, "B-Pod, control."

The door to B-Pod slid open, and he took Alexander to his cell. "B-one-eighteen, control."

The cell door slid open, and Alexander stepped inside. The door closed behind him before Officer Mason removed his handcuffs and closed the trapdoor. Alexander sat on the bed and stared blankly at the wall.

Hours later, the trapdoor swung open, and Officer Jones called Alexander to the door. "Merchant. Merchant," he called.

Alexander didn't move. He was still sitting in the same position.

Officer Jones tapped his baton on the door. "Merchant," he yelled.

Alexander looked up.

"Come on," Officer Jones yelled.

Alexander stood and stumbled to the door.

Officer Jones closed the handcuffs around his wrist and took him to the lieutenant's office.

Lieutenant Stroman sat behind a wooden desk. "Have a seat," he said.

Alexander sat across from him.

A notepad sat on Lieutenant Stroman's desk, and he held a ballpoint pen in his hand. He looked Alexander over before he spoke, "Do you care to tell me what happened?"

Alexander didn't speak.

"You really hurt those three boys bad, Merchant. I need you to tell me what happened," he said.

Alexander remained silent, looking through him as if he wasn't there.

"Look at this, dammit," Lieutenant Stroman yelled. He slid a picture of Reese's mangled body across his desk.

Alexander looked away.

Lieutenant Stroman rounded his desk and pressed his finger into Alexander's chest. "Look at what you did to him. That boy will never walk or wipe his own ass again," Lieutenant Stroman said.

"No," Alexander screamed. He stood and spun away from him.

Lieutenant Stroman grabbed Alexander and slammed him back down into the chair. "I'm gonna see to it that you are charged with attempted murder, and you will stay in prison for another twenty years, you animal."

"Fuck you," Alexander screamed. He tried to stand, but Lieutenant Stroman pressed his weight down on top of him. Multiple officers ran into the office and grabbed hold of Alexander. They dragged him down the hallway and placed him back into his cell.

Officer Ward removed his handcuffs and the officers tossed him across the room, the door slamming shut behind him.

Alexander stood and kicked the door. "Fuck you," he screamed. He kicked the door again, and again. "Fuck you. Fuck you," he screamed and kicked. The thunderous sound bounced off the concrete floors and cinder block walls filling the building.

Lieutenant Stroman trotted over to his cell. "Stop kicking my door, Merchant," he said.

"Fuck you," Alexander screamed. He kicked the door again and again.

Lieutenant Stroman opened the trapdoor. "Cuff up, Merchant," he said.

"No," Alexander screamed.

"Don't make me have to come in there, Merchant. Cuff the fuck up."

"No," Alexander screamed and kicked the door again.

"Suit up," Lieutenant Stroman yelled, pointing his finger towards the officers standing around him. Five officers trotted over to the supply room and suited up in riot gear. They wore stab-proof vest, elbow pads, knee pads, and helmets with face shields.

Officer Boyd, who was built like an NFL linebacker, held a large plastic shield. The other officers lined up behind him and marched to Alexander's cell. Officer Hunt followed closely carrying a video camera. The five-man team stacked up outside of Alexander's cell door.

"Last chance, Merchant. Cuff up."

"No," Alexander screamed, rolled up a sock and bit down on it.

The other inmates started kicking on their doors and flooding their toilets. Water ran down from the upper tiers.

Lieutenant Stroman grabbed his radio. "Pop the door, Control."

The door slid open, and the five-man team rushed into the cell.

Alexander lowered his shoulder and rushed towards the shield. The collision was heard throughout the pod.

The inmates cheered Alexander on. "Yeah, A-Rod."

"Fuck 'em up, A-Rod," they yelled.

Alexander pushed against the shield, but the five-man team was too much for him. They drove him back onto his bed.

Officer Boyd pressed the shield down on top of him. They cuffed his hands and feet, and carried him out to a holding cell where a large concrete block sat in the middle of the room. They laid him down on his back and placed him in four-point ambulatory restraints.

Alexander struggled, but there was no use. He lay there, spread-eagle like Da Vinci's Vitruvian Man. He closed his eyes and blacked out.

Warden Murphy arrived and made his way over to the cell. He looked in and saw Alexander lying there asleep and wondered how he had been so wrong about Alexander's character.

Captain McDowell arrived soon after.

Lieutenant Stroman filled them in on what had happened. "He won't speak to anyone," Lieutenant Stroman said.

"Where's your wife?" Warden Murphy said to Captain McDowell.

"She's home sleeping," Captain McDowell said.

"Doesn't she have a rapport with him?" Warden Murphy asked.

"Yes, sir."

"Well, get her down here," Warden Murphy said.

Captain McDowell went to an office and dialed his wife.

She answered the phone groggily.

"Hey baby, it's me. The warden wants you here, ASAP," he said.

"What's going on?"

"It's Merchant. He really fucked up three inmates earlier. He broke one of their necks with a pipe, and then acted out in seg. A team had to go in on him, and now he's in four-point restraints."

"Merchant did that?" she said, in disbelief.

"I know it's crazy, but now he won't speak to anyone. No one knows what the hell set him off. The Warden thinks he may speak to you," Captain McDowell said.

"Okay, I'm on the way," she said.

When Ms. McDowell arrived at the institution, she was briefed on the situation and reviewed photos of the inmates Alexander had harmed.

Captain McDowell sat across from her. "I didn't think he was capable of this sort of thing. He struggled a bit after losing his mother, but he seemed to be doing okay. I wonder what the hell happened. Has he said anything?" she asked.

"Not a word," Captain McDowell said.

"Where is he now?"

"In the conference room. He's ready for you," Warden Murphy said.

The McDowells followed the warden into the conference room where Alexander, still restrained, sat in a chair.

Warden Murphy and Captain McDowell stood on the wall behind Alexander, and Ms. McDowell sat across from the young man she had grown fond of.

"Merchant," she said.

Hearing Ms. McDowell's voice, Alexander looked up.

She returned his gaze with soft eyes. "Tell me what happened," she said.

Alexander shook his head and looked away.

"Come on, Merchant. Something must have happened to make you do what you did," she said.

Alexander's eyes turned glassy, and tears flowed down his face. "They were raping me, Ms. McDowell. I was in the shower, and they attacked me. They started beating me, and then they raped me. I had to get them off me—I had to." Alexander lowered his head and slumped his shoulders while a steady stream of tears flowed down his face. "I didn't mean to hurt..." his words trailed, and he sobbed uncontrollably. All the pain and suffering he felt burst out of him.

Ms. McDowell looked to Warden Murphy.

Warden Murphy turned to Lieutenant Stroman. "Did you do a rape kit?" he asked.

Lieutenant Stroman shrugged his shoulders. "We didn't know what had happened, sir," he said.

"Get him over to medical and have it done now," he barked, "And get those damn handcuffs off him."

"Yes, sir," Lieutenant Stroman said.

Officer Jones removed the handcuffs before Ms. McDowell helped Alexander to his feet. "Come on, son," she said, and helped escort him to health services where Nurse Rodriguez stood waiting.

Nurse Rodriguez took Alexander into an exam room. He removed his clothing and stood on a large sheet of butcher paper. She placed his clothes in plastic bags and sealed them. She swabbed around his rectum, genitals, lower back, upper thighs, and placed the swabs into plastic containers. She combed his body hair, scraped under his nails, and sealed the collected samples in a plastic box. She took photos of his injuries and uploaded them to a computer file.

Alexander sat quietly with red puffy eyes.

Nurse Rodriguez stepped out into the hallway where Warden Murphy, Captain McDowell, and Ms. McDowell stood waiting.

"What did you find?" Warden Murphy asked.

"It is hard to say, sir. At this point, much of the physical evidence is probably contaminated. However, he has abrasions and a slight rectal tear, which is consistent with anal sexual assault. He will require sutures to repair it and we'll start him on post-exposure prophylaxis to guard him against possible H.I.V. transmission," Nurse Rodriguez said.

Warden Murphy glared at Lieutenant Stroman.

The lieutenant averted his eyes. "Thank you, Ms. Rodriguez. Please, have your report on my desk before you leave."

"Yes sir, I will," she said.

Warden Murphy turned and stormed off.

Alexander was treated for his injuries and returned to his cell where he slept for 33 hours.

Officer Mason opened the trapdoor. "Merchant. Merchant, wake up."

Alexander sat up and rubbed his eyes.

"Cuff up," Officer Mason said.

Alexander stood and went to the door, turned and stuck his hands through the trap.

Officer Mason closed the cuffs around his wrists. "Open B-one-eighteen, control," he said.

The door slid open, and Alexander backed out of the cell.

Officer Mason went into his cell and collected his belongings.

"Where are you taking me?"

"You're moving to HCON," Officer Mason said.

"What's HCON?"

"Maximum control," Officer Mason said.

"Why am I going there?"

"I don't know."

"What do you know?" Alexander said.

"I'm just following orders, man. You can ask the lieutenant when you get there."

When Alexander arrived at the Highly Intensive Maximum Control Unit, he was placed in a holding cell.

Officer Ross stood at the door and looked him over. "Size thirty-four pants?" he asked.

"Yes, sir," Alexander agreed.

"What size shoes do you wear?"

"Eleven."

Officer Ross disappeared, later returning with a set of clothing. "Stand up," he demanded.

Alexander stood in the middle of the cell, and before officer Ross could speak, he removed his shirt and handed it to the officer. He removed his pants, his socks, and his underwear, handing them over, too. He ran his fingers through his hair, raised his arms above his head, opened his mouth and stuck out his tongue. He turned and raised his feet and wiggled his toes. He bent over and spread the cheeks of his buttocks and turned to face the officer.

Officer Ross never said a word and handed Alexander a new set of clothes and turned away from the door.

"Officer Ross, may I see the lieutenant, please?"

"I'll tell 'em," Officer Ross said over his shoulder.

Three officers returned to the cell.

"Turn around and cuff up," Officer Ross said, then closed a pair of handcuffs around Alexander's wrists.

The door opened and the officers pushed Alexander forward into the cell. They secured a black box over his cuffs, wrapped a Martin chain around his waist, and secured his handcuffs to the Martin chain.

Officer Cox kneeled behind him and closed a pair of leg irons around his ankles.

"Is all this necessary?" Alexander asked.

"It's policy. Everyone is treated the same," Officer Cox said.

An officer stood on both sides and held onto his arms. The third officer stood behind him holding his baton at the ready position.

"Let's go," Officer Cox said.

They marched Alexander down the corridor to his cell, where Lieutenant Harris stood waiting.

"You wanted to see me?" Lieutenant Harris said.

"Yes, sir. HCON is for your most dangerous inmates, so I don't understand why I'm here," Alexander said.

"It's for your own protection. After what you did, there may be a threat against your life. So, we need to keep you here until everything is sorted out," Lieutenant Harris said.

"How long will that take?"

"As long as necessary," the lieutenant said.

Alexander nodded.

"Is there anything else?"

"No, sir."

The officer removed the black box, the Martin chain, and

the leg irons. The cell door closed, and Officer Ross removed the handcuffs and closed the trapdoor.

Alexander looked around the five-by-ten cell. He saw a stainless-steel sink and toilet, a metal framed bed, a metal desk, a stainless-steel shower, and a small rectangular window. He stepped over to the window and looked out, seeing only the exterior wall of another range and the grass between them. He sighed and sat on the bed.

Over the next three days, Alexander mostly slept, stared at the ceiling, and slept some more. Meals were delivered to his cell three times a day. Most of his meals were inedible. He would pick out whatever he could stomach and send the rest back to the kitchen. On his third day in the Highly Intensive Maximum Control Unit, Alexander was sitting on his bed when he heard a tap on the door. He looked up and saw Ms. McDowell. He rushed to the door. "Hi, Ms. McDowell."

"Hey, Merchant. How are you doing?" she asked.

"I've been better," he said.

Ms. McDowell looked at him with soft eyes.

"How long do I have to stay in here?"

"We don't know yet. It depends on the outcome of the investigation, and if the district attorney decides to file charges against you."

"What could I be charged with?"

"Aggravated assault. Or worst-case scenario, maybe attempted manslaughter—but that's highly unlikely, especially if it happened the way you described."

Alexander felt lightheaded. He leaned against the door and steadied himself. "I was defending myself," he said.

"I believe you were. Again, it's highly unlikely you would be charged, but I want you to be prepared for what could happen," she said.

"Is he really paralyzed?"

"Yes, he is."

"To what extent?"

"From the neck down," she said.

"I didn't mean for that to happen," he said.

"I know," she mumbled. "You did what you had to do, but that's not necessarily how the D.A. will see it."

Alexander nodded.

"I'll keep you informed. Just keep your head up, okay?" she said.

"I will. Thank you." Alexander went back to the window, looking out at the grass below.

"Young man," a voice said.

Alexander turned and stepped back to the door, but he saw no one. "Young man, up here," the voice said again.

Alexander looked up at the vent above his desk. He stood on the desk and placed his ear to the vent. "Yes," Alexander answered.

"What's your name?" the voice said.

"A-Rod."

"No boy, what is your God-given name?" the voice said.

"Alexander Merchant," he said.

"It's good to meet you, Mr. Merchant. My name is Frank Mitchell."

"It's good to meet you, Mr. Mitchell."

"What are you doing in HCON?" Frank Mitchell asked.

"I was involved in a fight," Alexander said.

"It sounds like more than a fight to me. You hurt someone really bad, huh?" Frank Mitchell asked.

"Yes, I did, unfortunately."

"Did he have it coming?"

"Yes, he did."

"Did you have a choice in the matter?"

"No, I don't believe so," Alexander said.

"Then forget about it. Shit happens in prison. Making it home in one piece is all that matters, and you must make sure you walk out of here the way you walked in. You understand?" Frank Mitchell said.

"Yes, I understand."

"Good," Frank Mitchell said. The vent went silent.

TWENTY-FIVE

The sun dipped below the trees, and a heavy fog rolled over the hillside and covered the compound. The air in HCON was thick and murky, making it difficult for Alexander to breathe. He lay in bed holding his chest, and beads of sweat covered his body. He stood at the window drinking a cup of water. Peering out through the heavy fog, he could only see the distant glow of the area lights. He lied back down and tried to sleep. As he was drifting off, he heard frantic screaming, followed by a succession of thunderous kicking on the cell door from the man across the hall.

"Get me outta here. He's gonna kill me," the man screamed. Bang, bang, bang, he kicked and screamed.

Alexander climbed out of the bed and looked through the window across the hall. He saw Officer Fitch rush to the door.

"What's wrong with you?" Officer Fitch asked.

"He's trying to kill me," the inmate screamed.

"Who's trying to kill you?" the officer said.

"Him," the inmate said.

Alexander watched Officer Fitch peer through the glass window, looking around the dark cell.

"There's no one there," the officer said.

"Yes, he is," the inmate screamed. He pulled on the door handle and kicked some more.

"Stop kicking the damn door, Russell. You're gonna wake everyone up," the officer said.

The third shift lieutenant came to the cell. "What the hell is going on?" he said.

"He says someone is trying to kill him," Officer Fitch said.

"Who's trying to kill you?" the lieutenant said.

"Him," the inmate pointed. "He's gonna kill me, and it's gonna be your fault," the inmate screamed.

Lieutenant Swiney shook his head. "All right, we'll move you. Just quiet down," he said, turning to the officer. "Just put him in the holding cell until he cools down."

"Yes, sir."

Lieutenant Swiney spoke into his radio, "Officer Roberts, step over to cell one-thirteen," he said.

Officer Roberts arrived in time for Lieutenant Swiney to open the trapdoor. "Turn around and cuff up," he said. They restrained the inmate and took him to a holding cell.

"Thank God," Alexander said, and climbed back into bed.

"Mr. Merchant," Frank Mitchell said, through the vent.

"Yes," Alexander responded.

"That inmate has been here too long. He's losing his mind," Frank Mitchell said.

"Yes, I see," Alexander said.

"He wasn't always like that. He used to be a sharp fella, but he couldn't hold it together."

"How long has he been here?"

"A lot longer than I have, that's for sure. Do you have any books, Mr. Merchant?"

"No," Alexander said.

"Okay, I'll send you over something. You must keep your mind sharp. Read everything you can get your hands on, or you will end up like him. The mind isn't made for long-term solitary confinement. It needs stimulation, you understand?" Frank Mitchell said.

"I don't have that long—only have a few months left," Alexander said.

"How many months?"

"I'm not sure. I was down to three months before I got into trouble. I have a twenty-four-to-thirty-six month sentence, and now I wonder if I'll have to do the entire thirty-six."

"I've seen men lose their minds in less time than that. Read. Stay sharp."

"Yes, I will. Thanks," Alexander said.

ALEXANDER AWOKE AT DAWN. As he lay in bed thinking about his current circumstances. He could hear heavy breathing coming through his vent, so he climbed up on the desk and placed his ear to the vent. He could hear Frank Mitchell grunting and breathing hard. It sounded like he was in the middle of an intense workout.

"What's wrong, Mr. Merchant? Do you need anything?" Frank Mitchell asked.

"No, nothing is wrong," Alexander said.

"Are you sure?"

"Yes, all is well," Alexander said. He wondered how Frank knew he was there. He lay back down and went back to sleep. Forty-five minutes later, Alexander awoke to a knock on his door and the trapdoor opening.

"Chow time," the officer said, as she placed a tray on the trap.

Alexander stood and grabbed his tray. He ate the runny eggs, grits, and toast, and washed it down with the strongest coffee he had ever tasted. Just as he finished eating, the trapdoor opened, and he returned his tray.

Officer Porter handed Alexander a book. "It's from inmate Mitchell next door," she said.

"Thank you." He smiled for the first time in days.

She smiled back and closed the trapdoor.

So, Frank Mitchell is real, he thought. He held the book in his hands and read the title: *Long Walk to Freedom*, by Nelson Mandela. He lay across his bed and opened the book to chapter one. He read for several hours before stopping to shower. He dressed himself and climbed up on the desk.

"Mr. Mitchell," Alexander said, into the vent.

"Yes."

"Thank you for the book. It's fascinating."

"You're welcome, Mr. Merchant. Stay sharp, young brother."

"Yes sir, I will."

"Do you play checkers, Mr. Merchant?"

"No, not really. I know how to play, but I prefer chess," Alexander said.

"Even better. Hold on, I'm gonna send you a kite," Frank said.

"A what?"

"A kite."

"What's that?"

"Just hold on," Frank said.

Moments later, a homemade chessboard slid underneath Alexander's door.

"Did you get it?" Frank said.

"Yes."

"Detach the string." Alexander disconnected the string from the board and watched the string disappear underneath the door.

"How did you do that?"

"Many years of experience. Hold on, there's more to come," Frank said, before a stream of homemade chess pieces came sliding underneath Alexander's door. They were made of dried toilet paper and wax.

Where he had gotten the wax from, Alexander didn't know.

"Set up the board and call out your moves. Do you want black or white?" Frank asked.

"I'll take black."

"F-two to F-four," Frank said.

Alexander moved Frank's pawn to F-4.

"D-seven to D-five," Alexander said.

"G-one to F-three," Frank said, bringing out his knight.

"G-seven to F-six," Alexander said, also bringing out his knight.

"G-two to G-three."

"C-eight to G-four." Alexander moved his bishop deep into Frank's territory.

"F-one to G-two," Frank countered.

"B-one to C-three," Alexander said.

"Aggressive move," Frank murmured. "F-three to E-five," Frank said, moving his knight into Alexander's territory.

Alexander felt pressed. He moved the board to his desk and sat in front of it. After weighing his options, he retreated his bishop from G-4 to F-5.

Frank laughed and moved his pawn from C-2 to C-4.

"E-seven to E-six," Alexander said.

Frank brought out his other knight to C-3.

"F-eight to E-two."

Frank castled to G-1. Alexander castled to G-8.

"D-two to D-four."

"G-seven to G-six," Alexander said.

Frank Captured Alexander's pawn on D-5 and threatened Alexander's knight at C-6. Alexander captured Frank's pawn on D-5. Frank moved his pawn from E-2 to E-3, and Alexander moved his knight from F-6 to G-4. Frank moved his knight from E-5 to G-4, capturing Alexander's knight. Alexander was forced to retreat his bishop from F-5 to D-7. Frank captured Alexander's pawn on D-5 with his knight. Frank laughed again, which annoyed Alexander. He moved from H-7 to H-5.

"G-four to E-five," Frank said.

"C-six to E-five," Alexander countered, capturing Frank's knight.

Frank took Alexander's knight at E-5.

"E-seven to G-five," Alexander said.

"D-five to F-six, check," Frank said.

Alexander moved his king to H-8. Frank captured Alexander's pawn at H-5. Alexander took Frank's knight at H-5, falling for Frank's trap. Frank moved his queen from D-1 to H-5.

"Check," Frank said, laughing again.

Alexander moved his bishop to H-6, blocking Frank's queen.

Frank took his bishop. "Check," he said again.

Alexander moved his king to G-1.

Frank moved his bishop from G-2 to E-4.

"F-seven to F-five," Alexander said.

"E-four to D-five," Frank said.

"D-seven to E-six," Alexander said. He was feeling the pressure and desperately looking for a way out of this mess, but nothing presented itself—Frank was too good.

Frank took his bishop at E-6, forcing Alexander to move his

rook from F-1 to F-2. Then, Frank moved his rook from F-8 to F-5.

Alexander was under assault, so he moved his queen from D-8 to F-8.

Frank moved his rook to G-5. Alexander moved his queen from F-8 to G-7. Frank moved his queen from H-6 to G-7.

"Checkmate," Frank announced.

Alexander sat staring at the board and wondering where he got himself into trouble. It was the first match he had lost since coming to prison.

"Good game, Mr. Merchant. You played well, starting off strong, but you got rattled and started playing scared. That's what I took advantage of," Frank said.

"Yes, good game, Mr. Mitchell. I'll get you next time," Alexander said.

"Don't bet on it," Frank said.

"Let's go again," Alexander said.

They set up the boards and played another game, which Alexander again lost. After his third loss, he decided to take a break. His brain was hurting, and the losses were aggravating.

On the following day, Alexander and Frank played again, making it a part of their daily routine.

Alexander sat at his desk, reading *A Long Walk to Freedom*, and taking notes. The trapdoor opened, and an officer sat a tray of dinner and a drink there. Alexander stood and retrieved his dinner. He sat at the desk and removed the lid from the hot tray. Upon seeing what was on the tray, he slammed the lid back down and dropped it on the floor. He kicked the tray, sending it sliding across the room and slamming it against the cell door.

"Merchant, what's going on over there?" Frank asked, through the vent.

"This damn food. It's unbelievable," Alexander said.

"What is it?" Frank asked.

"It's the same thing you have," Alexander said.

"It's not what I have," Frank said, laughing.

"What do you have?"

"I have steamed broccoli, rice and a quarter leg of chicken," Frank said.

"How did you get that?"

"It's a kosher meal."

"Kosher? Are you Jewish?"

"Never ask a man about his religion, Mr. Merchant. Religion is the third rail of any conversation," he said, laughing.

"Seriously, Mr. Mitchell. How did you get it?"

"You must write a letter to the chaplain and tell him that you have been studying Judaism and you want to convert. He will send you a questionnaire. Fill it out and return it, and if you answer the questions correctly, he will add you to the kosher list. The kosher meals are prepared and packaged by an outside vendor," Frank said.

"I don't want to change my religion," Alexander said.

"Are you a Christian?"

"Yes, I am," Alexander said.

"Then don't worry. It's the same God. You'll be fine in the afterlife," Frank said laughing.

I can't go on eating like this, Alexander thought.

"You must take care of your body as well as your mind. Do you workout?" Frank asked.

"Yes, I do."

"What's your regiment?"

"I don't really have one. I just workout when I can."

"I workout six days a week. I do two thousand push-ups on Mondays and Thursdays, one thousand pull-ups and sit-ups on Tuesdays and Fridays, and one thousand squats and dips on Wednesdays and Saturdays. Eat and exercise like me, and by the time you get out of prison, you will look the way I do," Frank said.

"How do you look?"

"The way Adam did when God sculpted his body out of clay."

Alexander laughed.

"We start tomorrow morning at daybreak. Get some sleep," Frank said.

Alexander sat at his desk reading until the sunlight faded from his window. He flipped on his light and lay across his bed, reading until the words no longer made any sense and the book transformed into a pillow. As he lay there smiling at dreams he would not remember, he was awakened by inmate Russell's screaming across the hall,

"Stay your ass over there, motherfucker. Don't you move," he screamed. "Stay right there."

"Not again," Alexander said, rolling over on his side and placing his pillow over his ears.

"Get me outta here," inmate Russell screamed and kicked the door.

"Shut the fuck up," an inmate screamed from down the hall.

Inmate Russell kicked the door and screamed for help, but no help came.

Alexander tried to sleep through it, but there was no use. He sat against the wall and stared into the darkness.

When morning came, Alexander woke with heavy eyes.

"Mr. Merchant," Frank said.

Alexander didn't answer.

"Merchant, are you up?"

"Yes, I'm up," he said, groggily.

"Are you ready?"

"Ready for what?"

"How many push-ups can you do?" Frank asked.

"Shit," Alexander dropped his head, remembering he had agreed to exercise this morning. "I don't know, about fifty, I guess," he said.

"How many pull-ups?"

"Fifteen or twenty," Alexander said.

"Sit-ups?"

"Forty or fifty."

"Okay," Frank said.

Moments later, a piece of paper slid underneath Alexander's door. He disconnected the string and unfolded it.

Week 1

Monday:

10 sets of 10 wide arm push-ups.

10 sets of 10 medium wide push-ups.

10 sets of 10 close push-ups.

10 sets of inverted push-ups (feet on bed).

10 sets of 10 high inverted push-ups (feet on wall).

10 sets of 10 dips.

10 sets of 20 sit-ups.

Tuesday:

5 sets of 5 wide chin-ups.

5 sets of 5 medium chin-ups.

5 sets of 5 close chin-ups.

5 sets of 5 wide pull-ups.

5 sets of 5 medium pull-ups.

5 sets of 5 close pull-ups.

10 sets of 10 wide reverse push-ups.

10 sets of 10 medium reverse push-ups.

10 sets of 10 reverse sit-ups.

Run in place for 30 minutes.

Wednesday:

10 sets of 25 squats.

10 sets of 10 left leg split squats (right foot on chair).

10 sets of 10 right leg split squats (left foot on chair).

10 sets of 1-minute lunges.

10 sets of 20 side to side lunges.

10 sets of 10 side leg raises.

10 sets of 10 left leg step-ups.

10 sets of 10 right leg step-ups.

50 high knees.

10 sets of 10 calf raises.

10 sets of 10 jump knee tucks.

30 seconds of scissors.

30 seconds of flutter kicks.

10 seconds of reverse flutter kicks.

Thursday:

10 sets of 10 wide arm push-ups.

10 sets of 10 medium wide push-ups.

10 sets of 10 close push-ups.

10 sets of inverted push-ups (feet on bed).

10 sets of 10 high inverted push-ups (feet on wall).

10 sets of 10 dips.

10 sets of 20 sit-ups.

Friday:

5 sets of 5 wide chin-ups.

5 sets of 5 medium chin-ups.

5 sets of 5 close chin-ups.

5 sets of 5 wide pull-ups.

5 sets of 5 medium pull-ups.

5 sets of 5 close pull-ups.

10 sets of 10 wide reverse push-ups.

10 sets of 10 medium reverse push-ups.

10 sets of 10 reverse sit-ups.

30 seconds of scissors.

30 seconds of flutter kicks.

Run in place for 30 minutes.

Saturday:

10 sets of 10 wide arm push-ups.

10 sets of 10 medium wide push-ups.

10 sets of 10 close push-ups.

10 sets of inverted push-ups (feet on bed).

10 sets of 10 high inverted push-ups (feet on wall).

10 sets of 10 dips.

10 sets of 20 sit-ups.

10 sets of 25 squats.

10 sets of 10 left leg split squats (right foot on bed).

10 sets of 10 right leg split squats (left foot on bed).

10 sets of 10 lunges.

10 sets of 20 side to side lunges.

10 sets of 10 side leg raises.

10 sets of 10 left leg step-ups.

10 sets of 10 right leg step-ups.

Sunday:

1 hour of Meditation.

1 hour of Yoga.

"Did you get it, Mr. Merchant?" Frank said.

"Yes, but I don't think I can do this," Alexander said.

Frank laughed. "I don't expect you to. It's only your initial goal, and the goals are progressive. For now, just work towards completing each set of exercises, and whenever you complete a set, you increase it the following week. For instance, once you can complete ten sets of ten push-ups, you increase it to ten sets of eleven the following week. Keep a chart to track your progress. You continue increasing the sets until you reach your final goal of ten sets of one hundred. It could take years." Frank laughed.

Alexander nodded. "That doesn't sound so bad after all."

"I'll teach you some Kemetic Yoga exercises before Sunday, and I'm sending over a book on meditation by Master Thich Nhat Hanh," Frank said.

"No need. I'm well-experienced in that regard," Alexander said.

"Really?"

"Yes. My mom practiced yoga and taught me when I was younger, but I'd still like to see the book."

"All right, I'll send it over. Now, let's get to it. First set of ten, let's go," Frank said.

Alexander assumed the push-up position and completed his first set.

Weeks later, Alexander sat at his desk revising his workout plan. He was pleased with the progress he was making and was determined to push himself as far as he could before his release. He had progressed from 10 sets of 10 push-ups to 10 sets of 23, and from 5 sets of 5 pull-ups and chin-ups to 5 sets of 15.

Officer Porter opened the trapdoor. "So, you're Jewish now?" she said.

"I'm sorry?" Alexander said.

Officer Porter placed a black plastic tray on the trapdoor. "It's kosher," she said, sarcastically.

"Oh, yes," Alexander said, springing to his feet and darting towards the door. He grabbed his tray and sat at his desk. He grabbed ahold of the plastic cover and peeled it back. Steam rose from the dish, and he inhaled the aromas and smiled. His kosher meal consisted of a rosemary chicken leg, rice pilaf, and steamed broccoli. He held the chicken leg in his hands and sank his teeth into it. The flavors of lemon, garlic, and rosemary resurrected his taste buds. He closed his eyes and moaned in pleasure. He swallowed and quickly bit into it again. He heard Frank laughing through the vent.

Later, Alexander sat on his bed, full and satisfied, wishing he had converted to Judaism sooner.

"Did you enjoy your meal, Mr. Merchant?" Frank asked.

"That was the best meal I had in years," Alexander said.

Frank laughed some more.

Alexander climbed up to the vent. "Mr. Mitchell, may I ask you a personal question?"

"Depends on the question," Frank said.

"How did you end up in HCON?" When Frank didn't respond, Alexander said, "I'm sorry. I shouldn't have asked. Never mind."

Frank remained quiet.

Alexander showered and brushed his teeth. He read for a few hours before climbing into his bed and closing his eyes.

"Mr. Merchant, are you awake?"

"Yes."

"Have you been to The Castle?"

"The Castle?" Alexander repeated.

"Central Prison?"

"No, I've been by it, but I've never been inside," Alexander said.

"It's a real hellhole. It was built in the late eighteen-hundreds by inmates. Can you imagine having to build the prison that will hold you captive for the rest of your life? That has to be the cruelest punishment of all, don't you think?"

"Yes, I imagine so."

"That place is a dungeon. It's dark and murky and designed to make a man miserable. A man could lose his mind in a place like that, that is, if he doesn't lose his life first. Imagine the *Shaw Shank Redemption* but worse," Frank said.

Alexander shuddered.

"I was there for six years—the darkest years of my life. One day I was attacked by several inmates and was taken to the outside hospital for treatment. During the trip, the officer stopped at a restaurant and went inside to get food. He left me in the car alone, and while he was gone, I kicked out the window and made a run for it. I never made it out of the parking lot before the police were on my ass. I was charged with attempted escape and an additional twenty-five years was added to my sentence. I've been on lockdown ever since, and when this place opened, I was sent here," Frank said.

Alexander lay in bed listening to Frank's tale until he heard Frank climb down from the vent and climb into bed. Alexander turned over on his side and closed his eyes.

Uneventful days and indistinguishable nights slowed time to a crawl and Alexander wondered if his sentence would ever end. His release date had come and gone as he waited for the district attorney to make a decision on his case. He sat staring at the chessboard, plotting his next series of moves. His rook was under attack, and Frank had only left him two viable options. He could take Frank's knight and lose his bishop in the process, or retreat and give up valuable territory. He retreated and moved his rook back out of danger. He stood at the window and leaned his head against the glass, waiting on Frank to make a move. The cold glass against his skin told him that fall was setting in, and although he couldn't see the trees beyond the fence line, he knew autumn would soon set the hills on fire.

Frank called out his move, and Alexander went back to the board and saw that Frank had taken his pawn. Alexander gritted his teeth.

"What's wrong?" Frank said.

"Nothing," Alexander said.

"You're playing like something is wrong."

"I just want to get out of HCON." Alexander sighed.

"Why do you want to go out there? You're better off where you are. Believe me."

"Why do you say that?"

"You must learn to make it work for you. Listen, I don't know what led you to do what you did, but I can imagine you were no different than I was when I first came to prison. Before coming here, the only crimes I had ever committed were traffic violations, but when I came to prison, I had to run with the wolves to survive. The things I had to do still give me nightmares. But in segregation, I choose how I do my time, no one else does. My only enemies are those officers' batons and these four walls. I make it work for me, just as you must make it work for you. Now, make your move," Frank said.

CHAPTER

TWENTY-SIX

Alexander finished his morning workout and was sitting on his bed reading when Officer Ward tapped on his window.

"Get dressed," Officer Ward said.

Alexander put on his shirt and tied his shoes.

The trapdoor opened, and Officer Ward peered into his cell. "Cuff up, Merchant."

Alexander stuck his hands through the trap and felt the cold handcuffs closing around his wrists.

Officer Ward held onto Alexander's wrist as the door slid open.

Officer Jones enclosed a black box onto the handcuffs, while Officer Ward wrapped the Martin chain around his waist and secured his hands to it with a padlock. Officer Jones kneeled and secured a pair of leg irons to his ankles.

The officers brought him out of his cell and escorted him down the corridor.

Alexander peered into Frank Mitchell's cell and saw a slen-

319

der, chiseled man with a grey beard and long grey dreadlocks peering back at him.

"Where am I going?"

"To see your case manager," Officer Jones answered.

Alexander was placed in a holding cell, where he waited for his case manager to arrive.

"Who's over there?" the inmate next door said.

"Merchant."

"Okay, I'm Cheese. What's good?"

"Nothing. I'm out here to see my case manager. How about you?" Alexander answered.

"Disciplinary hearing," Cheese said.

"For what?"

"Gassing a CO."

"That was you?"

"He had it coming."

"Did he?"

"Yup, he's disrespectful. I told him to stop fucking with me, but he wouldn't listen, so I mixed up a cocktail of piss and shit and gassed him," Cheese said.

Alexander grimaced and turned away without answering.

Minutes later, Cheese broke the silence, "Merchant, I'm going out to the hospital tonight."

"Are you?"

"Yeah. Would you like me to get a message to anyone?"

"Are you sick?" Alexander asked."

"No, nothing's wrong."

"So, why are you going to the hospital?"

"I just want to see what's new out there," Cheese admitted.

Alexander shook his head in disbelief. *This guy is crazy,* he thought.

"Do you want me to get a message to anyone?" Cheese repeated.

"No, I'm good," Alexander said, incredulously.

"Suit yourself," Cheese said.

Moments later, Officers Jones and Ward came back to the holding cell.

"Turn around and face the wall," Officer Jones commanded.

Alexander turned and waited. The cell door opened, and the officers grabbed a hold of his arms and escorted him out of the cell. He was brought into the conference room where Case Manager Cunningham, Sergeant Powell, and Lieutenant Swiney sat waiting.

Officers Jones and Fitch placed Alexander in a chair and stood behind him, holding their batons in the port arms position.

Alexander saw his file opened in front of Case Manager Cunningham.

"How are you, Merchant?" Cunningham asked.

"I'm well," Alexander said.

"We heard from the D.A.'s office this morning," Lieutenant Swiney said.

Alexander shifted in his seat.

"The district attorney declined prosecution of the assault on Marqueese Young. Therefore, you're being released on Thursday," Swiney said.

Alexander gasped and lowered his head towards the table. His eyes filled with tears and liquid ran from his nose.

"We need to go over your release plan, Mr. Merchant," Case Manager Cunningham said.

"Okay." Alexander wiped his face on his sleeve and looked up.

"I have a release address listed at seven-fifteen Woodburn Road, Raleigh, North Carolina, two-seven-six-o-one," Case Manager Cunningham said.

"No, that house was lost in foreclosure after my mother passed," Alexander said.

"Where do you plan to live?"

"I don't know," Alexander said.

"Do you have any family?"

"No, I don't."

"Will you be homeless?"

"May I use the phone? I need to call a family friend. I'm sure I can live with them for a while."

"What's the name?"

"Orlando Connerly."

"What's the address?"

"Eight-forty-one Woodburn Road, Raleigh, North Carolina, two-seven-six-o-one."

Case Manager Cunningham wrote down the name and address. "Is this public housing?"

"No. It's a private residence," Alexander said.

"Are there any other felons living there?"

"No."

"Okay, there also can't be any firearms in the house."

"I don't believe there are, but I'm not sure," Alexander said.

"That's fine. Your release plan must be approved by the Department of Probation. I'll send your release plan over to probation today, and they will set up a home inspection. They will have to approve your release plan before you could live there, okay?"

"Yes, sir," Alexander said.

Case Manager Cunningham typed Alexander's information into a computer program, printed out his release plan, and set it down in front of him. He then looked at Officer Jones and said, "I need him to sign it."

Officer Jones held Alexander's arm and said, "Stand up."

When Alexander rose to his feet, Officer Jones placed a pen

in his hand, which was still secured by handcuffs and padlocked to the Martin chain around his waist. Officer Jones moved the release plan closer to the edge of the table.

Alexander leaned over, struggling to sign it.

"I'll be in touch," Case Manager Cunningham said.

"Take him back to his cell," Lieutenant Swiney said.

"Lieutenant, may I ask you something?"

"What?"

"What's Mr. Mitchell's story. Why is he in HCON?" Alexander asked.

"That's none of your business," Lieutenant Swiney said.

"He told me what he did. I just want to know if it's true," Alexander said.

"What did he tell you?"

"He said he was being driven to the hospital, and the officer left him in the car while he went inside of a restaurant. Mr. Mitchell kicked out the back window and tried to escape, but the police caught him before he got away."

"That's mostly true. What he left out is that the officer tried to stop him, and when he did, Mitchell beat him within an inch of his life. He then sat down next to the officer and waited for the police to come and get him."

Alexander nodded his head.

"You be careful around him," he said.

Alexander was brought back to his cell where the shackles were removed, and the door closed behind him. He clapped his hands and paced back and forth in his cell.

"What happened, Mr. Merchant?" Frank's voice came through the vent.

"The district attorney declined to prosecute me with new charges. I'm going home on Thursday," Alexander said, happily.

"Great news, Mr. Merchant. Great news," Frank said.

Two days. Just two more days, Alexander thought. He sat on his bed and looked around his cell. *Two more days. What am I going to do? What if Orlando says no? Where will I go? Where will I work, and how will I take care of myself?* Alexander asked himself. Alexander realized he didn't have a plan, and his excitement quickly turned into fear.

He sat and weighed his options, of which, there were few. *Howard and Orlando are all I have. They would certainly help me get on my feet, and my church family will help, too. Maybe Reverend Talbert will help me find work. I'll get a job and get my own place. Maybe I'll even buy our house back one day,* he thought.

He looked at the clock and saw that it was 3:01 P.M. He went to the window and tapped on the glass as the officer passed by, making her rounds. "May I have some cleaning supplies please?" he requested.

She nodded and continued her patrols.

Alexander sat and waited. She eventually returned and opened the trapdoor and handed him a netted bag of cleaning supplies. The bag included a spray bottle of pink cleaning solution, a scrub brush, a toilet brush, a can of scouring powder, two trash bags, a few rags, a hand broom, and a dustpan.

"I hear you're going home," Officer Cheeks said.

"Yes, ma'am."

"How long have you been down?"

"Thirty-six months," Alexander answered.

"Good luck. Take care of yourself, okay." She smiled at him.

"I will. Thank you."

Alexander spent the remainder of the evening cleaning his cell. He cleaned the shower, the sink, the toilet, and his desk. He swept the floor, sprayed it with cleaning solution and scrubbed it clean. He showered and cleaned the shower again. Finally, he returned the cleaning supplies and sat quietly on his bed.

When the lights went out, he lay in his bed and tried to sleep, but it was useless. His mind was racing, and he couldn't turn it off. He could only lie on his back and stare at the ceiling. A shadow passed by his window as an officer made his rounds. Alexander glanced at the clock. It was 3:01 A.M. Moments later, he heard the officer banging on a cell door.

"Doran, look at me. Wake up, Doran."

There was more banging, then Alexander heard him say, "Assistance needed on B-Block, cell one-twenty-six. Attempted suicide, cell one-twenty-six." Alexander sprang to his feet and ran to the window as several staff ran by.

"Watcha got?" Lieutenant Swiney said.

"Inmate Doran cut his wrists. He's bleeding out," Officer Fitch said, into his radio.

"HCON to all radio units. Attempted suicide, B-Block, cell one-twenty-six. Attempted suicide, B-Block, cell one-twenty-six," the control room officer announced.

Alexander saw more staff run past his cell, followed by two medical staff, wheeling a gurney.

"Open cell one-twenty-six, control," Lieutenant Swiney said.

Moments later, staff raced by Alexander's cell, with inmate Doran strapped to the gurney. A trail of blood streamed down the corridor behind them. Alexander watched with wide eyes.

"Mr. Mitchell, are you awake?" Alexander said, with his face close to the vent.

"I'm here," Frank said.

"He told me he was going to the hospital tonight," Alexander said.

"Did he?"

"Yes, he did. He said he just wanted to see what was new. He asked if I wanted him to get a message to anyone. I thought he was crazy and blew him off," Alexander said.

"He is crazy. Do you remember when I told you to keep your mind sharp? That's why. That's what happens when you let your mind go. You must stay sharp on the outside, too, Mr. Merchant. It's not easy out there. Far too often, I see guys released from prison, and they're right back in here after just a few weeks. Sometimes they violate on purpose, just because they couldn't handle life on the outside. They become too institutionalized to function in the real world. They are so used to being told when to wake up, when to eat, and when to sleep, so they can't function on their own. So, you stay sharp out there, you hear. And always remember that no matter how hard it gets, even your worst day out there in that world, is better than your best day in here. You understand?" Frank said.

"Yes, I do," Alexander said.

"You better, because I like you, young man. But, if I ever see your ass in here again, I'll kill you myself. Do you understand?" Frank said.

"Yes sir, I understand," Alexander said.

"Good. Is there anyone waiting for you on the outside?" Frank asked.

"No, not really. Not any family anyway," Alexander said.

"No lady friend?"

"No, not anymore. She's long gone," Alexander said.

"So, you had someone before?" Frank asked.

"I did."

"You should find her," Frank said.

"No. I have nothing to offer her. Besides, she moved away after I came to prison," Alexander said.

"So, find her. It shouldn't be that hard."

"You have no idea."

"Where is she now?"

"Sweden," Alexander said.

"Oh, damn."

"Exactly," Alexander said.

He hadn't thought of Natalie in months, and he didn't want to think of her now. He thought she was better off without him, and he didn't want to ever think of her again.

"What about you, Mr. Mitchell? Do you have a lady friend?"

"I was married when I came to prison, but she is long gone, too. One day after work, some friends and I went out to a bar. I drank entirely too much and got sick. I called a cab and went home. When I got there, my wife was upstairs in the shower. She must not have expected me home so early, because she had left her email open. I read through them and found some messages between her and another man—explicit messages. They discussed what they would do to each other when she arrived at his house. I felt like a damn fool. I had been faithful to her no matter how badly she treated me, and yet she was out doing God knows what with God knows who. I was so distraught I didn't have the energy to confront her. While she showered, I grabbed what I could and stuffed it into my car. I intended to drive to my parents' house and stay there until I got things sorted out, but along the way, some kid rode his bike right out in front of me. I felt the impact before I saw him. Maybe if I hadn't been drinking, I could've reacted faster, but I don't know how anyone could have reacted. I was charged with vehicular homicide and sentenced to fifteen years. I've been incarcerated ever since."

"How long have you been down?"

"Seventeen years," Frank answered.

"I'm sorry that happened to you," Alexander said.

"Yeah... Well, shit happens. All we can do is take it on the chin and move on." Frank said, and then fell silent.

Alexander knew not to speak. He would let the long night speak for them both.

On the following morning, Alexander rose early and completed his workout regimen. He showered and dressed, and separated his personal belongings he intended to keep from those he would throw away. He placed some letters, photographs, and his General Education Diploma in a bag, and he trashed everything else. The trapdoor swung open, and Alexander saw his case manager peering in at him.

"Hi, Mr. Cunningham," Alexander said.

"Hey, Merchant. Your release plan was approved. Mr. Connerly will be here to pick you up tomorrow morning," Case Manager Cunningham announced.

"What time do I release?"

"Seven-thirty," Case Manager Cunningham said.

"Thanks for everything," Alexander said.

"You're welcome. Good luck, young man," he said.

Alexander sat on his bed and waited for dinner. He was feeling anxious. His long nightmare will soon be over, and he was ready to get on with his life. Although, what was coming next, he didn't know, but he knew he would embrace whatever God had in store for him.

As Alexander consumed his evening meal, he thought about some of the places he would eat when he got home. He climbed up to the vent and called over to Frank, "How about giving me one more shot at the title?"

"Are you sure you want to leave here disappointed?" Frank said.

"More like on a high note, Mr. Mitchell," Alexander said.

"Best two out of three?"

"You got it."

"Set it up."

"I'm ready," Alexander said.

"D-two to D-four," Frank said. It was the queen's gambit.

TWENTY-SEVEN

Alexander strutted out of Rolesville Correctional Institution and stood in the parking lot. He didn't see Orlando, so he stood a few minutes and waited for his arrival. The sun was fighting back some rain clouds, and Alexander was sure he would get soaked if Orlando didn't arrive soon. The wind was blowing steadily, and Alexander closed his eyes and enjoyed the warm sun on his face.

A blue Toyota Camry slowed to a stop. The window lowered and Alexander grew tense. Peering into the vehicle, he was relieved to see Orlando sitting behind the steering wheel.

Orlando climbed out of the car with a huge grin on his face. "Where did those muscles come from?" Orlando asked, grabbing both of Alexander's arms.

They embraced, climbed into the car, and drove away.

"How do you feel?" Orlando inquired.

Alexander sighed. "I was worried this day would never come, but I'm excited. I'm glad that chapter of my life is over, and I'm ready to move on," Alexander answered.

"We're glad to have you back, and you're going to do well. Looking back on this will prove to be no more than a bump in the road," Orlando said.

"I certainly hope so."

"Don't hope, Alexander—believe God. He'll see you through," Orlando said.

When Orlando pulled into his driveway, they climbed out of the car. Alexander looked around. He was pleased to find the home just as he remembered, but the yard had changed a little. "What happened to the tree?" Alexander asked.

"It came down in a storm. We were lucky it missed the house," Orlando said.

Alexander looked around and took it all in. The furniture was mostly the same, but the cabinet which concealed the television was gone, and in its place, a large flat screen television hung on the wall. He looked at the photos displayed on the tables and walls. His eyes rested on Howard's graduation photos, and he sighed.

"The guest room is all set up for you, and there is a box of some of your things in there, too," Orlando said.

"Thank you."

Alexander went into his room and took it all in. He sat on his bed and saw a box sitting against the wall. He opened it and examined the contents. He found some clothes, some of which he could no longer fit, and some of which he wondered why he had ever worn at all. He separated the clothes he wanted to keep and decided to donate the rest to charity. He also found photo albums and a box of keepsakes.

He looked through the photos, which were mostly photos of himself, and some were of his mom and dad. He placed a photo of Emily in the corner of the mirror and placed an old, framed family photo of himself and his parents on the nightstand. The box of keepsakes contained some of Emily's jewelry.

He found her wedding ring, a gold necklace, a pearl necklace, a gold ring, a broach, some hairpins, and some small items of sentimental value. He slid the gold ring onto his pinky finger and clasped the gold chain around his neck.

Alexander found a smaller metal box holding his passport, social security card, birth certificate, and driver's license, which was still valid. He also found a bank card in his name. He picked up the phone and called the 1-800 number on the back of the card. The balance was $3,028. He put everything away and lay back on the bed.

Orlando knocked on the door and looked in. "Can I get you something to eat?"

"No, thank you. I'm going out in a little while. I've been craving Snoopy's," Alexander said, laughing.

"Really?" Orlando said, smiling. "Do you need any money?"

"No, I'm all right," Alexander said.

"All right. Howard says he'll call you this evening."

"How is he?"

"He's fine. Chuck is keeping him busy," Orlando said.

"Chuck?"

"Charles Terry," Orlando said.

"*Congressman* Charles Terry?" Alexander asked.

"Yes," Orlando said. "Didn't he tell you?"

"Tell me what?"

"He works for him."

"No, well we haven't talked in a while," Alexander said.

"I'm sure he'll tell you all about it." Orlando knew that Howard often felt embarrassed whenever he shared his accomplishments with Alexander. He didn't want to make him feel worse about his situation, so he kept his accomplishments to himself.

Alexander showered and dressed before going out. Walking around, he was astonished by how much the city had changed since he was gone. He saw sprawling apartment buildings where private homes once stood. He saw new hotels, restaurants, and shopping centers. He felt the new structures closing in, sucking up the air and suffocating him. He saw a neon sign across the street which read, Mobile 1. He crossed the street and looked through the window at an advertisement for the iPhone 3. *That's a phone?* he thought. He went inside and looked around.

"May I help you?" a man asked.

Alexander turned and saw a young white man with long blonde hair approaching him. His name tag said, Dan. "Yes, may I see the iPhone three?" Alexander asked.

"Sure. It's right over here," Dan said.

He picked one up off the shelf and handed it to Alexander.

Alexander held the phone in his hands and looked it over.

"Nice, huh?" Dan said.

"How much?" Alexander asked.

"Three hundred dollars," Dan said.

"Three hundred dollars for a fucking phone?" Alexander snapped. When Dan's face turned red, Alexander felt embarrassed. "I'm sorry. I just can't believe it's so expensive," Alexander said.

"I get it. I have a used one you can have for one-fifty," Dan said, and reached behind the counter and handed Alexander a used, second-generation iPhone. Dan leaned over and whispered, "Listen, I get off at six. Meet me down the street, and I'll give you a brand new one for the same price," he said.

Alexander chuckled. "Nah, man. I'll take the used one," he said, and paid for the used iPhone, and waited for Dan to activate it.

Dan handed him the phone. "Here you go, my man. Enjoy," he said.

Alexander took the phone and left the store. He wandered

some more and looked around. Approaching Hillsborough Street, he was relieved to find Snoopy's standing in its original form, unaffected by the surrounding modernity. The small yellow building with bold red and white stripes satisfied the familiarity he craved. Alexander stood at the window.

"May I help you?" the window attendant asked.

"Yes. I would like two famous hotdogs, add ketchup, fries, and a Coke."

"Do you want to make it a combo?"

"Yes, please."

"Anything else?"

"Make my fries, chili cheese fries, and add a cinnamon-sugar apple turnover, please," Alexander requested.

"Coming right up," she said.

Alexander stood to the side and waited. When his ticket number was called, he retrieved his food and sat at a small table. He raised a hotdog to his face and looked it over. He saw the steaming chili, onions, ketchup, and mustard swirling together and dripping over the sides of the bun. He inhaled, filling his nostrils with its aroma. He stuffed the hotdog into his mouth, licked his fingers, and smiled.

Alexander moseyed around some more before heading home. The sun was setting, and he was growing tired. He had seen enough change for one day. So many things looked different, and the city felt different, too. The people were different. They seemed more uptight and less friendly. He reflected upon these changes along the way, and before he knew it, he found himself standing outside of his old home, which had also changed. The left side of the front exterior was now cobalt blue, with white trim and white shutters. The right side of the front exterior was covered with white vertical shiplap, and an olive-green door. A new front porch covered the right side of the house, and it was also painted white—and Emily's rose garden had been removed.

From the sidewalk, he peered through the window and saw that the interior wall, which had separated the living room from the kitchen, had been removed, creating an open living space, and he could see straight through to the back of the house. The floors had been replaced with dark hickory colored hardwood, and the kitchen was gleaming with new modern finishes and appliances. Alexander noticed the new home-owner peering out at him, so he turned and hurried off.

Alexander returned home and rang the bell.

Orlando opened the door. "You don't have to ring, just use your key and come on in," he said.

"Sorry," Alexander smiled.

Orlando sat in front of the television and continued watching the evening news, so Alexander joined him.

"Where did you go today?" Orlando asked.

"I just walked around a bit."

"Lots of changes, huh?"

"Oh, yes. I'm not quite sure what to make of it," Alexander said.

"Neither am I." Orlando sighed. "There are some advantages, certainly more job opportunities." Orlando winked.

"Yes, I'll start looking for work tomorrow."

"Good. You can borrow some of Howard's dress clothes if you need to."

"Thanks," Alexander said. He leaned back and filled his nose with the aromas coming from the kitchen. "What's cooking?"

"Go have a look," Orlando said.

Alexander went into the kitchen and found Mrs. Connerly basting a pot roast and rolling dough.

"Hi, Alexander." She smiled and wiped her hands, and then wrapped her arms around him. "It's so good to see you."

"It is good to see you too, Mrs. Connerly. And thanks for letting me stay here."

"Don't mention it. You just make yourself at home."

Alexander leaned back against the countertops and crossed his arms. He looked around the kitchen and found it exactly as he remembered. From the yellow-painted walls and yellow-flowered wallpaper, to the magnets on the refrigerator. He had always felt at home there, but he missed his own home and his own kitchen dearly. Now when he thought of his home, which was now a shell of itself, it saddened him.

The three of them sat around the kitchen table to eat. They reminisced about Alexander's and Howard's mischief growing up, and they also remembered Emily. Alexander asked about Emily's funeral service, so they filled him in on all the details, including the eulogy, the songs that were sung, and of her sorority sisters who filled the church with pearl necklaces, pink dresses and green wide-brimmed hats. Alexander wanted to know everything.

"I'll go visit her this weekend," Alexander said.

"I can show you to the gravesite," Orlando said.

"No, thank you. I'll find it. I assume she's buried towards the back of Oakwood Cemetery, in the newer section," Alexander said.

"Yes, on the back side, near the wall," Orlando said.

Alexander nodded and filled his plate for the third time.

"Save some room for dessert," Mrs. Connerly suggested. She crossed the room and returned carrying a sweet potato pie. She sat it in front of him and smiled.

Alexander smiled widely.

Alexander was lying across his bed dozing when he heard

the phone ring. Moments later, Orlando knocked on the door and handed him the cordless phone.

"Hello."

"Hey, bro," Howard said.

"Hey, Howard."

"How does it feel to be home?"

"It feels great," he answered, although he was growing tired of the question. "When are you coming?"

Howard sighed. "Between work, school, and preparing for the LSAT, I'm not quite sure," he said.

"Your dad says you work for Congressman Terry?"

"It's an internship, but yes," Howard said.

"How did you land that?"

"I started out as a volunteer for his campaign. He took a liking to me, and I ended up managing a satellite campaign office here in the Bronx, not far from my apartment. Later, after his reelection, I applied for an internship, and he hired me."

"What do you do?"

I answer phone calls and letters mostly, and I sometimes act as assistant to his assistant, which means running lots of errands," he said laughing. "But it's been great, and you wouldn't believe the people I've met or the events I've attended," Howard said.

"It sounds amazing."

"Oh, it is. But, enough about me—I want to hear about you," Howard said, hoping to downplay his accomplishments.

"There isn't much to tell. I'm just trying to figure some things out," Alexander said.

"Everything will work out," Howard said, awkwardly.

"We'll see."

"Oh, that reminds me. I have some letters for you from Natalie. I'll drop them in the mail for you tomorrow," Howard said.

"No, I don't want them," Alexander said.

"Why not?"

"It would bring up too many bad memories. She needs to move on with her life. We both do," Alexander said.

"So, what should I do with the letters?"

"Throw them away or send them back. I don't care, but can we change the subject?" Alexander asked.

"Sure," Howard mumbled.

They talked for several hours before Howard had to go.

On the following morning, Alexander arose early and went to Cameron Village and picked up applications from The Flying Biscuit Café, the Village Draft House, the Cameron Village Bar & Grill, Ten Thousand Villages, and Accipiter, Fine Crafts and Lighting. He entered Accipiter and saw a middle-aged woman sitting behind the counter cleaning her glasses.

She put her glasses on and the corners of her mouth turned upward. "May I help you?"

"Yes, may I have a job application, please?"

"I'm sorry, but we're closing soon," she said, with sadness in her eyes.

"Should I come back tomorrow?" he said, perplexedly.

"No, I mean we are closing for good."

"Oh." Alexander sighed. "My mother used to bring me here all the time when I was a kid. She loved this place," he said, nostalgically.

"Yes, I think I remember you," she said.

"Why are you closing?" Alexander asked.

"Business isn't what it used to be. We just can't compete with the online markets anymore," she said.

"What a shame." Alexander looked around the store for the last time when his eyes fell on a set of glow-in-the-dark ice cubes. It was just the sort of thing he would expect to find at

Accipiter. He returned with them to the counter. "I'll take these," he said.

"Go on and take them. It's on us," she said.

"Thank you," Alexander said.

"Good luck finding work," she said.

From there, he crossed over to Hillsborough Street, picking up applications from the Readers Corner, Nice Priced Books and Records, the Irregardless Café, and The Flying Saucer.

He stood at the corner of Glenwood Avenue, exhausted and hungry when he saw dark clouds rolling in from the east. He sighed. *I'll come back and do Glenwood tomorrow,* he thought.

Heading home, the aroma of the Mellow Mushroom pulled him inside. "How many in your party?" the hostess asked.

"Just me, and may I eat outside?"

"Sure. Follow me," she said, carrying a menu.

Alexander followed her to the outside dining area and sat at a table in the corner of the patio.

"I'll be right with you," the waitress said.

Alexander looked over the menu.

"Hi, I'm Shanice. Are you ready to order?" the waitress asked.

"Yes, I am." He smiled. "I'll have the Kosmic Karma and a Coke."

"Coming right up," she said, smiling.

Alexander watched cars and people go by when Shanice returned with his pizza and sat it in front of him.

"Do you always eat alone?" Shanice asked.

"Not always." Then Alexander asked, "Who do you usually eat with?"

"I go out with my girlfriends sometimes, but no one else at the moment." She winked, turned, and tended to her other customers. Alexander noticed her hourglass shape and thick thighs as she moved about. Shanice later returned and refilled his glass of soda.

"How do you like working here?"

"It's not bad. I can work around my school schedule," she said.

"Where do you attend school?"

"Shaw U," she said.

"What are you studying?"

"Architectural design."

"Interesting," Alexander said, smiling.

There was a twinkle in her eyes as she met his gaze. "Can I get you anything else?"

"Just the check."

"I have it right here." She placed his bill on the table.

He looked the bill over and handed her his debit card.

"Right back," she said.

Alexander finished his last slice of pizza and washed it down with his Coke.

"Have a nice day, Alexander," she said, reading his name on the card before handing it back to him.

"You too," he smiled. He found Shanice's phone number written on the back of his receipt, and a note.

Call me if you ever need a friend to dine with.

TWENTY-EIGHT

On the following morning, Alexander reported to the North Carolina Department of Community Corrections. He sat in the waiting room, scrolling through his phone as he waited for his probation officer to call him.

"Alexander Merchant."

"That's me." Alexander stood and faced the man standing in the doorway.

"I'm Officer Maurice Taylor."

Alexander shook his hand and followed him into his office. Officer Taylor was impeccably dressed; Alexander noticed the crisp white shirt, spread collar, blue striped tie, and cufflinks. He wore blue slacks and shiny loafers and Alexander compared what he wore, a pair of grey slacks and a button-up shirt, wondering if he should have worn a tie.

"Have a seat," Officer Taylor said.

Alexander sat across from him.

"All right, Mr. Merchant. I am your probation officer. You recently finished a thirty-six-month sentence for indecent liberties with a child. You are beginning a sixty-month term of probation," he read from the papers in front of him.

"Yes, sir," Alexander said.

"You were released on Tuesday?"

"Yes, I was."

"And you're staying with Orlando Connerly?"

"Yes, sir."

Officer Taylor sat back in his chair and gazed at Alexander. "What have you done since you were released?"

"Not much—I applied for a few jobs."

"Oh yeah, where did you apply?"

"A few places in Cameron Village, on Hillsborough Street, and Glenwood Avenue."

"Were you honest about your criminal history?"

"I checked the felony box and said I would explain upon request."

"That's good." Officer Taylor nodded. "So, let's talk about your supervision. I'm going to explain the conditions of your supervision, so that you understand your requirements and what is expected of you. Okay?"

Alexander nodded.

"I see that you have no other criminal history and no history of drug use or alcohol abuse. You were a straight A student before your arrest, and you earned your GED at Rolesville Correctional Institution, right?"

"Yes, sir."

"All right. Now, let's talk about your crime. I've studied your case and I've read your Pre-Sentence Investigation and the statements of everyone involved, so we don't need to relive all the details. But I need to make sure you understand the law and why what you did was a crime."

"If I may, sir," Alexander said.

"Go ahead."

Alexander sat up in his seat. "I assure you that if I had understood the law at that time, it would not have happened, and I promise you it will never happen again. Furthermore, if you studied my case, then understand that essentially our relationship was illegal for a span of two weeks. Now, please, understand that I'm not making excuses for what happened, and I know that ignorance of the law is no excuse, but if I had known the law, I would not have gotten sexually involved with her," Alexander said.

"Are you claiming innocence, Mr. Merchant?"

"No sir, I take full responsibility for my actions, but I want you to know that I'm not out preying on underage girls or anything. It was a mistake and it's not who I am," Alexander insisted.

"Well Mr. Merchant, you don't strike me as a predatory offender, however, due to the nature of your offense, you are not a candidate for unsupervised probation at this time, but you may qualify at a later date. So, I'm going to place you on a modified supervision plan. This means I'll need to meet with you every thirty days during the term of your supervision. You must be on time, and you cannot miss any appointments without approval. Failing to keep your appointments will violate the terms of your supervision and you'll be sent back to prison. Do you understand?"

"Yes, sir."

"Also, you may not change your place of residence without prior approval. Doing so will violate the terms of your supervision and you'll be sent back to prison. Do you understand?"

"Yes, sir."

"You must maintain employment. I want a list of everywhere you have applied, and I want to know about any job interviews—and you must let me know when you are hired. If you lose your job, you need to inform me within twenty-four hours, okay?"

"Yes, sir."

"You must abstain from all illegal substances including marijuana. You will submit to random drug tests, and if any illegal substances are found in your system, you will be in violation of your probation and sent back to prison. Do you understand?"

"Yes, sir."

"Finally, you are required to register as a sex offender in any county where you reside for the rest of your life. Failure to do so, will lead to your arrest and possible prosecution. Do you understand?"

Alexander felt all the air emptying from his chest.

"Do you understand, Mr. Merchant?

"Yes," he said, and sighed.

Officer Taylor slid a piece of paper across his desk. "Sign here."

Alexander signed the registration form before Officer Taylor slid another form across his desk.

"Write down your job searches here, and if you need any help finding work, let me know. We have relationships with employers that hire offenders. It may not be the type of work you're interested in, but it will be honest work. Here's my card. Call me if you have any problems, and I want to see you again here on the fifteenth of next month at nine o'clock A.M."

"I'll be here," Alexander said.

"Good luck." Maurice Taylor stood, and extended his hand.

Alexander shook his hand and left.

Over the coming weeks, Alexander continued looking for work. However, when he inquired about the applications he submitted, he was told that all positions had been filled. In some cases, the help wanted signs were still displayed in the windows. Alexander attributed his bad luck to his lack of work history. For he was a man who had never held a job, and he knew most businesses were looking for candidates with work experience. He also knew that a man with no work experience and a felony record barely stood a chance. *If I could only get an interview, I'm sure I could convince someone to take a chance on me,* he thought. But with each rejection, he grew less optimistic.

Eventually, the Bywater Cafe called and scheduled an interview, leaving Alexander excited about the opportunity. On the day of the interview, Alexander dressed in blue slacks, a white dress shirt and a blue striped tie. He arrived early and went inside.

"May I help you?" the barista asked.

"I'm here for an interview."

"Okay, have a seat. I'll let Ms. Brown know you're here," she said.

Alexander sat and waited. Moments later, a slender woman wearing red glasses and shoulder-length micro-braids came over.

"Are you Mr. Merchant?" she asked.

"Yes." Alexander stood to greet her.

"I'm Desirae Brown," she said, smiling.

"It's nice to meet you." Alexander followed her to a table.

"Would you like something to drink?" she asked.

"I'll have a coffee, please," he said.

"Monique," Desirae called to the barista, "two cappuccinos, please." She glanced over his application and pursed her lips. "Mr. Merchant, do you not have *any* work history?"

"I had a summer job as a counselor at Jaycee Park once, but that was over four years ago," he said.

"Nothing since?" Desirae asked.

"No ma'am, but I assure you I am very eager to work and

learn, and if you were to hire me, I would work very hard for you."

Desirae smiled and rested her crossed arms on the table. "I must tell you, Mr. Merchant, I found your application very intriguing. I thought, either this guy is lying, or he has a story to tell. That's why you're here," she said.

"Everything on my application is true," he said.

"I see you attended Broughton High School, but you didn't finish?"

"Yes, ma'am. I received my GED from Rolesville Community College."

"What were your grades like at Broughton?"

"I had straight As."

"What was your GPA?"

"Four-point-nine." Alexander noticed Desirae had already written down his 4.9 GPA on his application before he told her.

Desirae saw him looking at her notes. "I have a friend at Broughton. She wasn't there when you were, but she looked up your grades for me." She picked up her notes. "Have you lived in Raleigh all of your life?"

"Yes, ma'am."

"I'm from New Orleans. My people are Creole. Do you know anything about Creole people?"

"Yes, a little."

"Selon votre candidature, vous parlez couramment français et espagnol," Desirae said.

"Oui c'est correct. J'ai étudié le français à l'école primaire et l'espagnol au collège et au lycée," Alexander answered.

"Your French is good."

"Thank you."

"But that's just the thing, Mr. Merchant. Reading your application, I thought, why does a kid who speaks both French and Spanish fluently and gets straight As in school, drop out and get his GED from community college, yet never works anywhere? Then I noticed your felony conviction, and I realized you went to prison—and that's where you got your GED. Do you care to tell me what happened?" she said.

Alexander sighed and explained to her the circumstances of his case, and the two-week window that made his actions a crime. "So, please understand that it was a mistake, and I just want to get past it," he said.

"Can you work weekends?"

"Yes, I can."

"We showcase local artists on Saturday nights, and I would need you here until midnight. Is that okay?"

"Yes, ma'am. That is fine. What type of artists?"

"Mostly Jazz, R&B, and Neo Soul."

Alexander nodded. "I'm available anytime you need me," he said.

Desirae tapped her elbow and stared at him for a moment.

Alexander felt his heart beating in his chest.

"Okay, right now I need someone to bust tables and help in the kitchen. If you do well, we'll train you to make coffee," she said.

Alexander clasped his hands underneath his chin and thanked her sincerely.

"Can you start Monday?"

"I can start right now if you like."

"Be here Monday at seven A.M.," she said.

Alexander spent the weekend learning about coffee. He read articles about where the best coffee beans were grown and about various coffee bean roasting techniques. He read articles touting the importance of using fair trade coffee beans and protecting small coffee farmers from corporate conglomerates trying to shut them out of the market. He read about the process of organically certifying coffee farmers, and learned about various brewing techniques, including the pour-over method, French press, and cold brew. He found online forums where people argued over which brewing method was best. They seemed evenly divided between pour-over and French press, and they all scoffed at the more common drip method. Some espoused their hatred for corporate owned cafés and discussed how café chains were ruining coffee.

"These people are crazy," he said, sitting in front of Orlando's computer.

"What did you say?" Orlando asked, looking up from his newspaper.

Alexander explained to Orlando what he was reading. "I never knew people cared so much about coffee," he said.

"People will always find something silly to argue about," Orlando said.

"You're right about that."

"Have you ever had French press?" Orlando asked Alexander.

"No, I haven't."

"Vivian has one in the kitchen," Orlando said.

Alexander went into the kitchen and found it. He watched a few videos on French press before attempting the brew. He poured two scoops of coffee beans into a grinder and ground it to a medium coarse texture. He poured the coffee grounds into the container and poured two ounces of boiling hot water on top of it, stirred the water, and waited thirty seconds. He poured the rest of the water into the container, stirred it, and set the plunger into place. He waited another three and a half minutes and pressed the plunger down into the coffee. He poured two cups of coffee, one for him and one for Orlando.

Orlando sipped the piping hot joe. "Not bad."

"Thanks," Alexander said, satisfied with his accomplishment.

Lying in bed, Alexander thought about his interview and the explanation of his crime. It made him wonder about Natalie Agadani. *What was she doing? Where did she live?* He searched for her on various social media platforms, but she wasn't there, making him wonder even more. He googled Natalie Agadani, University of Stockholm, track and field, and there he found her in various news articles, detailing her athletic achievements. She now held records on two continents, both in Raleigh and all over Sweden. As Alexander scrolled through the numerous articles, a warm smile formed on his lips. He searched some more and found articles she had written while in school. He read them throughout the night but then hit a block after her junior year—she seemed to have disappeared. *Was she still in Sweden? Was she back in Nairobi?* He didn't know.

ALEXANDER AROSE early Monday morning and dressed in a pair of blue jeans and a Bywater Café T-shirt. He walked over to the café and went inside, finding Desirae sitting in her office. "Good morning," he said.

"Hey, Alexander." She smiled and handed him several forms. "This is your W-four form, Employee's Withholding Certificate, and your Employee Profile form. Fill these out, please."

Alexander was at a table filling out the forms when he felt the need to relieve himself. He stepped over to the restrooms and paused outside the doors. He didn't know what to make of the signs on the doors which said: Male, Female, Whatever. He shrugged and chose the door on the left. He then returned and finished filling out the forms and returned them to his new boss.

Desirae looked them over closely. "Okay, everything looks good," she said. "Come with me."

Alexander followed her into the dining area.

"Have you met Monique? She's the best barista in town," Desirae said.

"We've met," Monique interjected, as she stood behind the counter, wiping down the machinery.

"We're opening in just a few minutes." Desirae continued, "Customers will usually order their coffee and food before finding a table. Your job is to locate the customers and deliver their orders. Just ask and make sure it's theirs before you sit it down, okay?"

"Yes, ma'am."

Desirae pointed. "Most customers will place their dishes over here in the pan when they're done, but some won't. Either way, wipe down the tables and wash the dishes."

"Yes, ma'am."

"Also, keep the floors clean. Sweep up periodically and clean up any spills. And if you work until closing, wipe down all the tables and chairs, and sweep and mop the floors before you leave," she instructed.

Alexander nodded.

Desirae led Alexander into a restroom and pointed to a chart hanging on the door. "The restrooms are to be cleaned every hour. When you're finished cleaning, initial beside the time slot here," she said, pointing to the chart. "If we're too busy and you can't get to it, that's okay. But clean it as soon as time permits. Now if there is one thing I cannot stand in any restaurant, is a dirty restroom. Also, dirty, sticky floors in the dining area. I will not eat anything in a place like that, so keep it clean, okay?" she said.

"Yes, ma'am. I've got it covered."

"I'm sure you do." She offered him a friendly grin. "Welcome aboard."

"Thank you." Alexander stood behind the counter and took note of what the customers ordered and where they sat. He delivered their orders, cleaned the tables, and washed the dishes. He gathered some cleaning supplies and prepared to clean the restrooms.

"No one's been in there," Monique said.

"Desirae said I had to clean it every hour."

"She is so O.C.D." Monique rolled her eyes. "Just stick your head in and if it needs to be cleaned, clean it. But if it doesn't, don't worry about it," Monique said.

"Got it." Alexander nodded and continued working through the end of his shift, as waves of customers continued to flow into the shop. When the flow of customers eventually slowed, Alexander stayed in the kitchen washing dishes.

"You can take off now. I'll see you in the morning," Desirae said, around five o'clock.

"Okay, I'll be here at seven sharp," Alexander said.

"Seven o'clock," she confirmed. "Good work today," she added.

Walking home, Alexander noticed the leaves covering the lawns. When he arrived at the Connerly's, he looked up at the trees surrounding their home and took notice of the autumn colors in full bloom. He had looked forward to fall when he was younger and wondered how he hadn't noticed its signs before. The temperature certainly didn't feel like autumn, at least not that he had noticed, but fall was certainly settling in.

He thought about the trips to the North Carolina mountains that he and Emily had taken every fall to see the leaves change. He remembered them strolling around Asheville and visiting Emily's friends who lived there. He remembered the trips to the Biltmore

Estate and driving along the Blue Ridge Parkway. It all seemed like another lifetime now, like the life of another person—a person who no longer existed. Prison had destroyed and buried that old version of himself, the version full of exuberance and optimism. But every so often, he felt the old Alexander clawing his way back.

In the following weeks, Alexander spent most of his time at the Bywater Café. He picked up extra shifts whenever he could, and when he was off, he often hung out there on weekends, listening to live music.

One busy morning, Alexander stood behind the counter arranging cups and saucers when a young woman took a seat at the bar.

"I'll be right with you," Monique said, as she worked on multiple orders of cappuccinos, lattes, and macchiatos.

Desirae stood arranging a batch of chocolate chip toffee cookies to go in the oven.

"No worries, I'll have a medium coffee when you get a chance," she said.

"Can you grab that, Alexander?" Monique asked.

"Sure thing," he said.

"Hi, Alexander," the young woman said.

Looking up, he saw Shanice from the Mellow Mushroom smiling at him.

"Hi... Shanice, right?" he said.

"That's right."

"I've been meaning to call you," Alexander said.

"So, why haven't you?"

"I don't really know," he said, feeling ashamed.

"It's cool. My number is the same," she smiled, her big, brown eyes fixed on him.

Alexander returned the smile and nodded. He took notice of her hair, which was pulled tightly into one thick braid, hanging on the left side of her face and past her shoulder, down to her chest. Her baby hair resting lightly on her brown forehead.

"I'll get that coffee for you," he said.

"Make it pour-over, please," she said.

"What roast would you like?"

"Yirgacheffe, please."

"Coming right up." Alexander poured a scoop of Yirgacheffe coffee beans into the grinder. He saw Desirae cut an eye at him, and Alexander met her gaze and winked.

Desirae crossed her arms and watched him intently as he ground the beans to medium coarse and placed a Chemex coffee filter into the mouth of a glass Chemex coffee maker. When the water began to boil, he rinsed the filter to seal it to the glass and rinse away any taste of paper. He poured the excess water out and emptied the freshly ground coffee into the filter. She noticed him pouring a small amount of water over the coffee grounds and waited thirty seconds for the coffee grounds to bloom. He set a timer to four minutes and slowly and methodically, he poured hot water on top of the coffee grounds in a circular motion, carefully watching to ensure the coffee grounds were evenly saturated. He waited one minute and poured in a second dose of water. She continued to watch as he waited ninety seconds and emptied the remaining water from the kettle over the coffee grounds. As the hot water filtered through to the bottom of the Chemex coffee vase, she saw Alexander remove the filter and place it in the trash. He then filled a mug with coffee and placed it in front of the customer.

Shanice added sugar and milk, and sipped the brew with a satisfied grin.

Desirae nodded with approval and placed the cookies in the oven.

"Have you worked here long?" Shanice asked.

"Just a few weeks. Have you been here before?"

"I stop in occasionally. I don't live far from here," she said, as her phone vibrated with a text message. She read the message and frowned, and angrily fired off a reply.

"Is everything okay?" Alexander asked Shanice, while rinsing the Chemex vase.

"I was supposed to meet two classmates here to work on a project. I haven't even been able to contact one of them all weekend and the other just cancelled without any explanation. I'm upset because the last time my professor grouped me with these two, I ended up doing all the work, and they benefited with the grade," Shanice said.

"Why did you agree to work with them again?"

"I didn't. I complained to my professor, but he didn't listen. I swear, he gives them preferential treatment because they're athletes. But this time, I'll complain to the department chair if they pull this crap again," she said.

"That seems only right," Alexander said.

She finished her coffee and stood. "It was nice to see you again," she said, offering another warm smile.

"It was nice to see you, too... And I'll give you a call," he said.

"Good. I'll talk to you soon," she said.

Alexander was still smiling as he watched her leave.

"She seems nice. I hope you're going to call her," Desirae said.

"I don't know. I feel like I need to get myself together first," he said.

"I wouldn't wait too long. I'm sure she has many suitors," Desirae said.

That night, as Alexander prepared for bed, he pulled open a drawer and found Shanice's phone number. He considered drafting her a text message, telling her how nice it was to see her again, and asking if she was free on Saturday night, but he decided against it. He thought he should first complete his registration to Wake Technical Community College, so that when she eventually asked about his future, he could present her with his plan. He would give himself a week to complete registration, and then he would call and ask her for a date.

TWENTY-NINE

Alexander finished his work and headed home. Along the way, he stood waiting at a traffic light when his eyes were drawn across the street to a light pole, covered in flyers. He had passed that light pole hundreds of times without paying it any attention, but on this evening, those flyers demanded his attention. As he gazed across the street, he saw himself staring back. He blinked his eyes and looked away before refocusing his gaze, and there, he saw again, his face staring back.

He crossed the street and approached the light pole, where a newly posted yellow flyer hung. The words across the top of the flyer in bold red letters, horrified him. It read "Sex Offender." Beneath was a screenshot from the sex offender registry website with Alexander's picture, front and center. The screenshot detailed his charges, and at the bottom of the flyer read, community watch. Alexander immediately ripped down the flyer, staring at it in disbelief. His head was spinning, and his heart pounded in his chest.

He turned around to see who was watching him. No one

was there, but halfway down the street, he saw another flyer. He ran over to it and tore it down, but at the end of the street, he saw yet another. Panic set in, and he ran home, bursting through the door in a state of delirium.

Orlando sprang to his feet. "What's wrong?" he asked.

Vivian rushed into the living room to see what was happening.

"Who would do this?" Alexander said.

"Who did what?" Orlando asked.

"This," Alexander said, shaking a stack of yellow flyers in his hand. "Who would do this?"

Orlando took the flyers from his hand and stared at them in disbelief.

"Oh, my gosh," Vivian exclaimed, shocked by what she was seeing.

Alexander backed up against the wall.

"Come and sit down, honey," Vivian said, grasping his hand.

Alexander pulled away.

She grabbed his arms. "Come on and sit down," she repeated, guiding him over to the couch.

Alexander sat, with the Connerlys across from him.

"They were all over the neighborhood. Everyone must have seen them," he said wide-eyed. "What am I going to do?"

"You're going to go on with your life," Orlando said.

"How can I do that? I'll be an outcast, don't you see?"

"No, you'll get past this," Vivian said.

"But who would do this?" Alexander mumbled.

"I think we have an idea. She has a history of this sort of thing," Vivian said.

"Who?"

"She's a bit of a vigilante in these matters. We'll talk to her," Orlando said.

Alexander got up and went into his room, closing the door behind him. He sat, rocking on the edge of his bed, staring at the wall.

On the following morning, Alexander arose early for work. Along the way, he kept his eyes open for more flyers. He didn't see any but knew they were out there. It was a big neighborhood, and he hadn't searched all of it. He arrived at the Bywater Café and went inside.

"Hey, Monique," he said.

"Hey, Alexander," Monique said, smiling.

Although she smiled, Alexander noticed Monique didn't make eye contact when she normally did—she made a point of it, and it sometimes felt as if she were looking right through him. He went on with his morning routine of taking down the chairs and setting up the tables. He rolled silverware and spruced up the bathrooms.

"Hey Alexander, would you step back to my office, please?" Desirae requested.

"Sure." Alexander followed her into the office and took a seat.

She looked at him with sympathetic eyes. She pursed her lips and reached into a drawer and pulled out a flyer with Alexander's face on it.

His heart sank and his stomach turned.

"I found these plastered on the door this morning," Desirae said.

"They're all over the neighborhood. I found some last night on my way home," Alexander confessed.

"Do you know who did it?"

"No, I don't. But, Mr. and Mrs. Connerly have an idea." He watched Desirae stick the flyers into a shredder. "I'm sorry. I know this can't be good for your business," he said, with glassy eyes.

"You let me worry about that. You just keep doing what you've been doing. We'll get past this," Desirae said.

"No," he said, shaking his head. "I can't put this on you."

"I knew about your history when I hired you," she said.

"No," he repeated. "Thanks for everything, but I have to go." He stood and rushed out.

At home, Alexander lay across the bed. Feeling restless, he decided to go outside and rake up the fallen leaves. As he raked, a young neighbor, Cory played with a football next door. Cory tossed the ball high into the air, caught the ball, and ran around imaginary defenders, all while providing his own commentary and cheer. Alexander focused on his task. As Cory ran by, he fumbled the football in Alexander's direction. Alexander kneeled to pick up the ball, and Cory stopped and smiled.

"Hi, Alexander," Cory said.

"Hey, Cory," Alexander tried to hand over the ball, but Cory turned and ran.

"I'm going deep," Cory said.

Alexander threw the ball high into the air and Cory caught it and ran for a touchdown. Cory trotted back over and tossed the ball back to Alexander.

"I'm going to run a post route this time."

"Okay." Cory stood on the line of scrimmage with one foot forward and his arms hanging at his sides.

Alexander stood beside him and surveyed the field. "Blue forty-one. Blue forty-two. Hike," Alexander called out.

Cory took off like an arrow and turned slightly towards the center of the field, and Alexander threw the ball. Cory caught it and ran for another touchdown. He spiked the ball hard and celebrated with a dance.

As he trotted back over to Alexander, Cory's mother

stepped out onto the front porch. "Cory, get over here," she yelled out.

Cory stopped and trotted over to her.

"What did I tell you?" she scolded.

"We were just playing catch," Corey said.

"I don't care," she grabbed his hand and pulled him into the house.

Alexander threw up his hand and waved but Cory's mother cut her eyes at him and furrowed her brow. She yanked Cory inside, and Alexander understood why. He lowered his head, picked up the rake, and continued gathering leaves. When he finished, he went back to his bedroom and didn't come out until dinner was served. He sat twirling his fork into the spaghetti with meat sauce, but he didn't have much of an appetite. He ate a portion of his food and excused himself. He returned to his bedroom where he remained for the next twenty-four hours.

On the following day, Alexander stayed in bed until noon. He knew Orlando and Vivian had promised to talk to the vigilante that evening, and he was anxious to hear how the discussion had gone. When he heard them enter the house, he waited for them to call him out, but they never did, and this made him worry.

Finally, Vivian knocked on the door and called him out to dinner. He sat down at the table and ate his food, all the while waiting for them to fill him in on their conversation. The subject was never broached, and Alexander had lost patience. He had to know, so finally, he asked, "Did you speak to her?"

Orlando and Vivian glanced at each other and nodded.

"Well, what did she say?"

"She was unreasonable, as I thought she would be," Orlando said.

"Unreasonable how?"

"We were unable to convince her to stop posting the flyers —but I'm sure with a little time, she will stop and move on to someone else. Just give it some time," Orlando said.

"I don't have time. People are looking at me like I'm a monster," Alexander said.

"They'll get over it. You are not the only one in the area she has done this to," Vivian said.

"Some of them deserved it, but you don't," Orlando said.

"But I will always be grouped in with them, don't you see?" Alexander said. He got up and went back into his room.

ON FRIDAY MORNING, 72 hours later, Alexander arose early and decided to go to work. He thought it would help get his mind off things. Along the way, he saw fresh flyers stapled to the light poles. He tore them down and continued on his way. He was the first to arrive at the Bywater Café, and again, he found more flyers plastered on the door. Instead of going inside, he continued down the street. He made his way to Hillsborough Street and disappeared into a greenway where he hiked in solitude all morning. He contemplated his next move and moving away was what he thought best. He went home and packed his belongings in a suitcase and took off.

He went to Wake Tabernacle and found Reverend Talbert sitting in his office.

Reverend Talbert surveyed Alexander's suitcase and empty eyes. He had never seen Alexander so distraught. He stood and gathered himself before speaking, "Alexander." He smiled half-heartedly and said, "Come—have a seat."

Alexander sat across from Reverend Talbert and opened his mouth to speak, but nothing came out. Tears filled his eyes and ran down his face.

"What's wrong?" Reverend Talbert asked.

Tears flowed harder. His shoulders slumped and he sobbed uncontrollably.

Reverend Talbert stepped around his desk and placed his hand on Alexander's back while Alexander told him about his troubles, and Reverend Talbert listened sympathetically.

"So, I can't stay there anymore," Alexander said.

"Where would you go?"

"Can I stay here for a while? I'll earn my keep. I'll clean and take care of the grounds for you."

"Where would you sleep?" Reverend Talbert asked.

"I thought I could sleep in the basement. There's a bed in the closet I could use—just until I figure things out," he pleaded.

"Sure," Reverend Talbert said, "But eventually, you will have to face it and get on with your life, you know."

"Yes, I know. But I have to get away for now," he said, sobbing.

"Of course," Reverend Talbert said.

They went down into the basement and into a storage room where a folding, twin-size bed stood against one wall and the other walls were lined with stacks of crates and boxes.

Alexander looked around and nodded. "This is fine."

"No, it's not." Reverend Talbert stepped across the hallway and opened a door to an empty office. "This would be more suitable," he said.

Alexander settled into the empty office, feeling it was all he needed. Just a place to lay his head as he figured things out. He busied himself with janitorial duties around the church. He vacuumed, swept and mopped the floors, cleaned the bathrooms, and wiped and polished the pews. He performed maintenance duties and landscaping and worked in the kitchen, preparing Sunday meals and for other church functions. Sometimes, when there was nothing else to be done, he would sit at the piano and play late into the night.

WINTER WAS SETTING IN, the trees were bare, and a polar vortex pushed down into North Carolina, bringing unusually cold days and nights. The old boiler pushed heat into the upper levels of the church but sent very little to the basement. Alexander lay in bed under a thin blanket, watching his breath rise into the air. He recalled seeing a space heater in the basement once. He climbed out of bed and searched the storage closet—it wasn't there. He looked around the basement before giving up and climbing back into bed. He would have to deal with the cold and try to sleep through it. He awoke the next morning with stiff bones. He dressed and went up to the sanctuary where the temperature was more suitable. He worked the cold out of his hands on the piano. He sat playing various songs he had learned over the years and worked on a few new songs he had heard during service.

"I didn't know you could play so well," Sister Becky said.

Alexander turned and saw her sitting on a pew. "I'm sorry. I didn't know anyone was here."

"No apologies. You sounded good."

"I wouldn't say I sounded all that good, but thanks."

"Do you think you could fill in for Paula today? She has to work," Sister Becky said.

"Fill in for what?"

"Children's choir rehearsal."

"Oh, I'm sorry. I forgot that's today."

"So, can you fill in on piano?"

"Sure," Alexander said, happily.

The kids slowly filtered in. Some parents dropped them off

and left. Others waited in the parking lot, and some waited inside the church. Becky ushered the kids into the choir stand and handed Alexander a stack of sheet music. "This is what we'll be rehearsing today. Now do you read music or play by ear?"

"Both, although I'm a little rusty."

"That's okay." She smiled. Sister Becky stood before the choir wearing a long, grey skirt and a white blouse. She was a slim, late-middle-aged woman with black shoulder-length hair. "Okay kids, we're going to start with *The Light*."

Alexander looked at the sheet music and pressed down on the ivory keys.

The choir swayed left to right. The altos started it off.

Altos: "One day when I was walking along."

Choir: "I saw the light from heaven come down."

Altos: "I heard a voice, but I saw no one."

Choir: "I saw the light from heaven come down."

Altos: "My hands were attached to the gospel plow."

Choir: "I saw the light from heaven come down."

Altos: "And I would not turn away from my journey now."

Choir: "I saw the light from heaven come down."

Altos: "I saw the light."

Choir: "I saw the beautiful light."

Altos: "I saw the light."

Choir: "I saw the light shining all around me. I saw the light, hallelujah, I saw the light from heaven come down."

Altos: "I saw the light."

Choir: "I saw the beautiful light."

Altos: "I saw the light."

Choir: "I saw the light shining all around me. I saw the light, hallelujah, I saw the light from heaven come down."

Sister Becky gave the sign to repeat the chorus, and the children followed suit. When the song ended, Sister Becky beamed with joy. "Wonderful job. Wonderful," she said. "Lonnie, soften your voice a little. Jamal. Sing from your diaphragm, okay?"

"Yes, ma'am," Jamal said.

"From the top," she said.

Rehearsal went on for another hour and when it concluded, Alexander went downstairs and prepared to go out and look for a new job. He wouldn't look so close to home this time. He put on his coat and went outside.

"Alexander, do you have a minute?" Sister Becky called after him.

"I have to catch a bus," he said.

"Where are you going?"

"To North Hills to check on some job applications."

"Can I offer you a ride?"

"Sure, thanks."

They climbed into her car and set off.

"Thanks for your help today," she said.

"You're welcome. I enjoyed it."

"Oh, good. Can you play tomorrow?"

"Sure."

"Oh, wonderful. Paula cannot make it tomorrow either. Her work schedule changed, and she can't always be here on Sundays."

"I'm available anytime you need me, but please, let Reverend Talbert know first. Also, you are aware that I can't be left alone with any children, so another adult will always have to be present," Alexander said.

"I, and other parents, will always be present," she said.

"Okay. In that case, I can do it," he said.

"Thank you so much," she smiled.

"You can let me out here," he said, as they approached Six Forks Rd.

"I'll see you tomorrow."

Reverend Talbert officially made Alexander an employee of the church. This satisfied his probation officer, but it didn't satisfy Alexander. For if he could ever afford a decent apartment, he would need to make more money. He submitted applications all over town, but no one called. Orlando's friend, the landscaper, would need help in the spring, but Alexander needed work now. He increasingly regretted leaving the Bywater Café. Desirae was the only person to give him a chance, and he should have stuck it out like she suggested. He wanted to crawl back and ask for his job, but how could he face her now? She was willing to fight for him when he wasn't willing to fight for himself, and a woman like Desirae couldn't respect a man who wasn't willing to fight. So, he couldn't ask for his job back now, besides, it was too late anyway. She had already replaced him with someone else, and that opportunity had passed. *Lesson learned,* he thought, as he stood outside the church trimming the hedges.

Using wooden stakes and strings as a guide, he trimmed the hedges back to the base of the shrubs in a straight line. He stood back and examined his work. Satisfied with the outcome, he removed the stakes and raked up the clippings.

"A-Rod," someone called from the sidewalk.

He paused. It was a name he hadn't heard since he left prison.

"Yo, A-Rod," he heard again.

He stiffened and turned to see Moe coming towards him.

"What's up, Moe?" Alexander said.

They slapped five and embraced.

"It's good to see you, man. I didn't know you were out," Moe said.

"Almost six months now," Alexander said.

"What are you doing here?"

"I grew up in this church. I help out with maintenance and stuff."

"Okay, that's cool. We should catch up over drinks," Moe said.

"Yeah, that sounds good. Just let me know when."

"How about now? There's a brewery right down the street," Moe said.

"Oh, I can't now. I have some more work to do."

"Come on, man. It looks good out here."

"All right. Just give me a minute to finish up," Alexander said, reluctantly. He finished raking the clippings and put away the tools.

He and Moe strolled over to the brewery and sat at the bar. Moe ordered a cream stout and Alexander ordered a Belgian ale.

"I normally don't see anyone who reminds me of prison, but it's good to see you, A-Rod."

"It's good to see you, too. I don't know how I could've made it without you looking out for me."

"Ahh, don't mention it, man. You didn't belong in there," Moe said.

"This system doesn't care whether we belong there or not. It will eat you up either way," Alexander said.

"That's the truth. Here's to freedom," Moe said, holding up his glass. They toasted and drank to freedom. "How are you getting along?"

"It's been rough," Alexander admitted.

"Where are you staying?"

"At the church," Alexander said, solemnly. "I'm still trying to find work, but no one wants to hire a felon."

"Tell me about it. They make it so hard to succeed. It's like they want us to fuck up, just so they can send us back, you know?" Moe said.

"Yeah, I know what you mean."

"Well A-Rod, if you need work, I can put you on," Moe said.

"Put me on with what?"

"I could use a courier."

"A courier?" Alexander said, incredulously.

"Yeah. I need someone who wouldn't draw suspicion to deliver packages to some associates."

"What sort of packages?"

"Don't worry about what sort of packages. Just make the deliveries and you get two hundred dollars."

"Two hundred dollars per package?"

"Yeah. It's easy money."

"How many deliveries are we talking about here?"

"Once or twice a day."

"That's potentially fourteen hundred to twenty-eight hundred dollars a week?" Alexander asked.

"Potentially, yes. What do you say?"

The work sounded easy, but it also sounded like trouble. "Thank you, but that type of work is not for me."

"That's cool, but if it gets rough out there, give me a holler. I got you," Moe said.

Later, Alexander lay in bed thinking of Moe's offer. It sounded so easy, and it would give him what he needed to get on his feet. He could get an apartment and maybe a car, but what of the consequences? There were always consequences, like going back to prison, and nothing was worth that. He pushed the offer out of his head, but on difficult nights, when he was hungry and cold, the offer crept back in.

Alexander reported to his probation officer for his monthly visit. He sat in the waiting room until Maurice Taylor called him back into his office. Alexander saw that Officer Taylor was impeccably dressed as usual, but several cardboard boxes aligned the wall.

"Are you going somewhere?" Alexander asked.

"I'm getting deployed back to Afghanistan," Officer Taylor informed him.

"How long will you be gone?"

"Six months, if I'm lucky," he admitted.

"I'm sorry to hear that," Alexander said.

"It's no big deal. It's part of the job," he said.

"Are you in the Army?"

"The Reserves," he answered. "How are things going for you?" he asked Alexander.

"I'm still staying and working at the church until I find something else," Alexander said.

Maurice Taylor took in a deep breath and nodded his head. "I know Reverend Talbert well, so I'm good with that," he said.

"Who should I report to now?" Alexander asked.

"I'm moving you to unsupervised probation for the remainder of your term. Therefore, you no longer need to check-in every thirty days, but you still must register in whatever county you reside, and you can't leave the state without permission. Do you understand?"

"Yes, sir," Alexander answered.

"Also, if you get arrested for any reason, that could violate your probation and you could be sent back to prison. You got it?"

"Yes, sir," Alexander answered.

"Good." Maurice Taylor picked up the phone and dialed a number. "Hey Teddy, will you step over for a minute? Mr. Merchant is here," he said.

Moments later a stout white man with a bald head stepped

into the office. His necktie hung loose around his neck, and his shirt sleeves were rolled up to his elbows.

"This is Mr. Teddy Nivinsky," Maurice Taylor said. "If you need anything, you can contact Mr. Nivinsky."

Alexander shook Teddy Nivinsky's hand. "Yes, sir, I will."

Teddy Nivinsky handed Alexander a business card and left the room.

"Thank you," Alexander said.

"Don't make me regret my decision," Maurice Taylor said.

"I won't, sir. I promise. And good luck in Afghanistan," Alexander said.

Alexander left the probation office feeling excited. It was the first good news he had received since he had found those damning flyers plastered all over his neighborhood. He felt that things may be finally turning around.

Paula's work schedule kept her away from service more and more, and Alexander was becoming the full-time pianist. Sometimes he played the organ, but he was much better on the piano. Reverend Talbert pushed Alexander to play the organ more, but Alexander was no gospel organist. A gospel organist requires a touch from God, an innate skill set that's almost impossible to learn, you either have it or you don't. One rarely sees a gospel organist reading sheet music. Like a jazz musician, the organist uses improvisations to drive the service. They underscore the sermon, pushing the tempo to stir up emotions. The organist feels and interprets the spirit of the congregation and knows when to heighten it up or tone it down. Working in concert with the preacher to bring on the desired effect, which is sometimes a quiet moment of reflection, and at other times a burst of kinetic energy that runs through the church like a herd of wild horses. This was not Alexander's skill set, but he tried his best.

When Sister Becky's father passed away unexpectedly, and

she needed to travel up to Chicago to settle his affairs, she told Alexander she wasn't sure when she would return and needed him to take over the children's choir until she returned. "I left instructions for the parents to stay at the church during rehearsal," she said.

Reverend Talbert made the announcement during service and informed the parents the children's choir rehearsal would take place at its regularly scheduled time, Saturday mornings at 10:00.

Alexander spent the week preparing for his debut as the children's choir director. He studied the catalog of songs, praying all along that the weather didn't disrupt his debut. The polar vortex pushed deeper into the state, bringing record low temperatures along with it, and to make matters worse, the worst snowstorm in a quarter of a century had North Carolina in its sights. He monitored the weather closely, and when the meteorologists estimated the storm's arrival to early Monday morning, he sent out a group text message to all the parents, informing them that rehearsal was still on.

He arose early Saturday morning and practiced the music some more. He opened the church and waited for the kids to arrive, but they never did. He sent out another text message and waited some more, and when he concluded that no one was coming, he went outside and prepared for the storm. He figured the children's parents were preparing for the storm, too, which explained why no one showed up. He imagined they were at the grocery store, trying to get their hands on whatever supplies were left. The grocery store shelves were certainly bare by now because no one panicked like southerners when a snowstorm was upon them. He laid out the snow shovels and spread rock salt around the walkways and parking lots. Although the storm wasn't expected until early

Monday morning, one could never put too much faith in the local weather person, so he thought it better to be prepared.

On Sunday morning, Alexander opened the church and prepared the sanctuary for service. He sat at the organ and guided the service along the best he could. He played through the morning worship, devotional service, and offering. The deacon stood at the podium and called on the children's choir to come up and sing a selection. It was the moment Alexander had been waiting for, he stood smiling, and beckoned the children forward, but no one came.

The deacon again called the children's choir forward. Several children stood, and a few came forward, and the other children were pulled back into their seats by their parents.

Alexander stood perplexed, not entirely certain of what was happening.

Reverend Talbert came to the podium and addressed the congregation, "I'm not sure what's going on here, but Sister Tina called the children's choir to sing. Please, come forward now," he said, sternly.

The parents sat stone-faced and held their kids where they were.

Alexander looked to Reverend Talbert and back to the congregation, and it was at that moment the realization set in, and he understood what was happening. The parents did not want their children around Alexander. He slowly backed up towards the organ and sat down. He tried to play, but he couldn't focus, and he fumbled his way through the remainder of the service.

Reverend Talbert called an emergency meeting with the parents immediately after service and the parents and church leadership all gathered in the dining hall downstairs.

Alexander quietly slipped in and sat near the door.

Reverend Talbert stood facing them. "Will you all please tell me what that stunt was all about today?" he asked, angrily.

No one spoke.

Reverend Talbert stood, surveying the room. "It was obviously a planned occurrence, so someone please tell me the purpose of that spectacle?"

"With all due respect, Pastor Talbert, we are uncomfortable with Brother Alexander working so closely with our children," Brother Tony said.

"You have all known Alexander since he was a child. Sister Becky is out of town, and she asked him to fill in for her until she returns. What is the problem with that?" Reverend Talbert said.

"Be that as it may, sir, we are still uncomfortable with a sex offender hanging around our kids," Tony said.

The word sex offender hung in the air like a cloud of smoke and Alexander sunk further into his chair.

Reverend Talbert stood, shocked by what he was hearing. "The boy made a mistake—years ago, for that matter. Have none of you ever made a mistake?"

The parents were unmoved.

Alexander had heard enough. He left the church, not even stopping to get his coat. He aimlessly stumbled around the city. He had no destination in mind, he just had to keep moving. *Lord, will I ever escape this misery?*

The cold air had set in. It hung thick and heavy, almost visible. Snow fell but he barely noticed. Dark thoughts filled his head, and he was losing the will to go on. The wind blew harder as the snow swirled around him. It was falling in thick flakes, and a layer was forming on the streets and in the folds of his dress shirt. He found himself near the Boylan public housing projects. He recalled Moe saying that he lived there. He stepped inside the development and looked around. Suspicious eyes watched him closely. His tie hung loose from his neck, and his white shirt clung to his skin. Kids ran past him, playing in the snow, and a man stood in a doorway intently watching him.

Alexander went over. "Hey, is Moe around?" he asked.

"Who the fuck are you?" the man shouted.

"Alex," he paused, "A-Rod. I just need to see him."

The man pulled back his coat, exposing the handle of his nine-millimeter. "Get the fuck out of here."

Alexander backed away frantically.

"Hey, chill man, that's my boy," Moe said, sticking his head out the door.

"You know this fool?" the man asked.

"Yeah, he's cool," Moe said.

"Don't you know better than to walk up in here like that? You better call first next time," the man said.

"Come on in, A-Rod," Moe said.

Alexander stepped inside.

"Damn you look fucked up. Rough day?" Moe asked.

Alexander nodded.

"Have a seat."

Alexander sat on the sofa in front of an assortment of liquor bottles covering the coffee table. The bachelor pad was slightly decorated. There was a black leather couch and a matching leather chair, a fifty-gallon fish tank with two snake-head fish circling each other, and a painting of a shirtless Jesus, with dreadlocked hair and his hands bound together by a rope. Alexander stared at the painting, and the painting stared back at him.

Moe handed Alexander a glass. "Help yourself," he said.

Alexander filled his glass with whiskey and drank it down.

"Have all you want," Moe said.

Alexander refilled his glass and leaned back on the couch.

Moe turned on the television channel to Sunday Night Football. "What do you think these Panthers gonna do?" Moe asked.

"I really don't know."

"Yeah, they've been on some bullshit this season," Moe said.

"They have a weak offensive line, and he doesn't have anyone to throw to," Alexander said, watching the quarterback on the small screen.

"They need to fire that damn coach," Moe said.

As they settled into watching the game, Moe cut open a cigar and emptied the contents out on the table. He filled the cigar with marijuana and rerolled it, lit it, and sucked in the smoke. He took another drag and handed it to Alexander.

Alexander filled his lungs with the marijuana smoke. He took another drag and handed it back.

"Do you want that gig we talked about?"

Alexander let out a heavy sigh.

"We'll talk about it. Just chill," Moe said.

Alexander drank more whiskey. The weed and liquor lessened his pain, but he knew the relief was only temporary, and pain would soon come stampeding back.

The man from outside came in and sat next to Alexander on the worn sofa.

"Pelon, this is A-Rod. He's our new courier," Moe said.

"That's what's up," Pelon said, and he and Alexander bumped fists. Pelon rolled another blunt and passed it around.

"How's traffic?" Moe asked Pelon.

"It's kind of slow," Pelon said.

"It's the weather, but you know they're coming to get that high," Moe said.

"Yeah, I'm going back out in a few. I just need to warm up a bit," Pelon said. He had a few drinks and watched the game.

The wind was howling outside, and snow built up on the windowsills.

"Do you have any hand warmers?" Alexander asked.

"Any what?"

"Hand warmers. They come in plastic packs, and when you break them, they warm up. You can put them in your pockets and in your boots to keep your hands and feet warm," Alexander explained. "You can get them at any sporting goods store."

"Best believe I'll get some tomorrow," Pelon said.

They smoked another blunt, and Pelon went back outside.

The air was thick with smoke and Alexander sat staring through the window at the snow swirling outside. Dark thoughts filled his brain and gripped his soul, pulling him down into a deep, dark place of anguish and despair. Tears filled his eyes and he wiped them away. "I have to go," he said, standing up.

"You going out in that storm? You can crash here if you need somewhere to stay," Moe offered.

"No, I'll be all right," Alexander said.

"A'ight. I'll text you when I have a package ready, okay?" Moe said.

Alexander nodded and dropped twenty dollars on the table and took a bottle of Jack Daniels with him.

Stepping out into the night, he treaded along in knee-deep snow, with only the whiskey to keep him warm. The streets were empty, the stores were closed, and the merchants were long gone. Nothing else moved except Alexander treading aimlessly in the night.

He lost his shoe in the snow. He dropped to his knees and searched for his shoe, but he eventually gave up and treaded on. He eventually came upon a familiar sign with an arrow pointing to the right, the Raleigh Rose Garden, where he and

Natalie had had their first date. *The Rose Garden, where it all began,* he thought, *can't think of a better place to end my misery.* He turned towards the Rose Garden and treaded on. He fell and got up, he fell again and crawled before getting up to continue.

Alexander made his way across the parking lot and down towards the stage of the amphitheater. He continued past the stage and into the garden of dried stems buried in the snow. He sat at the base of the redwood tree and lifted the bottle to his mouth, but it was empty. He tossed it aside and gazed at the dunes of white snow glowing in the night. He thought it was beautiful, certainly the most beautiful night he had seen in years.

The snow continued to fall, blanketing his legs and his arms. He could no longer feel his hands and feet. Nature was taking its course, and his pain and suffering was floating away. *It's a good ending,* he thought, *a good ending to a troubled life.* His core temperature decreased so his arms and legs stiffened as the snow gathered upon him. By morning, he would be completely covered, becoming one of the snow dunes he marveled. He closed his eyes as his consciousness drifted away.

CHAPTER

THIRTY

Masoud Amini peered out of the window in the direction where the young man had disappeared. He paced around his living room and looked out again. *He can't still be down there. He can't,* he thought. He sat on his worn sofa and reached for the Holy Quran, as he did on most nights, but he couldn't concentrate on his studies. His mind kept drifting to the young man he saw disappear behind the blinding snow. He peered out again and thought, *He could be in trouble.* He put on his coat and went out to see where the young man had gone. Visibility was low and the once visible footprints had mostly disappeared, but there were remnants of them leading into the garden. Masoud Amini followed his trail, all along, praying to Allah that the young man had safely passed through the park and made it home.

The garden was as still as an icy lake. Masoud Amini surveyed the landscape, looking for anything that didn't belong, a flash of color, a bump in the snow. He pushed deeper into the garden, which looked completely undisturbed. *He is not here,* he thought, breathing a sigh of relief.

Masoud started towards home when something caught his eye. It was a mound covered in snow at the base of the redwood tree. He knew the garden well. He knew all the bushes, the trees, the ferns and the plants, and there was nothing at the base of the redwood tree that would form that shape in the snow. *Is it a log? A bundle of trash?* He moved closer and saw that the shape outlined a human body. He darted towards the figure, dropped to his knees, and brushed the snow away from the young man's body.

"Please, be alive," he said, "Please, be alive." He felt for a pulse. Feeling nothing, he shook the young man and tapped his face. "Hey, wake up. Wake up," he screamed. He placed his ear at the young man's mouth, listening for breathing. Masoud heard nothing, but when he saw the chest rise by just the slightest measure, he knew the young man was alive.

"Praise Allah. All praises to Allah," Masoud Amini exclaimed. He hoisted the limp body onto his shoulder and carried him down the street to his small-one level home and placed him in front of the fireplace. He picked up his phone and dialed 9-1-1 but heard a busy signal. He removed the young man's wet pants and shirt. He wrapped him in blankets and poured warm tea into his mouth.

When the young man coughed it up, emptying the contents of his stomach onto the floor, Masoud said, "That's good. It means your body wants to live." He put the cup of tea back up to the young man's mouth and was relieved to see he kept it down this time. "Good. Good," Masoud said.

He watched him through the night, but the stranger never moved except under his eyelids. Masoud was encouraged. He stoked the fire, keeping watch until daylight crept through the window.

"Grandfather Mountain..." the stranger mumbled.

Masoud hopped to his feet and rushed over to the limp

body, finding him fast asleep. He added wood to the fire, all along, praying to Allah for help. He rubbed Alexander's hands with anointed oil and checked for frostbite. The stranger continued to sleep, his eyes moving rapidly under his eyelids. Masoud kept watch.

Hours later, the stranger's eyes fluttered open, and he rushed over. "What is your name, young man?"

The stranger looked through him.

"Your name? What is your name?"

"Grandfather Mountain. Take me to Grandfather Mountain," the stranger repeated in a state of delirium.

"How do you feel? Can you sit up?" When the stranger didn't answer, Masoud said, "I'll get you some soup." Masoud rushed into the kitchen, but when he returned with the bowl of vegetable soup, the young man was fast asleep. Masoud Amini kept the soup simmering on the stove, and he sat watching for the stranger to awaken, but his eyes grew heavy. The fire warmed his face, and he, too, slept.

When Alexander opened his eyes, he sat up and looked around the unfamiliar room and at the strange man sleeping in a chair across from him.

"Where am I?" Alexander said in a raspy voice.

Masoud Amini awoke and gazed at him.

"Where am I?" he repeated.

"I found you buried in the snow. I thought you were dead. When I realized you were alive, I brought you back here."

Alexander was perplexed. "Where did you find me?"

"In the Rose Garden," Masoud Amini said, pointing toward the window.

Alexander had no recollection of entering the Rose Garden.

Sitting with Moe was the last thing he recalled. "How did I get there?" he asked.

"I saw you walk by and enter the garden. I could tell you were heavily inebriated, and when I didn't see you return, I worried that something bad had happened, so I went into the garden to look for you. I found you covered in the snow," Masoud said.

Alexander tried to remember how he had ended up in that predicament, but it was all a haze. He had blacked out, and the last twelve hours of his life were lost to him.

"What is your name?"

"Alexander Merchant."

"I am Masoud Amini. It is a pleasure to meet you."

"The pleasure is mine," Alexander said.

"Are you hungry?"

"Yes, I am."

Masoud went into the kitchen and returned with a bowl of vegetable soup and a cup of chai tea, placing them on the table. "Can you walk?"

"I think so," Alexander said. He stood with the blanket still wrapped around him and went over to the table.

Masoud joined him at the table.

"Is there someone you wish to call?"

"No," Alexander said.

"Do you have any family? Someone who may be looking for you?"

"No. It's only me. I don't know what I was doing in the Rose Garden, and I shudder to think what my intentions were, as I was in a very dark place... I want to thank you for saving me, Mr. Amini. I owe you a tremendous debt of gratitude," Alexander said.

"You are welcome. I have been in a dark place a few times in my own life, but our God sees us through," Masoud said.

Alexander pressed his lips together and looked away.

"Are you not religious?" Masoud asked.

"I am. I have been all my life, but I don't believe I've benefited much from my devotion," Alexander said.

"The Almighty's grace is not always apparent, but it is there. Whether we see it or not," Masoud said.

"I suppose so," Alexander said, dubiously.

"Where is your home?"

"I don't have a home—I've been staying in the basement of a church," Alexander said, finally picking up his spoon to eat.

"I see. As you were sleeping, you continuously spoke of Grandfather Mountain. Is that where you are from?"

"No, I'm from here. I grew up nearby, in fact."

"Where is Grandfather Mountain and what does it mean to you?"

"It's a state park in western North Carolina, but it doesn't mean anything to me. It's about a four-hour drive from here."

"Do you have family or friends there?"

"No, I don't know of anyone who lives there."

"Then why did you want to go there?"

"I don't."

"You asked me to take you there."

"I did?" He placed the spoon on the table.

"Yes, several times. It was all you said."

"I honestly don't know. My pastor grew up there, but..." he paused, "Yes, my pastor grew up there before it was named Grandfather Mountain—he told me once about a monastery there." He sipped his tea.

"A monastery?"

"Yes. He had attempted to join the monastery, but later realized it wasn't for him. Yes, I do want to go there. Will you take me? Will you take me to Grandfather Mountain?"

"For what purpose? Do you want to live as a monk?" Masoud Amini asked.

"I have nothing else. There is nowhere else for me to go." Alexander placed the mug on the table.

"That is a big step, Mr. Merchant. Monasticism is a hard life. It is not for everyone," Masoud said.

"It's for me. It would offer me more than this life here ever could," Alexander said.

"Okay. If that is what you wish. I'll take you as soon as the roads are passable," Masoud said.

"Thank you, Mr. Amini. Thank you so much."

Alexander spent the afternoon imagining his life in a monastery. There would be no more judging, no more exclusion, and no more fighting to survive. He was done fighting. He only wanted to live in peace, and if moving to a monastery was necessary to find that peace, then he would turn away from the modern world, and embrace monasticism wholeheartedly.

All afternoon, Alexander watched Masoud in the kitchen cooking their evening meal. The aromas of saffron, turmeric, and lamb filled the house. The aromas lured Alexander into the kitchen. "Can I help with anything?" he asked.

"No, I have it," Masoud said.

"What are you cooking?"

"Baghali polo and lamb. It's a traditional meal in my homeland."

"Where's your homeland?"

"Iran." Masoud took two plates from his cupboard and motioned for Alexander to sit.

"How long have you lived in the United States?" Alexander asked, taking a seat.

"Twenty-seven years."

"Do you miss it?"

"Every day."

The baghali polo enraptured Alexander's taste buds. "This is amazing," Alexander said.

Masoud grinned and nodded. "Mr. Merchant, you say you were in a dark place when I found you. May I ask you the cause of your darkness?"

Alexander sighed and looked away.

"My apologies, Mr. Merchant. I don't mean to pry."

"It's okay. I was just trying to take my mind off it for a bit, but I can never seem to escape it for long," Alexander said.

He told Masoud his tale of Emily, her death, and of losing their home. He told him of Natalie—how they met, and of his crime, and the life sentence which he believed he would never get beyond. He told him about prison, the choices he had to make, and the things he had to do to survive.

Masoud listened intently.

Alexander went on, telling him about Buff, the assault, and of his attackers, one of whom would forever be bound to a wheelchair. "It is the worst thing I have ever done, and I barely remember doing it. I remember the attack, the violation, but the rest of it is a blur. One moment I was being attacked, and the next, I was locked away in segregation. I was told what I had done, and I saw the report, but it's like I was lifted away, like my mind went somewhere else," Alexander explained.

Masoud poured tea as Alexander continued, "My case was referred to the district attorney for prosecution, and I was certain I would spend an additional twenty-five years in prison because of it, but the district attorney declined to prosecute, so I was released. I thought I was given a second chance, a chance to do something worthwhile with my life. I found work, was about to enroll in school, things were going well, but society wasn't done with me. Society won't let me move on."

"How so?"

Alexander told him about the flyers. How the vigilante

forced him out of his neighborhood and into the basement of the church. He told him about the children's choir and how his own church family didn't want him there.

"So, I left. I went out into the storm, just wanting it to be over. I smoked marijuana and drank more whiskey than my body could handle, and the rest I don't remember. When I came to, I was here with you."

Masoud said nothing. He only sipped his tea and stared into the flames.

Alexander watched the flames flickering in Masoud's squinted eyes. He sensed a shift in Masoud's attitude, and he wondered if his tale had conjured up some dark memories from Masoud's past. They sat in silence for some time before Masoud excused himself and went off to bed. Alexander sat up alone. He wondered if he had shared too much of his story, and if Masoud still wanted him there after learning of his transgressions. He wanted alcohol, but there was none to be had in the strict Muslim home, so he sat by the flames until he dozed off to sleep.

The next morning, he was awakened by Masoud running water in the Kitchen. Alexander got up and folded his blanket. "Is there someplace I can put this?" he asked.

"You can take it into the guest bedroom. You can sleep in there tonight," Masoud said.

"And would you mind if I used your shower?" Alexander asked.

"No, of course. You'll find everything you need in there," Masoud said, pointing to the bathroom.

"Thank you," Alexander said.

"You are welcome. I have to go out for a while. I'll be back in a few hours," Masoud said.

Alexander went into the bathroom and climbed into the shower. The hot water felt good on his dry skin. When he emerged from the bathroom, Masoud had already gone. Alexander found a pot of coffee and a bagel waiting for him. He sat and ate and reflected on his decision to leave Raleigh for Grandfather Mountain, and the idea excited him.

Later on, after dinner, Alexander and Masoud sat near the fireplace.

Masoud sat pensive, staring at the flames. He hadn't said much since returning home, and Alexander wondered if he was wearing out his welcome. "Mr. Amini," Alexander said.

"Call me Masoud," he said.

"Okay, Masoud. I know that my request for you to take me to Grandfather Mountain is a lot to ask, and I no longer think it's necessary."

"Do you no longer wish to go?"

"I could take the bus. I feel that I've burdened you enough."

"Nonsense. I will take you as I promised."

Alexander nodded graciously.

"You know Alexander, your story is not much different from my own. I grew up on a farm near Sari, Iran. We grew figs, pomegranates, and apricots."

"What's it like there?" Alexander asked.

"The farm overlooked the Caspian Sea, and the land is more beautiful than you could imagine—so much that I lack the English words to describe it. I had worked the farm all my life. It was all I had ever known, and all I had wished to know. When one labors in paradise, on his own land, it never feels like work at all, because we are laboring out of love, the way a parent does for a child you see. We didn't work to build wealth, but we worked to cultivate our relationship with the land, because it is that relationship that sustained us, and afforded us the wonderful life we had. We worked the land, harvested our crops, and took them to market. Although I never enjoyed going to market, at least not early on. The market, where we sold our crops, was in the city center of Sari, and people in the city were not as nice or as friendly as the people who lived in the countryside.

"One day, as I was manning our produce stand, a woman approached wanting to purchase some apricots, and the girl standing behind her was the most beautiful girl I had ever seen. I stood mesmerized by her hazel eyes and her olive skin. So much that I was unable to calculate the cost correctly, nor could I calculate the proper change. My father eventually brushed me aside and completed the transaction himself," Masoud chuckled.

Alexander sat up in his seat listening to Masoud's tale.

"A few weeks passed before I saw her again. She was again with her mother, and as they passed, her mother never looked in our direction. I realized that my moment of opportunity was passing, and I needed to act quickly. I asked them if they would like some fresh figs. I told them we had picked them that morning. They kept walking. 'The apricots are fresh too,' I said. This got her attention, and they came over to our stand. My father took the woman's order as I stood gazing at her daughter. She told me her name was Samira, and from that moment on, she was all I thought about."

"Was she a local girl?" Alexander asked.

"She didn't live far from the market, but I didn't know that at the time."

Alexander sat listening.

"There was a dairy farm adjacent to ours, which produced mostly goat milk and cheese products. It was twice the size of our little farm. The Rahbars, who owned the dairy farm, had only one child, a daughter. Therefore, my dad would often send me over to help with the management of their farm. Over time, my knowledge of dairy farming increased, and Mr. Rahbar depended on my help more and more. Mahasti, his daughter, protested her dad's dependence on my labor because she felt she was as capable of managing the farm as I was, but Mr. Rahbar saw no value in teaching Mahasti. He knew she would eventually be married away, so instead, he focused on training me, and she resented him for it. She was always nearby listening and watching everything he taught me, and when he wasn't around, I would teach her all that I had learned.

"We grew close, and I came to think of her as a younger sister. In fact, she would often introduce me as her brother to her classmates," Masoud said, smiling. "As she grew older, she became interested in special cheese blends, using figs and apricots from my family's farm in her creations.

"Her father resisted her creations at first, but her cheese blends became popular, often selling as quickly as she could produce them, and she eventually began taking her cheeses to market, where their popularity increased even more, and it was at that time, when Mr. Rahbar decided on Mahasti's future.

"Meanwhile, my relationship with Samira blossomed. Sometimes I would walk over to her school during recess and talk to her through the fence, and we often left letters for each other in the hedges outside of her house. One day, I planned to ask her to be my wife. We both matriculated into the University of Mazandaran. There, I studied business and industrial management, as it was my hope to transform our family farm into a commercial operation. I saw no use in going to market every day and haggling over prices, when we could sell directly to global suppliers," Masoud said.

"That sounds like the smart thing to do," Alexander said.

"Yes, but when I tried to convince my father, he wouldn't hear it. He felt that our current model had provided all we needed, and he saw no point in changing it. But one day, I knew the farm would be mine to manage, and I planned to get the most out of it.

"Samira studied Persian language and literature. Her brother escorted her to the university and back home each day, which is custom in Iran, but we were able to meet between classes without the presence of a chaperone, as long as we discussed our studies, but any real privacy was impossible. I grew tired of stealing moments to be together, and I decided I would ask for her hand in marriage on the day of my graduation, and not a day later.

"One evening, back at the farm, I found my father sitting on a bench, overlooking the Caspian Sea. It was his favorite place in the world. I told him that Samira and I wished to be married after graduation, and I asked him to speak to her father and arrange it for us, but he refused. He said that I would marry Mahasti instead. But, I couldn't marry Mahasti. I thought of her as a sister, not as a wife," Masoud said.

"Why was he against you marrying Samira?" Alexander asked.

"Samira was from a higher class. Her father was an important businessman in Sari, and my father felt that Samira, who knew nothing about living on a farm, wouldn't be a good match. He also felt that Samira's father wouldn't allow her to marry a farmer. He felt that Mahasti was a better fit and little did I know, he and Mahasti's father had already discussed the matter, and had agreed to merge the two farms after our marriage, giving me the land I needed to transform the farm into a global supplier," Masoud said.

Sounds reasonable, Alexander thought.

"I told him I didn't care about the farm. I only cared about Samira. I pleaded with my father to reconsider, but he wouldn't hear it. His mind was made up.

"Samira did not return to school for the spring semester.

She had given me no indication she wouldn't return, and I wondered what had happened to her. I asked her friends and classmates, but no one knew why she hadn't returned. Her grades were excellent, and she was highly motivated to earn her degree. I left letters in the hedges near her house, but I received no response. She abandoned me with no explanation. I couldn't eat or sleep or focus on my studies. None of it mattered. I just needed to know what had happened to her, and if she was okay.

"One morning, a fellow classmate handed me a letter from Samira. The letter informed me that she was engaged to be married. She was marrying the son of her father's colleague, and therefore, she was not returning to school. I knew the marriage had been arranged by her father, but I didn't understand why she had agreed to it.

"I wrote her letters pleading for her not to marry this man, but to marry me instead. I received no reply, and when I saw the engagement announced in the newspaper, I knew I had lost her. I no longer wrote to her after that, and as her wedding day grew closer, I grew more and more depressed.

"I lay in bed one evening unable to sleep, when I heard tapping on my window. I looked out and saw Samira standing outside. I thought my prayers had been answered. I thought she had called off the wedding and had come to marry me instead. I rushed out to her. I hugged her and kissed her and told her I was glad to see her.

"We walked in silence for a while, neither of us quite knowing what to say. I held her hand and guided her through the dark fields, until we came to the bench where I had asked my father to arrange our marriage. We sat and looked out at the dark sea. She wanted to explain the engagement, but I told her she didn't have to explain. I asked her to run away with me to Tehran or to America where we could be together. She said she didn't want to marry him, but she felt she had no choice in the matter. She couldn't defy her parents. Tears ran down her face.

"I told her how much I loved her, now sobbing with her. She kissed me and laid her head on my chest, and we sat holding each other close. Realizing that was our last moment together, we didn't want to let go. We went into the barn and made love. Afterwards, I took her home, and we said our final goodbyes.

"A few days later, as I sat in class, Samira's friend ran into the classroom screaming that I had to come with her. She said that they were beating Samira at the town square. I rushed out of class. I jumped on a bicycle and rode as fast as I could. When I reached the town square, I saw a crowd dispersing after witnessing some sort of spectacle. I didn't know what was happening, but I knew I had to get there and stop it. I pushed my way through the crowd, but I was too late. I saw Samira lying on the ground in a pool of blood. Her head had been smashed in by a large stone. I rushed to her, wanting to help her in any way I could, but there was nothing to be done. She was already gone. At that moment two men dragged me off of her and started beating me. They hit me with sticks and threw stones at me. I didn't know what to do, and like a coward, I ran away," Masoud said, his eyes burning in anguish.

Alexander hung on to Masoud's every word.

"I later learned Samira and I had been found out. Her brother had found a letter she had written to me, and in that letter, she had referenced the night we spent together. Therefore, her brother and her uncle had killed her in front of everyone. They called it an honor killing, but what honor could come from such a barbaric act? It was at that moment, I decided to leave that god-forsaken country, and to never return.

"I made my way to America. I settled in New York. I found a job and rented a small apartment in Queens. I was getting along well for some time in New York, but after the attacks on September eleventh, it became very difficult for Muslims to live there. I lived under constant scrutiny and suspicion. I was harassed and accosted in the streets. I no longer felt safe, so I came here to Raleigh, and here is where I remained." Masoud Amini stood and went into his bedroom. "We leave tomorrow," he called out, and closed the door behind him.

ON THE FOLLOWING MORNING, Alexander and Masoud prepared for the trip to western North Carolina. They stopped by the church so Alexander could gather his possessions. They loaded them into the back of Masoud's pickup truck and Alexander searched for the address online but found no reference of the monastery.

"I can't find it," he said.

"How much do you know about this monastery?" Masoud asked.

"Not much. I only know that it's at the base of Grandfather Mountain," Alexander said.

"It's a big mountain? Did you ask your pastor?" Masoud inquired.

"No, I'm sure he would have tried to talk me out of going. Besides, I don't want anyone to know where I'll be. When we get there, I'm sure one of the park rangers can direct us." Alexander set the GPS to Grandfather Mountain State Park, as they turned onto Interstate 40.

Climbing up into the Blue Ridge Mountains, the hills were covered with fresh snow. They stopped at the entrance of the park, but found it closed due to the storm. They drove along the exterior of the park, looking for a marker or a road sign pointing them in the right direction, but they saw nothing.

"Did the reverend give you any clues of where to look?" Masoud said.

"No, he didn't. I know he grew up in Linville, and the monastery wasn't far from his home, so we should probably start there," Alexander said.

"Don't worry. We'll find it," Masoud said, holding tightly to the steering wheel.

Getting low on gas, they drove into Linville and pulled into a gas station. Alexander climbed out of the truck and placed the gas nozzle in the tank and filled it up. When Alexander and Masoud went inside the store, a group of men stood near the counter chatting with the cashier. They watched Masoud suspiciously.

"Excuse me. Do you know where I could find the monastery?" Masoud asked.

"There are no mosques here," the cashier said.

Alexander spoke up, "We're not looking for a mosque. We're looking for a Christian monastery. I understand it's near the base of Grandfather Mountain."

"There is nothing like that here," the cashier said coldly.

"Okay, thank you," Alexander said, before they left the store and climbed back into the truck. "What do we do now?" Alexander asked.

Masoud sat with his hands on the steering wheel, not knowing where to go when an old man shuffled out of the store and came over to the truck.

Alexander lowered the window.

"You say you're looking for a monastery, are you?" the old man said.

"Yes, we are. Do you know where we can find it?" Alexander asked.

"Well, there were some monks around years ago, but I don't know what became of 'em. I haven't seen them around in years," the old man said.

"Where did they live?" Masoud asked.

"There's an old church off of highway two-twenty-one, near the Linn Cove Viaduct. Go past the park entrance, and just around the bend, you'll see a dirt road on the right. I believe it's back there somewhere," the man said.

"Thank you, sir," Alexander said, just before the old man waved and walked away.

Masoud turned onto highway 221, towards the Linn Cove Viaduct. After passing the entrance to the park, he slowed down looking for the dirt road the old man had described.

"He said it should be just around the curve," Alexander reminded Masoud.

"This road is full of curves," Masoud said.

As they rounded a sharp curve of almost 180 degrees, the Linn Cove viaduct came into view. The clouds hanging low as they were, made the Viaduct appear to descend from the heavens.

Alexander sat mesmerized by the scenery. "If heaven truly does exist, it must be here in the Blue Ridge Mountains."

Masoud nodded slowly.

"There," Alexander said, pointing.

Masoud stopped the truck and followed Alexander's pointed finger. He didn't see it at first. The road had been grown over, and it appeared to be more of a path than a road. But, peering through the bare trees, he could see an old building perched on top of a hill. Masoud shifted into four-wheel drive and turned onto the road. They slipped and slid along the path until they came to a clearing. A stone wall surrounded the property.

Alexander then recalled Reverend Talbert mentioning the stone wall in his story. "This is it."

"Are you sure?"

"I'm certain." Alexander smiled.

Masoud parked next to a stone rectangular building. A small stone chapel stood at the top of a hill.

They climbed out of the truck and looked around.

Alexander knocked on the door. But when no one answered, he pushed it open and went inside. The wind blew inside the building, stirring up a cloud of dust.

"There is no one here—it's abandoned," Masoud said.

Alexander sighed.

They went from room to room, gazing back in time at what was once a simple existence. They entered a large room and stood next to a grand fireplace stained with soot from heavy use. Several wooden tables and chairs were stacked along a wall.

"This was the dining hall," Alexander announced.

In the kitchen there was a sink, an ice box, a wood burning oven, and a brick oven built into the exterior wall.

Masoud opened the oven door, examining everything closely. "It is in good shape," he said.

Beside the dining hall, stood a wooden door with a stained-glass cross at its center. Behind the door was a small empty room with a cross built into the stone wall. "This was the inner chapel," Masoud said.

On the opposite end of the corridor, they found the sleeping quarters. In each small room, there was a single bed, a chest of drawers, and a nightstand.

Masoud ran his hands across the furniture, admiring its craftsmanship. At the end of the corridor was a closet. Several brown robes hung inside, and a box filled with sandals sat on the floor. "Let's see the main chapel," Masoud said.

They went outside and climbed the hill towards the chapel. As they grew closer, they saw the cause of the abandonment. The chapel stood in ruin. Inside, the floor of the chapel was covered with snow. The interior walls were charred from a fire, and the roof had collapsed into the sanctuary.

Alexander fell to his knees and leaned back against the wall. He felt utterly defeated. "I thought this was my answer," he said.

"It is the answer, don't you see? All praises to Allah—it is the answer." Masoud clasped his hands together.

"How could this be the answer? There's nothing here," Alexander said.

"Yes, but we will rebuild. We will make it a place of interfaith worship, where both Muslims and Christians could come and worship together," Masoud said.

Alexander squinted his eyes in confusion. "A monastery for both Christians and Muslims? How could that work?" Alexander asked.

"I thought you were more open minded than that, Alexander. You are a Christian, because you were born in America, and your parents were Christians. Perhaps, if I were born in America, I would be a Christian too, but I was born in Iran. Therefore, I am a Muslim, but the Almighty does not care where we were born, or what name we call Him. He only cares about what we do with our lives. Don't you understand that?" Masoud said.

"Yes, but I've never heard of such a thing. Besides, I don't know anything about building churches, and where would we get the materials?"

"Look," Masoud said, wiping away the snow beneath them. "These floors are made of stone, and they are good." He placed his hand on the wall behind Alexander. "And these walls are crumbling, but the stones are still good. They can be repurposed," Masoud said.

Alexander looked dubious.

"Christians and Muslims have been fighting each other for centuries, Alexander. Don't you think it is time that we come together?" Masoud asked.

Alexander stood and took in his surroundings.

"For twenty-seven years, I have prayed to Allah for direction. I have prayed for some purpose in my life, and I believe this is why we were brought together. Why else has God taken us through these tribulations?" Masoud said.

"Would people come?"

"Yes, they would. God will send them," Masoud said.

"I suppose we have everything we need in the other building," Alexander concluded.

"Yes, we can start restorations there. It doesn't appear to need much work. Some roof repairs maybe—and we can start working here as soon as the weather improves," Masoud said.

Alexander considered Masoud's proposal and nodded at the possibilities.

They went into town and gathered supplies—food and cleaning products mostly. They returned and gathered firewood for the fireplace and the oven. Once the fire was going, they spent the remainder of the day cleaning the kitchen and the living quarters. After sundown, they sat near the fire and enjoyed their first meal together as brothers of a new order.

"Have you given any thought to the main chapel?" Alexander asked.

"Only that it will require a great deal of work," Masoud chuckled.

"I think we should convert it into an outdoor worshiping area. A place for silent reflection and meditation," Alexander said.

Masoud nodded. "As you said before, these mountains are quite heavenly. We should have enough stone for it, and it would require very little lumber," Masoud said.

"Are you experienced with masonry?" Alexander asked.

"Yes, I learned from my father," Masoud said.

"The interior chapel could be used during inclement weather and for seminary instruction. Perhaps we should establish a schedule for our respective faiths," Alexander said.

"Naturally," Masoud nodded.

DAYS LATER, the snow eventually melted away and Alexander and Masoud went up to the chapel and assessed the work to be done. They climbed the hill and entered the sanctuary.

"What do you think?" Masoud asked.

Alexander shrugged and surveyed the ruined chapel. He ran his hands over the stones and fallen debris. He went out and viewed it from a distance. "The existing stonework sort of reminds me of the Temple of Apedemak," Alexander said.

Masoud looked confused.

"It's a Kushite temple in the valley of pyramids of ancient Nubia."

"I know the Egyptian pyramids," Masoud said.

"No, not the Egyptian pyramids. The Nubian pyramids. The ancient Kingdom of Nubia was in modern-day Sudan. They are smaller in stature, but quite impressive," Alexander said.

"Yes, of course," Masoud said, feeling embarrassed.

Reflecting on his extensive reading, Alexander continued, "Also, not far away in the City of Naqa, the Nubians constructed the Temple of Apedemak, which also doesn't have a roof, and the masonry is similar to this chapel. Here, I'll show you." Alexander sketched the Temple of Apedemak on a sheet of paper.

Masoud looked it over. "I see. I think we can do this."

They continued their work on the lower building, cleaning the interior and making the necessary repairs. As they worked on the roof, two men arrived in a pickup truck. The driver climbed out and looked up at them, but an old man stayed seated in the passenger seat.

Alexander and Masoud climbed down from the roof and introduced themselves to the visitors.

"What are you doing here?" the younger man said.

"We are restarting the order," Alexander said.

The man looked at them in confusion. "What order is that?"

"There was once a monastery here, and we are rebuilding it," Masoud said.

"With whose permission?" the man asked.

Alexander felt a sense of panic setting in. A series of bad outcomes filled his head. He heard his probation officer's warning, *"If you get arrested for any reason, that could violate your probation, and you could be sent back to prison."*

"My family owns this land, and there hasn't been any brotherhood here for quite some time, so it appears that you are trespassing," the man said.

Alexander spoke up, "We don't mean any harm, sir. My pastor told me about this monastery years ago. He's from Linville you see, and he came close to joining the brotherhood, but after spending a year under the tutelage of Monsignor Gilbert, he decided against it."

The young man's face softened a little at the mention of Monsignor Gilbert's name, but he still looked upon them with suspicion.

Alexander continued, "My friend brought me here to join

myself, and after finding it abandoned and in its current condition, we decided to rebuild and restart the brotherhood."

"An interfaith brotherhood," Masoud added.

"Yes, here, both Christians and Muslims will worship together," Alexander said.

The old man finally climbed out of the truck and ambled over to them. "Tell me about this interfaith brotherhood," the old man said.

Alexander and Masoud passionately explained their vision for the interfaith brotherhood while the old man nodded politely.

"What's your pastor's name?" the old man asked.

"Daniel Talbert," Alexander replied.

The old man looked pensive for a moment, and nodded his head. "Oh yes, I remember Brother Talbot," he said.

Alexander was astonished. "Are you Monsignor Gilbert?" Alexander asked.

"No, my name is Edwards. I lived with the brotherhood for eighteen years. After the fire, the brotherhood disbanded, and only Monsignor Gilbert and I remained. When he died, he left the property to me, with instructions that it could only be used for Christian worship, he said.

Masoud stiffened.

"But knowing Monsignor Gilbert as I did, I don't believe he would object to your vision," the old man said.

"Dad, you're certainly not going to let these two stay here, are you?" the younger man asked.

Mr. Edwards waved him off. "I will pray to the Lord for guidance in this matter, and if it is His will for you to remain, I shall not interfere. We will evaluate this experiment over time."

The two men climbed back into the truck and left.

Alexander let out a sigh of relief.

"Have faith, Alexander. We are doing important work here," Masoud said.

Later, they prepared dinner and sat to eat by the fire.

Alexander was exhausted. He had not considered the amount of work the project would require, working continuously since they arrived at the old monastery. The list of projects seemed endless, keeping them busy for as long as the sun hung in the sky. With no electricity, the nights were reserved for fellowship and spiritual reflection. They were not sure when they could begin work on the outer chapel because there were more pressing issues to tackle first.

"We must produce our own food and become self-sufficient," Masoud advised.

"I've been thinking about that. We should get started on a garden as soon as spring arrives," Alexander said.

"We will need more than that. We must build an enclosure for chickens and other livestock," Masoud said.

"What sort of livestock?"

"For starters, we will need a few hens and a rooster. One will never go hungry with chickens," Masoud said. "Goats will provide milk and cheese, and eventually meat, as will sheep," Masoud added.

Alexander agreed.

"What if after we make all the improvements, Mr. Edwards doesn't allow us to stay?" Alexander asked.

"That will not happen," Masoud said, confidently.

Alexander wasn't so sure.

They eventually separated to read their holy texts and pray before going to bed, as would become their nightly routine.

On the following morning, they surveyed the property to identify the best location for a livestock enclosure, settling on two square acres on the northeast end of the property.

"We'll install a barbed-wire fence along here," Masoud

said, pointing along the base of the hillside and around the open field. "Dividing the sheep from the goats along here," he said.

Alexander followed along with his eyes and nodded.

"The job should take three or four days," Masoud said. "I suppose we could use the shed for the chickens and build an enclosure around it, too," Alexander said.

Masoud agreed.

They went into town and purchased supplies for the enclosures, returned and began installing the fence post along the base of the hillside. The rocky terrain proved more difficult than they had anticipated, extending the job by two and a half weeks. Upon completing the enclosures, they purchased six hens, a rooster, and two goats. The sheep were harder to find, but they eventually acquired an ewe and a young ram near the Tennessee border.

The surrounding fields bloomed with an assortment of wildflowers, and spring green leaves painted the hillside. Alexander and Masoud prepped the soil for the vegetables, soon to be planted. Using hand tools found in the barn, they tilled the soil and mixed in organic matter, working the soil until Masoud was satisfied. Once the seeds were sown, they would at last focus their attention on the monumental task of constructing the outdoor temple.

Alexander drew detailed plans of the outdoor temple. "I thought we should replicate the front exterior of the Temple of Apedemak, but lower the sides and the rear wall to three feet tall, with two pillars at the rear corners of the temple, like so." Alexander showed Masoud his designs neatly drawn on a piece of paper.

Masoud studied the plans, and after altering a few minor details, they agreed on the design. They started by deconstructing the chapel one stone at a time, until only the stone floor remained. They sorted the stones, separating them into two sections of either usable or unusable.

Weeds pushed up through the temple's floor, exposing the need for further restoration. They chiseled around each stone, removing the old mortar, which had held the floor in place for over a century. The August sun bearing down upon them made the task seem unbearable, but they pressed on. They applied fresh mortar, resealing the stones in place. They built two pillars at the rear corners of the temple and built a multi-faith altar between them. The altar pointed east. They added the side walls and completed the project by topping the pillars at the rear with a crescent moon and star on the left and a cross on the right.

CHAPTER
THIRTY-ONE

On the following morning, Alexander and Masoud arose early. They dressed in brown habits and went up to the temple to pray and reflect on what they had been called to do. They reflected on all they had accomplished since arriving at Grandfather Mountain eleven months ago, and with the temple now completed, it marked the first day of true monastic life.

After morning prayer, they went inside and had breakfast. Breakfast consisted of fried eggs, toast, goat's milk, and coffee. They cleaned the kitchen and went out to tend to the livestock. The 7 chickens had multiplied into 19. The doe was preparing to give birth to two kids, and the ewe was pregnant with a single lamb. They fed the chickens, collected a few eggs, and left the others for incubation. They fed and collected milk from the goat and released the sheep to roam free for a while.

Afterwards, Alexander and Masoud worked silently in the garden, harvesting a selection of winter crops. The winter garden consisted of lettuce, carrots, potatoes, parsnips, cabbage, beets, spinach, parsley, sage, cilantro, oregano, and thyme. Upon completing their work in the garden, they set out on their daily silent walk, Alexander's favorite part of their daily routine. The variety of trails surrounding Grandfather Mountain provided them with many options.

They returned to the monastery for noon prayer. They washed their hands, faces and feet, as was their custom, and ascended to the sanctuary. They removed their shoes, entered the sanctuary, and kneeled before the altar. Masoud prayed to Allah, as Alexander prayed to Jesus Christ, but they prayed together, as was also their custom.

As they descended to the lower building, they found Mr. Edwards standing near the door. He was wearing his habit, and a small bag sat near his feet.

"Brother Edwards," Masoud said, smiling. "Are you staying?"

"If you'll have me," Edwards said.

"Of course," Masoud said, embracing him.

Alexander embraced him also. "We wondered when you would come."

"I couldn't stay away," Edwards said.

"We are glad to have you," Alexander said.

"We were heading in for lunch. Have you eaten?" Masoud asked.

"I could stand a bite," Edwards said.

"Good, come," Masoud said, smiling. He pushed open the door, and the aroma of chicken vegetable soup filled the air.

Edwards smiled.

"You may choose any sleeping quarters you like, and meet us in the dining hall," Alexander said.

Edwards found his old sleeping quarters clean and just as he had left it years ago. He sat on the bed and looked around. Years of memories flooded his head. He saw the faces of all the brothers that had once filled the corridors of the old monastery. He sighed and made his way to the dining hall where Alexander and Masoud sat waiting. Brother Edwards filled his bowl and joined them. "You have made tremendous progress," he said, looking around.

"There is much yet to be done, but we'll get there, God willing," Masoud said.

"What was the cause of the fire?" Alexander asked.

"Some say it was a lightning strike, but I'm not entirely sure. It happened during the High Peak Fire over in Burke County," Brother Edwards said.

"What happened there?"

"A gentleman was burning brush on his property and the fire got away from him. The fire raged for seven days, burning over five thousand acres, and destroying twenty-seven homes. As the High Peak Fire raged in Burke County, a small brush fire started not too far from here. Although it normally would have been quickly extinguished, all of the state's resources were over in Burke County. The fire came over the hill and took out the church before it burned out at the river," Edwards explained.

Alexander couldn't help but wonder how God had allowed it to happen. *Why didn't God protect the church? Why didn't He protect my mother?* he thought, but then pushed those ideas out of his head.

"I would like to see what you've done with the old abby," Edwards said.

They finished eating and went up to the sanctuary. They removed their shoes and entered.

Brother Edwards strolled around and examined the space. He had initially felt uncertain about Alexander's design, but after seeing it completed, he now understood. The surrounding mountains and the rolling hills made the sanctuary feel like an extension of heaven on earth. He didn't speak but was visibly full.

"Take your time, brother. Alexander and I must tend to the livestock. We'll return for five o'clock prayer," Masoud said.

Brother Edwards nodded.

Alexander and Masoud herded the sheep into their enclosure. They fed the animals and milked the goats before returning for evening prayer.

That night, they sat by the fireplace and listened to stories about the old monastery. Brother Edwards spoke of the brothers who had lived there years ago. He spoke of their triumphs, as well as their difficulties and hardships. "Monasticism is not an easy life. Not everyone is suited for it. One should take great care in choosing this lifestyle, as the cost of it could be quite burdensome for many people. You will miss your family and friends, and you'll miss all that society has to offer. For the temptations of society don't go away. In fact, seclusion is likely to strengthen temptations, not lessen them. Which is why we must remain in a constant state of prayer and continuous study," Brother Edwards said.

Alexander felt the weight of Brother Edward's words and wondered if he was strong enough to endure the austerity.

Seeing the distress on Alexander's face, Brother Edwards leaned forward and placed his hand on Alexander's shoulder. "You'll be fine, young man," he said.

Alexander nodded and smiled.

"Do you also keep the Islamic prayer schedule?" Edwards asked.

"Yes, we try to pray together," Alexander said.

"That is good. I admire the conviction of the Salah prayer schedule," Brother Edwards said.

"It keeps us grounded with a daily, common purpose," Masoud said.

"The schedule could benefit all faiths," Alexander said.

"Then, I shall also observe the schedule," Brother Edwards said.

The addition of Brother Edwards raised the spirits of Alexander and Masoud. It served as confirmation that their efforts had value to the religious community, and if Brother Edwards saw value in it, others would too. His presence also lessened their workload, leaving more time for worship and study, and although Masoud had grown incredibly fond of Alexander, he was happy to have a more experienced person around.

As for Alexander, he valued Brother Edwards' biblical expertise and spiritual mentorship. Alexander and Brother Edwards spent a lot of time together discussing biblical theory, ethics and morality, and Alexander appreciated Brother Edwards' applications to the modern world.

CHAPTER

THIRTY-TWO

Natalie Lindestam, MD, arrived at Raleigh Durham International Airport. She navigated through customs, rented a car, and set off towards downtown. The traffic along Wade Avenue moved slowly, and when she arrived at her destination, she sat in her car confused—the house was not as she remembered it. She checked to ensure she was on the right street. She saw a man in the driveway washing his car, and she realized the person she had traveled across the world to see, was no longer there. She sighed and drove away. When she arrived at her parents' home, she was delighted to find her old neighborhood had not changed much at all. She climbed the stairs and went inside, finding no one was there. She looked in the garage and saw her father's car wasn't there. She took out her phone and dialed her mother.

"Hey, Mamma. I'm here."

"Hey, dotter. How was your trip?"

"It was okay."

"Good. We are at the grocery store. We'll be home soon."

"No need to hurry. I am tired. I think I'll lie down for a while."

"Okay. We'll see you soon."

Natalie went up to her old room, finding it just as she had left it. Old memories filled her mind, triggering emotions she had securely locked away. The grief she felt, had almost forced her to flee, but she steadied herself, lay across the bed, and went to sleep. She awoke a few hours later and went downstairs, finding her parents sitting in the family room, watching the evening news.

They embraced and all sat on the sofa, Natalie between them.

"How long are you staying?" her father asked.

"I'm due back on Monday," she said.

"That's no time at all," her mother said.

"I called in a favor to get this weekend off," Natalie said, as her mother wrapped her arm around her shoulder and squeezed. "I'm so hungry," she said, looking towards the kitchen.

"I made reservations for seven-thirty," her father said.

"Reservations where?"

"At Second Empire," he answered.

"I can fix you something," her mother said.

"No, I can wait," she said, just as the news caught her attention.

"The governor called state lawmakers into a special session today to discuss the state's voting districting maps three federal judges ruled unconstitutional. Victoria Aiden is standing by with an update. Victoria," the news anchor said.

"Lawmakers only have until tomorrow to meet federal guidelines after the recently drawn maps were ruled unconstitutional. The governor called lawmakers here for this special session to discuss redrawing the maps, and representative Connerly says his party is

unhappy that these maps are being pushed through so quickly," Victoria Aiden said.

Natalie Lindestam turned her attention to the television in astonishment, as representative Connerly addressed the reporter.

"It is very clear that our colleagues on the other side of the aisle drew these maps to benefit the rural counties of North Carolina and themselves, and my colleagues and I are prepared to keep them here all night, if necessary, until more fair and equitable district maps are produced," representative Connerly said, and then the reporter was again on the screen.

"This special session is expected to last for hours, and as Representative Connerly suggests, could last throughout the night. Reporting live from Raleigh, I'm Victoria Aiden."

"I'll be damned," Natalie said. "I'm sorry, but I have to go," she said, rushing towards the door.

"What about dinner?" her father said.

"I'll meet you at Second Empire," she said. She climbed into her rental car and drove directly to the North Carolina Legislative Building. She parked across the street and went inside. A security officer was busy directing the media, so she passed the officer's station without looking in his direction and continued directly to Representative Connerly's office, where she was greeted by a receptionist.

"May I help you?"

"Hi, Margaret," she said, glancing at the nameplate on the desk. "I need to speak to Congressman Connerly, please," she said.

"I'm sorry, but he's in session right now," Margaret said.

"That's okay. I can wait."

"Do you have an appointment?"

"No, I do not."

"Then you will have to come back another time," Margaret said, sternly.

"I cannot come back another time. This is a matter of urgency, and if you would tell him I'm here, I'm certain he would want to see me," she said.

"What's your name?"

"Natalie Lindestam."

"Do you have any identification, Ms. Lindestam?"

"Yes, I do," she said, placing her identification on Margaret's desk.

Margaret examined her identification, and looked over Natalie Lindestam, wondering what the purpose of her visit was, and what made this woman feel so entitled to see the congressman. "May I ask what all of this is about?"

"It's a personal matter, and I won't leave until I see him," she said sternly.

Margaret's face turned red with anger, and her anger quickly turned to fear—fear of what bombshell this woman was capable of releasing, and with the news media nearby, she thought she had better notify the congressman and let him decide how to proceed. She picked up the phone and dialed his number.

"I'm sorry to bother you sir, but I have a Doctor Natalie Lindestam here to see you," Margaret said.

"I'm in session, Margaret," Howard, said angrily.

"I understand that sir, but she's refusing to leave without seeing you, and she says she has an urgent personal matter to discuss with you."

"I don't know any Doctor Lindestam, Margaret. Please, tell her that I cannot see her today," Howard said.

Margaret felt relieved. "I'm sorry ma'am, but you're gonna have to make an appointment," Margaret said, still holding the phone.

"He knows me as Natalie Agadani," she said.

Margaret looked confused.

"Tell him, it's Natalie Agadani," she said.

"Sir, she says you know her as Natalie Agadani," Margaret said.

Howard was silent.

"Sir?"

"I'll be up as soon as I can," Howard said.

Margaret took a moment to steady herself. "Have a seat, ma'am. He'll be over soon," she said.

Relieved, Natalie sat and waited.

Howard eventually rushed into the office. "Natalie, is that really you?" he said, smiling broadly.

"It is so good to see you, Howard," she said, as they embraced.

"Natalie is an old family friend, Margaret," Howard said.

Margaret smiled dubiously.

"Come on in," he said, taking her into his office.

Natalie stepped in and scanned the photos aligning his walls and on his desk. Her eyes fell on a photograph of Howard and his family.

"Is that Allyson?" she asked.

"Yes. We married after college," Howard said.

"And the boy?"

"That is Nicholas. He's a year old," Howard said.

Natalie smiled and pressed her hand to her chest.

"You should come over for dinner. Allyson would love to see you," Howard said.

"I wish I could, but I'm only here for a few days. I have to get back to Sweden," she said.

"Is Lindestam your married name?"

"Yes. I *was* married, but not anymore." She continued glancing at the many photographs. "He was a good man, but

I just didn't," she paused, "He just wasn't..." she paused again.

"He wasn't Alexander," Howard said.

Natalie nodded. "Is that why you're here?" Howard asked.

"Where is he, Howard? I can't find him," Natalie said.

"I don't believe he wants to be found," Howard said.

"What do you mean?"

"He has had a tough time since you left, Natalie. He stayed with my dad for a while after he was released from prison, but he had a hard time getting back on his feet. Some members of the community didn't want him around. It eventually became too much for him, and he disappeared a few years ago."

"Have you tried to find him?" Natalie asked.

"I respected his privacy, besides, it's complicated," Howard said, taking a seat behind his desk.

"Complicated how?"

"When he left, he may have violated the terms of his probation, and there may be a warrant for his arrest. My finding him may cause more harm than good."

"I see..."

"And there is a matter of his registration," Howard said.

"What registration?"

Howard sighed. "Due to the circumstances of his offense, Alexander has to register as a sex offender in any county where he resides. If he failed to register wherever he's living, it could bring additional charges," Howard said.

"I had no idea." Natalie bit her lower lip as tears welled in her eyes before running down her face. She wiped them away and said, "I need you to find him."

"What will you do when he's found?"

"I'm taking him back with me to Sweden," she said.

Howard stood and rubbed his clean-shaven face as he considered. "Okay, I'll find him."

"And one more thing," she said.

"What's that?"

"I want you to get his charges expunged," she said.

"I don't have the power to do that," Howard said.

"You are a congressman, Howard. I'm sure you know someone who does," she said.

"I'm only a freshman congressman," Howard said.

"He needs a fresh start, Howard," she said, pressing him. "He doesn't need that hanging over his head anymore."

Howard shoved his hands in his pockets and breathed in and out heavily. "Okay. I'll do what I can."

A FEW DAYS LATER, Howard went to visit his father. When he and Orlando stood in the kitchen drinking beer, he said, "Natalie came to visit me."

"Natalie who?" Orlando asked.

"Alexander's Natalie," Howard said.

"What did she want?"

"She wants me to find Alexander so she can take him back with her to Sweden."

"Really?" Orlando took a long swig from his bottle of beer.

"Yeah. She also wants me to get his record expunged, but I'm not sure I have enough political capital to pull it off. If the press finds out about it, it could ruin my career." Howard placed his empty bottle on the table.

"So, what are you going to do?"

"I don't know."

"Remind me again why you went into politics?" Orlando asked.

"To help people."

"And to make the system work for people it normally works against, right?"

Howard nodded.

"Then stick to your principles, and do what's right, and if you have to take the hits for it, then so be it. You'll survive it," Orlando said.

Howard sighed and reached for another beer.

CHAPTER

THIRTY-THREE

Howard sat in his office at the North Carolina Legislative Building, working on a proposal to deliver a light rail system he had promised during his campaign. The proposed rail system would connect Raleigh, Durham, and Chapel Hill, North Carolina. He had spent the morning on the phone with the chancellor of North Carolina Central University, who had wanted assurances that the path of the rail line would provide access to her students. He previously met with the president of Duke University about his own list of assurances. Howard sat wondering how to appease them both.

Margaret knocked on the door. "Don't forget about your meeting with Judge Gregory," she said.

"Yes, thank you." He looked at his watch and sighed. It was 11:30 A.M., and his meeting would start in 45 minutes. He reached into a draw for a hairbrush, brushed his hair a few times, and returned the brush to the draw. He ran his fingers over his wavy hair and let out a deep breath. He turned off his computer, grabbed his briefcase, and went out to his car. He turned onto South Salisbury Street and headed downtown towards the Wake County Superior Court building, parked his car, and went inside.

It was a busy day in the court building, as many citizens rushed to receive their judgments. Some of them appeared happy and confident, while others appeared sad and worried. Howard's countenance was the latter. He climbed into the elevator and ascended to the top floor, entered the chambers of Judge Roger Gregory, and approached the receptionist.

"Congressman Connerly to see Judge Gregory," he said.

"He's expecting you." She smiled and picked up the phone. "Congressman Connerly is here, sir." She hung up and stepped around the desk. "Right this way." She led Howard to the judge's office door.

Howard went inside and found the judge putting a golf ball across the office floor and into a device that spit it out back at him. "Hello, sir," Howard said.

"Hi, Congressman. How are you?" the judge asked, extending his hand.

Howard shook the judge's hand and took a seat.

Judge Gregory returned to his golf ball and putted it across the room. He smiled when it landed in the hole. "How's your game?" the judge asked.

"It's coming along, although I am not very good," Howard said.

"This game, I tell you. One minute I'm hitting them like the pros, and the next minute, I can barely find the fairway." The judge smiled.

"I've seen you play, sir. I think you're being modest," Howard said.

The judge laughed. "Bourbon?" he offered.

"Sure, I'll have a little." Howard glanced around the room at several pictures of Judge Gregory standing next to several former North Carolina governors, United States senators, and another picture of the judge happily standing with President Barack Obama. The brown-skinned judge standing next to the brown-skinned president was a sight he never thought he would live to see. And now, there he was in the room, wielding his own influence. He could barely believe it.

The judge poured two glasses of Blanton's bourbon and handed one to Howard, before sitting across from him.

"What can I do for you, congressman?" he asked.

"It's not for me, sir. I'm here for a constituent," Howard said.

"Is that right?" The judge smiled and crossed his leg.

"Yes, and in full disclosure, he is a close family friend who was sentenced in your courtroom back in two-thousand-six."

"What about him?" the judge asked.

Howard glanced at the calendar on the judge's wall. "It was a little over seven years ago when he accepted a plea bargain to indecent liberties with a child and was sentenced to a term of twenty-four-to-thirty-six months."

"Then he's already done his time." The judge leaned back and folded his arms across his chest.

"He has."

"Then what's this about? "

"The girl who was involved in his case came to see me a few weeks ago."

The judge sat up in his seat. "How is she? I hope she's been able to get on with her life," the judge said.

"Yes, she's doing quite well. She lives in Sweden, a medical doctor now, completing her first year of residency."

"That's good," the judge said, nodding his head. "But why did she come to see you? What does she want?"

Howard reached in his bag and handed him Natalie's

written affidavit. "She's requesting that you expunge his charges so he can return with her to Sweden," Howard said.

"Why on earth would she want to do that?" the judge asked.

"She still loves him. And I'm certain he still loves her, too."

"What was the offender's name?"

"Alexander Merchant," Howard said.

The judge shook his head in disbelief. He drank his bourbon and read over Natalie's affidavit. He rubbed his chin and looked away. "Alexander Merchant," he said, thoughtfully.

"Do you remember the case?" Howard asked.

The judge stood and poured himself another glass. He picked up the phone and called his receptionist. "Will you be a dear and look in my files for a letter from an Alexander Merchant? Yes, that's right. Thank you," he said, and hung up the phone. He sat back down across from Howard and crossed his legs. He sipped his bourbon and furrowed his brow.

Howard said nothing.

Moments later the receptionist came into the office and handed the judge an envelope. Howard watched the judge open the envelope and look it over. He handed it over to Howard. Howard looked at the letter and immediately recognized Alexander's handwriting.

"I received this letter over five years ago and held on to it," the judge said.

Howard read over the letter in disbelief. It explained the circumstances of Alexander and Natalie's relationship. How they had met, how they had fallen in love, the two-week window that had made their relationship a crime, and of the act that had changed his life forever.

"What does Mr. Merchant say about this?" the judge asked.

"He doesn't know about it. You see, after his release from prison, he lived with my parents for a while as he tried to get his life back on track, but he had a very difficult time. He finally found work, but the neighbors eventually ran him out of the neighborhood," Howard said.

"Ran him out how?" the judge asked.

"The neighborhood watch posted flyers, warning the neighbors he was a sex offender. He went to his church for help, but they ran him away too. I believe it became too much for him, so he left," Howard said.

"He absconded his supervision?" the judge asked.

Howard let out a deep sigh. "I'm not completely sure. I have not spoken to the probation officer," Howard said. "And I'm not certain of his whereabouts."

"I see. I'm gonna have to think about this, and first, speak to his probation officer," the judge said.

"Yes, of course. I'll set up a meeting." Howard handed the letter back to the judge and shook his hand. "I'll be in touch," Howard said, and exited the chambers.

THIRTY-FOUR

Alexander sat in the temple, meditating. He concentrated on the air flowing in and out of his body, the inflation of his lungs and his heart beating in his chest. He cleared his mind. He relaxed his forehead, his eyes, his cheeks, and his mouth. He relaxed his neck, his shoulders, his arms, and his hands until he could feel the energy of life pulsating through his fingers. He became aware of rotary blades whirring overhead. Looking up, he saw a helicopter, hovering above. He watched it circle the property several times before flying away.

On the following day, Alexander, Masoud, and Edwards went up the hill to the temple for noon prayer. Soon after, a news van arrived, and a reporter approached Alexander and requested an interview.

Alexander agreed, and a cameraman began filming. He explained why they initially came there, and why they had stayed to refurbish the property. He showed the work they had done, from rebuilding the temple to restoring the abbey. They toured the gardens, the livestock, and the abbey.

"Both Christians and Muslims worship here together?" the reporter asked. "How does that work?"

"It works because we are all here for the same purpose, which is to be closer to the Almighty God, regardless of what we call Him," Alexander said.

"Have you had any conflict?"

"There isn't any conflict. We are not here to convert each other, or to prove whose religion is greater. We are here for the tranquility it provides, and the quiet reflection so difficult to find in the modern world," Alexander said.

"Are all faiths welcome?" the reporter asked.

"Any faith that is moral and good, or anyone who wants to worship peacefully and respectfully is welcome," Alexander said.

The story aired the following evening, and soon after, visitors from across the country began to arrive. Many were Christians and Muslims who believed in what they were doing at the monastery. Others were Buddhist, Hindus, Yogis, and spiritualists alike, who were looking for a place to meditate and be one with nature and the universe. Some were only looking to add to their social media profiles, but a few stayed on in order to decide if monastic life was right for them.

HOWARD ENTERED his office and sat behind his desk. He picked up the phone and dialed Natalie in Sweden.

"Halo, Doctor Lindestam," she answered.

"I found him," Howard said.

"Where is he?" Natalie asked.

"He's living in western North Carolina. You won't believe this, but he was featured in a news story. I'm emailing you a link now. It will explain everything," Howard said.

"Have you reached out to him?" Natalie asked.

"I thought I should leave that to you," Howard said.

"And what of the expungement?" she asked.

"The order to vacate his sentence is sitting on the judge's desk. He will be signing it any day now."

"Will I need to testify?"

"That won't be necessary. The written affidavit you provided was enough. There was also an outpouring of community support. My family, our pastor, his old boss, and even his probation officer all spoke on his behalf." Howard said.

Natalie cupped her hand over her mouth to conceal the emotions she felt. "Thank you," was all she managed to say.

"When can you be here?" Howard inquired.

"I'll be there in two weeks," she said.

CHAPTER

THIRTY-FIVE

Alexander sat in his sleeping quarters studying *On the Trinity* by Augustine of Hippo, when he heard a knock on his door. "Come in," he called out.

Masoud pushed open his door. "You have a visitor," he said.

Alexander put away his book and sauntered out into the corridor.

"She's outside," Masoud said.

"She?" Alexander asked.

Masoud placed a hand on Alexander's shoulder and nodded.

Alexander felt uneasy as he slowly opened the door and stepped outside where Natalie stood waiting.

Natalie met his eyes and smiled broadly. "Hi, Alexander," she said.

Alexander found himself unable to move or speak. He just stood there, staring at her, as if he was seeing a ghost. She looked just as he remembered. She wore red rectangular glasses and her thick, curly hair hung at her shoulders, her frame still slender and firm.

"What are you doing here?" Alexander managed to ask.

"I came to see you," Natalie said.

"From Sweden?" Alexander asked.

Natalie nodded. "Can we talk?" she asked.

"Yes, just give me a moment," he said, and went back inside and stood with his head against the door, breathing hard. He took several deep breaths to steady himself, and when he was calm, he went back outside.

"Let's walk," he said.

They made their way around the property, neither knowing what to say.

"Did you build all of this?" Natalie asked, breaking the silence.

"Masoud and I did," Alexander said.

"How long did it take?"

"We've been here for three years now," he answered.

"How long do you plan to stay here?" Natalie asked.

"This is my life now," Alexander said. "I have no plans to leave."

"Not ever?" Natalie asked, wringing her hands.

Alexander sighed. "I didn't think I'd ever see you again."

"Did you *want* to see me again?" she asked.

"Of course, I did. I just didn't think I would," he said, as they stopped and gazed at the sheep.

"I guess I didn't either," she said.

"Then, why are you here?" he asked.

Natalie nervously pushed her hands into the back pockets of her jeans and took in a deep breath. "I am here, because I want you to come with me to Sweden."

Alexander was astonished. "I can't go to Sweden," he managed to say.

"Yes, you can," she announced.

"No," he shook his head. "You don't understand. I am on probation and cannot leave the state, let alone the country."

"You're not on probation anymore, Alexander." She reached in her purse and handed him a legal document. "You are free to go wherever you like," she said.

"What is this?"

"It is a court order, vacating your sentence." Her lips curled into a radiant smile.

Alexander read over the document in disbelief. "But how did you get this?" he asked.

"Howard did it. We went to the judge and asked him to vacate your sentence, and the judge did. So, as far as the court is concerned, it never happened. Your record has been expunged," Natalie said.

"But it did happen. I have the scars to prove it," he said, turned and entered the temple.

Natalie followed. "Talk to me, Alexander. Please."

He turned to face her. "Thank you, Natalie. This means more to me than you could ever imagine, but this place is all I have. I have nothing to offer you. I can't take care of you," he said.

"I don't need you to take care of me. Not monetarily anyway—I can do that myself," she said, and held his gaze for a moment before continuing, "Do you know I was married?"

"No, I didn't," he said, his eyes lowered.

"We met in medical school, and he could give me anything I wanted. Anything except the one thing I wanted most of all— which is you," she said, wrapping her arms around him, burying her head in his chest.

Slowly, his arms went around her waist.

"Come back with me, Alexander," she said.

"What would I do in Sweden?" he asked.

"You could start anew. Finish school or open a café. You'll be free to do whatever you like." She backed away from him and looked around. "I mean, are you really gonna stay here forever?"

Alexander couldn't help but laugh. The idea somehow seemed absurd now. "I'm not the same person you knew in high school, Natalie. I've changed. Life and the system have changed me into someone even I barely recognize sometimes," Alexander said.

"I wrote to you before I was married. I wanted you to know before I went through with it. If you had told me not to marry him, I wouldn't have, but every letter came back unopened," she said, with a flash of anger in her eyes.

Alexander remembered his conversation with Howard. *Were those the letters he returned?* "I thought you needed to move on," he said.

"That's not what I wanted," she said.

Alexander sighed.

"You are still the person I love. Nothing could ever change that," Natalie said.

"I love you, too," Alexander mumbled, afraid to say it aloud.

"Then will you come?" she asked, looking up at him.

Alexander met her eyes and the corners of his mouth went up. "I will."

They embraced and stood, holding each other as they had both dreamed of doing for many years. They finished surveying the property and filled each other in on their lives—their accomplishments and failures.

"I will have to find a way to tell Masoud. I'm not sure how," Alexander said.

"We'll tell him together," Natalie said.

"No, I'll handle it," Alexander said.

Alexander found Masoud and Edwards sitting inside the interior chapel. "I need to speak to you," he said to Masoud.

Masoud looked up at him in anticipation.

"I don't know how to tell you this, but I have decided to leave," Alexander said.

"Where are you going?" Edwards asked.

"To Sweden with Natalie," Alexander announced.

"Are you sure?" Masoud asked, standing to face him.

"I'm sorry... But, yes, I'm sure," Alexander said.

"No need to apologize," Masoud said, embracing him. "I'm happy for you."

Alexander held his embrace.

"Tonight, we will have a feast in your honor," Masoud said.

Natalie stood nearby listening, but then stepped outside, took her cell out, and phoned Howard. "Hi Howard, I'm here."

"Have you spoken to him?"

"Yes, just now."

"What did he say?" Howard asked.

"He agreed to come back with me."

"When are you leaving?"

"Our flight leaves tomorrow morning."

"I'd like to see him before you go," Howard said.

"That's why I am calling. They're planning a goodbye meal for him tonight. Can you guys come?"

"Sure. We can be there by seven," Howard said.

"Good. We'll see you then," she said, ending the call.

Natalie went back inside, finding the group of men sitting around socializing. The scene was more jovial than before, as the brothers broke from their normal silent routine. They eventually dispersed in preparation for the evening meal. Brother Edwards and Natalie worked together in the kitchen. Edwards prepared baked chicken, roasted vegetables, baked potatoes, and pasta salad, as Natalie made red beans and rice, lentil tabouli salad, biscuits, and apple pie. Masoud slaughtered a lamb. He seasoned two legs of lamb with salt, pepper, garlic, and rosemary, and then placed them inside the oven.

Howard, Allyson, Orlando, Vivian, and Reverend Talbert arrived, joining the celebration. They all sat around the table, and for the first time in many years, Alexander had everyone he loved in one place, everyone except his mother. Reflecting on Emily made him sad, but he could feel her there, sitting amongst them. The feeling grew stronger, and he realized she had been there with him all along. Joy washed over him. It was a joy he hadn't felt in years. He looked around the table and smiled.

The End

ACKNOWLEDGMENTS

First, I want my wife, Karine, my son, James, and my daughter, Victoria, to know how much I appreciate their continued support. Thank you to the early readers of *Grandfather Mountain*: Janice Erlbaum, Jada Kaye Martinez, and Ronald Byron Norwood. All your valuable feedback and encouragement during the early stages of the manuscript is greatly appreciated. I would like to thank the editors at Before You Publish – Book Press for holding me to a high standard and patiently helping me realize my vision. I would like to thank Joe, Tenisha, Stephanie, and the Harris family for their reliable friendship. Finally, thank you to the brothers of Gamma Beta Chapter of Alpha Phi Alpha Fraternity, Inc. and my NCCU family for the continued inspiration.

ABOUT THE AUTHOR

Wynton Sellers started his career working in a youth prison, much like the one Alexander was in. During this time, he saw many young men incarcerated for the same crime as Alexander: indecent liberties with a child. In his discussions with these inmates, he found some offenders knew they were breaking the law and deserved their fate. However, for many offenders, no one had taken the time to explain the law to these young men, leaving them ill-equipped to weigh the consequences of their actions. This was the original inspiration for the book. Sellers wants parents to know the importance of explaining the law to their sons and daughters, so they won't make the same mistake as Alexander. *Grandfather Mountain* also looks at the effects the modern-day prison system has on people, regardless of whether they deserve to be incarcerated or not, raising the question, is prison reform necessary? *Wynton Sellers lives in North Carolina with his wife and children.*

facebook.com/Wynton-Sellers-

instagram.com/wyntonsellers